The Feather N
One love

About the author

Gabriella Marshall lives in Surrey with her husband, two gorgeous sons, Jeff the cat and a tortoise called Fred. Originally from Dorset, Gabriella is the youngest of what she terms 'a wonderfully interesting family'. Along with the normal chaos of home life and writing her novels, Gabriella is also a complementary therapist and tries to perfect the one and only cake she has ever mastered – the Dorset apple cake.

The idea for the *Feather Necklace* series came to her in a dream, so vivid was it, she felt she had lived it before. The characters still come back to visit her…

This paperback edition first published in the UK in 2020
by ACT Publishing House

Copyright © Gabriella Marshall, 2020

The moral rights of Gabriella Marshall to be identified as the author of this work has been asserted in accordance with Copyright, Designs and Patents Act of 1988.

All rights reserved. No part of this publication may be reproduced, stored in a retrieval system, or transmitted, in any form or by any means, electronic, mechanical, photocopying, recording, or otherwise, without the prior permission of both the copyright owner and the above publisher of this book.

This is a work of fiction. All characters, organisations, and events portrayed in this novel are either products of the author's imagination or are used fictitiously.

Paperback ISBN: 9798636850229

Chapter 1

Cap Ferret, Southern France, May

Joey knew her breathing was ragged as she watched this irresistibly handsome man ease himself out of the water, grab his towel and walk towards the lower gardens.

What just happened? She splashed some cool water from the pool on her face in an attempt to refresh her bewildering thoughts, then touched her lips where, just moments ago, he had so passionately kissed her. She was cold, really cold, and slowly she swam towards the steps and climbed out of the tranquil swimming pool. Joey languidly walked towards the sun lounger to retrieve her towel. Looking towards the lower garden and waiting for her breathing to return to normal, Joey hoped to see him return.

How do you explain it when a man, and not just any man, but this seriously hot, out of her league man, looked at her the way he just did? Kissed her the way he just did? Pressed his incredible body against hers the way he just did? She knew he wanted her, she could feel his attraction, but why had he pulled away from her just as quickly as he had embraced her?

Joey decided he wasn't coming back anytime soon and she wasn't going to risk being rejected again, so she headed back into the villa glancing over her shoulder once more as she pulled back the French sliding doors.

Drinking a large glass of cool water, Joey allowed her mind to return to *that* moment. His arms were so strong and protective, his lips soft yet demanding. Her skin felt sensitive to the touch and her body tingled all over. She heard herself sigh out loud with the memory and was slightly taken aback to see that her hand, which held the now empty glass, shook.

'Get a grip!' Joey murmured to herself. She placed the glass on the worktop with more force than necessary and turned to walk up the imposing staircase, back to her room.

What was he thinking? How had he allowed things to get that heated and out of control, that quickly? He just walked. He had no idea where he was heading but he had to put some distance between himself and Joey or he knew he would *have* to take her there and then.

He reached the edge of the garden and took in the sea breeze air. At least his body was physically returning to normal, his mind, however, was wild with emotions. He hadn't felt the desire to be with someone quite this badly before. Yes, he had made love to women in the past but this was different. This feeling wasn't a *want*, it was a *need*. How was he going to survive the next few hours and night in her company? He couldn't just scurry away and hide; she deserved more respect than that. He'd just have to stay focused and maintain a civil distance. At least this evening she'd have more clothing on…

Joey must think he was very strange to have left her so suddenly like that. He looked out to the sea as if he were searching for an answer, but received no response. With a sigh he turned and walked back towards the villa. He would have to talk to her, but firstly he needed a shower, and possibly a drink to calm his nerves.

Joey stepped out onto her balcony and the intense heat beating down from the cerulean blue sky caught her by surprise. Her eyes wandered to the pool and to where she had last seen him disappear between the trees.

She wondered what he was doing now. Was he regretting the kiss? Was she too forward? Was that why he had moved away from her as if he'd been stung? She leaned against the railing and looked out to the beautiful sea. What should she do? Oh God, was it that big of a mistake? Maybe she should leave now before the pleasure they had experienced was totally ruined.

As she looked out onto the vast horizon of the Mediterranean Sea her mind continued to give flashbacks from the last three weeks. Never in her wildest dreams did she imagine her life would have taken this turn. She remembered the first time she saw him; she had never seen anyone look as striking as he did.
There was no denying there was a strong attraction between them. Joey decided to see what mood he was in before dinner and to take it from there. If they were both uncomfortable she'd ask him to take her to the airport and their paths need never to cross again.

As Joey turned and walked towards her room to run a bath she didn't see him emerge from between the trees and look up towards her window.

Relaxing in the warm, soapy water, Joey allowed her mind to relive the past few weeks.

It was May. The beautiful, historic city of Bath was drenched in a heavy, spring shower, the kind of shower that saturates every layer. An English monsoon…

Chapter 2

Bath, South-West England, May

It was a Tuesday afternoon as Joey scurried out of Stones into torrential rain. Bustling past busy shoppers and tourists, Joey seethed under her breath as she fought to put up her umbrella. They appeared oblivious to her desire to get out of the rain as quickly as humanly possible. These people kept getting in her way or stopping suddenly making it nigh on impossible to keep a steady pace. Eventually Joey reached her haven and entered the much-needed dry and peaceful ambience of The Pig's Head.

After quickly scouting the room she realised she'd made it to the pub before Lucy, so she walked up to the bar to order their regular: two large glasses of Pinot Grigio. Whilst trying not to spill a drop, Joey picked a table, which would have the best view of Dave.

Dave, or Dishy Dave as Joey affectionately called him, is a senior architect at Stones, where they both work. He had only been working there for four months but already he has made quite an impression on both employers and Joey. Although it seemed, *he* still hadn't noticed *her*.

He was the one and only birthday present she really wanted, but so far all she'd received was a reputation for hanging around the bar nursing her single glass of wine until it was warm and rancid.

After taking a sip of her presently chilled wine, Joey sighed, replacing the glass on the table, turning it slowly by its stem. She'd not passed many birthdays as a singleton and she had hoped to celebrate her thirtieth with a man who was potentially the love of her life and who would be father of her children. Her mum had reminded her on many occasions: *Josephine, if you want a family then you'd better find Mr Right pretty damn quickly!* But does Mr Right exist? What is ideal?

Knowing where these negative thoughts would lead, she pulled out her phone and began to pass time skimming the news on social media. Reading through dull, celebrity feeds she sensed something behind her. Joey furtively looked over her shoulder and saw three men. They had olive colour skin and long, straight, black hair, which was pulled off their faces. Joey couldn't remember seeing them before and they certainly didn't look local, they were quite exotic.

The men were strangely fascinating and Joey couldn't resist another look. She surreptitiously ogled them, finding them curiously alluring. The first had a thin, pointy face and piercing, rat-like eyes that darted from side to side as if waiting to pounce. The second had a friendlier face, the sort that instantly warmed you to them, a full mouth and laughter lines etched around his large, brown eyes. The third had the blackest of black hair, an aristocratic nose and eyes that seemed too intense, too… cold. As Joey glanced at him her body shivered.

She tried to focus on her phone again but found she couldn't resist another peek.

Joey was forcefully dragged back into reality when she heard Lucy. 'Sorry I'm late.'

'That's fine,' Joey replied, 'I've been admiring the scenery.' She nodded discreetly in the direction of the three dark strangers.

'Oh,' Lucy said, glancing dismissively at the three men sitting in the corner. 'Any sign of *you-know-who*?' she murmured.

'Not yet. He's finished his perspective and I overheard him talking to Bas about meeting here later.'

Joey couldn't help but be drawn to the mysterious men. The cold one looked totally bored as he turned a beer mat round and round his fingers, the other two oblivious of his unease.

Suddenly, a blast of cool air reached Joey and she looked around to see who had opened the door. She momentarily stopped breathing as Dave and Bas confidently bowled through the door. She was openly staring but she couldn't help it as he shook rain from his blonde, slightly wavy hair.

Joey loved his body, tall and athletically built, but it was Dave's eyes that melted her into a pool of goo. His eyes were the palest ice blue she had ever seen. Dave and Bas walked past her and Lucy towards the bar where they then ordered their usual ale.

The women looked longingly at the men; the men looked longingly into their pints.

- - -

The rest of the week passed in much the same mundane manner until Friday, and for once it wasn't actually raining,

Joey's hair flew loose about her face as she ran to The Pig's Head for 80's night. *Kids in America* was blaring out as she stopped abruptly outside. She ran her hands through her hair and took a deep breath trying to find some composure before wrenching open the door.

As she moved into the heaving pub towards her normal vantage point, she realised that she couldn't see Lucy anywhere. Damn it was noisy; she thought to herself as she made her way through the throng of people, maybe this wasn't such a great idea. That was when she noticed Lucy's frantic waving from the other side of the room.

The place was packed with students. Joey had never seen the pub like this. There were people everywhere – in front of the bar and around the surrounding tables. Joey took her glass of now warm wine from Lucy and asked if she had seen Dave. A quick nod and twist of Lucy's mouth said it all before Joey had even turned around. Reluctantly, she followed Lucy's gaze and saw Dave talking and laughing with a leggy blonde. Their heads were practically touching so as to hear what each other were saying. In a split second decision Joey downed her glass of now warm Pinot and headed to the bar for another.

What was the point? Joey thought to herself, as she finished her second glass of wine, he'd only end up using and cheating on her anyhow. It would become too uncomfortable to work together so one of them would need to leave their job, and Joey could guarantee it would be her. To add insult to injury her mum would also add: *Never mix business with pleasure.* And, *It was bound to happen anyhow. You can never trust a man. When will you learn?*

'Joey, want to take a breather?' Lucy asked.

'Nope.' Joey felt slightly squiffy and knew she should walk away, but she couldn't. Somewhere in the depths of her being she knew that Dave just needed to notice that she existed. She grabbed Lucy's hand and started to dance. She knew she had rhythm, better than that leggy blonde for starters.

'Okay, you may not have got Dave's attention, but you sure have the cold, mysterious stranger looking at you,' Lucy teased Joey.

'Who?' replied Joey never taking her eyes from Dave.

'The strangers, remember them? Your 3 o'clock, to the right.'

It always took Joey a while to work out these riddles. Why can't people say, 'over there, to your right'? Once Joey had worked it out, she glanced over and saw the three brooding men from a couple of nights before. The cold one looked up catching her peek.

He held her gaze uncomfortably, until Joey had to look away. It felt like her eyes had been burnt.

'Um, yes, I see them,' Joey shivered; it felt as if all her nerve endings had been exposed to hot metal. 'Why do I attract the wrong men? I mean look at him, he's so cold I bet he's never smiled in his life.' Joey looked more closely at him; 'Look he hasn't one line on his face?'

'Haven't looked hard enough to notice,' Lucy replied.

'You've got to be kidding, *Bonnie Tyler*!' Joey moaned to Lucy and the surrounding mass of people around her.

Then to Joey's total surprise she heard a very deep voice behind her say – 'May I have this dance?'

Chapter 3

Kari could not sit any longer and watch this pretty young woman self-destruct. He had to do something. He knew what he wanted to do. This woman was desperate for Bland Man to notice her and maybe, just maybe, he could grab his attention and literally put her in the man's hands. Kari waited for the next slow song. Thankfully he didn't have to wait long, a slow piano tune began to throb from the speakers and he decided to take action. He pushed his chair back and without saying anything he moved towards the brunette. Instinct overtook him.

'May I have this dance?' he asked the brunette.

She didn't say anything. She just stared at him. Was he really that intimidating? He couldn't go back now. He stared into her startled eyes as he passed the nearly empty wine glass to her friend before guiding the brunette to the dance floor. He could feel her body was ever so slightly trembling and he wanted to put her at ease. He didn't want to frighten her… he wanted to help her. With no sign of haste they moved in time to the music – a slight shuffle side-to-side.

His two companions, Henrique and Lacroix, could not believe what they were witnessing. One minute Kari was sitting with them, the next he had finished his drink, placed his empty glass on the table and got up towards the bar area. At first they thought he may be going to the bathroom, but then he rarely used public facilities. Maybe he wanted another drink but someone else always got the food, drink or whatever was required. Kari didn't have to do anything except his work.

It was with total bafflement that they watched him approach a young woman, say something to her, pass her glass to another young woman and then proceed to take her by the hand and dance. They watched in stupefied silence. They should probably go over to get ready to leave, but neither of them wanted to bare the wrath of Kari. So instead they just sat and watched, along with everyone else it seemed.

It was at that moment Kari realised they were the only two dancing and everyone seemed to be watching them, including Bland Man. Kari was used to standing out from the crowd, it happens when you're 6ft 2" and look nothing like the locals. Well apart from his two colleagues who were now staring and willing him to sit down, or better still, leave. Henrique looked like he was physically struggling to remain seated. But with every step he could feel the tension ease from the brunette. The music swelled and dipped very dramatically.

'Are you alright?' he said to the brunette staring deeply into her beautiful eyes. A nod of her head was the only reply he received. If only she would relax.

Now he was this close to her he could see her face in fine detail. Her nose was small; her mouth had the most perfectly shaped lips he'd ever seen and her eyes a stunning shade of aquamarine. She was wearing too much makeup as far as he was concerned, but he just couldn't take his eyes from hers. It didn't help with the lyrics mentioning *bright eyes* over and over. As he gently held her body he felt the hairs on the back of his neck stand up. This woman made him feel things that he wasn't used to.

What was happening was all Joey kept thinking. Where did he come from? She wasn't meant to be dancing with him, she was meant to be with Dave. She didn't even know where to put her hands. He was so tall. Being fairly petite herself he was nearly a foot taller. She knew she was trembling and just hoped to God he didn't feel it. She didn't want him getting the wrong idea. She was not trembling in trepidation; she was in fact very nervous and now aware everyone was watching them, including Dave.

For the first time in her life Dave had seen her, but this wasn't good, she was in another man's arms. *No, I'm still available Dave* she wanted to shout, but her mouth was dry. She needed a drink.

They were dancing very closely and he hadn't moved his gaze from her face. That's when she noticed his eyes. His eyes were like that black precious stone Obsidian, Joey thought it was called. The whites of his eyes were crystal clear and his pupils dissolved into the sparkling brown black of his irises. She found she couldn't pull her eyes away from his - they were almost hypnotic - intense in his gaze. They weren't cold as she had presumed, but warm, inviting, intense and interesting. The sort you hear people would dive into and get very, very lost… as she was beginning to feel.

She managed with sheer will power to move her eyes to the rest of his face. He had a long, straight nose, almost aristocratic. His lips were perfectly formed and full. *I bet he kisses well…* Joey thought - No! She couldn't think about that… then there was his smell. Not expensive or cheap aftershave, just a warm, clean, fresh smell. Perhaps not a perfume at all, but there was just something… she wasn't sure what. She knew it wasn't bad, though. Maybe it was manly, whatever manly meant. Not sweaty, but not perfumed, just right. He was also very strong. She could feel his back and forearm were rock solid.

To begin with, Kari couldn't stand the song, but as time passed he began to actually quite enjoy it. When she finally relaxed he discovered the brunette had rhythm and the experience was very pleasurable. But he also knew he had to steer them towards Bland Man. If his memory served him correctly he should be just behind him after three steps, if not he was about to upset an innocent bystander - three, two, one, yes, target, hit.

Joey wasn't sure what happened next, all she knew was that the man she was dancing with had bumped forcefully into Dave of all people. She was totally unaware they were that close to him, she had been in her own world.

'I'm so sorry,' said the stranger to Dave before turning back to Joey and saying, 'How rude, please forgive me?' After a small silence, he added, 'I don't even know your name?'

At which point she was about to reply when Dave interrupted, 'It's Joey.'

Oh my God, Dave knows I exist and he knows my name!

'Thank you, Joey, for the dance,' the stranger said politely to her before walking back to his table where his two friends were getting their coats ready to leave.

'Can I buy you a drink, Joey?'

'Yes please,' was all she could say. She was stunned; Dave was offering to buy her a drink! How did that happen? Joey turned around just in time to see the strangers leave. The one she danced with glanced over and smiled, the warmest smile she had seen in a long time. He nodded his head and followed his friends. Would she ever see him again?

'There you are,' Dave handed Joey a large glass of red wine. Red wine, she thought to herself, she'd been on white all night, hadn't he noticed? But then again he didn't notice her until the stranger bumped into him.

Once outside, Henrique turned to Kari and through clenched teeth, 'What the fuck was that?' he spat.

'Me having fun,' Kari replied with a hint of humour in his tone.

'Well it entertained a lot of people, that's for sure,' Lacroix said quietly smiling to himself.

Chapter 4

Joey should have been over the moon… this was what she wanted, but she awoke with a start in the early hours of Saturday morning from a dream where she was kissing the mysterious stranger. Those eyes. She couldn't stop feeling the dark depth of them penetrating her mind…

It was on the Wednesday when Dave sidled up to Joey as she photocopied Cedric's latest presentation. He kissed her on the cheek before saying in a hushed whisper, 'Fancy a weekend in a cosy tent, fantastic music and me – what more could you want? It will be amazing. Have you ever been?'

Joey looked at him blankly.

'The Fiesta!' was his reply, holding up his hands enigmatically.

Joey continued to look blankly at Dave.

'Well trust me, it's a blast. I go every year. You'll love it.'

'What?' she asked again.

'Coming to the music festival with me at the weekend. My mate has a tent we can borrow and I've got a sleeping bag,' he said giving her a knowing look.

'I'm not sure,' she replied, 'I've done camping once before and didn't really enjoy it.'

'But this time you'll be with me.' Dave looked eagerly into her eyes, 'Go on say yes, you know you want to,' before wafting away with one of those 'cat that got the cream' looks, leaving his expensive aftershave lingering.

- - -

The following day she wandered to The Pig's Head and to her relief had beaten Dave. At least now she could buy her own drink and sit at a table of her choice. As she turned from the bar her eyes locked with the dark stranger. She smiled at him and his friend and in return they smiled back.

Thank God Pointy Face didn't appear to be there, he gave her the creeps. Joey sat with her side to the strangers so she could see them clearly in her peripheral vision. She noticed they were casually dressed tonight, wearing jeans and t-shirts.

As Joey waited for Dave she racked her brains trying to think of a nice way to let him down gently regarding The Fiesta. What was the point, she reminded herself, she'd probably end up going.

The day had gone well. Kari was happy that he and Lacroix had achieved more than they had hoped in the attics at the museum. They worked well together. He was feeling the most relaxed he had felt in ages. Lacroix didn't question why they went to the pub again, he just followed, as Kari would expect.

Tonight, he observed Joey. She was nearer in proximity and was companionless. Kari sat alone for a minute or two as Lacroix went to the restroom. He sighed, put down his drink and walked to where Joey sat.

'May I?' he said as he pointed to an empty chair at her table.

'Feel free.'

As Kari sat down he asked, 'How are you?'

'Well, thank you. And you?'

'Good, thanks.'

There was a moment of silence.

'So, you're alone tonight?' Kari asked.

'Seems that way.'

Kari assumed she would rather be alone, as she wasn't giving much away. He stood up to leave her in peace.

'Wait!' said Joey suddenly; 'thank you for the dance the other evening.'

'You're welcome, Joey.'

'Please, will you join me?' Joey indicated to the chair Kari now stood behind.

He smiled and sat back down.

'You know my name, but I don't know yours.'

'Kari,' was his brief reply.

Kari, Joey thought, she'd never heard that name before, but then he didn't look like your average kind of guy. Mark would never have suited him. Noting his accent she asked, 'And where are you from, Kari?'

He liked the way she said his name. 'Well, originally from Canada but I spend a lot of time travelling, hence I'm in this beautiful city of Bath.'

Joey couldn't get over the soft depth of his voice. It was the sort of voice you heard on audio books. The sort that sooths and sends you into a blissful sleep. Joey noticed the friendly one return from the toilets, look across to Kari before sitting alone at a table.

'So, why are you in Bath?' Joey asked.

'Business.'

'What kind of business?' she probed.

'This and that.' Kari replied before looking away.

Joey was no mind-reader but she got the distinct feeling he didn't want to talk about his business.

'Where's your friend tonight?' Kari asked, his eyes returning to look directly at her. He did not want to talk about his business.

His eyes, Joey thought to herself as he held her gaze. 'Lucy? Oh she's with Susie tonight. Susie's having man trouble and Lucy is lending her ear.'

'I see. But I meant your man friend.'

'You mean Dave?'

'The blonde gentleman you were having a drink with when I left last Friday.'

'Yes, that's Dave. He's working late tonight but he may pop back to my flat later.'

'I see,' was all Kari said.

'No… not in that way. I mean he's popping back to mine later but only for a chat. Nothing, like you know… no, it's not like that. He's nice and everything but no, we haven't, you know. Not through lack of trying on his part but no, we haven't. Not that I wouldn't because he's very nice, but no, no…' Why couldn't she stop talking!

Kari smiled at the way Joey blushed so brilliantly.

'The thing is,' her brain was saying stop talking but her mouth didn't take any notice. 'I'm in a dilemma. I like Dave, I have for a while now, and he's asked me away this weekend but I'm not sure I want to go.'

'So don't.'

'But I can't just say no. It would hurt his feelings.'

'You'd rather put yourself through misery just to keep Dave happy?'

'When you put it like that then yes.'

'Well it appears you have no dilemma.'

'I do. It's The Fiesta.'

'Ah,' Kari smiled and nodded, he understood. By all accounts it was a fantastic music festival but you had to be prepared for rain. If it rained The Fiesta could quickly lose its pull.

'Yes, and I don't like camping. Also if I go with him he may have expectations if you know what I mean.' Why was she telling him this, he was practically a stranger but she just found herself unloading on him anyway.

Kari didn't say anything he just nodded.

'And well… I don't want to… you know.'

'I still don't see why you can't just say thank you, but no.'

'Well, it's not that simple. We work together and I don't want things to get messy,' Joey looked down, she felt foolish.

Kari waited until she looked back up at him and simply said, 'It could get a whole lot more messy if you go away and things don't work out. I find it's always best to be honest from the start but most importantly to look after yourself because there aren't many out there that will.'

'What do I say?' Joey asked him.

'You have the choice to continue with your life as it is or accompany Dave to the Fiesta.' He looked at her intently and added, 'Or you could come to France, with me?'

Joey, choking on her wine, spluttered as she placed the glass back on the table. She looked at Kari and said, 'Yeah, right?'

'I'm serious, I have a place in the South of France.'

Still Joey said nothing.

'I'll be working most of the time so you'll have the place to yourself. Well, my housekeeper will be there. Think of it as a mini break.' He then saw the look on her face, 'And it's not an invite with expectations as you put it, just a friendly gesture with absolutely no strings attached, I promise.'

Joey could not believe what he had said. A relative stranger had just invited her to his place in the South of France! France or The Fiesta?

'I can't.'

'Why, scared I'll expect things from you?' Kari smiled at her.

Somehow she knew he didn't. 'How would I get there?'

'Simple, I'll leave a return flight ticket for you at Bristol airport ready for your collection. I'll arrange for you to be met from Nice airport to take you to the villa,' Kari looked at Joey and he could see she didn't know what to say or how to react.

'Honestly, the villa is quite large and you can come and go as you like. I promise I will not make a pass at you or insist we even eat together. As I said I'll be working a lot and it seems you need a plausible reason for not going to The Fiesta.'

Joey couldn't believe it. Kari was offering to buy her flights to and from Nice, let her stay in his villa, all with absolutely no strings. It would also be an honest reason for not going to The Fiesta with Dave tomorrow night. She would have other plans. She felt excited.

'So I'd be able to come and go as I please and have the weekend to relax, nothing more?'

'Exactly.'

'Why?'

'You look like you need time out. I appreciate you don't really know me but I have a lot of privileges and I'd like to give you the opportunity to experience some this weekend. Alone.' He paused a moment and then added, 'Think about it. Speak to Lucy. The tickets will be at the airport tomorrow if you're interested, no pressure. If I don't see you, it's been a pleasure meeting you, Joey. Just remember, know your self-worth.'

Chapter 5

As Joey entered the arrivals hall at Nice airport, it suddenly occurred that she wouldn't know the person coming to collect her... what if there weren't anyone waiting for her? She guessed if that were the case she could just catch the next plane back, curse Kari and hope for his sake she'd never see him again.

Perhaps if there were someone, would they be holding up a big piece of card with *Josephine Lewis* scrawled across the front? She felt more nervous than brave.

Joey scanned the mass of faces waiting to collect loved ones. She felt a wave of relief when she recognised Friendly standing with a woman – thankfully they didn't have a card sign!

'Did you have a good flight?' Friendly asked, his tone warm, his accent similar to Kari's.

'Yes, thanks.'

'Here, let me take your luggage,' he said as he reached for Joey's suitcase. 'Also, allow me to introduce myself, I am Lacroix and this is Solonge.'

'Welcome to France, Joey!' Solonge said cheerfully.

Joey instantly liked Solonge. She had a warm smile, the kind that instantly put you at ease. Solonge was very beautiful and obviously from the same ethnic group as Kari and Lacroix.

Joey smiled back and hoped she didn't look as nervous as she felt. She had no idea where she was going. Suddenly she had a vision of her mum on TV saying, *All we know is she flew to France to stay with some man called Kari, Kevin or something, and now my beautiful girl has gone missing.* Enough! Joey told herself, trying to put things into perspective. They seemed nice and couldn't be that bad, could they?

Joey followed Lacroix and Solonge to a Mercedes Benz with completely tinted glass - the sort of car the mafia would drive. She needed to rein in her imagination... They drove in silence for about forty minutes until eventually they pulled up at large, closed gates. Pausing for only a moment, the gates magically opened to reveal a long, sweeping driveway leading up to a very large villa placed at the top of the hill. Joey sat in stunned silence until Lacroix opened the car door to let her out. The only sound was the strange ticking from the cicadas.

Although it was late in the evening, the silvery moon and glistening stars dotted the dark void of the night sky causing a dramatic backdrop to the vast villa. Subtle lighting lit not only the villa but also the surrounding areas of the grounds. The smell of exotic flowers mixed with the fresh sea air filled Joey's senses.

'Please follow me,' Lacroix said as he carried the suitcase up the villa steps. He opened the door and allowed Joey to enter first closely followed by Solonge.

Even if they did turn out to be murderers at least they had impeccable manners, Mum would be impressed thought Joey.

'Would you like supper, Joey?' Solonge asked.

'I'm fine actually; I had something at the airport before I boarded the plane. I just feel a bit tired.'

'Of course, Solonge please could you take Joey to her room.'

Solonge took Joey's case from Lacroix.

'Kari asked me to remind you to make yourself comfortable. Please use the house and grounds as you wish and if you need anything Madame Dupre will be here tomorrow. She is generally found in the kitchen cooking all sorts of lovely food. We will stay until Kari returns later tonight. He is out most of the day tomorrow so you will have the place to yourself.'

Joey smiled before following Solonge up the impressive winding staircase. There were so many doors, how would she remember where to go?

'Here is your room,' Solonge said as she opened a door revealing a charming and spacious bedroom.

The room was furnished with white painted French furniture. An opulent bed dominated one wall with decorative end tables either side, each boasting an ornate lamp. A beautiful white and pastel blue floral throw covered the enormous bed invitingly. A grand wardrobe stood proudly against one wall, alongside a chest of drawers. There was a large open window in the far end of the room, fine sheer curtains blowing gently in the breeze. Joey felt instantly at ease.

'Relax Joey and remember to enjoy yourself. You have been given a very special opportunity so please make the most of it.'

'I will, I can assure you.'

'Good. Madame Dupre is lovely… very French! She cooks the best food you have ever tasted and keeps this house and Kari in good shape.'

Joey thought maybe Madame Dupre was Kari's partner if she was keeping him in such good shape.

'Anyway, I will leave you to it and don't look so nervous; we are good people, I promise.'

'Thank you, Solonge, you're all being very kind.'

Solonge quietly shut the door behind her and left Joey alone.

Joey sat on the large, comfortable bed and sent Lucy a text to say she'd arrived safely and was now at the villa. Then she explored what was behind the door to the right. She discovered an en suite which was modern and clean, complete with a generous TV imbedded in one of the walls. Joey smiled, she knew she was going to enjoy herself.

She glided over to the windows and discovered full-length French doors behind the billowing sheer curtains, leading to a small balcony with its own table, chairs and sun loungers. Was this place a hotel? Joey thought as she made her way back into the room to look for a kettle or mini bar but found neither. Before retiring to bed she unpacked the few things she'd brought with her, hanging her only dress.

Kari arrived at the villa shortly after midnight. He was exhausted and just wanted to crash but Lacroix and Solonge were waiting for him in the living room. 'I am shattered and François wants a breakfast meeting tomorrow at eight a.m. Does that man ever rest? Sorry Solonge, I haven't said welcome, how are you?' Kari crossed the room to greet her, kissing each cheek.

'I'm very well Kari. You are looking well yourself considering your hectic lifestyle.'

'Thank you, I'm grateful for you coming over at such short notice.'

'Kari,' Solonge said, 'she looked pretty nervous when we collected her. I'm sure it suddenly dawned on her what she was doing. Coming to a strange house, with strangers all around her. I encouraged her to relax and she has promised that she will.'

'I didn't think. I should have met her. At least she has spoken to me.'

'Yes, for all of ten minutes,' laughed Lacroix, 'I'm sure she'll be fine after she has spent time here tomorrow.'

'That reminds me, I was wondering if you both fancied coming for dinner tomorrow evening?'

Lacroix looked at Solonge and said, 'Yes, that would be lovely.'

'I'll invite Joey, she may decline but I'd appreciate your company,' Kari yawned. 'If you will please excuse me, I really need to sleep. Another very busy day awaits me tomorrow.'

Kari walked out of the room, followed by Lacroix and Solonge who then left the villa. They would return the next evening unless Madame Dupre called and said Joey needed something.

Joey woke to the sound of birds singing. She groped for her watch to find the time, but it fell to the floor. Muttering, she scrambled to retrieve it, gasping when she saw it was nearly eleven o'clock. Wow, she had slept for over twelve hours! Okay she knew she had been tired, but this was edging on lazy. She flung the duvet back off her bare skin, got out of bed and looked out of the window. In daylight the view was stunning. The surrounding grounds were beautiful - there was even a tennis court and a swimming pool. Why didn't she bring a swimming costume? *McFly*, she said to herself as she tapped her forehead, sometimes she just didn't think.

After a quick shower she dressed in shorts and a strappy top. Today she intended to read her book, explore the grounds, and eat some of Madame Dupre's delicious food followed by more snoozing… well, they did say relax and she was most definitely going to try!

As she made her way out of the room she made a mental note of the door to her room. Opposite the door was a console table with a blue vase containing a colourful display of fresh flowers.

Feeling like a bloodhound she allowed her nose to lead the way down the stairs, enticed by the most delicious smell of fresh baking.

'Ah Bonjour,' a very rotund, very French lady said to her as she stepped into the kitchen.

'Bonjour,' Joey replied politely.

The French lady then rattled something off in French at a zillion miles per hour to which Joey just stood and stared. She let the lady finish and then weakly tried to explain she was English and didn't understand, but put a *pardon* at the end for good measure.

This didn't seem to upset the French lady, she merely laughed, clapped her hands together and spoke in French about the English. Though Joey still didn't really understand what she had said.

With very broken French and ad hoc sign language Joey managed to make out that the lady was in fact Madame Dupre, clearly not Kari's wife, unless Joey had seriously mistaken him. Joey also managed to interpret that she must eat more food because she looked too thin and she must also go outside and enjoy the beautiful weather.

Madame Dupre added another croissant to a plate which she had already laden with various fruits. Joey gratefully accepted the large glass of freshly squeezed orange juice Madame gave her and ventured out into the heat of the midday sun. It was blissfully warm. Joey found a swing chair, tucked her legs under herself and proceeded to eat everything including the second croissant. She wondered if the sea air was making her extra hungry.

Whilst she ate she looked at her immediate surroundings. It felt as if she were sitting in a famous Chateaux garden. She took her empty plate back to Madame Dupre who was clearly delighted she had eaten everything. Joey retraced her steps outside and continued to the pool. The water looked so inviting, but looks can be deceiving. If Joey swam, which wasn't often, the water had to be warm – she did not do cold water!

Joey spent the afternoon wandering around the various levels of the garden. The different levels each took inspiration from different cultures across the world - a Japanese section, a tropical garden and many more. After a while she felt tired and found a particularly comfortable looking sun lounger in the shade, which was perfect for her to read her book. She just settled down when Madame Dupre appeared with half a baguette filled with Brie and salad along with a jug containing water, ice and fruit and sage leaves. Joey thanked Madame Dupre and watched as she bustled away. To be honest Joey wasn't very hungry but there was no way she was going to upset the lady of the house, and it did look very good.

After eating a good chunk of the baguette Joey lay back, placed her open book on her lap and gave way to the sensation of sleep invading her body.

As Joey began to open her eyes after a brief sleep stretching her stiffened body she heard Kari's voice say nonchalantly, 'I'm glad to see you've taken my advice and relaxed,' and looked up to see him drinking a cup of coffee.

Joey sat bolt upright, causing the book to fall from her lap. Kari bent down to retrieve it and handed it to her.

Rubbing her eyes Joey asked, 'I didn't know you were back. How long have you been here?'

'Long enough to know you snore.'

'I don't! Do I?'

'No, not as far as I'm aware. I've been here five minutes or so and the only sound I heard was from the birds and crickets. Here, I've brought you a coffee,' Kari said as he handed her the hot drink. 'How are you?'

'Sleepy,' Joey replied, squinting her eyes.

'Sorry, I hope I didn't disturb you?'

'No, that's fine. I can't spend all day sleeping. Madame Dupre will think all I do is eat and sleep.'

'Well, you haven't eaten all of the baguette I see she made you. She won't be happy. It was one of the first things she said to me just now, *that English girl is too thin; she needs more meat on her bones,'* chuckled Kari.

'I knew that's what she was saying to me. I didn't pay much attention to my French lessons when I was younger therefore my French is very limited.'

'Ah, Madame Dupre's English is non-existent.' They were quiet for a moment, just the sound of the crickets breaking the silence which hung in the air. 'I'm glad you decided to visit France. It's nice to see you again.'

'Likewise. It is truly beautiful here. You are lucky to own such a place.'

'I don't own the villa, it belongs to my parents. It's a handy place to stay when I have work in Europe'.

Joey looked at her book although she couldn't concentrate on the words. She felt strangely nervous. It was Kari who spoke again, 'So, what did Dave say when he found out you weren't going to The Fiesta?'

Joey smiled and looked back towards Kari, 'He wasn't too impressed. I don't think he takes rejection well. He looked like a sad puppy when I said I had other plans.'

Kari raised his eyebrows, saying nothing. He liked Joey's strange little sayings.

Joey continued, 'But as soon as it was out in the open I felt an enormous relief. I told him to have a good time and to hope it didn't rain.'

'Well the forecast suggests it's raining in the south of England at the moment. I hope he wasn't too upset you turned him down.'

'Oh, Dave will be fine. Besides he's probably found another woman to share his tent and to stroke his ego.'

'Really? He'd do that to you and think nothing of it?'

Joey snorted, 'Knowing my luck, yes.'

Kari shook his head, he felt it was very wrong for a man or a woman to be dating and even consider sleeping with another. It's something he didn't agree with or believe in. Deciding not to air his opinion instead he said, 'Madame Dupre's has Saturday evenings and Sunday off. I have invited Lacroix and Solonge for dinner tonight. You are very welcome to join us or you can eat alone if you prefer?'

'That would be lovely, thank you.'

'Which would be lovely?'

'Eating with the three of you. Solonge seems very nice.'

'And Lacroix and I are not?' Kari teased.

'No, I didn't mean it like that. You both seem very nice, it's just, well you're men, and I don't really know you both. Not that I know Solonge but it's easier to relate to another woman. Does that make sense?' Joey knew she was digging herself into a massive hole.

Kari smiled at her, 'Of course, I understand. No need to explain.' He finished his coffee and stood up stretching to his full height.

Woah, Joey thought, he's massive!

'I'm off to shower and change. Lacroix and Solonge are due at seven, feel free to join us whenever you're ready.' He picked up Joey's unfinished lunch and walked back towards the villa.

Joey watched him stride away. He had a lovely walk, sort of gliding. His legs moved but his body didn't seem to move up and down much. It almost looked like he was on a travellator.

She decided to wait another ten minutes before heading back into the villa to shower and change. Thankfully one advantage of not packing very much meant she couldn't waste a lot of time deciding what to wear!

Chapter 6

Joey noticed that she'd caught a little sun, which gave her a healthy glow as she dressed in white linen trousers and a black, strappy top. It was just before seven o'clock and she wondered whether she should go down and see if Kari was there, but then again how would she find him? Even with his unique smell, she didn't think she'd be able to track him down using just her nose. So, she decided to wait until Lacroix and Solonge arrived, then she could venture downstairs and follow the sound of talking. What if they didn't talk? Her imagination began to run away. If that were the case, she would open every door downstairs until she found them!

Bang on seven, Joey heard the front door open followed by muffled voices. Here was her chance – oh, but she had better go to the loo just one, last time. A few minutes later, Joey descended the stairs, straining her ears to listen for their voices, but she couldn't hear a thing!

Okay, nothing for it but to open every door. She started at the first door in front of her and tried to open the door – locked. She went to the next but it was also locked. Were they playing some cruel joke and watching her make a fool of herself? Or maybe this is the kind of entertaining they do, everyone to their own rooms, not that they would of course as they all seemed so welcoming, but still, the thought made her chuckle.

'And what is so funny?' Kari appeared from behind her, holding a bottle of wine in one hand and a corkscrew in the other.

'Oh, nothing, just a private joke.'

'As intrigued as I am, I won't insist. Solonge and Lacroix have just arrived, they're in the kitchen.' Joey followed Kari as he walked away.

'Hi Joey, have you had a good day?' Solonge asked as she greeted her with a kiss on either cheek.

Slightly taken aback by Solonge's kiss Joey said, 'I've had an amazing day not doing a great deal, thanks!'

'Kari mentioned he found you asleep down by the Japanese garden,' Lacroix said warmly.

'Thanks, Kari! Well, everyone kept telling me to relax and take it easy, so I did.'

'And you look well,' said Solonge.

'Shall we,' Kari said and pointed in the direction of the terrace.

It was a beautiful evening. The sun was setting slowly, the birds squawking their goodnight and the cicadas beginning to work themselves into a frenzy. The table had been laid for four people. Unsure where to sit Joey hung back slightly and waited to see where everyone else sat. Solonge noted her unease and said, 'Joey, come and sit next to me.'

Joey smiled and gladly took the seat Solonge offered.

'And,' Solonge continued as she made herself comfortable, 'we can talk about anything we like and not have to listen to their boring stories of sport!'

'We are able to talk about subjects, Solonge,' commented Lacroix as he sat opposite Joey.

'Really!' teased Solonge.

'Yes!' Both Lacroix and Kari said in unison.

'Well, Joey and myself look forward to your scintillating conversation,' Solonge added, looking directly at Lacroix.

Any remaining tension Joey felt began to fade as she watched Lacroix affectionately flirt with Solonge.

Kari began to offer the wine to the table but momentarily stopped. 'Would you prefer white wine, Joey?' he asked, 'I noticed that's what you drank at The Pig's Head.'

'No, red is perfect, thank you,' enjoying the fact that he remembered what she normally drank.

'So, be honest Kari, did you prepare everything for this evening or did Madame Dupre?' Lacroix asked Kari as he reached for his glass to take a sip of water.

'A little bit of both,' Kari replied, 'Madame Dupre prepared the main course which I just need to re-heat. The wine I chose, the cheese I prepared and I also dressed the table. Impressed are we, Lacroix?'

'I am slightly. I'm still waiting to taste one of your infamous meals that you make from scratch, though.'

'They're rare, Lacroix, but worth the wait!'

'How many more years do I have to wait?'

Kari smiled and the conversation started to flow freely. Solonge spoke softly to Joey whilst the two men invariably talked sports. Joey only knew one sport well and that was tennis which, unfortunately, didn't seem to crop up in conversation.

During quieter moments Joey was able to observe. Lacroix and Solonge must be a couple - if they weren't, they should be. They both smiled at the same things and moved at the same time. Joey decided she liked them both very much. They were easy to talk to and entertaining.

Kari, well, she thought she could watch him all day and still be fascinated. He looked full of health tonight. He was wearing loose, white linen trousers, a look most men can't pull off, however he did. He wore a fitted, white t-shirt that did little to hide his toned body. On his feet was a pair of expensive looking leather flip-flops; no squashed, hairy toes, just neat and well proportioned. His jet-black hair was still slightly damp from his earlier shower and it hung loose like a sheer, black curtain down his back. He was also smiling a lot and Joey could see crow's feet around his eyes. Maybe he was human after all.

Kari was the perfect host and he continually asked if Joey was all right. The wine flowed and the mouth-watering duck was cooked to perfection. Kari cleared the table of plates before bringing out a cheese board and a decanter of port. It was perfect. The lights illuminated automatically when darkness began to fall.

By ten o'clock the cicadas were in full song. Joey shivered as she began to feel cold.

'Shall we go in?' Kari suggested.

'Actually, I'd better take Solonge back to the hotel. Try as she might, I can see she's fighting a losing battle to keep her eyes open,' Lacroix said. Joey hadn't noticed until that point that Lacroix had not drunk a drop of wine all evening.

'Jet lag?' Joey asked Solonge.

'Yes. I flew in from Canada yesterday and I think it's starting to creep up on me,' Solonge admitted.

'I had no idea. And there's me sleeping most of the day and I've only come from England!' Joey said, making them all laugh.

They walked into the villa and Solonge and Lacroix made their way to the front door. 'Thanks for a wonderful evening, Kari,' Solonge said as she kissed him on either cheek.

'You're welcome,' Kari replied as Solonge hugged and kissed Joey.

'It was lovely to spend some time with you, Joey. Enjoy and make the most of tomorrow.'

'I will, thank you, Solonge.' Joey said as she watched Kari and Lacroix do a typical manly hug – the sort where they grasped hands whilst slapping the other jovially on the back. Joey hoped Lacroix wouldn't expect this from her! Thankfully Lacroix gave Joey a polite nod and said he and Solonge would pick her up tomorrow at three to take her to the airport.

Kari closed the door behind them and as he turned to Joey and said, 'Fancy another glass of port?'

'That would be lovely, thank you.' Joey didn't want her evening to end just yet. They walked back through the kitchen to retrieve their glasses. Joey noticed Kari clock all the washing up that had to be done and she began to rinse the plates.

'It's okay, I'll do this later,' Kari said.

'You have been a perfect host,' replied Joey, 'you've fed me and let me use your house, so the least I can do is help clear up.'

'No seriously, it's fine… if I allowed that then I would no longer be the perfect host as you say.'

'No, you'd become a stubborn one!' retaliated Joey.

'Okay, you win, but it's not as bad as it looks, a lot goes in the machine.'

Together they cleared through the piles of cutlery, plates and pans. Kari brought everything in from the table. He wrapped the remaining cheeses and put them in the fridge. They worked in companionable silence.

Once finished, Kari poured the two glasses of port and they went back out onto the terrace. Joey found a blanket in the kitchen and wrapped it around her to keep out the chill.

'Are you feeling more relaxed?' Kari asked Joey.

'Like you wouldn't believe, and to think I could have been in a smelly tent instead.'

'You can tell me to mind my own business but it doesn't sound like you're particularly interested in Dave.'

'You're bang on there!'

Again Kari smiled at another strange saying he'd never heard before.

Joey sighed and looked up into the clear night sky. Every sound seemed to drift away as finally Joey looked towards Kari. She was once again caught in his hypnotic gaze, try as she might, she could not pull her eyes from his. His eyes sparkled, like the stars above them. Silence hung in the cool, night air. Eventually Joey found her voice. 'I thought he'd be more interesting than he really is. He's actually quite dull.'

'Bland, you could say,' Kari offered.

'Exactly.' Joey took a deep breath in an attempt to control her thoughts. Kari was far from dull or bland.

Kari smiled.

'I don't know, I'm not very good at finding the right man. I always seem to go for the wrong sort... but, ah... I wont bore you with my sad love life. I've had a lovely day and I don't want it to end with you feeling sorry for me. How about you, is there a Mrs Kari out there?

'No.'

'A girlfriend?'

'No.'

'A man of few words. Well for what it's worth, I'm surprised. I mean you've got everything - the house, an interesting lifestyle, great friends and *the looks*. Plus, you've welcomed a complete stranger into your house and it's not been awkward. To top it all, you even know where things live in the kitchen – I'm waffling now, aren't I?'

Kari smiled throughout her little speech and only looked up when she mentioned he had *the looks*.

Silence fell between them. Joey finished her drink and stood to leave. Being ever the gentleman, Kari also stood.

'Thank you for giving me this opportunity, Kari, I've had a wonderful day and a perfect evening. I know I will sleep well tonight.' Acting on instinct Joey went to kiss him goodnight on the cheek, to thank him. At that moment, Kari also went to kiss her and they ended up clashing noses and becoming embarrassed, never actually kissing each other. They both smiled and Joey walked away to her comfortable bed in her beautiful room in the magnificent villa, occupied only by her and this gorgeous man.

Chapter 7

Joey slept with the window open, she loved listening to the sound of the cicadas and the haunting hoot from an owl. As she woke she tried to decipher the new noise that broke her sleep. She lay holding her breath as daylight broke through the gap in her curtains. She reached for her watch and saw it was half past eight. Thankfully she hadn't over slept today otherwise she would earn the reputation of a sloth.

Slowly Joey got out of bed and wandered to the window, pulling back the curtain just as Kari was getting out of the pool. For a moment she couldn't move. She stood gaping at what she saw.

As her senses returned she dropped the curtain quickly blocking the view. She inhaled deeply and pulled the curtain back again. There in full glory Kari stood breathing deeply from excessive exercise. She had just witnessed him pull himself out of the pool and to say *Daniel Craig* coming out of the sea as *Bond* was a sight to behold, well so was this!

Joey knew Kari would have a good body, but she didn't expect to see it quite this early in the morning. He was stunning. If Joey closed her eyes she could relive the full experience in technicolor - his back and arms rippled as he pulled himself out of the water. His skin was soft brown in colour and to say he was fit was an understatement. And to top it all, he was wearing a relatively tight pair of black Speedo shorts.

Taking another deep breath she headed for the shower. Kari was a friend, clearly well out of her league and she had to try and wipe that vision from her mind. She tried, she really did. Coffee would help. So after a shower and dressing she made her way downstairs suddenly remembering they were alone. Not to worry, she thought to herself, continue as if he were an unattractive male friend that happened to be taking a swim.

'Good morning.'

Joey nearly dropped the kettle. 'Oh, hi,' she turned around only to turn back again quickly to what she was doing. He was there in the kitchen with a towel around his waist but his bronzed, beautiful body was on full display. 'Fancy a, umm, coffee?'

'Yes, that would be lovely thank you,' Kari replied. 'Not sleeping in this morning then?'

'No, not today.'

'It's going to be a beautiful day,' Kari said, oblivious of his near nakedness.

'I'm sure,' stuttered Joey. 'Any plans?'

'Well, I have a rare day off and I was wondering if you fancied going out for lunch?' He saw Joey freeze. 'No strings remember, I just don't fancy cooking and if you're up for it I know a lovely restaurant not far from here.'

Joey still didn't reply.

'But if you'd rather stay here alone then that is fine.'

'No, I'd love to go out for lunch, thank you.'

'Great. I'm off to shower. Help yourself to breakfast,' he said taking his coffee before leaving.

Joey realised she hadn't said much at all; she hoped she didn't appear rude, but to be honest she was lost for words.

She made herself some breakfast and headed out to the terrace desperately trying to wipe the vision of Kari's body from her mind. She was doing quite well until he reappeared, fresh, clean-shaven and dressed in white, linen trousers and shirt. How could she relax knowing his body was hiding beneath those fibres?

He sat opposite her and quietly ate brioche and fruit. They lapsed into silence, each absorbed in their own thoughts.

Kari was confused – had he said or done something wrong? He didn't mean anything by going out for lunch. Last night he enjoyed her company and thought it would be a nice thing to do. She seemed very happy when she went to bed yesterday evening but this morning she seemed out of sorts.

Feeling decidedly plain in comparison Joey said to Kari, 'What should I wear to lunch?'

'What you're wearing is fine. It's a very simple fish restaurant not far from here which I go to frequently, especially if Madam Dupre is having a day off.'

Joey looked at what she was wearing. Did that mean he thought what she was wearing was simple. Should she make more of an effort? She could wear the dress she packed, but she didn't want to look keen or like she wanted to impress him. Because she wasn't, she liked him as a friend that was all. A friend who happened to have an amazing body, a great voice, a kind nature, totally kissable lips…

'If it's okay with you I thought we could head off in half an hour?'

Joey wasn't entirely sure what Kari had said; she had been in gaga land. 'Sure, yes I can be ready soon,' Joey answered but really it was a question.

'Great. Have you finished with that?' he pointed to her half eaten breakfast. She replied with a nod and he took the plates away.

Joey walked to the edge of the balcony. She had to get a grip. A few deep breaths later she went to her room to brush her teeth and compose herself before going out with Kari.

Joey sat next to him as he drove the sleek, understated, black Audi R8 coupe. He loved this car, it was his and his alone. He also loved the opportunity to drive, which he rarely did because there was always someone there to do it for him. It was on occasions like this he was almost able to be normal. They drove in silence to the small town of Pontrains. Kari parked the car and got out. The time it took for him to walk around the car and open her door he discovered she'd already stepped out of it. There was a brief, 'Oh sorry,' passed between them.

'Fancy a walk to the beach?' Kari asked as he locked the car.

'A walk sounds perfect.'

Kari held out his hand to indicate which way, and it wasn't long before a small group of children excitedly ran up to them both. As he bent down to their level they showered him with hugs and kisses. Joey couldn't understand what the children were saying as they spoke extremely fast and in French, so she just stood back and waited for the mayhem to calm down.

A beautiful, little girl, who looked about five, was giving Joey evil looks. Kari noticed and spoke to the girl. The girl replied, never taking her eyes off Joey.

The little girl walked forwards and said to Joey, 'Bonjour, je m'appelle Claudine.'

'Bonjour, Claudine.' Joey replied, the little girl smiled. All eyes were on Joey, including Kari's. Joey crouched down to Claudine's level noting the well-worn, well-loved teddy bear the little girl held comfortably to her nose. 'Comment tu t'appelle ton dodo, mademoiselle?'

'Pippy,' Claudine, replied quietly.

'Est ce que je peux rencontrer Pippy?' Joey held out her hand hoping Claudine would allow her to see her teddy.

Claudine looked up to Kari for reassurance. Kari smiled warmly and nodded. With a degree of trepidation, the little girl passed Pippy to Joey.

Joey's smile reached her eyes as she held the bear gently. 'Enchanté Pippy. Qu'est ce qui as?' Joey said, pretending he was whispering something in her ear. 'Tu veux voler la plage?' Joey moved the bear's head in agreement.

Suddenly all the children burst into peels of laughter. Joey looked up towards Kari who was also laughing quietly. 'What did I just say?' she asked, instinctively knowing she'd said something in error.

Kari smiled, 'Apparently, Pippy would like to steal a beach!!'

'Oh no, I'm so sorry! I said my French was very limited.'

'I'm impressed you tried.' Kari crouched down next to Joey, 'What did you mean to say?'

'That Pippy would like to *go* to the beach!'

Kari smiled and reached for Pippy. Holding the loved bear gently and pretending to speak his voice he said, 'Claudine, ce que je veux dire c'est j'ai envie d'aller à la plage. Dis donc, je sais bien que tu peux pas voler une plage!'

The little girl giggled and took her bear back from Kari. After a quick snuggle with her bear Claudine placed one of Pippy's hands in Joey's whilst she held the other. The bear swung merrily between Joey and Claudine as they led the lively group towards the shoreline. Kari carried a small boy on his shoulders, the boy's persistent laugh showed he loved every minute of the ride.

They must have spent the best part of an hour splashing in the sea with the children. Kari enjoyed chasing various children along the beach and swinging them high in the air to a mass of giggles. It was a lovely sight. Joey didn't understand what they were saying but she could see Kari was very loved, she was discovering it was hard not to. She felt very out of breath so after a while sat quietly on the sand. As she watched them all laughing and shouting for Kari's attention it occurred to Joey that they all seemed to be of the same ethnicity. They really were quite a beautiful sight to see. At one point Kari had obviously said he needed five minutes peace and he joined Joey.

'You okay?' Kari said breathing heavily as he'd just done a major work out with kids.

'I'm fine thank you. It's lovely to see you having such fun. I had no idea you were such a big child,' Joey teased.

With that Kari pushed Joey to the side, laughing as he did it. Joey laughed as she righted herself.

'I'm assuming you don't really understand what the children were saying?'

'You're right, but I can see they like you a lot.'

Kari smiled, 'Claudine is convinced I'm going to marry her and she was concerned as she'd never seen you before and she thought you are very beautiful. She was worried I was going to forget her and marry you.'

'Oh, is that what that was all about.'

'Yes, I said you are very beautiful but assured her you are only my friend.'

A little boy and Claudine ran over to where they sat and pulled Kari to his feet whilst rambling away in French, Kari answered the boy in French and then proceeded to chase the giggling little boy back to the group of children.

Joey watched the joyful scene and was happy but a little sad at the same time. He said she was beautiful, correction very beautiful but they were only friends. Exactly right - they were only friends, but she couldn't help it if she fancied him. Yes, she officially fancied him but knew it was only a dream she would have to hold in her memory forever.

Joey continued to watch Kari play with the children whilst she plaited Claudine's hair. A short while later Kari returned and pulled Joey to her feet suggesting they go and eat as he was starving.

The children ran off down the beach and left Kari and Joey to walk to the fish restaurant. The restaurant owner greeted them with great warmth. So much so that Joey felt as if she was a long, lost friend who had finally returned. They sat at a table for two near the back of the restaurant, away from the general passing public. The restaurant was very French and tribal decorations adorned the walls. Joey looked at the menu and really wasn't sure what to order.

'Any recommendations?' she asked Kari.

'It's all wonderful, but you can never go wrong with fish of the day. It will be freshly caught and cooked to perfection, that I can promise you.'

'Okay, fish of the day it is then!'

A waiter brought them a basket of bread and a bottle of water. Kari asked if Joey wanted wine, she declined and said she'd stick with water. They gave their order and were left in peace.

'So, do you come here often?'

'Yes, when I'm in France I try to visit at least once.' Kari smiled, 'You are aware that sounded like a really bad chat up line aren't you.'

'Yes, as soon as the words left my mouth I realised,' Joey said as she helped herself to a piece of bread. 'Kari?'

'Yes.'

'I hope this doesn't come out the wrong way, but I couldn't help but notice everyone in this village appears to be of the same ethnicity as you, Lacroix and Solonge.'

'Very observant of you,' Kari replied with a slight edge to his voice.

'I didn't mean to sound rude, far from it, I'm just interested. Is there a small pocket in this part of France which are, I'm not sure what your ethnic origin is, but are you all related in some way?'

At which point Kari burst out laughing, 'No, we're not all related, there's no inbreeding if that's what you mean. We just happen to be similar people who like this part of the world and have therefore built a community here.' Kari smiled and took a large bite from his piece of bread.

Joey could tell that was the end of that subject. She wanted to know more but could feel the door shut from Kari as far as he was concerned. She decided to change the subject.

'Well, I've decided it's time for a change. I'm going to dump Dave and look for another job.'

Kari nearly choked on his bread and had to drink water to remain from dying from asphyxiation, 'Really, are you sure?'

'Absolutely. I've made the most of my two days down here in France and one thing is clear, I need to move on. I'm not getting any younger. I'm bored at work and need a new challenge. I'm not sure what it is yet, but it begins with binning Dave off for good and then handing in my notice.

'Poor Dave.'

'Don't go sticking up for your fellow men,' Joey warned looking directly at Kari. 'I texted him last night simply to say hi and hoped he was having a good time and seconds later I received a text back saying he was having a wonderful time.'

Kari nodded, 'That's good.'

'Not when it was signed Michelle who then sent another text informing me exactly how wonderful a time he was having, with her.'

'Oh.'

'So he's dumped.'

'You don't want to wait for an explanation?'

'Nope,' Joey said as she tore her bread in half. 'No trust, no man.'

'That simple.'

'That simple,' Joey added as she popped the bread in her mouth.

'But what will you do for work?'

Joey finished her mouthful before replying, 'I've hardly seen anything of the world and I'd really like to travel. But travel costs money so that's not really an option unless I volunteer somewhere like Africa and help others, just for a year or so. That way I can become completely independent and look after myself for once, but at the same time doing some good. Does that make sense?'

'Wow I didn't expect this weekend to be so life changing for you.'

Little did he know, Joey knew her life would ever be the same again after meeting Kari.

Lunch was really pleasant and conversation flowed easily. They talked about Africa, volunteering, art, music and anything that wasn't directly personal to either of them. Whilst drinking their coffee Joey asked about Lacroix and Solonge. 'Before I leave today I just need to ask one thing,' she saw Kari tense up.

What did Joey want to ask he thought? Did she want to know more about his work, did she want to see him again, his mind raced.

'Solonge and Lacroix, are they an item?'

'No, but they should be. What makes you think they are?'

'They seem perfect for each other. I watched them yesterday and they seem so in tune with one other. She moves her leg, he moves his leg and so on,' she replied.

And Kari thought he was observant, 'I know what you mean. They have known each other all their lives. They have had partners but nothing serious. I guess they're waiting for the right one to come along and it's obvious to both you and me that it's staring them both in the face.' His eyes narrowed, clearly deep in thought. After a moment's silence he looked at Joey through his furrowed brow and said, 'I've just had a fantastic idea.'

'What?' Joey asked curiously.

'Next week I have to go to the Nice ball.'

'And?'

'Well, we all have to stay here in France for the week and travel back to Canada next Monday. I was going to take Lacroix with me anyway but why not include Solonge?' Kari looked very pleased with himself, 'It's a pretty major event and they'll have to go together and who knows, they may just notice each other in a different light.'

'That sounds perfect,' Joey enthused, she felt annoyed with herself for feeling slightly jealous. 'I really hope your match making works, they should be together, anyone can see that. Gosh, talking of Lacroix have you seen the time? We had better head back otherwise he'll think you've kidnapped me.'

They finished their coffees and said their goodbyes to the restaurant owner. Joey noticed Kari didn't pay for the meals, she assumed he had a tab and settled at the end of the month or something.

The drive back to the villa was too short as far as Joey was concerned. This may well be the last time she saw Kari and she wanted to savour every moment. From his unusual delicious smell to the muscles of his thigh, which tensed every time he changed gear. Kari seemed lost in thought too, probably thinking of work or not long now until I say goodbye to Joey and never have to see her again.

They got back to the villa and again Kari walked around to open Joey's door but again she was out before he had a chance. Kari wasn't used to this in women.

Once inside the villa, Joey turned to Kari and said, 'Just in case I don't get a chance later I want to say a very big thank you for a really perfect weekend. It was just what I needed and it gave me the chance to make some very important decisions. Also lunch was really good, the fish of the day was perfection as you said it would be.'

Kari smiled warmly at her, 'You're welcome.'

'I'd better go and pack my things,' Joey said as she began to walk up the stairs.

'Before you go, I've something I'd like to ask you?' Kari called after her.

Joey turned to look at him. He looked at her with dark, penetrating eyes leaving her feeling very vulnerable and weak. Right now if he asked her to strip naked she would. She looked back at him with as much effort as possible to keep eye contact and not lower her eyes to the floor.

'It's just a thought, but would you consider being my date next week for the Nice ball?'

Joey's eyes widened and she just stared right back – not sure she had heard correctly.

'Not *date* date, but date as in no strings attached unofficial date date?'

'So, not a date, but someone to accompany you, that's all?' Joey clarified.

'Yes.'

'How posh is this ball, what would I be expected to wear, how would I come back, when is the ball?'

'Posh, a dress, you'd fly and it's next Saturday,' replied Kari with a smile.

'Okay,' Joey said her eyes narrowing as she tried to match his answers to her questions.

'Let me clarify. It is a very posh event and you would need to wear a knock out dress. I would pay for the dress and your flights. You wouldn't need to do anything except arrive, accompany me – no strings – and shop for a beautiful gown.'

'Well, when you put it like that it's a no brainer, but I can't let you pay for my plane ticket again or dress. I'd feel like I'm sponging off you.'

'Honestly, I wouldn't be happy unless you let me pay,' he replied looking hurt.

Joey walked back down a few stairs until she was eye level with him. She didn't want to upset him, 'Honestly I don't mind…'

'You need to save your money if you're going to Africa. Please accept this gift from me. I'm putting you out, it's the least I can do in return,' Kari replied and gave her a really warm smile.

Joey smiled back at him, 'In that case, yes. I'd love to be your no strings date.'

'Excellent,' Kari wanted to hug her, but he remained where he was. 'I'll get Lacroix to buy your plane tickets when he takes you to the airport shortly. Solonge can take you shopping next Saturday for a gown and we can all go together. That way we can both watch and see if Solonge and Lacroix get together,' he added with a mischievous glint in his eye.

'If you're sure, then that will be lovely.'

'I am. It's probably best if you fly in next Saturday and leave on the Monday. Although the ball is Saturday evening we probably wont be home until the early hours and knowing you, as I'm beginning to, you'll need Sunday to sleep!'

'Cheeky,' Joey said as she skipped up the stairs to pack. A few moments later she heard Lacroix and Solonge arrive to take her to the airport. She looked around her beautiful room really excited to think she'll be back next week. She could feel her face flushing with joy.

As she walked downstairs she noticed Lacroix and Kari were deep in conversation.

Solonge asked what Joey had done today and Joey explained they had lunch at Pontrains. Solonge said nothing but the *oh* was written all across her face. They waited for the men to finish their conversation, and then Lacroix said they had better get going. He took Joey's suitcase and he and Solonge left to wait by the car.

'So,' Joey said, 'it's not goodbye just yet, but see you next week.' She shuffled uncomfortably from side to side. Should she shake his hand, give him a hug, kiss his cheek or just wave and say see you soon? Thankfully Kari could see her unease and took the initiative - he held her shoulders still whilst he kissed her on both cheeks - no clashing. Mind you Joey didn't move a muscle throughout the whole blissful moment. In fact she thought she might have even stopped breathing.

Kari stepped back and held out his arm for her to leave. Thankfully she wasn't wearing heels as her legs had gone just a wee bit jelly like. Lacroix opened her car door and closed it behind her. Joey belted herself in and waved goodbye to Kari as Lacroix pulled away.

'I hear we're to see you again next week,' Lacroix said warmly.

Chapter 8

When Joey returned on the Sunday evening she went straight round to Lucy's and relayed every detail, paying particular attention to how fantastic Kari had looked in Speedos.

The following week seemed to fly by. Joey handed in her notice and tried to detox but ended up feeling sick, so she stopped because there was no way she was going to miss this weekend, come hell or high water!

At work, Dave appeared to be avoiding her and therefore made it blissfully easy not to talk to him until Wednesday when she felt she had to say *bog off.* When they met at lunchtime Joey told him it wasn't going to work. At first he seemed a bit pissed off but then proceeded to tell her all about The Fiesta and how she'd missed a fantastic event. *Perhaps* she thought, but then again I wouldn't have seen Kari in his Speedos or have the opportunity to go to the Nice ball this weekend!

When she challenged him about Michelle he had the audacity to try and deny that anything happened. But it didn't take long for him to come clean, putting the onus back on to Joey. He implied he wasn't getting any satisfaction from her even though she'd been after him for weeks - after all he was a red-blooded man who had needs and Michelle was able to meet them. Joey couldn't believe he'd known she'd fancied him for weeks yet he did nothing until Kari literally put her in his hands. She was better off without him and to think she had wasted months waiting for him to notice her!

When Joey flew into Nice airport on the Saturday, she was surprised to see that only Solonge was waiting to meet her.

'I'm so excited!' Solonge said with enthusiasm as she embraced Joey, 'I have never been to the Nice ball and it's amazing that Kari has given us this opportunity…. and the chance for us both to buy a beautiful dress!'

'So, Kari is paying for your dress too?' Joey asked.

'Yes.' Solonge replied as if it were natural for Kari to buy her dresses. 'We're actually going shopping before I take you to the villa. Kari wasn't sure if you needed someone to do your hair and make-up, I made the decision that you'd probably be happier doing all of that yourself, was that okay?'

'Absolutely.'

They wasted no time in heading to some chic clothing boutiques. Joey tried on, what felt like, ten dresses but none of them were quite right. Solonge had found her dress straight away and she looked amazing. Joey just wasn't sure what she wanted and the price tags sent shivers down her spine.

Solonge noticed that Joey was looking at the prices and returning the dresses back to the rail. Finding a seductively tight, sheer black dress, with a split up to the thigh and an overlay of lace, she handed it to Joey. 'Here, try this one.'

Instantly Joey looked at the price tag, 'I can't!' she said as she returned the dress back to the hook. 'Have you seen how much it is?'

'That doesn't matter. I know it will look fantastic on you. Try it?' Solonge said as she handed the dress to her again.

Joey shook her head and reluctantly took the beautiful dress from Solonge. Even before the assistant had fastened all the tiny buttons at the back of the dress, Joey knew it was perfect. She came out of the dressing room and Solonge took a deep breath and said something in a language she had never heard before – it definitely wasn't French.

'What do you think?' Joey asked.

Solonge simply walked up to Joey, took both her hands in hers and said, 'Perfect.'

Joey was so happy to be back in the beautiful bedroom and headed straight for the French doors. Opening them, she headed out to the balcony replaying the memory of Kari pulling himself out of the pool. Sadly, he wasn't there, but he would be back soon, ready for the ball. It had been arranged that Solonge and Lacroix would pick both her and Kari up at eight p.m.

Joey now had three blissful hours to get ready. She immediately phoned Lucy to update her, explaining that she had arrived safely and was going to be wearing a gown that cost as much as a small deposit for a flat in Bath! Joey wondered what time Kari would be back? *Stop*! She thought, I must start getting ready.

She had a shower and began to use her straighteners to curl her hair into loose waves. It always took ages and she was beginning to wish that she did have someone to do it for her. She was sure she heard the front door open, closely followed by footsteps running up the stairs. Could it be Kari? Her heart began to hammer; she half expected a knock on her door. Nothing came.

She peeled herself into the sleek, ebony black gown, worrying how she was going to do up all the tiny buttons – a dress like this definitely required a second pair of hands. After 15 minutes, sheer determination, will power and a fair bit of swearing, she managed to fasten all the tiny buttons.

With one last trip to the toilet to re-apply her lipstick, she was ready to go.

As Joey started to walk down the hallway, she heard voices downstairs. She now recognised it was Solonge, Lacroix and Kari. How she loved the tone of his voice - it was so deep and sultry. She gave herself a quick shake and walked down the stairs.

Kari was talking as she rounded the corner but stopped abruptly when he saw her. Joey also thought she saw his mouth pop open! *Woah, how bloody gorgeous did he look* she thought whilst desperately trying to steady her feet on the stairs. She held onto the balustrade with a vice-like grip whilst trying to look graceful. Kari's weighty gaze held hers until she eventually reached the bottom of the stairs. With his hands placed gently on her shoulders, he kissed her on either cheek. She was glad he had regained control. But he didn't remove his hands and it felt like her skin was beginning to burn from his simple touch.

He looked deep into her eyes and said simply, 'You look exquisite.'

Kari was still holding Joey when Lacroix said, 'It's lovely to see you again, Joey. And may I say, both yourself and Solonge look a million dollars.'

Lacroix couldn't properly greet Joey because Kari had kept hold of Joey; his touch was now scorching Joey's shoulders. She stood transfixed, as she felt the fire spread to the pit of her stomach. She couldn't tear her eyes away from his, which glinted with mystery. It was Lacroix who coughed, breaking the spell by murmuring that they should leave. Kari took Joey's arm and escorted her to the black Mercedes. He opened her door, she slid in and he closed the door behind her, before walking round to the other side and joining her in the back of the car.

'How are you?'

'I'm very well, thank you. I've had a productive week. I'm now single and jobless, or at least working out my notice.'

'You don't hang about, do you?'

'What's the point - I realised that last weekend. How about you, have you had a good week?'

'Very good, thank you. Everything just seemed to fall into place.'

They lapsed into a companionable silence for the remainder of the short journey, each absorbed in their own thoughts. The car cruised smoothly along the Cote d'Azur, lights from the expensive motor yachts dotting the sea. Tourists enjoying an evening walking along the promenade des Anglais. As the car began to slow, it joined a small convoy of expensive looking cars and sleek limousines. Eventually the car halted outside the Musee d'Art Contemporain, their destination.

Joey looked out of the window and saw a red carpet leading to the entrance between the two imposing white façades of the gallery. Either side of the red carpet were journalists and photographers eagerly waiting to pounce on the next person to arrive at the ball. She looked across to Kari, who remained poker face and seemingly at total ease with the situation they were about to walk into.

Uniformed attendants opened the car doors simultaneously and Lacroix handed the keys to one, whom Joey assumed would park the car. As Joey went to step out of the car Kari, thankfully, reached forward and offered her his arm. 'Are you okay?' He asked her, concern evident in his eyes.

Feeling very out of her depths she nodded. But as she held onto Kari's arm her confidence began to grow. She held her head high and together they began the short walk towards a large modern gallery. Flashbulbs of the photographers were lighting the space all around them. Journalists and TV crews vying for attention. Joey felt like a celebrity... but it wasn't her name they called, it was Kari's. He wore a blank expression and without stopping to pose or answer any questions walked, with a steely determination, into the art gallery where the ball was being held.

As they ventured further into the doorway, it began to dawn on Joey just how posh the event was. They waited quietly in line; Kari didn't utter a word, instead, he gently squeezed Joey's arm in reassurance.

Oh crap, thought Joey, a very smartly dressed attendant was announcing people as they arrived. Joey looked at Kari and grinned. He smiled back. She was so excited. Lucy would never believe her when she told her about this!

Mr Kari Qaleti Kutan and Miss Josephine Lewis, said the announcer as they approached.

Joey felt like she should bow or wave, but thought better of it as Kari gently pulled her along. Damn, she'd been so caught up in the moment that she'd missed Kari's surname! She couldn't ask him now, in case someone over heard her and thought it was very odd that she was accompanying a man without knowing his full name!

The evening was magical. Everywhere she looked there were glamorous people. Beautiful people. Famous people. She recognised extremely famous film stars, top musicians and beautiful models. Although politics isn't one of her strong points, she certainly recognised many world leaders including the American President!

A live band played soft sultry jazz music as people mingled and made polite conversation. Many people vied for Kari's attention and he politely conversed with them, however, being ever thoughtful of Joey's presence.

The room was filled with class and sophistication. There were moments when Joey felt able to look around and just soak up not only where she was, but also whom she was sharing the evening with. Her senses were over powered. The aroma of expensive perfume and cologne mixed with the distinctive fragrance from the great oil paintings caused powerful artistry for her sense of smell. The gentle sway of the Jazz music blurring with many multi-national accents created a deeply sexual ambience. Powerful Pop art paintings by Andy Warhol and Roy Lichtenstein caused an intensely dramatic backdrop to the rich and famous. She smiled to herself as she thought it ironic to be in an art gallery yet her senses were creating their own art, cementing the experience to memory forever.

The evening continued with an eight-course dinner. Joey sat opposite Kari and she thought he was easily the most handsome of the men sat at their table. In the candlelight he looked utterly delicious. The warm candle glow drew attention to his chiselled features and highlighted his deep dark eyes. She found it hard not to watch him, and tried in vein to converse with her immediate neighbours; she didn't want to let Kari down.

The food was exquisite, she wasn't sure if she had ever tasted such fine food before. The first course was a small amuse-bouche followed by a fresh oyster. As the beautifully presented oyster served on a nesting of seaweed was placed in front of her she looked up and saw amusement in Kari's eyes. He could see this was another new experience for her. Joey smiled and lowered her eyes, yet when she returned them his gaze was still transfixed on her. Without uttering a word he picked up his oyster and ate it, his eyes never leaving hers. Bravely she did the same. As she swallowed she tried not to gag. A smile teased

Kari's lips as he watched her reach for her champagne glass. He mirrored her and said, 'To you,' as he raised her glass to her's.

The remainder of the courses was divine and immaculately presented, each an individual piece of art. Joey particularly enjoyed the pork tenderloin with roasted vegetables as well as the simple cheese course served with a selection of dried fruit and nuts. Even though she had eaten eight courses, Joey was surprised not to feel as if she had overeaten. She had surreptitiously watched Kari throughout the evening. As music began to play again, people were moving away from the tables to dance. She wasn't sure if Kari would ask her to dance, besides he was engrossed in conversation with a man that had to be a politician, the poor man looked so terribly dull compared to Kari.

It wasn't long before she was asked to dance by many different men, and she rarely had a moment to catch her breath, but still Kari never approached her. She hoped it was because he was busy and not because he didn't want to dance with her.

As she danced she was able to observe Solonge and Lacroix. She noticed that they had danced together all evening, in fact they only had eyes for each other.

After dancing for nearly an hour Joey decided to take advantage of being where she was and took the opportunity to look at some of the exquisite art pieces. She smiled as she walked around the gallery looking at the imposing paintings and sculptures. She was happily emerged in her own world, when she heard, 'Are you hiding too?' It was Kari.

'Not really, more… taking a breather! Why? Are you?'

'Yes.'

'From whom?'

'The French Head of State. I really don't want to talk about work all evening, I think I'm entitled to some fun!' Kari smiled at her. 'If you see a serious looking, grey haired man walking this way, please, tell me?'

'Okay, deal.'

'Besides, I haven't spent any time with the most devastatingly gorgeous woman in the gallery.' Kari said, looking at the painting they were standing in front of.

Joey felt a surge of jealously course through her body. 'Well, I'll keep an eye out for the serious French man and you go find her,' Joey replied, in a polite but clipped tone.

Kari turned to look at her, 'I have. I'll let you in on a secret; it's my *no strings* date! She looks ravishing tonight.'

Joey couldn't help but blush, she replied, 'Have you had your eyes tested recently or have you been drinking?'

'Yes, to both questions, but my sight is perfect and I've only had two glasses of Champagne.' He was still looking at her. Joey moved to the next painting to create distance between them, she was feeling slightly tipsy and didn't want to make a fool of herself. Kari followed.

'Do you like this one?' She asked.

'Yes, the longer you look, the more interesting it becomes.'

Joey nodded, but stopped when she realised he was still looking at her. As she turned, she saw a grey haired, serious looking man making his way determinedly towards them, 'I think it may be time you made your exit.'

At first Kari was confused, had he said too much? Then he saw in his periphery, the French Head of State about to walk over to him.

Kari grabbed Joey's hand and leading the way he pulled her towards the dance floor, politely excusing them both as people parted like waves before them. The band was playing a beautiful piece of classical music, though it could have been *Bonnie Tyler* and Joey would have still danced.

Whilst twirling her around in a fluid motion, Kari pulled Joey tight against him and leaned down to whisper in her ear, 'You do realise you have danced with many different men tonight, and some more than once, but this is our first dance. Was my dancing really that bad at The Pig's Head or are you scared I'll bump into some poor, unsuspecting man?'

'So, you've noticed I have been dancing? I wasn't sure you had. I was beginning to think *you* didn't want to dance with *me*.'

Kari stopped abruptly, gently pulling himself back from her so he could look into her eyes, he said, 'I wouldn't want to be anywhere else in the world than right here.' and then continued to dance.

Joey wasn't sure what to say. Her mouth had gone horribly dry.

Kari changed the subject, 'Have you noticed how much time Lacroix and Solonge have spent together?'

'I have.'

'It seems like we were right. I wonder if Lacroix will take Solonge back to his tonight?'

'That's none of our business.' Joey admonished, they continued to dance in silence until she said, 'Kari?'

'Yes.'

'Have you noticed how many people are staring at you?'

'Yes, but it's not just me they're staring at, it's you as well.'

'Why me? I'm just Joey Lewis.'

'Yes, but *who* is Joey Lewis? They have never seen you before. They're trying to work out if you're a model, film star, or my date!' Joey teasingly slapped his arm, 'Okay, but trust me, they're wondering who you are.'

Like I'm trying to work you out, thought Joey.

As the music ended, Kari kissed Joey's hand, 'Now if you'll please excuse me I had better talk to the French Head of State.'

The rest of the evening flew by in a swirling blend of dances. Joey noticed that Kari never asked anyone else to dance with him, and every time she looked over, she caught him watching her. All too soon three o'clock struck, signalling the end of the event and slowly the Musee d'Art Contemporain began to empty.

Lacroix dropped Joey and Kari back to the villa and said they would return Monday morning to take Joey to the airport. Solonge wished them good night and the car drove off.

Kari turned to Joey, 'Definitely back to Lacroix's.'

Joey playfully swiped his arm.

They were still laughing when they stumbled inside the front door and Kari turned off the alarm.

'Right, I'm going to bed.'

'Of course, you need your eight hours of sleep!' Kari teased.

'No... well, yes, but it's going to take me ages to get out of this dress!' Joey looked over her shoulder to indicate all the tiny buttons on the back of the dress.

'Do you need a hand?' Kari said, simply.

If only Joey had thought before answering, but instead, she quickly said, 'No, I'll be fine. I got into it so I'm sure I can get out. But, I'll take you up on that kind offer tomorrow if I'm still wearing it at breakfast.' Joey tried to make light of what could be a very dangerous suggestion.

'Breakfast, you'll be up for breakfast?' Kari joked, with mock surprise.

'Yes, but I may not look as good as I do now.'

'Honestly, rest and take your time; there are no plans for tomorrow. I thought we could relax by the pool.'

'The pool, yes... okay.' Suddenly Joey had the vision of the Speedos again and started to blush.

'You did bring your swimming things this time, didn't you?' Kari questioned, noting her change of expression.

'Yes, but you forget, I may still be wearing this!' Joey held open her palms and pointed to the dress.

'Well may I say, one last time, that you look incredible tonight and I was proud to have you on my arm. Thank you for being my date.' He said, sincerely.

Date! What happened to the no strings part? Joey thought. 'Thank you for my invitation. I had an amazing time, I really did.' She knew she should say goodnight and go to bed, but for some reason the look in Kari's eyes had rooted her to the spot. His eyes sparkled, but not with mischief, it was more... lust. She noticed a slight tick in his cheek as if he were also fighting emotion. Seconds passed, but they felt more like minutes. Eventually Joey said, 'Well... goodnight.'

They stood looking at each other, she couldn't move, she appeared hypnotised by Kari's deep, searching eyes. He looked at her with an intensity that could be mistaken as desire. Very slowly Kari closed the distance between them. He tenderly lowered his head towards hers, obviously with the intention of kissing her goodnight. Joey panicked, she wasn't sure what to do. Which cheek should she kiss - left or right? Right felt more natural, but it was wrong - they clashed! Kari didn't move his head he just smiled, Joey laughed, nervously.

She felt his hands gently cup her face. He regained control. She didn't have time to think as his lips brushed hers. Oh shite, she thought, he was really kissing her! His lips were so soft as she yielded to his intense kiss. Joey closed her eyes and felt her legs turn to jelly.

He pulled back slightly and simply said, 'Thank you, goodnight.'

Joey smiled and concentrated on every step she took as she walked carefully up the stairs to her room, the kiss had seriously thrown her off balance. Inside her body a whole host of fireworks exploded. Once safely behind her closed bedroom door she did a dance of victory. Kari had kissed her! She fell on the bed, no longer caring about the dress as she touched her lips, losing herself to the memory.

Chapter 9

Joey didn't get much sleep; her head was spinning too much. At a sensible hour she decided to change into her bikini and a kaftan, picked up her sunglasses and headed for the pool. She didn't want to miss the chance of seeing Kari in his Speedos! She waited about an hour and, just as her thoughts turned to hunger, Kari appeared, carrying a silver domed platter and a jug of coffee. Despite the fact food and coffee were coming her way, Joey was disappointed, why, she thought silently to herself, was he was wearing shorts and a t-shirt!

'Good morning, sleep well?' Kari asked Joey.

'Once I managed to get my dress off, yes, thanks.'

'Well, I did offer to help.' Kari replied, throwing her a look as he set the silver platter and coffee down on the little bistro table, next to Joey's lounger.

Joey thought it was better not to answer.

'I didn't expect to see you for hours so I was pretty surprised to see you down here when I opened my balcony doors. But, I didn't think you'd eaten yet, so, perhaps we can share a less conventional… breakfast.' He paused before continuing, 'down here beside the pool!' He smiled as he lifted a silver lid to reveal pancakes laced with maple syrup.

Why was it every time he spoke now, Joey's head had to turn it into something sexual? Joey's over active imagination was off again. He didn't want to undo her dress, whip it off her and for him to have his wicked way. He meant breakfast, not sex… the two *could* be combined, she thought, as her mind wandered away again!

'Thanks, good thinking,' was all Joey could manage as Kari handed her a delicious, mouth watering pancake oozing with maple syrup. Silence lapsed between them as they ate until Joey asked politely, 'Which is your room?'

'The doors which are two down from yours,' he replied, finishing his pancake and licking syrup from his thumb.

Joey was transfixed, how I wish you could lick that syrup from…

'Have you finished?' Kari said, breaking her train of thought.

'Erm, yes… delicious… you are, I mean they were delicious thank you.'

Kari smiled but said nothing as he took Joey's plate from her.

'It was an excellent event last night, I really enjoyed myself, thanks again for inviting me.'

He nodded. Joey was desperately thinking of something to say but all her mind kept thinking was - you kissed me, Kari you kissed me! She didn't dare to open her mouth in case it betrayed her.

Kari pulled a sun lounger closer to the one Joey had been sitting on. 'It feels hot already.' he said as he strolled over to the pool and swished his foot through the water. 'Almost warm enough.' he said, mostly to himself, as he lay down on the sun lounger.

Joey's mind was racing; it's going to get a lot bloody hotter if your Speedos appear, she thought to herself. Now, should she remain sitting or lay down on the sun lounger, but if she lay down she would be directly next to Kari! Why think, she said to herself, just do. So she did. As she lay back she couldn't help but think this is what it would be like to lay next to him in bed. Really need to think of something else now…

Kari interrupted her thoughts, 'So I wonder what Solonge and Lacroix are doing?'

'Probably asleep,' replied Joey.

'You're probably right. I expect they're very tired.'

'What do you mean?'

'They've had a busy couple of days and a long night,' Kari suggested, innocently.

Joey was sure he meant they'd been busy last night having sex. She closed her eyes and soaked up the warming rays of sunshine. The next thing she knew, Kari was up, testing the water again.

'Perfect!' he exclaimed and whipped off his shorts, folding them neatly on the chair where he'd eaten breakfast, then proceeded to remove his t-shirt, his back rippling.

Joey thought she was going to implode… or *explode*! She had no idea how long she had held her breath. He was even more impressive close up, and she meant impressive in *every* way. He walked over to the edge of the pool and dived in as gracefully as a professional diver. She watched him swim length after length. It must have been a good twenty minutes or so. Eventually he stopped and, looking at her with his arms folded on the ledge of the pool, said, 'So, are you coming in or not?'

'How warm is it?' asked Joey.

'Gorgeous. Here!' he said, as he tried to splash her.

The water did not feel gorgeous, it actually felt quite cold, 'Stop, it's cold!' Joey screamed, 'You're going to wet my top! I think I'll leave it a little while to warm up further.'

Kari didn't reply, and instead returned to swimming lengths. After removing her kaftan and applying sun cream to the areas she could reach, Joey decided to lie back and watch the erotic sight in front of her whilst sunbathing.

The rest of the morning was spent in relative silence; Kari joined her on the sun lounger and sunbathed. She noticed he applied sunscreen too; she was very tempted to offer her services, but thought better of it.

They may well have both dozed, neither seem to be aware, but as the sun climbed higher in the sky, Joey felt she was beginning to burn. She sat up and pulled her kaftan back on. Kari looked at her and asked if she fancied something to eat.

'You know what, I think lunch sounds like a great idea.'

Kari jumped up and redressed in his shorts and t-shirt, much to Joey's dismay, and proceeded to walk towards the villa. Joey followed.

'No it's okay, you go back and relax. I'll bring lunch out.' Kari said to Joey.

'It's not that I don't trust you to make a good lunch, I thought I'd lend a hand.'

'There's really not much to do.' Kari continued to walk to the house, Joey followed.

'Oh, it's another Madame Dupre re-heat?'

'It's not. In fact, it's a salad that I often make for myself. Also, for your information, I will be cooking from scratch tonight.' He continued to walk; he then stopped as he noticed Joey had. He turned around; she was staring open-mouthed at him.

'Really? From scratch, no re-heating?' asked Joey.

'No re-heating.'

'You mean you've never cooked for Lacroix yet you're going to cook for me tonight, from scratch?' Kari didn't answer.

'Well, I am truly honoured,' Joey said, as she walked past him and into the kitchen.

If only she knew how I felt, Kari thought. He wasn't sure how long he could keep up this detached façade.

She watched Kari prepare a deliciously fresh, salad niçoise with a homemade dressing. He poured them both a glass of white wine and they ate under the shade of dappled vines on the terrace.

'You know, you do make a very fine lunch, Kari, but tonight you really must allow me to help in some way. You are beginning to spoil me and it will only hurt more when I have to crash back into reality next week.'

Kari just smiled at her, wiping his mouth on the napkin, 'What would you like to do this afternoon?' Kari asked.

The honest answer would have been, rip your clothes off and make mad, passionate love, instead she replied, 'How about a walk around the gardens? I did notice that they're themed and I'd be interested to know more.'

'It would be my pleasure,' Kari said as he pushed his chair back and took their empty bowls into the kitchen.

'I'll confess, I don't really know much about these gardens; the gardener tends to them, under my mother's very strict instruction. She's visited many parts of the world and likes to recreate a little piece of the beauty she has seen into these gardens here in France.'

'It is amazing, I've never seen anywhere quite like it.'

They strolled leisurely for a good hour, talking about places they'd visited. Kari, it seemed, had been all over the world, whilst Joey explained that she'd only been to Bayeux on a school trip.

She discovered that Kari loved to horse ride and rode as much as possible. His younger brother was called Luca and was an artist, currently living in Paris. He never disclosed anything about his work life or why he was so well travelled.

He was still a mystery. He seemed to clam up and carefully control what he said when the subject of conversation switched to him.

Joey, on the other hand, thought she had said everything about her life. Well, he knew already she was unlucky in love and she didn't enjoy her job. But she also told him that her father had divorced her mother when she was only five and that she hadn't seen him since. Kari didn't pry, but he listened, engrossed, as if she were telling the most interesting story in the world.

Joey said she believed she was the major reason her mother and father separated. They had desperately wanted a son. Her mum had told her more than once that her father was devastated when Joey turned out to be a girl and how their marriage had struggled from that point. She tried to make light of the fact her name, Joey, is also a boy's name, but Kari could detect the hint of sadness in her voice. Joey added that she wanted to meet a man who would love her forever, and respect her as a person. She then shirked the comment off, saying she was a true romantic. Kari said nothing.

They slowly rounded their way back to the sun loungers and Kari said, 'I fancy a lie-down, want to join me?'

Again, Joey struggled to rein in her imagination. 'Yep, I'd quite like to soak up some more rays, if that's okay?'

'Of course.'

He watched Joey remove her kaftan and begin to apply sun cream to her beautiful, creamy skin. She could easily burn, and without thinking he took the cream from her and started to apply it to her back.

'It's probably easier if you lie down on your front.' Kari suggested. So she did. She enjoyed feeling his strong hands rub the cream into her skin, and was in general bliss until she felt him undo the back strap of her bikini top. She wouldn't be able to get up! She panicked as she lay in his hands. He moved his hands to the backs of her legs and she nearly had to ask him to stop when he reached the top of her thigh. Thankfully, she heard the loud *snap* as the bottle lid shut, making her jump. Kari moved to lie down, next to her.

Chapter 10

Joey wasn't sure how long she had slept, but her neck was stiff when she awoke. She immediately remembered that her bikini top was undone, so, she refastened it quickly and rolled onto her back. As she put her sunglasses on, she looked across to where Kari was asleep, he looked so serene. She watched him, listening to his gentle, rhythmic breathing. Joey wasn't sure how long she had been staring at him, but when she refocused her eyes on his face, he was looking directly at her. She smiled at him and he smiled back, 'Was I snoring?' he asked.

'No, you looked very peaceful.' Joey replied.

Kari quietly laughed.

'What's so funny?' Joey asked.

'We've both seen each other sleep, yet we've never slept together.'

Choosing to ignore what *could* be a sexual innuendo, Joey pointed out, 'Well, we have, I was asleep, until a little while ago.' Kari simply broadened his grin.

'Are you hungry or thirsty?' He asked, touching her hand, which sparked shivers of desire running down Joey's spine.

'No, I'm fine, thanks. There is one thing I need to do, though.' Joey said, reluctantly.

'What?' He asked, hearing the apprehension in her voice.

'I should get in the pool.'

'You don't sound very enthusiastic?'

She let out a small sigh, 'I'm not keen on swimming and to be honest, I *hate* cold water.'

'I could hold your hand?' Kari replied, as he slowly reached out to grasp Joey's free hand and wove his fingers with hers, until their hands became inseparable.

Joey felt elated as she lay on her side, gazing at this impossibly handsome man, who was holding her hand and looking at her with hunger in his eyes. How she wanted him to kiss her again, to feel his lips on hers, to touch his skin… She closed her eyes and attempted to stop the thoughts, which began to rapidly race through her mind. 'I really need to cool off.' She muttered quietly to herself.

Easing her fingers from his, she sat up, and, resting on her elbows eyed the pool with the same conviction as a matador before a fight. She *had* to get in - she needed to cool off… in every sense of the word!

Joey sat happily on the vast steps, letting the cool water soothe her smouldering skin, mesmerised by the colours that were being reflected from the water, onto the wall tiles of the pool. Suddenly, Joey became aware that Kari was next to her. How was he so quiet?

'Brave, you're in danger of actually getting wet here!' said Kari, his eyes twinkling with humour.

'I had to move, I was beginning to fry!'

Kari gently scooped handfuls of deliciously cool water over her burning shoulders, 'I didn't put enough sun cream on you. I'm sorry.' he quietly said.

'No, it's not your fault, I know I easily burn, I should be more careful.' Peering into his eyes, she saw the humour had disappeared and instead had been replaced with desire.

With their eyes locked on one another, Kari eased himself into the water so that he was in front of her. Joey felt an invisible, magnetic force drawing them together. He was kneeling on a lower step, looking deeply into her eyes as the cool water gently lapped around him, making a lulling sound. An intense flow of energy coursed through her body and, without thinking, she wound her legs around him, until he was ensnared between her thighs.

An untamed passion radiated from his deep eyes with an intensity she had never seen before. She couldn't think. She couldn't breathe. As he stared into her eyes, it felt as if he were penetrating her soul.

Like the night before, he cupped her face in his hands and kissed her. His hands left her face and ran through her hair, round to the nape of her neck, before running down the length of her back, pulling her ever closer to him. As his mouth demanded more, his lips moved over hers with more passion. Joey melted into him. She had never been kissed so sensually before. It was simply erotic. Suddenly, he ripped himself away and swam to the other end of the pool, creating distance between them. Joey was left bewildered and surprised.

Something had moved deep inside his soul when he looked at Joey. He had tried to deny it but he had felt it last night before he'd kissed her, and just then too; it had taken all of his will-power to pull away. This was becoming too dangerous with so few clothes on! He tried to quash the feelings that were boiling in his blood *before* they spun out of control! He must remember she was just a friend, a friend with no strings! She trusted him. He took a deep breath and turned to look at Joey. He watched her shiver and hoped it was the cool water and not because he'd just kissed her, 'Are you okay?'

'A bit cold.'

He swam back to Joey and said, 'Why don't you swim around a bit, you'll soon warm up.'

'I'm not very good at swimming, you'll laugh at me.'

'I won't!' Kari protested.

'Yes, you will.'

'I won't, or at least, I'll try not to.' He added, with a smirk.

Joey slipped down into the water, gasping sharply as the water chilled her to the core. She then started to do a weird length of breaststroke up the pool. *Crap it's cold, just keep moving!* She told herself. Then, she noticed Kari laughing, 'See, I said you'd laugh!' Joey spluttered. 'Need the shallow end! Can't reach the bottom.'

In a flash, Kari was by her side and was holding her safely. She looked cross, which made Kari laugh even harder.

'I knew you would laugh.' Joey said, making her way out of the pool, trying her best not to sound like an angry child.

'I'm sorry, but from where I stood, it looked pretty funny. Hey, don't go! I promise I'll stop laughing.'

Joey halted, 'Promise?'

'Yes,' he said, trying to keep a straight face. He then smiled, 'I have an idea. Let me help you.' She was about to protest when he held his hand up to stop her. 'Trust me. I'll keep you buoyant by placing my hands under your stomach, this will give you the freedom to move your arms and legs like this.' He demonstrated what he wanted her to do. She was unsure, but nodded anyway.

He steadied her body. Tentatively, Joey began to move her legs.

'That's right, like a frog, good, keep going!' Kari said, encouragingly.

Joey started to laugh, big deep belly laughs, she felt ludicrous. She wasn't a child, yet here she was, swimming, as instructed, like a frog with the sexiest man she had ever met! She was laughing so much but knew she was out of her depth, so, she had no choice but to wind her arms around Kari's neck and hold on.

Kari started to laugh too, and found himself involuntarily bending to kiss her again. As his lips touched hers, Joey instinctively wrapped her legs around his waist. His legs weakened, as blood rushed to other areas of his body, desire coursing through his veins. Quickly he moved them both towards the edge of the pool, whilst continuing the kiss. When her back gently touched the edge of the pool, he allowed instinct to overpower him.

His hands grasped the sun-scorched side of the pool and he pressed his body to hers, the feeling of her wet body, pressed next to his, made him lose control. He wanted to kiss her everywhere as his passion over took him, but he satisfied himself with her neck and lips. In the depths of his mind, he knew he should stop, before the kiss got out of control.

Joey had no idea how she got to the side of the pool, but she did know that Kari was passionately kissing her. She let her hands wander down his strong, firm back, stopping before they could wander any further. His body, pressed against hers, felt incredible.

Unfortunately, it was over just as quickly as it started. Kari suddenly stopped and swam to the deeper end, pulling himself out of the pool altogether. She could see he was breathing deeply, trying to regain control. Wrapping a towel around his waist, he walked away into the depth of the gardens without so much as a word or even a backward glance.

What the hell just happened? Joey thought, as she splashed water onto her face. She tried to make sense of the desire she had felt from Kari, maybe she'd read the situation wrong? She allowed herself time to catch her breath before doggie paddling towards the vast steps to get out of the pool.

Chapter 11

After a warm and relaxing bath it was time to face the aftermath of that kiss. Putting a smile upon her face, Joey walked into the kitchen to see Kari busy, preparing food. She was obviously still invited for supper.

'What can I do to help?' She asked.

But Kari had been so deep in thought, he hadn't heard Joey enter the kitchen. Her voice had taken him by surprise. Glancing over his shoulder, he said, 'You'll find some green beans in the fridge, they need to be washed.'

Conversation was going to be difficult, she could tell. Maybe she should say something, but what?

As if sensing her discomfort, Kari put down the knife he was using to trim the steak, washed his hands and walked over to her. 'I'd like to apologise, for my behaviour in the pool today.'

'There's no need to say sorry.' Joey assured him.

'It's not that I regret it, far from it.' He saw a look of confusion flash across her face. He took a deep breath and continued, 'I'm not sorry I kissed you, but I felt a little out of control, and I'm sorry if I made you feel uncomfortable.'

'I didn't exactly help the situation, I guess I kind of went with the flow…' Joey looked cautiously at him, 'Are we okay?'

'I hope so! I've really enjoyed your company and it would be a shame to spoil things because of one, slightly out of control, kiss.'

'I don't mind leaving now if it would make you feel more comfortable?' suggested Joey.

'Do you *want* to go?'

'No.' Joey immediately replied.

'Good, then please stay.' The sexual tension pulsated between them. Joey thought he was about to kiss her again, but instead, he moved back to chopping the steak.

'What delights are we having tonight?' *Why did that sound so suggestive!* Joey thought, as the words left her mouth. His eyes snapped to hers and again she saw desire etched within them.

He took a deep breath and said, 'Steak au Poivre, green beans and sauté potatoes.'

'Sounds delicious!' Joey spotted a radio and turned it on. A French station began to blare out some dreadfully depressing music.

Kari reached across, turned the volume down and pressed the auto tune button. The French DJ said, 'Bienvenue à Les *Grands Classiques*'.

'I love this song!' Joey exclaimed, as a popular song began to play. 'I'd invite this guy over for a cup of tea any day.' Kari looked at her strangely. 'I don't fancy him, but I imagine he'd be interesting to talk to.'

'Over a cup of tea?' Kari said slowly, shook his head and smiled, 'The English and their tea.'

Joey poured the French red wine, dressed the terrace table and lit the candles.

Kari was a man of many talents and he seemed to be an expert in the kitchen. As he cooked, he took the odd sip of wine and once again, they fell into companionable silence. They moved at ease with one another, always with enough space so as not to touch. She loved the look of concentration on his face as he sautéed the potatoes and made the sauce. His large masculine hands delicately served the food.

He then carried the plates to the table and she brought the carafe of wine. The food was delicious; the steak cooked to perfection, succulent and juicy. Conversation flowed freely, as if nothing had happened earlier that day to cause tension.

Joey was too full for pudding, but gladly accepted the port Kari handed her. The evening was warmer so they remained on the terrace. When Joey asked what plans Kari had for the following week, he stood up and walked to the wall of the terrace, putting a greater physical distance between them.

'I fly back to Canada tomorrow. My father has a new project he'd like me to work on. I have something of my own I'd like to look into.' He ran his hand down his face and sighed, 'I guess I'll have to do that in my spare time. Which is pretty limited to say the least. What about you?'

'Well, I fly back to England tomorrow… Doesn't sound quite as glamorous does it?' Joey shrugged her shoulders. 'Then, I'll begin rounding stuff up at work, look into voluntary work abroad and who knows where I'll be this time next month!'

They looked at each other as Joey pushed her chair back and walked towards Kari; she felt braver now she had wine running through her veins. 'I have loved every minute here, over these past two weekends. I feel like I have been given the opportunity to escape my life and I want to thank you from the bottom of my heart. Unless I get a serious case of amnesia I'll never forget the time I have spent with you.'

'You have loved *every* minute?' Kari asked cautiously.

'Definitely. I know all good things have to end, but I don't want to think about that right now. My bubble of happiness will begin to deflate as soon as I go to bed.'

'You don't need to go to bed just yet…' Kari said quietly, looking intensely into her eyes. They remained there, eyes locked on one another for a moment.

Joey could see pain in his eyes. 'Do you regret inviting me here?' She had to ask, she had nothing to lose.

Before answering her question, he put his drink on the wall beside him, took her hands and pulled her towards him. She took a step closer, and he said softly, 'No. How could anyone regret meeting you?'

Joey looked away, embarrassed by the compliment, 'Well, I could name a few I'm sure… Dave, for example. He said some harsh things…'

Her words were halted as Kari placed a finger gently to her lips, stopping her mid-flow, 'I don't regret meeting you.' He could feel her hand trembling in his.

He couldn't take it any longer and he gave way to what his heart desired the most; he kissed her, gently and softly. He pulled back, trying to assess her reaction and, as he looked into her beautiful eyes, a fire ignited within his body. He wanted her. Every muscle in his body yearned for her. He ran his hands down her back, then up into her hair as he lustfully made for her mouth. The kiss was deeper than the one they had previously shared. He wanted to taste her, share the same breath.

She responded with equal intensity. Their breathing became ragged and fast, their tongues probing and entwining. Joey's legs turned to jelly from the passion in his kiss and she thanked God that he was holding her so tightly.

His hands swept down the length of her back and in one, quick movement he lifted her up so she was sat on the wall. She wrapped her legs around his hips, as he cupped her face and kissed her passionately.

Her hands wandered over his defined chest, down the length of his body until she reached his belt. Her hands dived beneath the fabric of his shirt and swept over his warm skin. To feel his body pressing into hers was unthinkable as her hands explored his firm, sculptured form. Then, very slowly, Kari calmed the intensity of their kiss. So much so, he was now resting his forehead on hers. Joey opened her eyes and saw Kari looking intently at her.

'We can't Joey. Trust me, I want to, but we can't.' Kari said, breathlessly.

'I understand.' Joey said, as she reluctantly removed her hands from under his shirt. But, the fact was, she didn't understand. Kari held her hands but he'd stepped back, creating distance between them, once again.

'I think we'd better call it a night.'

Joey couldn't talk, she thought she'd cry if she did. She nodded and they went inside. Kari locked the doors behind them and they went upstairs together. Joey opened her bedroom door and said goodnight to Kari. Kari cupped her face in his hands and kissed her tenderly. Joey managed to strain a smile as she closed the door. She wandered to her en suite and, as she stared at her reflection, she noticed her pupils were wide with excitement.

Meanwhile, Kari was in his room pacing. He went out onto his balcony and stood, gasping for fresh air, desperately trying to clear his lust filled vision, before heading back into his room, continuing to pace.

How had Joey got so into his head, was it because she was out of bounds? He rubbed his hands over his face but, still, his body wouldn't let him forget her touch, feel and taste.

Without thinking, he dived into his bathroom. Wrenching open the top draw of a chest, he grabbed a box of condoms. His mind raced as he took out the first one, and then another, before deciding to shove a handful into his trouser pocket. He looked at his reflection in the mirror and saw his eyes were alive with desire. He shook his head and left the bathroom and then his bedroom. He knocked hurriedly on Joey's door.

Chapter 12

Joey opened the door in surprise as Kari stood before her. They exchanged gazes and in one swift movement he scooped her up in his arms, slamming the door shut with his foot.

He kissed her passionately and spoke in a language she hadn't heard before. Confused, Joey asked what he was saying between each demanding kiss.

He looked deeply into her eyes, 'I know I shouldn't, but I can't stop.' He carried her to the bed and placed her upon it.

'Why shouldn't you?' Joey said, nervously, 'Are you with somebody else?'

He looked at her confused, 'No, I'm not with anyone else, I haven't been for years.'

'Then why…'

'You're my no strings date.' Kari thought quickly.

'Consider the strings cut!' She replied, before pulling him down towards her. He kissed with a hunger she had never experienced before.

He kissed her lips passionately, then every inch of her face, whilst his hands slid gently over her supple skin. He loved the soft moans that escaped her lips; it spurred him on.

Joey began to touch him too. Her hands had moved under his shirt, familiarising themselves with his body. With shaking hands she undid the buttons, sliding the shirt from his arms and torso. He was now topless and Joey absorbed what she saw.

She gently pushed him onto his back and kissed every part of his body she could reach. His body was hot, firm, yet soft.

His hands swept over her clothes - but he wanted more, he needed to touch her skin. He sat up; pushing Joey back onto her heels as he tore the top she was wearing free from her body. The sensation surging through him was immense. He gently lay her down and began to kiss her newly revealed skin. He kissed her breasts and teased her nipples with his teeth, causing her to moan out loud. His hand glided down her leg, before tracing up the inside of her thighs, around to her bottom and pulled her closer to him.

Uncontrollably, he groaned as he pressed his groin against her. Slowly, he kissed his way down her body, dipping his tongue into her navel, causing her to giggle. Without her even being aware, he removed the rest of her clothing, leaving her naked. He looked down at her and loved what he saw.

Aware that Kari had stopped touching and kissing her, she opened her eyes and looked up at him, 'Kari?' She whispered questioningly as she wondered why he'd stopped.

'You are so beautiful.' he replied. As lust smouldered from his dark eyes, he began to sensually kiss her mouth again.

Joey felt tears well in her eyes. No man had ever said that to her before, with such sincerity. Kari made her feel beautiful, the way he kissed and stroked her body. She battled with the belt of his trousers, fast losing control of her shaking hands; her body was alive with incredible sensations that Kari was eliciting. He noticed and calmly undid his own belt and removed his trousers. He didn't remove his underpants, in a vain attempt to prolong the pleasure he was feeling.

Joey pushed him over and straddled him as he lay on his back. She kissed his features as he had done to her, before reaching his neck and collarbones. His skin smelt delicious. She wanted to taste him. As she licked and teased various parts of his body, she smiled to herself when he groaned with satisfaction. His body was perfect – toned and strong. His pecks were incredibly well defined. A subtle six-pack led the eyes to oblique muscles, which encouraged her eyes to look lower.

She could see he was incredibly well endowed as his boxer briefs didn't leave anything to the imagination… She swept her hand gently over his swollen groin, making him moan with desire.

His eyes opened as he felt her remove his underwear. 'Joey?' he said sitting up, 'Are you sure?'

She nodded in response to his question, unable to talk as she took in his full splendour.

Joey was motionless. He touched her face gently, 'If it's too soon…'

'No. Please, I want to, I want you.'

He searched her eyes as he stroked her cheek.

'Please.' She said, before he wrapped his arms around her body, kissing her passionately as he swept her beneath him.

An everlasting kiss began as her hands travelled down the length of his back, before reaching his firm bottom and pulling him hard down onto her body. With their torsos touching, he instinctively ground his hips against hers encouraging her to accept him. With tantalising control, Joey felt every inch of him deep within her, He held himself still for a moment before pushing further inside her, causing them both to gasp with pleasure. He ground his body into hers and Joey writhed with satisfaction. Slowly, Kari began to pull back, before easing himself deeper into the heat of her body once more. Clenching his teeth he groaned, it felt wonderful.

With a gentle rhythm, Kari made love to Joey. He wanted to take it slowly, to bring Joey to a climax first, but even with all his effort in trying to prolong the pleasure she was quickly throwing with the demands of her thrusting hips.

He was so close to losing control and pulled himself free from her kissing her deeply. Joey, however, had other ideas and suddenly pushed him onto his back, before plunging herself down onto him.

'Joey!' Kari called out, as she rode him with a demanding pace. He basked briefly in the wonderful sensations Joey was giving him, before holding her hips firmly between his hands, ceasing all movement as he fought not to ejaculate.

'Kari, please!' Her voice strangled with desire as she struggled to free her hips from his grasp.

Forcing her backwards, Kari stretched his whole body against hers as he lay on top of her. She felt more alive than she could ever remember. Tiny electrical sensations rippled from her stomach, to her most intimate area.

He kissed her forcefully. With one thrust, he immersed himself deeply into her, causing her to cry out. Instantly, he stopped he didn't want to hurt her. He looked into her eyes but she whispered, 'No, don't stop, please,' so he didn't. He began to move quickly as his release came ever closer. He seethed silently as he lifted her bottom, helping to keep the rhythm of his demanding thrusts, as he stroked a tender spot within her again and again.

'Ahh!' She cried, as his hips pumped against hers, demanding her body completely. 'Kari!' Her cry was lost as he growled a deep, primitive moan as he released.

Both glowing in sweat, they held each other tightly as they waited for their breathing to return to normal.

Kari kissed Joey with adoration, before rolling onto his back, taking her with him. As he held her in his arms, he asked, 'Are you alright?'

'Just perfect.' She replied, as she listened to his heartbeat return to a steady rhythm. Running her hand gently over his chest, she said, 'So, what exactly did you mean when you invited me here as your no expectations date?'

Kari positioned them both so they remained as one, but he could look into her eyes, 'Please, believe me when I say, I had no expectation or intention of sleeping with you.'

Searching his eyes for the rest of the sentence Joey said, 'But?'

'No buts,' he whispered before kissing her passionately. Looking directly into her eyes he made slow, sensuous, love to her.

Chapter 13

Kari woke a few hours later and gazed upon Joey as she slept peacefully. Gently he eased his arm from underneath her beautiful naked form; she stirred, rolling over but continued to sleep.

It wasn't a dream, Kari smiled in the semi darkness. They really had slept together! He had thought it was like the dream he'd had the previous night, but to his immense joy, it had obviously been real. He looked at Joey's naked back, finding it too irresistible not to touch. He had no idea what the future would hold for them, but he knew it felt right, in fact, it felt almost inevitable. It wasn't that he thought he wouldn't see her again, as he really hoped he would; he'd never had a one-night stand and didn't want to start now!

He knew his parents would more than likely disown him, but right now, laying here next to her, he was prepared to take the risk. He could resist her no longer, his body began to ache for hers again.

Joey stirred and, as she awoke, she realised she was naked. She could feel very gentle kisses, moving down her spine, sending a shiver of pleasure to her core, she liked it - a lot. She didn't want to move, she wanted to enjoy the sensation but her body wanted more, in any case she wanted to see Kari. She turned to face him and smiled, 'I was just having the most amazing dream, but, now I think about it, I was reliving an event.'

'Uh huh.' Kari said, between showering her face with small kisses, 'Me too. I think we had the same dream.'

'Um, did yours involve… exercise?' Joey asked.

Kari stopped and looked at her, 'Well, in a way, yes.'

'I remember us getting very hot and sweaty.' Kari grinned and kissed her again. 'Would you mind if we action replay?'

'Thought you'd never ask.'

Kari kissed her deeply. As their limbs entwined, they rolled around the bed, both wanting to satisfy the other. Pillows and bed linen were pushed aside, as their passion escalated. Joey captured his wrists above his head and held him captive, as she teasingly rubbed her body against his. Releasing his wrists, her hands wandered down his body, until she found his impressive erection. He was so firm, yet his skin felt like silk. Gently, she licked her finger and circled her thumb around his wet tip, causing Kari to gasp and falter.

Their eyes locked on each other as Joey gently rode him. Small gasps of satisfaction escaped his parted lips, as he watched her. He sat up, holding her hips to maintain a steady pace. He wanted to kiss her, but, with every movement she made, his breath was taken away. She dropped her head back, leaving her neck vulnerable - he kissed it softly.

Pulling her legs around his, he laid her back onto the bed. As he began to make love to her, he saw trust emanating from her beautiful eyes. He *wanted* her to trust him. He wanted to make her feel wanted and special, like the person he had come to know and respect. He kissed her lips, before continuing his descent to her small, pert breasts. He licked and teased her hard, aroused nipples.

She submitted her body to his pleasure, revelling in the quiet groans of delight that seemed to come from his core. Never before had she ever felt so wanton and desired. It seemed he wanted to familiarise himself with every inch of her body. His hands never stopped touching, probing and exploring her. His long hair tickled her warm skin as he kissed both arms and hands before taking each digit, in turn, deep in his mouth and sucking gently. As he did, she felt a strange stirring deep within her body she couldn't remember ever feeling before. Her muscles seized him internally, which felt wonderful; he started to grind his hips into her.

Once he had given her body the attention it deserved, he kissed her lovingly on the lips. With his weight supported by one arm, his free hand swept down her body, tracing the soft contours of her breasts, stomach and navel until he reached down between her legs. He felt her stiffen in surprise and he saw the look of question in her eyes. He kissed her tenderly to reassure her. 'Relax.' He said quietly, as his fingers applied gentle pressure and circled her clitoris.

His thrusts were slow and shallow as his fingers stimulated her further. He was sure she'd been satisfied earlier but he also knew she hadn't orgasmed, and he desperately wanted her to experience one with him. Pulling himself out fully from within her, he replaced the void with fingers. Again, he felt Joey tense up. He stopped and kissed her tenderly, before exploring the most intimate part of her body. 'Relax, Joey.' He whispered, as his finger beckoned her to a new level satisfaction. Calmly and expertly he increased the pressure on her tender spot and very quietly she began to moan with pleasure.

What was happening? Joey thought as she felt euphoria sweep through her body. She had never felt so desired. It seemed his sole focus was to satisfy her. He kissed her so tenderly as he encouraged her to experience new levels of fulfilment.

She could feel muscles deep within her core begin to clench and spasm. Without even realising it, she had become more vocal, as her body began to tremble. She had never felt sensations like this, ever before. She clung to Kari's body and pushed her head, hard, into the mattress. She felt she was about to burst, but somewhere deep in her subconscious, she didn't want to lose control.

'Don't hold back, just relax.' Kari reassured her, his body close to orgasm from watching her. He tried desperately to take her to fulfilment, but Joey pushed his hand away. Instantly Kari thrust into her. He placed his hands under her shoulders and she moved her hands to gently hold his face. They moved in synch, never taking their eyes off each other. It was intense and incredibly erotic. They could see what was turning the other on. His rhythm was unfaltering, as he alternated between shallow and deep thrusts, bringing them both overwhelming pleasure.

Kari was so turned on, he felt he may combust if he didn't release soon. He begged Joey to let go. He could feel the tightening of her muscles, clenching him, but he knew she was still holding back, just a little. Their rhythm increased and, as Kari couldn't hold on any longer he cried her name as he gave way to wave after wave of ecstasy.

Joey had never experienced anything like it before. Tiny explosions coursed through her body, Kari had so gently encouraged her to release, but she was scared, she didn't want to give herself to him completely, for him to then leave her. Never before had a man been so selfless in making love to her, never before had she felt those sensations.

He held her tightly in his arms and he could feel she was trembling. Once their breathing returned to more or less normal, Joey moved her face to look into Kari's eyes. She hated to ask, because she didn't like to sound vulnerable, but she *had* to know, 'Will I ever see you again Kari?'

'Do you really have to ask that question?'

She shrugged her shoulders, 'Yes.'

'I think you know the answer.' He said as he planted a kiss firmly on her lips. Kari held her tightly and they drifted off to sleep.

Chapter 14

It was early in the morning when Joey rolled over in the bed, so, she was surprised to find herself alone. Perhaps Kari was in the en suite? After a respectful amount of time, she knocked quietly on the door, but, with no response, tentatively opened it, only to discover that it was empty. She went to the window to see if he was in the pool. It didn't look like he was there either. 'Strange…' She muttered out loud.

She showered, dressed and ventured downstairs to try to find him. As she reached the bottom of the stairs, she heard someone call her name; it was Lacroix. 'Good morning!' he said breezily, as she walked into the living room.

'Morning,' Joey replied, slightly confused, 'I was wondering…'

'Kari caught the early flight to Canada this morning.' Lacroix interrupted before she could say anymore. 'He asked me to wait here for you and take you to the airport as planned. He also mentioned that he forgot to ask for your number. If you're happy to leave it with me, I can make sure Kari receives it.'

Joey looked at him blankly.

'Kari doesn't have a phone.' Lacroix explained, 'I do all external communications for him, but, I can assure, you he wants your number and I'll be in touch in due course.'

'Okay.' Joey gave Lacroix her number and watched as he entered it into his phone. 'Why doesn't Kari have his own mobile?'

'He has no need.'

Has no need! What human on this planet doesn't own at least one mobile phone? Joey thought, angrily. She'd just spent the night making mad, passionate love to a fully grown man who doesn't have his own mobile phone and someone else does all his external communications. Was *she* an external communication? Then, it dawned on her – this was probably Kari letting her down, gently. Who was she trying to kid; she was never going to hear from him again. He'd had what he wanted, and obviously she wasn't that great, so, he'd snuck out early and poof – gone! He didn't even have the decency to wake her up and say *thanks but no thanks*.

Lacroix saw the cloud fall across her face. He had to say something to ease the pain he assumed she was now feeling. He walked over to her, 'Joey, I swear Kari is currently en route to Canada. You would have been asleep and he wouldn't have wanted to wake you, just for your number. I am his trusted friend and confidant. He wants your number and, I also know, he wants to see you again.'

Joey smiled, 'You don't know how much I want to believe you, Lacroix.' Joey sighed and shrugged her shoulders. She couldn't help but feel as if her magic bubble had just popped. He never did answer her question; *I think you know the answer* had been his reply. Well, she did now.

Chapter 15

Joey went to work the following day, but found it really hard to get back into a routine. Not only because she was working her notice, but also, she had crashed back into reality from a wonderful weekend, like no other she had ever experienced. To top it all, she had no idea if she would ever again see the man she was falling in love with.

She knew she should feel on top of the world, but she didn't, Kari hadn't said goodbye to her. She felt cheated. Why had she slept with him so quickly? Joey tried to think positively – maybe he'd been too busy to contact her? Perhaps Lacroix had accidentally deleted her number? She couldn't help but feel they were hopelessly lame excuses. She had no way of contacting Kari; it was up to him to contact her, *if* he wanted to see her again – the proverbial *if*.

That evening, Joey invited Lucy to her flat for supper. As she recounted her weekend, she could tell Lucy thought she was exaggerating, that nothing could have been *that* wonderful. However, to Joey, it really had been! Joey could see the pity in Lucy's eyes as she looked at her; clearly Lucy thought Joey had been taken for a complete ride. But it wasn't like that; those two days she'd spent with Kari had been amazing. If two days were all she'd ever get with him, then it was better than nothing. Some people live a lifetime without experiencing what she had in just two weekends.

Joey was beginning to think she'd dreamt it all until Thursday morning when her mum phoned. Margaret never called during the day unless someone had died, was about to die or something major had happened.

She saw her Mum's number appear on her phone screen and answered with all the cheer she could muster. 'Hi Mum, who's died?'

'Josephine, I've just seen you in *'Out There'*, a magazine the boys have in their salon!' *The boys,* being two gay hairdressers her mum visited every week for a treat and gossip. 'You're in it, with some big, dark, brooding man!' She babbled, excitedly.

Joey suddenly sat up straighter, 'What?'

'I just told you. There is a picture of you with some man going to a French ball. Why didn't you tell me you were dating?'

'Mum, I'm not dating. Where is the picture?'

'In *Out There*. I'm looking at it now. Have you seen it?'

'No, but I'll have a look at lunch time.'

'So, who's this man? Gary thinks he's gorgeous. He looks a bit dangerous to me. Are you dating him?' Margaret probed again.

I wish, Joey thought... 'No, he's a friend, he needed a companion that night and he asked if I'd join him. I had no idea we'd be in *Out There*.'

'You've never mentioned him before. I'll read what it says; *Kari Kutan arrives looking as dashing as ever, with an English beauty by his side. Could this mean change in the Kutan household?* So, what does that mean?'

Joey replied, 'I have no idea. All I can say is, I had a great night and that's as much as I know. Look, Mum I have to go, I'm at work, but thanks for letting me know.' Joey said her goodbyes hurriedly and hung up.

Joey knew where she was going at lunchtime! So, she didn't dream it. She really did go to the ball. As soon as her chance came, Joey ran to the newsagents and bought a copy of *Out There*. Sure enough, there was a double-paged spread capturing the Nice ball. Various photos of celebrities featured and then there was Kari and herself. Actually, the photo did make them look like a good-looking couple, even if she thought so herself!

For the remainder of that day, Joey looked at the picture whenever she felt a bit low, and it spurred her on to look for volunteer agencies. There was no call from Kari and she was beginning to think she wouldn't ever hear from him again. However, late Friday evening, Joey and Lucy were drowning their sorrows at The Pig's Head, when her phone rang. An international number that she didn't recognise flashed across her screen. 'Hello?'

'Hi Joey, it's Lacroix.' At which point Joey nearly fell off her chair. 'Firstly, Kari said I must apologise on his behalf for him not saying goodbye on Monday. Secondly, apologies for not calling sooner and finally, he would like to invite you to Canada, as he would like to see you.'

Joey was speechless.

'Have you seen the English copy of *Out There* by any chance?' Lacroix asked.

'Yes.' As she hyperventilated and gesticulated to Lucy that it was Lacroix on the phone!

'I guess you have some questions?'

'You could say that. In fact, I have a fair few now I come to think of it.' Joey couldn't control the unnecessarily harsh tone of her voice. She hadn't heard from Kari all week, he had walked out on her without saying goodbye and now gets his friend, *friend*, to call and invite her to Canada? ... Of course, she knew she'd go, but still!

'I understand.' Lacroix replied. 'All I need to know is, would you like to come to Canada or not?'

'When?' Joey asked nonchalantly, she didn't want to appear too keen.

'Well, Kari wondered if you could make it for next weekend? Fly over Wednesday night, have a day or so to recover from the jet lag and then Kari should be free for the weekend. I'm not sure when he'll next be in France and he's desperate to explain things.' Lacroix offered.

'The thing is Lacroix, I'm supposed to be working my notice, so I can't just take time off. Can I ask you to leave it with me and I'll call you back once I've spoken to my boss, perhaps on Monday morning?' It was killing her trying to be this chilled about the situation. Every ounce of her body was screaming *Yes, of course I'll come*... But she needed to act cool and not appear desperate. She didn't want Kari to think she'd been pining for him, like she had been.

'Of course. I will explain the situation to Kari. Naturally, he will pay for your flights and if you did come, you would be invited to stay in their family home. I will call you again, your time, Monday at eleven a.m. That way we can plan our week.'

'That sounds excellent. Thank you, Lacroix, for being so understanding.' Joey was beginning to surprise herself, she sounded so in control.

'Until Monday, then. Also, Kari said to ask one more thing – Are you relaxing?'

At this, Joey laughed and blushed as she remembered when Kari had encouraged her to *relax*. 'Please tell Kari, I need more practice, but, I'm trying.'

They hung up. Joey dissolved into minor fits of laughter and proceeded to relay the strange conversation she'd just had with Lucy.

Joey hoped she hadn't blown it. The last thing she wanted was to be so cool and Lacroix not to call back. However, first thing Monday morning, she managed to strike a deal with work. If she could take the Thursday, Friday and Monday off, then, she would stay another week after her period of notice had finished. At first they weren't too keen, but Joey pointed out that they hadn't found a replacement yet, so surely, it would be better to have her for another week, than no one at all? They agreed, and at eleven a.m. on the dot, her mobile rang.

'Hi Joey, it's Lacroix. Not sure if you remember, I said I'd call back this morning to discuss whether or not you could visit Kari in Canada?'

'Hi Lacroix, no, I hadn't forgotten.' *Like heck would she forget,* she thought!

'We were just wondering if you'd made a decision yet?'

We, did he say *we* as in Kari and he? 'Yes, thank Kari for the invite, I'm pleased to say I have been able to arrange the time off work.'

'Excellent. I will arrange for the necessary tickets to be collected from the check-in desk at the airport. The flight from Heathrow to Vancouver leaves late Wednesday night, do you think you'll be able to make that flight?'

Darn it, how the heck would she get from Bath to Heathrow? The train, she guessed, even if she had to hitch-hike, she would! 'Yes, I'm sure I can.'

'Excellent. Solonge will meet you from the airport. Kari looks forward to seeing you next week. Goodbye for now.'

'Thank you, bye.' Joey couldn't hold it in any longer; she did a victory dance at her desk, just as Dave walked by. He looked at her as if she had a screw loose. Joey didn't care.

The remainder of the week passed quickly and smoothly, and before Joey knew it Solonge met her from the airport and greeted her like a long lost friend, it was very reassuring for Joey. They drove out of the city, through ruggedly wild countryside and eventually turned into a very long and sweeping driveway, leading to the most magnificent house, Joey had ever seen. Joey imagined it to be over a hundred years old and exceedingly impressive. 'Wow!' Joey said as Solonge pulled up.

'I know.' She replied. Solonge took Joey's suitcase and carried it to the house. Joey offered to take it from her but Solonge insisted and Joey didn't want to argue. Solonge pulled the bell cord. A young woman opened the door, and stood back to allow them into the house. Joey noticed the young lady didn't make eye contact with her.

'Welcome to Cha Tik Warro, home to the Kutan family.' said Solonge, 'I'll show you to your room.'

Joey just stared in awe. She didn't think she had ever been anywhere quite as grand before. The grandest house she had ever visited was *Longleat House* in Wiltshire. The hallway they entered was as big as a regular, three-bedroomed, family home in England! A massive, sweeping staircase flowed to the upper levels, branching in opposite directions, half way up. Ancient looking paintings decorated the vast walls. A large round wooden table dominated the lower hall, it was topped with an impressive vase of flowers. Joey followed Solonge in silence up the stairs taking the right hand sweep.

'You are in the west wing.' said Solonge. *West wing? Now this definitely sounds like something from a glamorous soap opera!* Joey thought, as she followed Solonge. She had no idea how many doors they passed, or, how many paintings come to think of it, but eventually Solonge stopped and opened a vast wooden door.

'Here we are, you are in the blue room, floor one of the west wing. Behind that door is your en suite. Please make yourself at home. Kari is away on business until tomorrow night, but his mother is here to welcome you. I will introduce you to her at supper tonight.'

'Thank you, Solonge, my room is beautiful.' Before Solonge left Joey asked what time supper was expected.

'Come down for eight o'clock,' Solonge replied, before leaving Joey to relax and settle.

Joey made herself at home, the bed was incredibly squeaky but it seemed comfortable enough. The en suite was four times bigger than her bathroom at home, stocking everything she could wish for! The room itself was tastefully decorated, but the old and dark furnishings were quite imposing in the room, Joey, however, was preoccupied by the amount of Native Indian artefacts. There were pictures, paintings, dream catchers, animal skins and a variety of miniature totem poles. Joey was in a modern day, Native Canadian's house. Kari really was from tribal descent, not that it bothered her. She was looking forward to meeting Kari's mother. She began to wonder what she was like, but nothing could have prepared her…

At eight o'clock Solonge introduced Joey to a much older lady than she imagined Kari's mum to be. She may not have been old in years, but she appeared old in nature. She looked nothing like her son. She was about 5ft 3" and had an extremely hard, weathered face. She didn't welcome Joey, she didn't even say hello, merely grunted, kept her arms crossed and walked away towards the dining room. Joey gave a pleading look to Solonge, who only nodded for Joey to follow Mrs Kutan.

On entering the dining room, Joey was mesmerised by the dominating portrait of a handsome Native. He looked vaguely like Kari, but more rounded and less chiselled. Joey wondered who it was, but didn't like to ask. At either end of the vast room, there were various animal heads, including bears and bison. In the centre of the room was an imposing oval table, with space for around twenty places, it was currently laid for three. Joey sat down and waited for the food.

A young woman brought forward a pot for Mrs Kutan to inspect. Joey watched her smell it, stir it and then dip her spoon and try it. Without saying a word she nodded and the woman left the room. She returned a short while later with a tray containing bowls; they looked distinctly like part of a skull from an animal. As the bowl-type object was placed in front of Joey, she noticed it was a soup and it smelt good. Joey watched as Mrs Kutan and Solonge tucked in. As the liquid entered Joey's mouth, it took all of her control not to spit it back out. It tasted rancid and very salty.

'This is very different to anything I've had before, what is it?' asked Joey. Mrs Kutan looked up, but, didn't answer and continued to eat.
Solonge replied, 'Caribou brain soup.'

Huh! How am I going to eat this? Joey thought to herself. Well, her mum brought her up to eat whatever was offered, so as not to offend. With a great deal of determination and a heck of a lot more water, Joey managed to eat most of her soup. She was hoping *Ant* or *Dec* would appear from behind the Bison's head, so she could say, *I'm a Celebrity Get Me Out of Here!* But they never did.

Without saying a word, Mrs Kutan got up and left the room. Joey looked at Solonge, 'Has Mrs Kutan finished?'

'Yes.' said Solonge. 'Was the soup okay?'

'Well, it's the first time I've had it,' said Joey, and hoped it was the last.

'I'm not too keen either. Sorry, Mrs Kutan hasn't said much, she is a lady of few words.'

Few words? Let's say no words! Joey thought.

That night she didn't sleep. Her overactive imagination convinced her that someone was watching, which meant that she was too afraid to even go to the bathroom during the night. She waited until the sun rose before leaving her bed. The hideous squeaking bed had also woken her every time she rolled over. Joey spent the day reading or trying to find where she imagined breakfast and lunch would be, but sadly she found neither.

At one point, she stumbled upon the kitchen, but the door was slammed shut in her face, so, she guessed she wasn't welcome there. In fact, there didn't seem to be anybody in the house. She couldn't find either Solonge or Mrs Kutan. Thankfully, she did find a bowl of fruit in the dining room and feeling positively starved, she took an apple and orange. Thankfully they were real and not wax!

Joey spent the remainder of the day in her room and at around seven in the evening, she heard voices coming from downstairs. They spoke in a language she didn't understand, but she could tell the conversation was heated.

At eight, Joey made her way to the dining room and thankfully she found Mrs Kutan and a man. She had no idea who he was and she wasn't introduced to him. Again, he was a native and Joey guessed he was around fifty.

Joey sat at the table. Like the evening previous, the serving woman came in, presented a pot of food to Mrs Kutan, who, in turn, smelt it, tried it and the woman went away again, returning with three plates of food. The only thing Joey recognised on the plate were the eyeballs, they were surrounded by fatty and grisly pieces of meat.

Joey tried to pick off what meat she could, but she drew the line at eyeballs. She saw Mrs Kutan and the gentleman eating heartily and nearly gagged when she heard the eyeballs pop in their mouths, as they chewed. Joey felt sick. Where was Kari? 'I was just wondering, when do you think Kari might be returning?' Joey asked.

'Tonight.' The stern man replied. Then, the man and Mrs Kutan proceeded to have a lengthy conversation in a language Joey didn't recognise. Joey felt isolated, and incredibly lonely.

She was just thinking of going to bed, when she heard the front door open and close. Heavy footsteps treaded the bare wooden floorboards growing ever louder as they approached the dining room. Suddenly, Kari filled the doorway. Joey wanted to run into his arms and say *Save me from these people!* But, she thought better of it, she stayed where she was and just smiled at him.

Her face began to ache as he failed to acknowledge her. She also noticed the discomfort in his stance, he wouldn't even look at her.

Chapter 16

After what felt like eternity, Kari finally spoke, 'I see you have eaten.' His tone was cold, he hadn't even said hello. Joey thought she might cry. She was hungry, tired, and lonely. She'd travelled over 4000 miles to see this man and all he did was stand in the doorway and say, *you've eaten*! Where was the hug? Where was the kiss she'd been dreaming of? Where was the Kari she had known in France?

The man spoke to Kari in the same, strange language. Kari seemed annoyed and replied in the same language before turning to Joey. 'My father says you didn't appear to enjoy supper.'

Father! That's your father! Joey thought. After a moment to collect her thoughts, Joey replied, 'I'm not sure what it was, but I've eaten enough, thank you.'

Kari muttered quietly to himself, too quiet for Joey to hear, before leaving the room. Mr and Mrs Kutan also left leaving Joey alone. Knowing she was on the verge of tears, Joey ran from the vast dining room and went to her room. She threw herself onto the bed and sobbed into her pillow, conscious of the dreadfully squeaky bed.

The next morning, Joey sat in her bed, bathing her swollen eyes with cotton wool and cold water. Why had Kari been so cold last night? She'd had romantic illusions of him sweeping her into his arms, taking her off to bed, so he could feed her chocolate and share wine before making love to her all night.

She decided there was no point going down to breakfast because there wouldn't be any. After an hour, curiosity and hunger got the better of Joey, and she ventured down to the dining room. *Thankfully the fruit was still there*, she thought as she chose a banana and an apple to eat.

Joey looked out of the window, whilst eating the fruit. The view was breath taking. She could see meadow after meadow of lush, green grass with a stunning mountainous backdrop. She was startled when she heard footsteps enter the dining room – she felt like Eve being caught eating the stolen fruit. It was Mrs Kutan.

'Kari has gone riding, he'll be back later.' She said frostily, before she turned and left. Great, a third day in the house of coldness! She decided to go outside to get some fresh air in an attempt to alleviate her hunger and cool, her still swollen, eyes.

Joey wandered around the grounds of the impressive estate. There was a large outdoor area centred around an enormous Totem Pole. The garden gave way to a river and miles of lush, green land, with an incredible backdrop of mountains. There was an expensive looking livery yard nestled in a grass valley, which any champion jockey would be proud to ride. The overall sense gave Joey a juxtaposition of grandeur and an untameable wildness – like Kari, thought

Joey. She wandered around for another few hours before heading back to her room.

At around 5 o'clock, Joey began to feel hunger pangs again and wondered what culinary delights she would be served tonight… In fact she didn't want to think about it! In the distance, she saw a horse and rider galloping towards the livery, jumping hedges with ease. They were so graceful, and as the horse and rider drew closer to the house, Joey suddenly realised it was Kari. It looked like a scene from an old Western movie. He looked incredibly handsome, with his jet-black hair streaming out behind him, his jeans tight around his thighs and a look of steely determination on his face. He slowed the horse to a trot as he neared the livery.

Joey wondered if he'd be joining them for dinner tonight. If he did, she had to talk to him. She couldn't go on like this. If he didn't want her here then fine, but why had he invited her? Maybe she should pack and go home? This was no fun. It would have been great if she'd wanted to lose weight, but Joey didn't - she loved food.

Like the two previous evenings Joey tentatively entered the dining room. To her amazement and joy, the table was laid for four. The question was, which four, who had been invited? She walked over to an overwhelming portrait above the vast fireplace. She could clearly see it was a portrait of Mr Kutan, wearing full tribal clothing. He wore a headdress of feathers and held a Tomahawk in one hand. He looked unbelievably threatening. His stature oozed power and determination; pride emanated from his cold, dark eyes.

Suddenly, Joey heard voices; it was Kari's parents, followed by him. His mother and father sat down and Kari held a chair back for someone. Joey didn't move. Was he holding the chair for her?

'Please, come and sit, Joey.' So, she moved to the table, noting his unfaltering manners. As he pushed the chair in, he caressed her shoulder. She gasped quietly, so powerful was the caress of his hand. At last, her friend had returned, or, at least, she hoped he had. She smiled at him as he sat opposite her and, at last, he returned the smile.

Again, the same ritual of the woman bringing in the food began. However, tonight the food was more appetising. Fish with a selection of root vegetables and some kind of wheaty pulp was served, much to Joey's delight. At last, the food was delicious, and Joey was so ravenous that she ate very quickly. She could feel Kari watching her, but she was so hungry she didn't care; she hadn't eaten properly for days. There wasn't much conversation, *perhaps this is how people eat here*, she thought. This was very odd for Joey because when she ate with her family and friends, it was the time to talk and share thoughts.

Mr and Mrs Kutan spoke to Kari in their native tongue, but Kari always replied in English; Joey was too scared to say anything.

When everyone had finished, Kari walked to the French doors, opened one and left. Anger swelled in Joey's stomach. She excused herself to Kari's parents and exited through the same door as Kari; Mr and Mrs Kutan looked shocked but Joey was past caring.

The air was cold and hung with unanswered questions as Joey stepped out, waiting for her eyes to adjust to the darkness. She couldn't see Kari, so she quietly called his name. No answer. She called a little louder and suddenly, he appeared in front of her. His black, sparkling eyes peered directly into hers. He didn't move towards her, touch her or say anything. Joey started to shake, not only from the cold, but also from rage, which was bubbling beneath the surface of her skin.

'Tell me you weren't leaving again without saying goodbye? I mean, it's becoming a bit of a habit, first France, then last night and again this evening. Also, you invited me to visit, but you weren't here to greet me, and when you did finally arrive, you didn't look pleased to see me, and all you said was *you've eaten,* before promptly disappearing off again. And today, today I thought you'd at least be around but, oh no, you went riding. I'm sleeping on the squeakiest bed known to man and I'm so bloody tired because every time I turn over, I wake up. I haven't had breakfast or lunch in days and, to top it all, I've been left on my own with *your* mum and dad, eating who knows what and not understanding a word they say.'

Kari stood there, waited a moment and then asked, 'Have you finished?'

'No. You don't owe me anything Kari. I did have a wonderful time in France, but frankly that's been clouded by the horrible time I've had here. I have one last request, I'd like to go home tomorrow, please?'

Kari could see the fury raging from Joey's eyes and it took all his strength not to pull her into his arms and kiss her passionately. Instead, he took a deep breath and asked again, 'Now have you finished?' He could see tears welling in the corners of her eyes; she didn't speak, just nodded.

He went to hold her hand but she shook him off. He beckoned her to follow him – she did. They walked silently towards an out building.

Eventually, Kari spoke. 'Joey, I want to say that everything is going to be all right but I can't do that. You've asked me a lot of questions and understandably deserve answers.'

Joey was about to interrupt but Kari held up his hand, 'Please, allow me to speak now.' Joey nodded, still fighting back tears.

Kari desperately wanted to hold her, kiss her, make love to her and dry the tears in her eyes, but he knew he had to firstly give answers to her looming questions.

'I left the room just now because I couldn't bare the tension any longer. I left via the garden doors because I was hoping that you would follow. The morning I left you in France was hell. I'd heard the entry buzzer very early, I have always been a light sleeper, but you didn't even stir. It was Lacroix and I had to leave immediately to catch a flight back to Canada, as something needed my attention urgently. I hated leaving you, but I only had ten minutes to pack my things. I couldn't bear to leave you alone in the villa, so, I insisted Lacroix stay and wait for you to wake up. I did go back into your room and kiss you goodbye; you were sound asleep. If I woke you, I knew I'd miss my flight because I wouldn't have been able to resist getting in the bed with you.' His voice rang with sincerity.

I drove myself to the airport and hoped that you would forgive me and leave your number with Lacroix, as I desperately wanted to see you, soon. What I had to deal with when I got back is another matter, but it wasn't helped with the fact that Lacroix had to catch a later plane and I was on my own. Once things had calmed down, I knew I had to see you, so, I asked Lacroix to phone you.

That weekend was hell, not knowing if you would come or not. I nearly stole Lacroix's phone to call you myself. The relief when I knew you were coming was immense. I tried to fit six days work into four, just so that I could be here with you. But as ever, my work life took over. When I walked in last night and saw what you had been given to eat, I was filled with rage. How dare my family serve you that disgusting food? I left to get you something more palatable, but when I returned, you'd gone.

This morning, I had an argument with my father. I had found out they had spitefully given you Caribou brain soup and that they hadn't made you feel welcome. I have no idea what else happened, I'm sure you could tell me, if you wish to. Anyway, suffice to say, I was in a foul mood and I did not want you to see me like that. I thought it was best if I let off some steam by riding my horse. Whilst I was out, I discovered a fence to one of our sheep herd had broken and I tried to rebuild it because otherwise, we would risk losing them to the wolves. I completely lost track of time.

I rode home as fast as I could to tell the kitchen to make something more appetising, and hopefully see you before dinner to explain where I had been. But I couldn't find you. I'm mortified you haven't had breakfast or lunch, and I can only apologise for my parent's intense rudeness. I understand if you want to go home. Tomorrow I will arrange transport for you.'

Kari looked at her intently, 'And, to top it all, as you say, I'm scared to touch you because I don't think I'll be able to stop.' At which point the tears slowly and steadily fell from Joey's eyes.

Joey could see a muscle pulsating in his cheek and his hands were clenched tightly shut in an attempt to retain control. She looked into his beautiful, dark eyes, which were oozing honesty, 'So don't stop.'

They stared into each other's eyes for a moment. When Kari looked away, Joey sighed and walked back towards the house.

'Wait.'

She stopped and turned, showing the tears which were streaming down her cheeks.

Kari walked up to her and unclenched his hands, hesitantly reaching for her shoulders. His touch was so light she could hardly feel it, and then slowly he bent his head, as his lips searched for hers. They melted into each other's arms as the distance and argument fell away, leaving nothing but the delightfully intense kisses of the present.

Kari gently pushed her backwards so she was pinned against the wall of the house. He instinctively grabbed the back of her thigh and pulled her leg up around his waist. He ground his body to hers and kissed her, fervently. His hands familiarised themselves with her body, face and hair. Joey thought they were about to re-consummate their bodies but, as suddenly as it started, Kari pulled away. He rested his forehead on hers as he panted deeply. His fingers wiped away tears from her face.

'Please, don't cry, I can't bear to see you cry.' He kissed her closed eyes and as she opened them, she saw passion shine from his. 'Tomorrow, I am free all day. Meet me in the dining room at seven o'clock; I will be there with breakfast. If you still want to leave, I will arrange it. But, if you're willing to give me another chance, then I promise I will make it up to you. I will pack a picnic of *edible* food and we'll ride up to the long meadows. There, I can tell you about my life and why things are so difficult for us, I promise.' Kari said, his breathing now normal.

'That sounds great but there is just one problem.' Kari looked at her quizzically, 'I can't ride.' Joey explained.

'You don't need to worry about that. We'll ride together on my horse. He can take the weight of us both, especially as you've been on a crash diet for three days. Madame Dupre would be most upset if she knew.'

Joey laughed. 'Okay, looking forward to it.'

Kari kissed her on the nose and sighed, 'I have to respect my family's wishes so we had better go in, to our separate rooms. However, I can assure you that although my body is in a separate bed to yours, my thoughts are not…'

He took her hand as they walked back into the house. Everything seemed quiet until Kari's father called out to him. Joey released his hand and Kari kissed her forehead, she continued to climb the stairs, with a new spring in her step, looking forward to tomorrow.

Chapter 17

Joey had the best night sleep since arriving in Canada. When she walked into the dining room the next morning, she was greeted with a banquet of food, plus a smiling Kari. His beaming smile seemed to light the room and as she sat down.

'Good morning, sleep well?' He asked.

'Much better, thank you. How about you?'

'Not so good, my body kept me up most of the night knowing you were sleeping in this house!'

Joey raised her eyebrows, 'Hmm, that's not good. Perhaps I should help you?'

His eyes glinted mischievously as he smiled at her, 'I wish.' He shook his head, attempting to erase the thoughts. 'I knew you were hungry, so, I've tried to cover all the bases. There's cereal, fruit, meat, cheese, pastries but I'm happy to arrange a cooked breakfast, if you'd prefer?'

'This is fantastic, no need to arrange anything else.' Joey looked hungrily at the choice of food, spread across the vast table.

'I saw how quickly you ate last night, I now understand that you were hungry and I'd hate to have to see you like that again.'

As Joey sat down, Kari stood, almost transfixed, to the spot. 'Please, tell me you're going to eat?'

'Yes, sorry I was just thinking how beautiful you look.'

Joey blushed.

Together, they ate as much as they could stomach. Kari excused himself from the table to retrieve the picnic and Joey gulped down the last of her tea. Whilst he was gone, Kari's parents entered the room. They looked at the vast array of food and Joey sitting alone. *Shite, they must think I'm a pig!* She worried. Standing bravely, she said, 'Good morning. You've just missed Kari, but he should be back any minute.'

They didn't reply.

Awkwardly she sat down and waited for Kari to enter the room again. When he finally did, Joey noticed that he was carrying a large wicker basket of food.

Addressing his parents, Kari asked, 'Are you not going to say good morning to Joey?' Neither did. They left the room but not without giving Kari a pointed look first.

'Again, I apologise for my parents rudeness.' Kari said, sternly. 'Come, let's ride,' as he held his hand out for Joey.

Kari led Joey to the stables where his horse, Kauto, was waiting for them. He packed the food in the saddlebags and pulled himself up and onto the horse. Joey looked up, 'And, how exactly am I meant to get up there?'

Kari leaned down and said, 'Put your foot in the stirrup, hold onto my arm and I'll pull you up, but you must swing your leg over.' Joey broke into peels of laughter. There was no chance. She tried a couple of times but without success. Kari dismounted, so that he could help her.

'Okay, that didn't work. Let's try something else. Keep your foot in the stirrup and I'll push you up.' Joey did as instructed, but when Kari pushed her bottom, she began to laugh again. They both stood chuckling for a while. Eventually, Kari led Kauto to a small, raised wall.

'If this doesn't work, I give up!' He said, as he got back onto the patient horse. 'Stand on the wall, foot in the stirrup, hold onto my arm and swing.' Joey tried again and this time, she managed to get up onto Kauto – Kari beamed at her, 'Now, perhaps we can escape this place for a few hours.'

They rode through the meadows in exhilarating silence, becoming freer with every step of Kauto's hooves taking them further from the house. Joey enjoyed holding Kari tightly around his waist. As they rode, he pointed out various interesting places, trees and animals and eventually, they stopped in a beautiful meadow of wildflowers. Kari jumped off the horse with grace and instructed Joey to swing her right leg in front of her and jump into his arms – he caught her, thankfully!

Kari lay out the picnic rug and food. Even though Joey had eaten a banquet at breakfast, she found she was still quite hungry and enjoyed the delicious meat pies. As they ate they made small talk. They talked about anything and everything apart from the actual reason why Kari brought Joey to the meadow in the first place. It hung over them like a heavy time bomb, waiting for Kari to ignite the fuse. After satisfying their hunger, Kari lay on the rug and stretched, Joey lay next to him.

They were both looking up at the fast moving clouds in the sky, when Kari said, 'Joey, I need to tell you about my life. Who I am. Why things have been… difficult for you. My life is complicated and you need to be aware of exactly who I am. I see that now… frustrating as it is.'

She took a deep breath, she desperately wanted to know the truth behind the man she had fallen in love with, but there was no denying the apprehension that filled her heart. Blissful ignorance suddenly felt quite appealing. Turning her head towards him she said, 'You don't have to tell me Kari.'

'I do, Joey, you deserve that from me. It will make things clearer, I hope.' He rolled onto his side and faced her. 'Please understand I've never had to tell anyone about me before. I've never needed to and, to be more frank, never wanted to.' Kari lovingly tucked a wayward lock of her hair back behind her ear. His eyes were full of honesty and wonder. 'I like you Joey and you deserve to know the truth.' A bubble of nervous laughter escaped his lips before he said, 'I'm not sure where to start?'

Joey shook her head and said nothing. This was Kari's moment. He needed to talk.

Mere seconds passed, but it felt like minutes before Kari drew a deep breath and said, 'My name is Kari Kutan, I am 34 years old and I am a son to the Chief of the Kutan Tribe, Gahenge Kutan. My mother is Aiyana Kutan and I have a younger brother, Luca. That makes me, the older son to the current Chief. When my father retires, it will be me who is expected to take over as Chief to the tribe. I have worked all my life for this, it is expected of me.' He paused, long enough for Joey to register what he had just told her.

'So, you're next in line to become Chief to your tribe?'

'Exactly.' confirmed Kari, 'But, I have additional boundaries. I am expected to marry and have sons to continue the Kutan bloodline. You're probably more familiar with the term Native Americans, American Indians, Aboriginal People, but we call ourselves The First Nations. Our Kutan Tribe is of pure blood and one of the last of its kind.' He saw a look of confusion flash across Joey's face. 'We don't mix blood in our tribe. In the past, many tribes, First Nation people, married and had children with the new settlers, Europeans, making the tribes mixed race.' Joey nodded showing that she understood and was following the story.

Kari continued, 'I am expected to marry a woman from the tribe. A native. I am not allowed to marry any other woman.'

'That's okay, we're not getting married, we're just friends.'

Kari laughed and rolled onto his back, 'Don't know about *you*, but *I* don't sleep with my other friends.'

'No, you know what I mean. Like when my mum saw the pictures of us in *Out There* magazine.' She heard Kari mutter something under his breath. 'Anyway, Mum thought we were dating and before long she'd want us to marry. Don't worry though, I quickly settled her nerves by assuring her that it's nothing serious. Can't we do the same with your parents? After all, we've only just met.'

He turned his head to look at her, 'Joey, I haven't been in a relationship for over four years. In that time, I've not been on many dates and I certainly don't sleep with someone lightly. My parents know that something's going on. The rest of the tribe are beginning to hear rumours. I don't normally spend the weekend with an English woman in our family villa in France and then fly her here, to stay at Cha Tik Warro. I like people, but I'm not that generous. I'm doing it for you because I like you, a lot.

My parents understand I wanted you to come here, so you can see my life, but they said they couldn't accept you. We came to an agreement that if I respect their wishes and keep our relationship platonic whilst you are here, then they will at least respect my decision and be civil to you. But, I am quickly becoming aware that this isn't the case, and my respect for them is diminishing.' Silence fell between them. Kari allowed Joey time to digest what he had just said.

'I don't know very much about native tribes, I assumed they were quite poor. But you seem so…'

'Affluent?' Kari offered. 'Our tribe is an original and we've managed to maintain a degree of wealth and independence, which we strive to continue. There are many other tribes that are not as fortunate as us. They struggle with poor health and poverty.'

He continued, 'For years, our tribe dominated this area. Between the fifteenth and nineteenth centuries Europeans arrived and land was taken. There was violence between tribes and the Europeans. The Europeans had brought diseases such as the pox, measles and influenza, which were fatal for the natives, because we had no natural immunity from them. We only wanted peace and to continue our lives as we had. The Europeans needed our help and at times there was peace. We taught them how to survive the harsh winters. We traded fur and food for metal tools, cooking utensils and other items. We also taught the Europeans how to hunt and make canoes. Simple enough tasks, but essential for survival.

Inevitably, disease was brought into our tribe. My ancestor, Chief Wah Chtun had a dream which told him that the Kutan tribe would only survive if they kept their people away from the Whites. Dreams are sacred and guide us to choosing the right path to follow in life. From that moment, only our Spiritual Leader and Elders were permitted to deal with the Whites. Many white men respected our wishes, but there were a few who didn't. Rape happened. This will sound cold and heartless, but if a woman was raped they had to be removed from the tribe. Our tribe could not risk the chance of disease spreading, let alone mixed blood from any child born from the rape.'

'But it wasn't their fault if they were raped!' Joey tried, but failed, to understand what Kari was telling her.

'I know. Many men lost their lives trying to protect their wives, sisters and mothers. Something had to change and therefore, a treaty was written. Basically, it says if a tribal man or a woman was to have any relations with a white person, be that consensually or not, they would instantly be dismissed from the tribe.'

'Harsh.'

'It is shocking, but true.' Kari sighed. 'The Kutan tribe also made treaties with the European Colonisation and eventually, we were able to maintain peace and our individuality. However, my ancestors also appreciated we had to move forward and learn new skills if we were going to, not just survive, but prosper. The Elders befriended a white family – The Walkers. Charles Walker taught us the skills we needed to build houses. In fact, he helped make the cottage, which still stands today - further up in the mountains. Libby Walker, Charles's daughter, taught us how to read, write and speak English, as well as French.'

Joey interrupted Kari, 'Why did the tribe accept The Walkers? They could have spread disease or raped the women.'

'Charles Walker desperately needed our help. His wife had been raped and killed by another tribe and he feared for his daughter's life. We needed the skills they could teach us and they needed our protection. They were subjected to a long period of quarantine before being integrated into our tribe.'

'Such heartache.' Joey said quietly, as she tried to imagine the difficulties both the natives and new settlers had to endure.

'As I said earlier, many treaties were written and another was formed when a group of French settlers wanted to build on part of our land. In return, they gifted us some of their land in the South of France, Pontrains.'

Joey nodded as Kari's life became clearer.

'Our land was, and still is, very prosperous and any money we make is continually invested.'

'What is it you're expected to do for the tribe?' Joey asked.

'Various things. Mainly maintain peace amongst my people, keep our investments viable and make them prosper. Make sure the world accepts our beliefs and respects them. Writing histories. My role is diverse. It ranges from world politics to intimate family matters. Helping families that are struggling either with health issues, money troubles... One day I could be in England, and the next in France, and perhaps a week later, I may be in Brazil or Canada. I fly around the world working with other world leaders to try and ensure peace is held. Not easy in the current world. It's demanding, emotional and very, very private. I know things that most people are unaware of. I constantly have to watch what I say and to whom. Our tribe prides itself on our commitment to each other.

'It's funny because although I'm expected to remain silent about so many matters, my private life seems to be in constant speculation.' He looked at her, 'I can't even go to the bathroom on my own whilst being out in public; I have to take a protector with me. I'm not supposed to be left alone unless I'm in a private residence.'

Joey interrupted, 'Did you just say... protector?'

'Yes, kind of like a bodyguard, I suppose you could say. Lacroix is my primary protector, but I also have Henrique and Solonge. If I go to a large event, I have several. Don't get me wrong, I respect what they do for me because they are selfless on an extraordinary level, but there is part of me that would like to be an unknown, even if just for a day or two.' He sighed.

'So, are they expected to die for you? Take a bullet in your place?'

'Yes, although, I'd gladly take it in theirs.'

'Wow.' said Joey, 'I had absolutely no idea. Now, I see a lot of things fall into place. So that morning you deserted me in France, you flew back to Canada on your own, just so I didn't wake up in an empty house.'

'Yes.'

'But, your father would have been furious.'

'That's putting it mildly. Lacroix wasn't too keen for me to go alone either, but at the end of the day, he has to respect my wishes or lose his post. My father was already livid, as word had got to him that I had taken an English woman to the Nice ball and she was currently staying at the French villa. He believes I was being disrespectful to the tribe.'

'Kari, I swear I had no idea who you were when I met you, absolutely no idea.'

'And, that's one of the things that drew me to you, Joey.' Kari replied and looked deeply into her eyes. 'Do you really think we're just friends?'

'Well, what would you say we are?' Joey threw the question back to him.

'We're seeing each other. We've slept together, so in my book, we're boyfriend and girlfriend.'

'Oh, don't say that, it sounds naff!' Joey cried.

'Okay, I'm not keen on the term partner and courting sounds too old.'

'How about friends with benefits?' Joey said winking, but Kari gently slapped her leg.

'Ow.'

'Ah, didn't like that did we?' said Kari.

'No.' Said Joey whilst rubbing her leg, thinking this man has no idea how strong he is.

'Well, I don't like friends with benefits. I'm a monogamous lover and I don't want you to have any other *friends* whilst I'm seeing you.'

Joey laughed as he reached out and poked her side, reiterating his point. Her laughing increased and she retaliated, tickling him hard in the ribs. To her delight, she discovered he was incredibly ticklish and soon, she had gained control. She pushed him onto his back and sat astride him. He protested, and being much stronger, he pushed her back. He sat astride her midriff and held her forearms above her head.

Still laughing, he instinctively leant down to kiss her. She responded passionately to his demanding, deep kisses. Before they even realised what they were doing, they had removed their jackets and were beginning to attack the next layer of clothing.

Kari lay on top of Joey. Her hands explored and felt his hardness through his jeans. Kari took a sharp breath, as if being jolted awake from a dream, and stopped kissing Joey, 'We can't.'

'I know, your parents wishes.' Joey replied feeling slightly annoyed.

'No, I mean I don't have any protection.'

'What, Lacroix has to be here!'

'No!' Kari said, laughing, 'I mean, I have no protection.'

'It's okay, I'm on the pill.' Joey offered, pulling Kari back into another deep kiss.

'That's good to hear but I cannot risk you getting pregnant, I would like to prevent that as much as possible.'

'I understand, the last thing I need is to get pregnant when I'm off volunteering.'

Instead they settled and lay quietly in one another's arms.

As Kari stroked Joey's hair, she asked, 'Where does the term *The First Nations* come from?'

'Our collective name is derived from the fact that we were the first people on this land. We, as in Native Indians, The First Nations and so on, were all indigenous to the Americas before the European Colonisation.'

She rested her hands on his chest, interested in what he was telling her. 'Please don't take offense, but when I was little, we called Native Americans, Indians.'

'And we chased cowboys with our bows and arrows!' Kari laughed. 'I'm not offended. It was Christopher Columbus who first called us Indians when he thought he'd landed in India, not realising that it was the Americas.'

'You learn something new every day.'

'How are the volunteering plans going?' Kari asked.

'Okay, I've made plenty of phone calls, written dozens of letters; I'm waiting for a job offer. I didn't think it would be this hard. I'm volunteering my services for free, surely someone in the world needs them?'

'I do.' Kari's look melted any resolve she was beginning to form from having sex. But, she didn't want to push him, so, kissed his nose and suggested they head back, before she ripped off his clothes and took him, protection or not.

They collected their things together and Kari helped Joey to get back onto the horse. As they rode back to the house, Joey took advantage of her position, sitting behind Kari and reached further forward, crushing herself into him so she could caress his thighs. The tightening of his jeans betrayed him as lust coursed through his veins.

Chapter 18

When Joey finally went back into the house, she was surprised to see Lacroix and Solonge, but not so happy to see the pointy-faced, narrow-eyed, Henrique. Lacroix and Solonge greeted Joey affectionately, but she could have sworn that she heard Henrique snarl from the corner of the room.

'Kari!' Boomed his father from further down the hallway. 'We need to talk. Now!'

'Father, can't it wait? I'd really like to shower and change before supper.' Kari replied loudly, knowing if he spoke to his father, he'd end losing his temper and he didn't want Joey to witness that.

'No. I have waited long enough.'

Joey could hear the harshness of Kari's father's voice. Kari turned to Joey and said he'd see her later. Joey watched as Kari pointedly looked at Solonge. Solonge replied with a slight nod of the head before ushering Joey to another room.

'Have you had a good day, Joey?' Solonge asked, as she closed the door.

'It's been good fun, I even rode a horse… well… sort of!'

Suddenly, they heard raised voices. The argument was heated. Joey could hear Kari and his father's voices, with occasional interjections from Henrique. She didn't know what was being said as they were shouting in their own native language, but whatever it was, it definitely seemed to be aimed at Kari and it didn't sound good.

Joey had never heard people shout so loudly before. The argument was so forceful; Joey thought any minute she'd hear the sound of gunfire or fighting. Solonge and Joey just looked at each other. 'Are they okay?' Joey knew it sounded pathetic, but she had to ask.

'Not really.'

'Is it because of me?' Joey asked.

Solonge just nodded.

'Oh, crap. Can I do anything?'

Solonge shook her head, 'I'm sorry you have to hear this, Joey.'

Joey didn't want to hear anymore. Wrenching open the door, she ran to her room. When she reached the privacy of her room, she tore off her clothes and bolted to the shower. At least, in the shower, she couldn't hear the shouting.

Dinner was as Joey hoped, thankfully no black eyes and everyone seemed present, so no deaths either. Joey sat next to Solonge and opposite Kari. Conversation stagnated. Joey could feel the tension emanating from both father and son. The food ritual began. *At least tonight, the food looked appealing. What the hell had they made her eat the first two nights?* Joey thought. Now Kari was home, the food seemed to be much more appealing and normal.

Kari tried to make polite conversation that involved everyone, but it only seemed to be Lacroix joining in. Joey was too scared. At one point, Kari asked Joey if she liked what she was eating, she was about to answer, but Kari's father cut across her, with a direct question to Kari in native tongue. Joey could see the fury beginning to build in Kari's eyes and she felt apprehensive. A little while later, Kari tried again to include Joey in a conversation he was having with Lacroix. This time his mother cut across Joey, so, Joey's response fell on deaf ears. Kari gave his mother a pointed stare.

With the food finished, Kari's father suggested that the men should retire to the smoking room to use the peace pipe. Kari snorted which resulted in Gahenge shouting at Kari, and Kari responding, equally loudly. Joey couldn't take the tension any longer. She hated arguments and wanted to escape. Her mother and her father always made her feel like every argument between them was her fault, and now she was the cause of this argument between Kari and his father. Unable to take anymore Joey made her excuses and left quickly, disappearing up to her room.

She didn't realise that Kari had followed her, until she was nearly at the top of the stairs. As he caught up to her, he saw tears falling down her face. He pulled her into his arms, letting her sob. 'It's because of me, it always is.' She said, over and over again.

Kari rocked her gently and when she had calmed, he led her quietly down the corridor, past many closed doors and into a completely different wing of the house. Eventually they stopped outside a closed door. He opened the door to the room and Joey knew instantly that it was *his* bedroom. It smelt of him and she could see the jeans he'd worn earlier, folded neatly on a chair by the window. Kari closed the door behind them.

Without saying a word, he pulled her into his arms and kissed her. Within seconds, their passion flared into intense flames. They tore at each other's clothing, pulling and tossing them aside. He lifted Joey to his bed and thrust deeply into her, the need to become one seemingly unavoidable. They wanted each other desperately and quickly. His cry of bliss as he climaxed, rang through her ears. When he was finally spent, he collapsed on top of her, too exhausted to move; she clung to him, never wanting to let him go.

After a short while, Kari moved and wrapped his arms protectively around Joey. He spoke, breaking the silence, 'I couldn't hold out any longer. You drive me wild with lust and I needed you. My parents broke their vow to be respectful to you, so, I have no qualms about breaking mine to them.'

Joey just snuggled closer to him, and fell asleep peacefully, knowing Kari would be there in the morning, when she awoke.

But during the night, Joey woke to find she was alone in the vast bed, and she began to panic. After her eyes had adjusted to the darkness, she noticed Kari standing by the window, staring down to the moonlight gardens. She could see the silhouette of his naked body, his broad shoulders forming a triangle as it dipped to his waist. His firm, round, tight buttocks led to long, muscular, powerful legs.

'Kari?' Joey whispered into the dark gulf between them. He turned, walked towards her, completely naked. He climbed back into bed and without uttering word, made love to her. Throughout the erotically charged experience they looked into each other's eyes and, unlike the time before, it was slow, considered, and sensual, eyes never leaving each other's. Afterwards, they lay together contentedly, their limbs still entwined.

In the morning, Kari was there, as promised. After taking a shower together, Joey returned to her room to get dressed and thankfully made it down the corridor into her room without being caught. After choosing an outfit for the day and changing into it, she ran downstairs for breakfast and found Kari alone in the dining room, waiting for her.

'Good morning.' He said, 'Sleep well?'

'Actually, very well, thank you.'

They ate breakfast alone, his mother and father didn't join them. Kari knew Joey had to fly back to England today; Lacroix and Solonge were coming to collect her in an hour. Kari said, unprompted, 'I'm not sure when I'm next free, but, I promise I will find time, and it will be soon, I need *you,* more than you realise.'

Joey didn't ask anymore, she wanted him as much as he wanted her and Joey was sure that he would find time to see her soon.

As Joey was about to leave the house, Kari pulled her into a side room and kissed her passionately. He didn't want to let her go, but he knew he had to… for now.

Chapter 19

The following week passed with relative ease. Joey ploughed on, working out the remainder of her notice, even though she was suffering badly with jet lag. She helped to interview a couple of possible candidates for her job, but neither seemed particularly great. All week, her mind constantly jumping into thought every time the phone rang, longing for *the* call from Kari; at least this time she felt more confident that it would come.

Over in Canada, Kari seemed like a different man. He was happier than usual, and neither distant nor reserved. He worked harder than ever, but this week, everything seemed effortless for him. The tension with his father had not decreased, so they avoided each other, where possible, however, Kari made sure his work didn't slip.

There were occasions when he almost divulged his feelings for Joey to Lacroix, but he didn't want to make him feel awkward, and therefore, decided not to.

But Lacroix knew. He had known that Kari had strong feelings for Joey for a while now and watched as, at times, Kari appeared to drift into another world. This, he imagined, was because Joey had had a profoundly positive effect on Kari, he was less tense and he even laughed more often. Lacroix couldn't help but wish Joey were a native to their tribe, their life would be so much simpler.

Joey invaded Kari's thoughts, especially when he was alone. When he thought of her, he could see her face in fine detail, he could even imagine her sweetly intoxicating smell. She had returned to England just five days ago, but he already missed her terribly. Towards the end of the week, he knew he *had* to see her. He asked Lacroix to rearrange his diary, so that he could be in France towards the end of the following week. Lacroix worked hard to accommodate Kari's wishes and, with a fair amount of juggling and commitment from Kari, he was able to.

Later that afternoon, Lacroix called Joey and, for her, it was like taking a breath of fresh air. She was so happy to hear from him, he could only imagine what reception Kari would get the next time he saw her… Lacroix explained that Kari would be in France the following weekend and had asked if Joey would like to join him. There was nothing planned, no social events, just a quiet weekend, together. Joey accepted immediately and Lacroix explained that the plane tickets would be waiting at the check-in desk, and she would be collected from the airport and driven to the villa. Joey smiled to herself as she thought of how easy and normal this pattern now seemed. She was over the moon. In just over a week she would see Kari.

As Joey flew to France the following Friday she reflected on conversations she'd had with both her mum and Lucy. They were both clearly concerned that she'd quickly fallen for a man, and not the sort of man that Joey would normally be drawn towards. Her mum was also growing increasingly insistent that she meets Kari. Joey smiled as she recalled her mum suggesting that maybe Kari would also like to treat her to a small holiday where they could *all* spend some quality time getting to know one another! She sighed as she tried to imagine how Kari would react if he were to ever meet her mum. Such stark contrasts… Kari a man of few words, whereas her mum could talk the hind leg off a donkey and more!

However, there was also no denying the nervous excitement she felt as she arrived at, the now familiar, Nice airport. She was astounded when she saw Kari waiting to greet her. He was alone and grinning from ear to ear. He met her formally, with a kiss, either side of her face, and took her bag. Various people watched, unconsciously drawn to the tall, striking man. Joey noticed paparazzi taking a few quick snaps.

'Surprised to see me?' Kari glanced across at Joey in the passenger seat, as they sped towards the villa in Kari's Audi.

'Very. How did you manage to make it alone?'

'Don't worry, Lacroix and Solonge are not too far away, they're the only two who know what I am doing this weekend. They're sworn to secrecy but, thanks to the local paparazzi, it won't remain a secret much longer.' Joey smiled across at him and he put his hand on her thigh. Joey wanted to feel his hands on the rest of her body, but she knew she had to wait. Collecting her from the airport was one thing, but making out in his car was another, besides, he was driving.

'I want us to be like a normal couple this weekend. Nobody else will be here. No protectors, no housekeeper, just you and me…' Kari said and looked wantonly across at Joey.

Joey felt her heart begin to race; she imagined being alone with him for two whole days and nights.

They pulled into the villa driveway and all was very quiet except for the hum of cicadas. He took her suitcase from the boot of the car and they walked hand in hand into the villa.

Once Kari had shut the door and silenced the alarm, he turned to Joey. 'And then, there was just two.' He threw the car keys onto a nearby chest.

Joey walked towards him, closing the distance between them. The passionate kiss led them to pull each other's clothes off. Almost animalistic in their frenzy, they sank to the bottom of the stairs where they passionately made love.

It all happened very quickly and they both knew, it wouldn't be long before they'd want to reunite their bodies again. Kari knelt on the floor, his head resting on Joey's lap whilst he waited for his breathing to return to normal. He looked up and said, 'Welcome back.'

They didn't make it back downstairs until the next day. Their clothes remained where they had dispelled them the evening before, scattered in the hall.
Throughout the night, they had continued to reunite their bodies, and now Joey looked at his profile; he truly was an amazing man in every way.

'I can't, not yet. I need breakfast, I need fuel.' Kari said, wearily.

'It's okay; I'm not after another session… just yet! I was thinking how truly gorgeous you look, especially after… last night. You have undeniable stamina.'

He was quiet as he reminisced. Smiling coyly he said, 'I particularly liked it when you… took control whilst I slept, shall we say. No wonder I'm hungry, what am I going to be like by the end of the weekend!'

'Let's see.' Joey replied, kissing him.

'Oh no, don't do that, we'll never eat. I'll be back in a moment.'

Kari pulled on a pair of boxer briefs and walked out of the room. He walked past the disarray they'd created the night before, chuckling to himself. He had never reacted so wantonly before and he liked it, yet it was so out of character for him. He made a pot of coffee, found some pastries and took them back to Joey. She was lying in his massive bed, looking thoughtful.

'Breakfast is served, Mademoiselle.' said Kari seductively, as he walked towards her and placed the tray on the bed.

Joey sat up and wrapped the duvet around her to hide her nakedness, *why*, she thought, he'd seen her naked just a few minutes earlier. 'I've never been in this room before. I like it, it's so peaceful, masculine.'

'As you may have guessed, it's my room.'

Hungrily they ate their breakfast, remembering that they had forgotten to eat the night before.

'So, is there anything you'd like to do today?' Kari asked. She gave him a lustful look, 'Except ravage my poor, battered body.'

'I am at your beck and call.'

'You may regret saying that.' Kari smiled. 'I know a quaint, French town, not too far from here. How about visiting, having a look around and perhaps a bite to eat? After which, we can come back and you have my full permission to do with me as you wish.' Kari suggested, with an enticing smile.

'Sounds good in every aspect.'

'But first, I need a shower.' Kari said, walking towards his en suite. Joey's eyes followed him as he exited. She waited until she heard the shower start and got up and joined him.

'I thought we were going to spend the entire weekend together.' Joey said as he turned around, surprised but pleased to see her.

Kari parked the car in a small side street in the French town of Antibes. It was a beautiful town, beckoning the rich and famous year after year. Incredible yachts dotted the harbour and intriguing side streets beckoned. The market was full of tables, selling interesting French trinkets. One moment the aroma of fresh fruit filled the air, the next a delectable stall offering the chance to taste and buy wonderful cheeses.

Joey was excited as Kari took her hand and they began to explore. Joey forgot whom she was with, until she noticed a lot of very attractive women, checking Kari out – who appeared to be oblivious to their stares. Joey was proud it was *her* hand he was holding.

They tasted various cheeses and fruit and she tried different wines. The freshly caught fish looked excellent and both agreed to pop back later to buy some for supper. Kari took her to a small, traditional restaurant where they ordered local salads and frites. It seemed natural for them to share each other's food. It wasn't long before watching the beautiful people and admiring the stunning scenery distracted Joey. Eventually Kari gave up reminding her to eat and decided to feed her instead. To be honest, Joey found it strangely seductive, the look of concentration on his face as he carefully fed her without dropping a morsel. It was perfect. The weather was hot, but it didn't affect them as they sat in the shade, eating their lunch leisurely.

After lunch Kari showed her some of the towns attractions including a small church and the Musee Picasso. They then walked, following a wall that traced the edge of the town with spectacular views overlooking the sea, admiring the Cote d'Azur.

'Have you ever been on one of those yachts?' Joey asked.

Kari nodded, 'Yes. If you fancy it, I'd be happy to hire one for the day?'

'I'd love to, but right now I'm happy just being here with you.'

He looked down at her and smiled, before they continued on their way. They walked past a young couple who were making out.

'I guess, you'd never be able to do that without the risk of being caught on camera.' Joey asked inclining her head towards the couple, as they passed them by.

'No, I'm not supposed to show any emotion in public. This,' he held up her hand which he held firmly in his, 'isn't an option, either. But today I don't care, I want to be normal.'

'You've never held hands with a woman in public?' Joey asked.

'Only experienced with you, Mademoiselle Lewis.' Kari replied. They stopped and looked at each other. Lust emanated from their eyes, 'I think it's time we headed back.'

Kari drove quickly back to the villa and they made it to a large sofa in the lounge, before reuniting their bodies. Their desire as strong as if they hadn't made love in a month, when actually, it was only hours since their last union.

The weather was perfect and Joey suggested heading to the pool for a swim – or rather, Kari swim, whilst she lounged by the side. They changed into their swimming outfits and headed outside. Joey admired the large, new rattan reclining seat; it was as big as a double bed, but round in shape. Kari explained he'd wanted something they could recline on together and Lacroix had the task of finding it. Joey was impressed.

'Poor Lacroix, I know he's one of your protectors but it must put him in a difficult position when your family isn't too hot on me, and he knows you're here alone with me. It doesn't take a genius to work out what we do.'

Kari turned to look at Joey, 'I have some fantastic news to share with you.'

'What?'

'Lacroix and Solonge are engaged!' Kari said, enthusiastically.

'What!'

Kari saw the look of disbelief on Joey's face.

'No! Really?'

Kari laughed, 'Yes really. They may have only been dating a short time, but they've known each other all their lives. They have also, as we suspected, admired each other from a distance for a very long time. Besides, they're perfect for each other.'

'But even so, it's very quick! Where I'm from, it generally takes months, *years* even, to get to that stage. What if they've rushed into it? What if they live to regret not waiting a little longer? What if... *what if...*'

'What if *what* Joey? Why live life by what ifs? Isn't it better to have experienced life and not regret what could have been? What is a life if it's a collection of missed opportunities?'

'But what if you regret doing something?'

'I'd rather live and learn than be afraid and stagnate,' Kari said warmly. His eyes searched Joey's as he tried to explain. 'In our tribe, we believe when you find your soul mate, the one you're destined to be with for eternity, why wait. If you love each other, what else matters?' Kari said, with a matter-of-fact tone.

'I guess, when you put it like that, but still!' Joey shook her head. 'So, when's the wedding?'

'In a month.' He saw the look of shock on Joey's face.

'You are kidding!'

He chuckled and said, 'No, Lacroix and Solonge will marry in a month.'

'Why do I get the distinct feeling there is still more you're going to tell me,' Joey was certain Kari was not telling her everything. What he'd said already was hard to comprehend.

His eyes sparkled with mischief, 'For one whole month, the engaged couple are encouraged... to be celibate, making the chances of conceiving on their wedding night greater.' This time, Joey felt her mouth gape open – she was speechless. Kari continued, 'You will love the Kutan Tribal wedding ceremony. Our tribe believe that in order for the newly married couple to conceive, every couple is encouraged to have sex on the wedding night.'

'Now you are pulling my leg?' Joey asked in disbelief. Even though Kari shook his head in denial, the humour in his eyes was evident.

'This ritual sends fertile energy to our Spirit Gods.' He laughed, as he watched Joey's mouth fall open, still in disbelief, 'You will be invited to the wedding because you were a key member in getting Lacroix and Solonge together, you need to be there to complete their circle. I look forward to that night.' Kari grinned at her.

Still unsure if Kari was teasing her or not Joey said, 'Forgive me, I'd love to be there for Solonge and Lacroix, but won't it make it a little awkward for your parents?'

'My parents have to accept you at the wedding. It's imperative you attend. You have to be there for the sake of Lacroix and Solonge. Without you, their circle will not be complete. Their marriage would be considered weak.'

Without another word Kari stretched, got up and dived into the pool. Gee, he is beautiful, Joey thought as she watched him swim, length after length. She knew there was more to the wedding than he was letting on, but she also understood he'd ended the subject as far as he was concerned and he'd tell her more as and when he was ready. Besides, what is the circle he mentioned and what the hell is the night of orgies all about? There was nothing she could do but wait and see what else would unfold within the ridiculously short engagement time.

Chapter 20

During the lazy afternoon, they sunbathed, dozed and discussed their pasts and their hopes and dreams.

'To become Chief of the Kutan Tribe has always been my destiny, as far as I'm concerned. It's all I've ever wanted, and been brought up to believe.'

'At least you never had to make serious career choices, like the rest of us minions.'

'Sometimes, it's nice to have choices, though.'

Joey noted his slightly sad tone as he made his last comment. 'So, when you become Chief, is there anything you'd like to change?'

Kari scoffed, 'Yes.'

'What?'

'I'd like the tribe that I lead, to become more open minded and to move forward to reflect the modern world that we are living in. But, I guess ultimately, I am happy with how things are being managed. As long as there is peace and harmony, and the tribe is allowed to live independently, then I'll be happy.'

'Sounds simple.'

Kari looked at her, 'If only it were.'

'I guess there's more to it than I appreciate.'

Kari smiled, but said no more on the subject. 'What about you, are you going to become the next leading volunteer for the British Red Cross or its equivalent?'

'I'm not sure about *leading* volunteer worker, but if I can do some good, then I'll be happy.'

'I know you don't crave power or fame.'

'No! I'm quite simple when it comes down to it. One day, when I'm old and grey, I'd like to look back on my life with happiness, knowing I fulfilled all my ambitions and I have no regrets. A chance for me to help those more needy than me, whilst giving myself some space to breathe, and really think about what I would like from life.' She sighed, 'I know, this is going to make me sound like a daft ol' romantic, but, all I want is contentment. I guess money helps, but… it's not everything. I want to meet a man who will love me forever and not walk out on me like my father did. Eventually, I'd like to have children but if that's not possible… well, I guess, I just want to be happy.'

'Sounds ideal.'

'That's what worries me, because ideals aren't real.' He watched, as her wistful look turned into a beaming smile.

'What are you thinking about?'

She giggled, 'Oh… another ambition.'

He narrowed his eyes and looked at her sceptically, she had a wicked glint. Joey grinned, 'Before I'm too old, I want to make love under a waterfall.'

Kari propped himself up on his elbow to face her, 'Why?'

'Imagine how it would feel - the sound, power and force of the water.'

Kari smiled, 'Well, I could help you with that ambition. There's a waterfall on the grounds of my home in Canada… but the water is really cold.'

Joey looked at him, 'You sound like you're speaking from experience.'

'Luca and I used to play there as children. But, no, I have never made love there.'

Joey was pleased to hear that. 'What about you, do you have any secret wishes?'

He sighed as he lay back down, 'Yes. I want to watch the sun rise over the Sacred Mountains at Cha Tik Warro with the love of my life in my arms, then I'll marry her and have many children. Now, that's my ideal. I'd also like to make-out with my wife in public and not worry about being photographed.'

They shared the afternoon together, eager to listen to what the other said.

At one point, Kari caught Joey looking at his body intently and said, 'Does something not meet your satisfaction?'

Joey blushed, she didn't realise Kari had caught her ogling him, 'Oh, no!'

Kari smiled but said nothing.

'It's just…' Joey said sounding mystified, 'How do you stay so fit and… perfect.' She knew she could go on, but felt it better to stop there before she got carried away.

'I'm lucky that I have access to a pool both here and at home, so I swim often. I also love to ride my horse and I practise yoga.'

Joey was impressed; 'So, you don't actively work out, by that, I mean running or weight lifting.'

'No, that'd be too dull.'

'Yoga is something that I've never tried.'

'I'll show you one day. It's great for the mind, body and soul.'

Joey nodded, 'Potential problem though, I'm not very flexible.'

Kari pulled his heart-stopping smile and replied, coyly, 'You'll be amazed what you can achieve with practice.'

Joey was convinced that he was implying other areas of life. 'We've discussed a lot of things, but not ex's…' Joey ventured, not sure if she wanted to hear his response. She knew Kari was an experienced lover, more so than herself, and she did have a jealous streak.

'Do we need to talk about them? They're part of the past.' Kari replied.

'I'm interested. You have way more experience than me and I'd kind of like to know where I stand in comparison to your past girlfriends. How old were you when you lost your virginity, have you dated many women, have you had your heart broken?'

'Really, I'm not keen to dredge up the past. I'd rather leave it there.'

He saw the look of concern on Joey's face as she said, 'Now, you're really scaring me. What's there to dredge up?'

'Not a lot, and honestly, nothing very exciting.'

'I'd like to know, that's all.'

He slowly exhaled the air from his body. Joey was obviously a girl who had trust issues in men, and although he'd rather not talk about his past relationships, he knew if he didn't tell her, her imagination would conjure up all sorts of wrong ideas. 'I lost my virginity when I was twenty-one, to a girl named Eyota. I have known her all my life and we were encouraged to get together. We did, but after a short while, we knew we weren't destined to be together, we were more like brother and sister.'

Joey could hear the warmth in Kari's voice, as he talked about his past. 'I have a great deal of respect for Eyota; she could have insisted we marry, and at the time, I may have. I was young, but she was strong and walked away. She is now very happily married, to a very good friend of mine, and they're currently expecting their forth child. I have a feeling you would like Eyota.' Kari stopped to breathe. Joey was feeling mildly jealous.

'Then, there was Arabella.'

Joey instantly didn't like her; she didn't like the way Kari said *then*.

'We had an on-off relationship for years. It finally finished about four years ago and I haven't had a relationship with anyone else, until I met you. Arabella is very hard work. I'm sure she was only with me because of my title. There were no true feelings in our relationship; it was purely physical, to be blunt. I was bored, I needed a woman in my life, or so I thought, and Arabella was there. I didn't love her and my blood runs cold, when I see her now. She's Henrique's daughter.' He added.

'Oh.' Joey said.

'So, rest assured, I haven't had loads of women in my bed. I have had dates, but nothing of any consequence, until I met you.' Kari looked at her, 'I haven't had my heart broken, yet.' He gently kissed her. 'So, now you've heard about my lack of girlfriends, I guess you want to tell me about your past relationships?'

'Not if you don't want to hear them.' Joey said, rolling onto her back.

Kari moved over her and said, 'I don't really want to know, but I'm inquisitive – I must warn you though, I can get insanely jealous.'

Joey looked him in the eyes and said, 'I was seventeen when I lost my virginity.'

'Ooh, young!' Kari said, teasingly.

'It was legal. Anyway, I was seventeen, he was eighteen and it was the first time for both of us; his name was Rob and, at the time, I thought he was the bee's knees. We dated for about three years and everything was fine until one day, he called me and said it was over; he'd met someone else. Yes, he did break my heart.'

'Bastard.' Kari said as he scooped Joey into his arms, hugging her tightly.

'I met Phil. He was okay, but to be honest, I think he was a rebound from Rob. We went through the motions, like sex and going out, but I didn't really like him. So, I dumped him.' She could feel Kari watching her intently, wondering what she'd say next. 'I've had flings with men since, but nothing of any note.' She felt Kari withdraw slightly. She turned onto her side to look at him. 'I'm no saint but I assure you, I haven't had scores of men in my bed, just a handful. None of them made me feel special. Well, take Dave for example.'

'I thought you didn't sleep with him.'

It was easy to hear Kari's cool tone. 'I didn't. He's a classic example of how guys make me feel rubbish. In fact, if it weren't for you, I don't believe he would ever have noticed me. Any dates I've had these last few years, have been relatively platonic, and if things did go further, the "relationship" only lasted a very short time. I have a horrible habit of breaking up with whomever I'm seeing, mainly because I don't want to risk falling in love and break my heart again.'

Kari moved her chin so she would look at him, 'Why?'

'I saw it happen to my mum and she's never got over my father leaving.'

Kari kissed her nose, 'I don't like to think of anyone else being with you. I hate Rob and I've never met him. How can anyone break your heart?'

'It mended a long time ago, I'm cautious, but being with you is definitely helping.'

He looked into her open and honest eyes, 'You are special, Joey, don't ever forget that. Never, ever let another human make you feel worthless.' Slowly he bent to kiss her.

As the sun fell deeper in the sky, they both prepared the beautiful sea bass they'd bought earlier at the market. Whilst they cooked, Joey played various songs from her iPod. At one point, she played the latest chart number one, a song, which Kari had never heard before. She danced seductively next to him, he nearly gave up what he was doing, forgetting about eating altogether, lifting her to his room... *What was it with this woman? She hardly moved and all he wanted to do was make love to her!*

They ate on the terrace and watched the sun go down. It was a beautiful end to an incredible day. After supper, Joey realised that Kari hadn't said anything for a good while. Instead, he was looking at her, very intently indeed.

Eventually, she said, 'Okay, either you've forgotten how to talk or I've bored you into silence!' He didn't answer, he just watched her with a pensive gaze. 'Kari, are you alright?' Joey asked, now feeling concerned.

'Wait here.' He murmured, walking into the villa. Her mind raced. What had she said to silence him? Quickly she re-capped, but she couldn't recall saying anything harmful. By the time he returned, she'd convinced herself that he'd have her suitcase, insisting she return home. But no, he returned, carrying only a small, folded pouch of beige leather. He knelt down in front of her, still with an extremely serious look on his face. As she looked into his dark eyes, she saw they reflected the same burning intensity, which he gave her after they'd just had sex.

He took her hands in his, 'Joey, I have a gift for you. It may not seem like much, but it means so much to me.' His hands shook just a little as he passed Joey the folded pouch. His voice was sincere when he said, 'Please, look?'

Carefully, Joey untied the leather binding that kept the pouch closed. She unfolded the leather to reveal a necklace, similar to the familiar design of a dream catcher. The main pendent was a thick, platinum ring. Intricate, spidery webs of silver threads spanned the ring. Tiny crystals - black, hues of brown, amber, deep magenta and clear crystal, floated along the fine silver threads. From the base of the ring hung a beautiful black feather with three strands of tiny crystals, hanging either side. The pendent itself was suspended from a simple, black leather lace.

Joey gasped – it was incredibly impressive. She looked up and saw emotion welling in his eyes, revealing just how precious the gift was and how privileged she was to receive it. She would almost swear his eyes were moist with unshed tears. Joey placed one hand on his face, 'It's beautiful, thank you.' Kissing him, desperate to show her love.

He received her kiss. She pulled back from him slightly, 'It's identical to yours.' She touched the feather necklace that Kari always wore; he never took it off, as far as she knew. She thought of the times that he had lain next to her, all of him totally naked, apart from the feather necklace.

He touched her hand that currently held his feather, 'I know, and it is so special to me. I want you to know you are also very special and mean so very much to me.' He kissed her softly, before moving silently behind her and placed the necklace around Joey's neck. She moved her hair to the side so he could tie the lace securely. There were no fancy clasps, but Kari knew how to tie the lace in an unbreakable knot. He kissed her neck as he let the necklace fall gracefully around it. She thought it was one of the most seductive gestures Kari had ever made.

He walked around to face her and pulled her to her feet, 'Perfect, just perfect.' He said, gazing into her eyes. Joey found she was very close to tears, tears of joy. It was the most unique present she'd ever received, and although he hadn't said anything, his eyes looked like they were bursting with love and pride.

'I want to make love to you, Joey – my way, like the natives from my tribe.' Kari scooped Joey up and into his arms as if she was as light as a feather, and carried her to his room.

Chapter 21

Kari gently placed her on to his enormous bed, kneeling opposite her. He gently held her hands as he explained; 'When a member of our tribe makes love with their partner, they connect with one another in a way that is more than just physical, it becomes a spiritual experience too. In order to achieve this, you give yourself entirely to each other. We begin by focusing on our breathing. You'll discover by satisfying their need, you satisfy your own. Touch each other's bodies, as well as your own, mirroring each other the whole time. Once we are spiritually one, we then physically join as one.'

Unable to speak, Joey looked nervously at Kari.

'I will guide you, but remember to trust your instinct.' He placed his hand on his own face and nodded to Joey to do the same. Joey was nervous, what if she went wrong? 'Relax.' he murmured.

At first it felt alien for Joey to be touching her body. She normally relied on her partner to touch and arouse her. But, as she watched Kari, she forgot it was her own hands on her skin because they felt like an extension of his. His eyes held hers as his hands traced over his body, encouraging her, silently, to copy him.

Kari moved closer to Joey and started to pull her dress off, over her head. Joey reached out and undid the buttons to Kari's shirt and shorts and removing them to reveal his incredible body. They drank in each other's bodies for what felt like minutes.

Moving in harmony, they touched each other's bodies, never losing eye contact. It was incredibly erotic and Joey had never experienced anything like it. They were breathing at the same rate, deeply and measured. Time seemed to slow until all that mattered was this moment of pure, simple pleasure.

He leaned closer to Joey and unclasped her bra, before easing the straps down, over her shoulders and off her arms. Joey thought she was going to pass out from his slow, tantalising touch. Kari then moved his attention to her knickers. She felt completely relaxed although every nerve ending was aroused and screaming for his touch. Unimaginable, incredible feelings pulsated through her body.

When he stopped and rested his palms on his thighs, Joey began to caress and massage him. She noticed his muscles clench and relax under the pressure she applied. He lifted her onto his thighs and she wrapped her legs around him.

They gazed into each other's eyes. With impossibly slow and careful caresses, Kari ran his hands and eyes from the very top of her head, down her face and neck, over her shoulders, back towards the hollow of her throat, where his fingers picked up her feather, before tracing down over her breasts, torso, waist, bottom, thighs and right to the end of her toes. Before he let go of her feet, his eyes flashed back to hers. Desire bubbled beneath their skin. She had never seen him so charged before; he seemed more intense than ever.

He took her hands and placed them on the top of his head, indicating for her to do the same. Slowly and seductively, Joey absorbed his body. She became aware of every muscle and movement – the muscle twitching in his cheek, his pulse pulsating strongly in his neck. His shoulders were broad and strong. She gently held his feather, before running her hands down his pecks, incredible six-pack, pelvis bone, bottom, thighs, long legs until she reached his feet, where she returned her eyes to his. Their eyes locked. Joey desperately wanted him. She had never felt so aroused. She began to tremble with anticipation.

Gently, he lifted her and held her, until their most intimate areas were millimetres apart. Not a sound could be heard apart from their beating hearts, which were pounding in their ears. They held their breath. Then, with a slight movement from Kari's hips, he entered, pulling her down onto him until he was penetrating her deeply. They both moaned aloud at the pleasure, finally uniting their bodies. Kari held her hips as he raised himself higher, so he was able to move back and forth with ease. Joey wanted to scream, her body was on fire - she had never felt such amazing, sexual sensations before.

He held her body close as he kissed her throat, before gently biting her neck - the pleasure increased as he continued to thrust, driving her to new levels of ecstasy. He kissed her passionately before laying her gently on the bed.

She was more relaxed than she had ever been with him and watched, through a sexual haze of contentment, as his fingers explored her intimately. With masterful touches of his fingers, he aroused her further and further, lovingly bringing her to utter fulfilment until she cried his name, begging him to come with her. Immediately, he thrust deeply into her, their stimulated bodies becoming one. He wanted to kiss her but the pull of orgasm constricted his mouth. Their eyes remained locked on one another's as their passion quickly built.

It only took a few strokes, before they were climaxing together. Wave after wave of ecstasy rolled over and through their bodies. Calling out each other's names between cries of pure, unadulterated bliss. Kari wrapped her tightly within his embrace, kissing her longingly.

Joey had never experienced anything like it. She remembered she had screamed out loud in pure wonder, she had never had an orgasm like *that* ever before. Her whole body tingled with tiny electrical shocks, dripping with sweat as she clung to Kari in a vain attempt to stop her satisfied body from shaking.

Chapter 22

Daylight streamed in through the windows as Kari woke the next morning. He looked across at Joey, who seemed to be deep in thought, holding her feather delicately between her fingers. He noted the bruised, bite mark on her neck that he'd given her last night whilst they were making love. He wondered what she would say when she saw it. As if sensing that he was watching her, Joey suddenly looked across at him and smiled. 'Good morning, beautiful.' Kari said, leaning down and kissing her.

'Good morning to you, too!' Joey said cheerfully, as she snuggled next to his warm body. 'Thank you for last night.'

'No. Thank *you*. I have never experienced anything like that before, I don't think I'll be able to stop grinning for days.' Kari pulled her closer to him.

Joey thought, *Well, I certainly have never experienced anything quite like it before*! She hadn't known that those sorts of sensations were even possible. 'Kari, was I okay?' Joey felt like a virgin, asking a very experienced lover.

Kari rolled over so he could face her, 'My beautiful Joey, you were incredible, in fact, more than incredible. Perfect sounds too lame but you were, you are! Last night was the best night of my life so far. I have never felt like that with anyone before. Can you feel how connected we are?'

'I guess, but you're so much more experienced than me.'

'Experience doesn't count, it's whether it's right or not and, to me, you feel so right.' He kissed her again. He wanted to share the same breath - taste her, be one with her.

They stayed in bed for the remainder of the day. Both aware this would be the last time they would be able to see each other for a while. They were eager to make the most of their private time together.

On a visit to the bathroom, Joey noticed the bite mark on her neck. She'd never had a love bite before because she wasn't too keen on them. But, she didn't mind this, whenever she looked at it, she would be reminded of their amazing lovemaking.

They continued to unite their bodies throughout the day, and during the afternoon, whilst lying in bed facing each other, Kari said, 'I'm not sure how I'm going to survive until I next see you.'

'I was just thinking the same thing. At least you'll be busy; I'm winding down at work and, in a week, I'll be jobless with too much time to think about you and wondering what you're doing.' Joey replied. 'What are your plans?'

Kari absent-mindedly tucked a wayward lock of her hair back behind her ear. 'I'm flying to Paris to see Luca. There are a couple of things I need to discuss with him. I'm also meeting the French President before returning to Canada.' He knew time was running away and soon, Joey would have a new venture in her life to concentrate on. 'I want to see you again Joey, soon, before you get too busy.'

'Me, busy!' Didn't she just say her work was coming to an end?

'Maybe the week after you finish work, you could fly to Vancouver?'

Joey looked at him in despair.

'What was that look for?'

'It's not that I don't want to see you, because, trust me, I do, but being with your mother and father again, on my own, doesn't fill me with joy. I'll probably starve again. I guess I could always pack a spare case of food.'

'I can only apologise for my parents' disrespectful behaviour. We have spoken and they've agreed that, when you return as my guest, they will be more accommodating.' Kari sighed, 'You have good reason not to believe me, but my mother and father are incredibly, lovely people; they're just very traditional when it comes to tribal values. The more they get to know you, the more they'll like you.'

Joey hoped Kari was right, but somehow she wasn't so sure, after all she was sleeping with their son and heir and she was not a member of the Kutan Tribe.

'We're going to have to get up soon, if you want to catch the plane on time.'

'Don't remind me!' Joey said, as she snuggled closer into his arms.

'Fancy a shower?' Kari said, mischievously pulling her chin up so he could see her face.

Joey liked the wicked glint in his eyes.

A short while later, Kari watched Joey dry her hair after their heated shower. For the first time in his life, Kari really didn't want to say goodbye. He had never before imagined that he would really enjoy spending such intimate and quality time with another person. He felt uneasy taking her to the airport, not knowing for sure when he'd see her next.

Joey caught Kari looking at her in the mirror reflection and smiled at him, he smiled back. He walked over and took the hairdryer, beginning to dry her hair. She loved feeling his fingers run through her hair, separating sections to ease the drying. His eyes were pensive as he concentrated on his task. As she watched him, she had mixed feelings – love, because she knew she loved him but these feelings were marred with waves of sadness. Sadness, because what they had shared, couldn't possibly continue.

She was so entranced in her mesmerised and hadn't realised that he'd already finished.

'Is that okay?' Kari repeated, and smiled at her mirrored image.

'Yes, perfect.'

He kissed her head and said quietly, 'You are.'

Kari spoke so quietly Joey wasn't sure if she'd heard him correctly. She was momentarily struck dumb, watching as he put her hairdryer in her suitcase, closed it and walked with it to the door.

'Ready?' He asked.

'No.' She walked towards him, stopping at the bedroom door which he was holding open.

They walked quietly along the landing and down the stairs and as Joey reached the bottom, she turned to Kari and said, 'It seems I'm always saying my little speech just about here.' She said, pointing to the floor. 'But, thank you again for a truly perfect weekend…' Her voice caught in her throat, her heart wanted to tell him she loved him, but her sensible head stopped her, she didn't want to scare him off.

Kari reached for her and pulled her into a firm embrace. 'Thank you, I have truly loved every moment. I don't want to say goodbye.'

'Me too!' She replied, her voice muffled as she spoke into Kari's chest.

'When I say goodbye to you at the airport, I'm going to want to hold you and kiss you but, please understand, I can't. I'm not supposed to show any emotion in public, but the paparazzi, no doubt, will be waiting to photograph us.'

'I know, I'm glad you show emotion in private.'

He laughed quietly because he'd never been so open and honest with his emotions, and it was so liberating.

Sure enough, as they arrived at the airport the paparazzi were waiting to take pictures as he pulled Joey's case and she walked demurely beside him. She checked in her luggage and said goodbye to Kari, who kissed her on either cheek.

Kari drove back to an empty and untidy villa. They hadn't even washed up yesterday evening's supper plates. He spent the next hour cleaning so that Madame Dupre wouldn't find the house untidy.

He reflected whilst he cleaned. He had never felt this way about anyone before. Joey had only been gone a short while and, already, he felt like half his soul was missing. He was glad he'd given her the feather necklace, but he was unsure if she realised its important meaning, but he'd tell her that next time he saw her in Canada. Right now, he didn't care about his future within the tribe and he hoped Luca would support him with his new project. He hoped the *tribe* would support him with his new project!

As Joey flew back to England, she had time to reflect on the weekend and how she felt. She knew she had fallen in love with Kari, in fact, if she were totally honest, she'd suspected it for a while, this weekend had only confirmed it. But, she couldn't admit her true feelings, even to herself. She knew it would only be a matter of time before Kari told her he didn't feel the same way. Yes, he'd he cared for her deeply, but he hadn't said he loved her. The closest he'd come to saying it was when he said he wanted to make love to her, just after giving her the beautiful and special feather necklace. Joey thought about the future, deciding that there was no chance of a future *together*; they had totally different pasts and futures. She was not a native, and never would be, therefore, there was no future for her and Kari. She must try to create distance because she knew it was going to hurt like crazy when she crashed back into reality.

'Joey, be *careful*, that's all I'm trying to say!' Lucy advised Joey as she watched her friend unpack her suitcase from the latest trip to see Kari. 'You seem to jump to his demands every time he calls, correction, every time his *Protector* calls. Don't you find it just a little bit odd he never, ever calls you? What if you're one of many women he uses?'

'If only you knew what he is really like, he's not the cold, hard faced man we thought he was when we first saw him. He is so warm and giving. I have never known a man like him.'

'Are you sure it's not just the fame?'

'No way!' Joey protested, 'You know me better than anyone. I had no idea who he was when he first invited me to France. I have grown to love the man I have spent time with. No pre-conceived ideas, I have fallen for a really decent guy… who also happens to be fantastic in bed.'

Lucy mimed being sick. Joey truly seemed to be in love and Lucy had never seen her this blissfully happy with a man before. If Kari was half the man Joey said he was, then he was a pretty special person. She didn't understand the feather necklace he'd given Joey though, surely a man of his wealth could afford a few diamonds? Still, she didn't want to be the one to rain on Joey's parade. And the love bite, what was that about? Good for her though, she deserved happiness. She only hoped that Joey wasn't heading for a broken heart, as she seemed to have fallen hard for this man.

Chapter 23

Joey's week flew by. She kept recalling the weekend she'd just experienced with Kari and what they had done together. Every time she felt unhappy, she would touch her feather necklace and the heart pain became a dull ache.

On Wednesday, Joey received a call from Lacroix.

'Lacroix! I believe congratulations are in order for both yourself and Solonge. I couldn't be happier!' She enthused.

'Thank you, but I'm sure I would still be pining after Solonge if Kari and you hadn't set us up! You will come to the wedding, won't you?' Lacroix asked.

'I will, if I'm allowed.'

'You have to be there, it's imperative. Anyway, I'm calling because Kari and I arrived back in Canada half an hour ago and he asked me to call you. Would you be free to fly here next week? Unfortunately, he has meetings that he's unable to reschedule, but he will try to get home, at least every evening.'

'Sounds great! Thanks Lacroix, I'd love to come over. I'm free from Monday, so what day works best for Kari?' Joey asked.

'How does flying over Thursday morning sound? I'll collect you and Kari will hopefully be at home during the evening. He wants to assure you that he will try his best to be there every evening because he knows it was difficult before.'

'Thank you, please tell Kari I appreciate that.'

'Kari will definitely be free all weekend to be with you, we will make sure of it. Until then, goodbye and see you next week.'

They both hung up. So Kari had just returned to Canada and he made sure Lacroix called her to arrange another visit, her heart sang.

Stones Architects arranged a leaving party for Joey - dinner at Michael's, followed by drinks at The Pig's Head, for those interested. She was given gift vouchers to spend at a large department store, a large bouquet of flowers and a massive card. The directors made a very lovely speech saying they were going to miss her and she was welcome back anytime. Most of the staff went for drinks at The Pig's Head, including Dave.

Whilst sitting in the pub, Joey looked across to Dave who had propped himself against the bar, nursing his usual ale. She tried but failed to see how he'd ever caught her eye. She smiled to herself as she compared Dave and Kari to chocolate. Dave was like white chocolate; pale, uninteresting and gave you the feeling that you needed to eat a lot, to achieve any sort of hit, often leaving you feeling slightly sickly. Whereas Kari would be dark chocolate, at least 85%, interesting and intense and you only needed a small chunk to get an extreme hit.

Dave caught Joey looking in his direction and assumed her misty-eyed look was for him. It was too late and before Joey could rearrange her expression, he sidled up to her and began flirting.

'I can't believe we're not going to see your cheery face around the office anymore. What're we going to do?'

Joey noticed he didn't make the statement personal, it was all "we" and never an "I". *Self centred bastard* Joey thought. 'Oh, I'm sure you'll survive without me.' Joey enthused, taking a big sip of her wine.

'I hope it wasn't the fact that I ended our fling that you feel you have to leave Stones.'

He! *He* ended their fling! It was her! 'Not at all, Dave. Let's say it was a convenient coincidence.'

'Ah Joey, you're not still jealous of Michelle.'

'Nope.'

'Because, nothing came of it. It was a crazy weekend where inhibitions were lost and everyone fucked each other.'

Joey raised her eyebrows but passed no comment.

'Now you, dear Joey, on the other hand was the fish that slipped through my fingers.' He said, reaching across and running his fingers through her hair.

Joey glared at him.

'You stalked me for weeks. I loved knowing that you'd be in here, waiting for me.'

'Nice Dave, real nice.' Joey said as she got up from her table and began to say her goodbyes to her ex-colleagues and leave Dave and the pub behind her. Little did she know, Dave had downed his pint and started to follow her.

'Joey, wait. Don't be like that. You didn't even say goodnight.'

'Goodnight, Dave.' Joey said wearily as she walked towards the bus stop.

He ran up to Joey and pulled her arm to stop her. 'You should have come with me to The Fiesta.'

'Should?'

Dave nodded.

'Here's a bit of advice Dave, no one should be told what she should or shouldn't do. Treat people with respect and it's amazing what you will receive.'

'I do. I respected you.'

Joey turned on him, 'When?'

'I took you out, I dined you.'

'Whoopee, and what did you want in return?'

'Come on, Joey, I'm a man.'

'And, I'm a woman!' She glared at him, before turning on her heel and walking away.

'It's not too late, Joey. Why don't we carry on where we left off.'

Joey actually felt bile rise into her throat. 'It is too late Dave, I'm no longer interested.'

'You were, I know you were.' He said as he walked alongside her.

Joey stopped. 'Just answer me: What changed? Why did you wine and dine me?'

Dave shrugged. 'I guess when I saw you dancing with another man I felt, I don't know…'

'Please don't tell me you felt jealous?'

'No. Yes. I don't know. It was clear he fancied the pants off you! He couldn't take his eyes off you and I thought if anyone was going to have you, it would be me.'

'I didn't even know him!' Joey said, reeling from Dave's observation that Kari fancied her all that time ago.

Dave's eyes were cold as he stood over her. 'You and he only had eyes for one another. Until then, you only had eyes for me.'

'True.' Joey whispered.

'Joey…' Dave said quietly as he ran his hand over her hair and bent to kiss her.

'No!' Joey said, pushing him off and walking quickly towards the bus stop and willing her bus to arrive.

'No one walks away from me, Joey. I always get what I want.'

Joey didn't like the look in his eyes. She checked her watch again and looked down the road, Where was the bus? She thought, beginning to panic.

'Let's get a taxi back to mine?' Dave leered at her.

'I'm tired, Dave. I just want to go home.'

'Fine, let's go back to yours then.' He smiled as he bent to kiss her again.

'No.' Joey said firmly as she dodged away from him.

'Playing hard to get?' He said quietly, too quietly for Joey's liking. The next thing she knew, he was lunging at her, forcing her back against the bus shelter as he brought his lips crashing down on hers.

'Noooooo.' She strangled out, her voice muffled by his vicious kiss. She tried to push him away but he was strong and, the harder she pushed, the more insistent he became. Tears began to well in her eyes as she felt him roughly pull her body tightly to his. She knew she was in trouble. Dave had drunk too much and God knows where he would stop – if he would stop.

An image of Kari flooded her mind. His beautiful, sculptured face, his dark intense eyes and she felt a strength she didn't know she possessed. Forcefully, she pushed Dave away, causing him to lose his balance and fall backwards. She spat, 'You step one foot towards me and I'll have you charged with sexual assault.' She glared, ready to fight him with all her strength. Thankfully, she could see her bus coming towards her.

'You don't know what you're missing.' Dave said, clearly his pride and ego had taken a major battering.

She held her hand out for the bus. As the bus stopped and the doors opened Joey said, 'Everything happens for a reason Dave, even if it meant I had to be with you for a brief while.' She turned, paid her fare and took a seat. As the bus pulled away she saw Dave punch the bus shelter window, sending a cascade of glass, smashing to the floor. She smiled to herself as she watched him clutch his bloodied fist, furiously trying to ease the pain.

She opened her purse and took out a folded piece of paper – it was a cutting from *Out There* magazine of her and Kari at the Nice ball. She couldn't wait to see him next week, how she wanted to feel safe in his arms. She needed him tonight more than ever. If only she could call him. If only he would call her. Would she tell him about what just happened? Probably not, after all, it was only a stupid, drunken kiss from an ex.

Chapter 24

Joey arrived in Vancouver, as planned, on the Thursday morning. She was looking forward to seeing Lacroix and wishing him well for his upcoming wedding, but as she walked towards where he normally met her, she was surprised and taken aback to see that Henrique was waiting instead.

He acknowledged her and asked her to follow him. He didn't offer to take her case, not that she minded, but she felt he was making a point. They drove to Cha Tik Warro in silence. Nearer to the house, Joey started to feel nervous. Where was Lacroix? Was everything okay? Henrique stopped the car, got out and walked to the house. Joey followed.

'You're in the same room as before,' Henrique muttered and pointed upstairs.

Oh joy the squeaky bed again, Joey thought, but then if Kari was home later, maybe she could go to his room? The thought of seeing him so soon made her heart quicken. She couldn't wait to see him.

Joey retreated into her room, until eight o'clock, when she thought she'd better see what awaited her in the dining room. She walked in and saw Kari's mother, father and Henrique already eating. 'Good evening.' Joey said politely, but she didn't receive any response, not even a smile. She sat down at the spare place setting, feeling decidedly unwelcome. She wasn't sure what supper was called, but it resembled meat and potatoes and tasted good. She tried to make conversation with Kari's parents throughout dinner, but was either cut off or ignored entirely.

She asked where Kari and Lacroix were, but sadly, received no answer. Joey thought it would be best to remain quiet and keep her head down, surely any moment Kari would walk through the door and sweep her off her feet. But, that didn't happen.

Henrique kept looking at her intensely, until she began to feel self-conscious. Her self-esteem plummeted further when Henrique said something in their native tongue to both Kari's parents, who also proceeded to stare at her. She dabbed at her mouth in case she had spilled her food.

'Is everything okay?' Joey asked, tentatively. They didn't answer but talked heatedly to one another in their native tongue so that Joey had no chance of understanding.

They were discussing the fact that Kari's feather was hanging around her neck. Things were more serious than they'd thought. If Kari had given Joey his feather, it was incredibly important. They also noticed the faint bruising on Joey's neck – an indication that Kari and Joey had made love; it was a classic mark from one member of their tribe to another. They knew they had to intervene and soon.

After what she hoped was a respectful time waiting for them to notice her, and enlighten her on the conversation they were clearly having about her, she excused herself and went to bed.

She'd never done it before but she decided to call Lacroix. Something was very strange and she had many questions: Why hadn't he warned her that it would be Henrique collecting her from the airport? Also, what time would Kari be home? Joey tried the number but, it was no good, her phone wasn't working properly. Feeling totally jaded, she climbed into bed and hoped Kari would come to her during the night, if not, she prayed for positivity for the next day.

Sadly, Kari didn't wake Joey during the night. After a fitful sleep, she dressed and went downstairs, hoping to see a friendly face and breakfast. Unfortunately like previous mornings, the dining room was void of food, a clear indicator Kari was still not home. She picked an apple and banana from the fruit bowl and felt a wave of déjà vu wash over her. Taking the fruit into the garden she walked to the meadows.

- - -

'What do you mean her number isn't registering?' Kari bellowed at Lacroix. He didn't mean to sound so angry but he was extremely unhappy that he'd had to stay in Calgary last night, due to a meeting that had overran, and today didn't bode well either.

'I have no idea. Both Solonge and I have tried Joey's number but, for some reason, it's not registering.'

Kari seethed under his breath. 'I spoke to father and he said she'd arrived. Henrique had collected her and she had eaten with them last night. But, I bet she hasn't had breakfast.' He was exasperated with work. 'Why can't people decide whether they like our proposition or not? Are they incapable of making a decision?'

He pressed his palms to his head in frustration. 'I'm sorry, I don't mean to lose my temper, but I see no point in us staying here. We could be here for days with them still not reaching an answer. It's not that difficult to decide. Some of us have lives we would like to continue!' Kari seethed, continuing to pace the room.

Lacroix hadn't seen Kari this anxious in years, he was clearly worried about Joey. If only he could speak to her, it would ease Kari's concerns. Lacroix had spoken to Henrique earlier but he wasn't helping, he would not play the same game for Kari. Henrique had admitted openly that he would not help Kari see or speak to Joey in any way.

Joey was just walking into the house when she heard her name being called. At first she thought she may be hearing things, but then she heard her name again, this time, louder and more insistent. She approached the room the voice came from and was greeted by Kari's father, mother and Henrique. They stood under a massive portrait of a Native Chief; Joey didn't have time to look at the picture, as her eyes were drawn to the three people who were staring at her.

'Sorry, did you call me?' Joey asked.

'We did. Please sit.' Kari's father said pointing to a chair by the window.

Joey sat. She was confused. Why did they suddenly want to speak to her? Had something happened to Kari? 'Is Kari alright?'

'Yes, he is well.' Gahenge replied. 'We must talk to you to make you aware of the impact you are having on my tribe. You must know that this...' He waved his hand as he tried to find the appropriate words to use, 'thing, whatever it is you and Kari are having, cannot continue. It has no future. You must be aware of that now you have visited our home - twice. I see no point in this continuing and wasting everyone's time, as well as causing a great deal of upset amongst my tribes people.' He looked at her - the same intense stare she'd received many times from Kari, but this time not with lust, but with concern.

'I'm sorry, I wasn't aware I was causing a great deal of stress.' Joey said quietly, almost to herself.

'You know what is expected of Kari. One day, he will become the Chief of the Kutan Tribe. He was born to take over from me when I retire. He has worked all his life for this and, if the prophecies are true, he will make one of the best Chiefs the tribe has ever seen. But, in order for him to complete his calling, he needs a native wife by his side, with whom will bear his heirs. If I'm honest, he should already be married with sons, but sadly, it is not the case. He knows he needs to find a wife and soon. However, whilst he is playing with you, he is not focusing on the task in hand.'

Joey nodded as if she understood, but it all seemed a bit fuzzy, she felt slightly faint.

Gahenge persisted, 'There is only one option. To stop this 'thing' and for him to find a wife.'

'But...' Joey started, the words catching in her throat.

Henrique cleared his throat and looked pointedly at Gahenge. Gahenge nodded and continued, 'If he stays with you, he will be banished from the tribe, his family and his life as he knows it. Do you really want him to have to choose?'

'No.' Joey said, in a strangled voice.

'Kari could never fulfil his destiny and become Chief of the Kutan Tribe. He will be dismissed and never allowed to return. Luca would have to become Chief. At first Kari may be happy with this decision, but years later he'll begin to resent you and then hate you for what you made him do. He is a very honourable man, he would not desert you, if you asked him to stay.' He took a step towards her. 'You need to be the strong one.'

Henrique interrupted, 'Why did he not come back last night? Why is he not here today? Does he regret inviting you? Is he hoping you would see that there is no point in staying and go back to your life. Out of interest, has he called you?'

'No,' Joey replied quietly, as Henrique's words registered in her brain. Maybe this was Kari trying to let her go...

'Well, well!' Henrique laughed. 'I spoke to him yesterday to say you had arrived and interestingly,' he sneered at her, 'he didn't make any comment about you.'

At that moment, Joey felt sick to her core, but, took deep breaths and waited for what would be said next.

'We will leave you for a moment to think. You can stay but Kari will be banished from the tribe and his future. Or, you can leave now and Henrique will take you to the airport.' Gahenge couldn't help but be moved by the pride Joey showed. Although clearly shaken and intimidated, she was determined not to break down in front of them and make a fool of herself. His tone was less harsh when he said, 'I know it will hurt, but the pain will be less now, than in years to come when Kari no longer looks at you with pleasure, but with hatred.'

'I wish I could talk to Kari, I wish he could explain, I wish I could explain…' Joey trailed off, not sure what else to say.

'You could write him a letter which I would give to him?' Aiyana offered.

'But, I would insist that, if you go, you must not contact him again. And remove all of our telephone numbers from your phone. Do you understand?' Gahenge said firmly.

Joey nodded. She took the paper and envelope from Kari's mother and gazed out of the window as all three exited the room. Suddenly she was alone, very alone.

She looked around the vast room. If only she could talk to Kari, maybe he could find a way for them to stay together. After all, they were only having fun, it didn't feel like it should end. She hadn't asked for marriage or commitment, and neither had he. She felt horrible, more worthless than she had felt ever in her life.

She glanced at the massive portrait of the Chief. She wondered who he was. As she moved towards it, she gasped; it was a portrait of Kari. He had a distant look in is eye, as if searching for something. His long jet-black hair fell over his naked chest. He wore ornate jewels and feathers around his neck, but his beautiful black feather stood out. To maintain his dignity, he wore a breechcloth made from beige buckskin and a length of animal fur balanced over one shoulder. One hand rested on his waist whilst the other held a spear. He looked intense, magnificent, worthy. Joey could not take him away from his world. The world he loved and had worked so hard for. She knew with, intense sadness, what she had to do. His father was right; it hurt now, so what would it be like if she left it any longer? She walked over to a small table and began to write.

Joey was crying as she sealed the envelope. It felt as if her heart was physically breaking - how was she going to carry on? After a few minutes, she went upstairs to pack her suitcase, leaving the envelope on the small table.

A short while later, she came back downstairs and saw the three of them waiting for her.

'I see you wrote a letter.' Kari's father said, holding the sealed envelope between his fingers gingerly, as if it were a grenade. 'I will make sure Kari receives it.'

'Thank you. I was wondering if you could help me remove the feather necklace Kari gave me. I know it's precious to him and I'd like him to have it back. I've tried but I can't undo the knot he tied.'

Aiyana assisted Joey, but also struggled.

Henrique came towards them with his knife. 'Here, let me cut it off.'

'No!' Joey and Aiyana shouted in unison. They looked at each other. For the first time, they finally agreed on something and Kari's mother saw what her son saw in Joey. She saw Joey loved her son very much and couldn't bear to ruin something as precious as his feather.

Aiyana persisted and eventually the necklace was freed.

'I'm sorry, I don't have the leather case it came in, Kari has it.' Joey said sadly, looking at the necklace for the last time.

'You are doing the right thing.' Gahenge said.

Henrique picked up Joey's suitcase and left the room, indicating for her to follow. She turned and looked at the portrait of Kari one last time, she smiled and said, 'He will make a wonderful Chief.' Then, without so much as a backwards glance, she turned and followed Henrique to the car. Her heart was screaming for her to stop, but her legs propelled her forwards.

Chapter 25

Kari was oblivious to the events which were unfolding at his family home. But, the meeting was dragging and he was close to saying, 'Stop! We will continue another day.' Kari had no interest in what Eric Paterson was saying, for the first time in his life, he didn't want to be representing his father.

He began to feel nausea washing through his body in waves. He looked over to Lacroix and spoke to him quietly, in their native tongue. 'I don't feel well, we need to wrap this up soon.'

Lacroix noticed the ashen colour of Kari's face and watched as beads of perspiration collected at the top of his forehead. Lacroix felt anxious and watched in horror as Kari suddenly groaned, unable to contain the pain that ricocheted out from within his chest. Lacroix was at his side in an instant whilst the others watched with fright. The two other members of the Kutan team, Philippe and Tak Tun stood, rooted to the spot.

After a few moments, Kari managed to catch his breath but was still physically shaking. An extremely anxious Lacroix encouraged Kari to drink water, before turning towards the board members and saying, 'I'm sorry, do you mind if we postpone this meeting until tomorrow?'

'Of course not!' Eric Paterson replied, concern for Kari etched onto his face.

'No, please give me five minutes and we can continue.' Kari replied, still clutching his chest, but adding to Lacroix, in native tongue, 'I *have* to go home tonight. I have to see Joey.' He excused himself and opened one of the large, sliding doors that led to an outside balcony. Lacroix followed, desperate not to leave him alone.

'Kari, I should phone for a doctor, you look incredibly unwell.'

'I'll be okay in a moment. I just need a little time and some air. Please, go back inside and insist Philippe and Tak Tun get the fucking contract signed. It shouldn't be difficult.' Kari said, angrily.

Lacroix agreed it shouldn't have taken this long. In fact, there had been points during the day when Philippe and Tak Tun seemed to be dragging their feet. He knew Kari was unimpressed with their work and he knew they would pay for it later.

Tak Tun was just finishing a conversation on the phone when Lacroix walked back into the room. 'Kari will not leave until the contract is signed.' Lacroix said to his colleagues, using their native tongue. 'How are you going to face Henrique? Besides him, you both know this contact better than anyone.'

Tak Tun pushed past Lacroix and took his seat at the large boardroom table. The atmosphere in the room was intense as they waited for Kari to return. The only sound came from the annoying *tap tap tap* Philippe made as he repeatedly drummed his pen against the table. Nobody uttered a word, nobody dared to make eye contact.

'That was Tak Tun.' Gahenge said to his wife. 'Kari is unwell. He has an immense pain in his chest.'

Kari's mother gasped and fell into a chair. 'Oh, Gahenge, what have we done?'

'I know, I know. There is nothing we can do now, though. Tak Tun is going to round the meeting off and they will all be home later.' Gahenge replied, comforting his wife.

Remarkably, the contract with the Paterson organisation was signed and sealed within ten minutes of Kari re-joining the meeting. Tak Tun surprisingly upped his game and suddenly from no-where everything was complete.

Why hadn't Tak Tun performed like this yesterday? Kari thought. He was going to look forward to the de-briefing they would have next week. Tak Tun saw the glare Kari gave him and he averted his eyes.

'Kari, are you sure you won't allow me to call a doctor, I mean, you kinda scared me for a moment,' Eric Paterson said to Kari as he walked over to shake his hand.

'No, really, I'm fine. It must be something that I've eaten.' Kari tried to re-assure him.

'Why don't you stay for the evening? We'd love to take you out for a celebratory drink?' Eric asked.

'Thank you, but we must return tonight. I have a friend waiting.'

'Does this mean the great Kari finally has a lady in his life?' said Eric, warmly.

'I hope so.' Kari replied, before thanking everyone and leaving the room.

Something is wrong, Kari thought, walking towards the car that was waiting to drive them to the airport. He wasn't sure what it was, but it felt very wrong. His first priority was Joey - he needed to see her. If he still felt unwell when he got home, then he would see a doctor, if only to keep Lacroix happy.

Joey cried during the entire flight. She no longer cared what anyone thought, her life would never be the same again. She'd bolted from yet another relationship, but this time it hurt, emotionally and physically. It felt as if her soul was being ripped from her core, her heart being torn in half. Her skin was sensitive to touch and pressure in her head was almost too much to bear.

Lacroix drove up Cha Tik Warro's long driveway, wishing he'd arranged for a doctor to be waiting for them. Kari didn't appear to be in pain, but he hadn't spoken once during the entire journey and although he tried to hide it, anyone could see he was not well.

Kari got out of the car before it had entirely stopped. He ran towards the house and banged on the front door. As soon as it was opened, he burst through the doors, followed closely by Lacroix, Philippe and Tak Tun.

'Joey!' Kari cried. He shouted up the stairs, into the main living rooms and dining area. He began to stride outside, when Kari's father came out of his study.

'Kari, she's not here.' Gahenge said, simply.

'What do you mean, not here? Is she out?' Kari asked.

'She's gone.'

'Gone? Where?'

Gahenge inhaled deeply. 'Joey has gone back to England.'

Lacroix watched as the colour drained from Kari's face for the second time of the day and he feared he was about to re-live what had happened earlier. Kari drew himself up to his full height, shouting, 'What did you say to her?'

'She went of her own free will.'

'I'll say it again because, obviously, you didn't hear me. WHAT DID YOU SAY TO HER?' Kari bellowed. The entire house seemed to shake with fear, as the sound of his loud voice reverberated off the walls.

Kari's mother rushed into the hallway, followed by Henrique. 'Kari, calm down, I hear you were unwell today?' Aiyana pleaded, alarmed to hear such anger in her son's voice. 'Please, come and sit, I need to see if you're alright.'

'I'm okay, but I need to know what YOU ALL said to Joey?' Kari stared at his father first, then his mother before finally turning his glare to Henrique.

'We explained the circumstances and she made an informed choice.' Henrique offered, feeling slightly unnerved by the look on Kari's face.

'I might have known you'd have something to do with it.' Kari said, pointing his finger at Henrique.

'Can I suggest we go into the sitting room to talk?' Aiyana urged.

'I don't want to talk. Lacroix, drive me to the airport. I'm going to England.' Kari announced, turning to his office door.

'Kari, wait!' Gahenge said, momentarily stopping his son in his tracks. Kari glared at his father. 'She gave me this to return to you.' Gahenge held out Joey's feather necklace, 'It's over, Kari.'

Silently, Kari walked to his father and took the necklace from him. He held it in his hands as if it were a frail, sick creature. Joey had returned his necklace. She didn't want him anymore. Slowly, he moved towards the drawing room, appearing smaller than his usual great height. He sat heavily in a chair and said simply, 'Why? What didn't I do?' He placed his head in his hands and said, 'Where did I go wrong?'

'You didn't do anything wrong, Kari. It was never going to work, you must know that.' Aiyana responded, kneeling at his side. She hadn't seen her son as devastated since he was fourteen years old, when his childhood pony had to be put down as a result of one of his adventures. She desperately wanted to ease his pain, but wasn't sure where to begin. She looked imploringly at Gahenge.

'Kari, it was a matter of time. I believe the sooner you both realise, the better.' Gahenge said.

Kari looked at his father. 'What do you mean, *the sooner we both realised.*'

'We simply told Joey that there would be no future in this *thing* you both thought you had. You are from different cultures. You need to find a native wife who will bear you the children you deserve and need.' Gahenge explained.

'We weren't getting married. I hadn't asked her to marry me. We were enjoying each other's company and having fun.' Kari said, coolly.

'But, you gave her your feather necklace, Kari, that, is a massive commitment.' His father said, continuing awkwardly, 'We also noticed the bruising on her neck. Clearly, you have been... intimate, shall we say. What if she were to fall pregnant?'

'We were careful. The last thing either of us wanted was to become parents, give us some credit.'

'You can't be sure. Some women get pregnant to keep hold of the man.' Jibed Henrique.

Kari didn't rise to Henrique's flippant comment. The look he shot him should have been enough to shut him up.

But Henrique chose to ignore this hint. 'You do realise that this gold digger had probably planned this from the start. She knew who you were, and slowly she spun you a line and you fell hook, line and sinker.'

Kari stood up and walked towards Henrique, his eyes locked on the smaller man. Through gritted teeth and with a voice as cold as ice, Kari said, 'I swear, Joey had no idea who I was when she first met me. It wasn't until she came to Canada that she realised who I am, and even then, I didn't tell her everything.' Lacroix held Kari's arm, halting him from going any further. Kari shook it off and walked away. Sitting back in the chair, he took deep breaths as he tried to regain control.

Lacroix spoke. 'For what it's worth, I can confirm what Kari says. Joey had no idea Kari was the future Chief of the Kutan Tribe. In fact, she was seeing someone else when she first met Kari. She is an innocent woman.'

'Not that innocent, she had two guys at the same time!' Henrique scoffed.

Kari was up in a shot and had Henrique by the scruff of the neck, pinned to the wall. 'Don't you ever say anything so degrading about Joey ever again, or I swear I cannot be held accountable for my actions!'

Tak Tun and Lacroix removed Kari's hands from Henrique's body and encouraged him to step away. Henrique looked shaken as he tried to shrug off Kari's assault.

Aiyana hated to see her son so upset and went to his side. Gently, she placed her hand on his arm she said, 'Joey wrote you a letter, I believe it explains why she left.'

His hand shook as he took the envelope from her. 'Ironic, this is the first time I've seen Joey's handwriting. Which room did she stay in whilst she was here?'

'The same as before.' Aiyana replied.

Kari laughed, bitterly. 'She was never made to feel welcome here, was she? I'm disappointed in you; the worst guest room, neither breakfast nor lunch and the most disgusting dinners. I suppose she had the same treatment this time?' Kari asked. The silence screamed the answer. He sighed, 'Why?'

He walked towards Lacroix and spoke quietly to him. 'Don't leave without me. I can't stay here.' Lacroix nodded and Kari walked away, drawn to the room where Joey had stayed.

Her smell hung heavily in the air and tears welled in his eyes as he walked into her room. He could almost imagine she was still there, hiding. He lay on the squeaky bed and buried his face in her pillow. If he closed his eyes, he could imagine he was lying next to her, but when he reached out, no one was there. He rolled over and opened the letter he didn't want to read…

Kari,

If you're reading this, it is because I have left. I have come to understand that we cannot be together. Your work and tribe are more important than me. I need somebody who will be there for me, always. I had hoped you'd return home last night, but you didn't.

Thank you for the time we have had together, it was fun.

Best wishes,

Joey

P.S. I will give your necklace back to your mother.

Chapter 26

Lacroix drove in silence as he took Kari to the apartment that he rented, in a nearby suburb. He'd already called Solonge and had asked her to meet them both there. He didn't elaborate, but he said Kari was in a bad way because Joey had left him.

Solonge was not prepared for what greeted her at the apartment; the lifeless shell of Kari arrived and sat, motionless, on the sofa. Lacroix took Solonge into the kitchen and explained briefly what had happened. Together, they walked back into the living room and Solonge sat opposite Kari, whilst Lacroix poured them each a whisky. Lacroix put Kari's drink on the small table beside him, his hands occupied with the feather necklace and letter.

Solonge had to speak, she had to try and break the wall Kari was beginning to build to protect himself. 'Kari, I am so sorry, I had no idea Joey would leave without saying goodbye.'

'Well, she did leave a note.' Kari gave Joey's envelope to Solonge. 'Here, read it.' Solonge wouldn't take it; she didn't want to read his private letter. 'Please.' Kari insisted. She took the letter, reading in silence as Kari took a big gulp of his whisky.

As she passed the letter to Lacroix, she said, 'Honestly, I don't believe Joey wrote this. It doesn't sound like her, at all. It's too cold and hard.' She shrugged, 'I know this is going to sound farfetched, but is there a chance that somebody else has written it?'

'I see what you mean.' Lacroix said. 'I don't know Joey as well as you, Solonge, but I can't hear her as I read it. What do you think, Kari?'

'I don't know what to think,' he said as he shook his head slowly. 'I've just had one of the worst days of my life. Firstly, we had the arduous Paterson meeting that dragged, then, I thought I was about to die from a stabbing pain; we finally get the deal signed, only to return home and find Joey has dumped me. I could have killed Henrique for his comments and then, I get this poor excuse of a goodbye letter.' Kari finished his whisky, getting up from his chair to refill his glass.

Solonge glanced at Lacroix and looked questioningly at him as if to say *should he*, Lacroix nodded.

'How are you feeling now, Kari?' Solonge asked.

'In truth, fucking awful.'

'We should get a doctor, Lacroix.' Solonge suggested. 'Are you still in pain?'

'No, that was probably nothing.' Kari said, trying to reassure Solonge. He did still have a pain in his chest, but that was the least of his worries right now.

'It didn't look like nothing to me, Kari.' Lacroix said quickly, 'I thought I was going to have to administer CPR! I do think we should get you checked out; it looked like you were having a heart attack. Please, can we go to the hospital?' asked Lacroix.

'No.' Kari replied sternly, carrying the bottle of whisky onto the balcony and closing the door behind him. He wanted to be alone.

'Honey, something's not reading right.' Solonge said to Lacroix as he wrapped an arm around her and pulled her tightly to him.

'I know. I can't put my finger on it, but I agree.'

'Okay, we didn't know Joey well, but I can't believe she would just go, without saying goodbye. Have you tried calling her?'

'Yes, but she wouldn't answer.'

Solonge ran her hand across his chest, 'It's weird how neither of us could get hold of her yesterday. I called at the house but they said she'd gone out walking in the meadows and they wouldn't let me in to see her.'

'Mmm,' Lacroix replied, deep in his own thought. 'Of course!' He said, sitting upright, disturbing Solonge from her comfortable position.

'What?'

'Kari!' He called as he quickly got up from the sofa and slid the patio door open.

Kari turned, hearing the urgency in his friend's voice.

'I've been thinking and I'd like to run my thoughts past you!' Lacroix said, quickly.

Kari nodded and followed Lacroix back into the living room and sat opposite his two friends.

Lacroix poured them all another whisky, before beginning. 'Firstly, why didn't Henrique go to the meeting, why send Philippe and Tak Tun? Also, don't you find it a little bizarre that the Paterson meeting lasted a lot longer than it should have? We were led to believe Philippe and Tak Tun were well briefed from Henrique, so why didn't they respond quicker to the questions that were asked? They only raised their game *after* you made your speech. When I went back into the boardroom, Tak Tun was finishing a phone call - who was he talking to?'

Kari shrugged, but sat up, listening carefully to what Lacroix was saying.

'Was it Henrique, or your parents? What if they purposefully dragged the meeting over two days, making it impossible for you to return home to see Joey yesterday? Thus, giving them time to persuade Joey to leave and Henrique was conveniently there to drive her to the airport. Tak Tun phones your home and they tell him Joey has gone. They can now round the meeting up as Joey is safely out of the picture. So when you arrive home, you are already too late.'

Kari and Solonge sat staring at Lacroix.

'Are you serious?' Solonge challenged Lacroix.

'Okay, maybe it's a bit farfetched but yes, that's what I believe,' was his reply.

'You're going to think I'm crazy, but can you please call the airline to make sure Joey boarded a flight back to England today and check the time?' Kari looked intensely at Lacroix.

'You're not suggesting they've done something to her are you, Kari?' Solonge asked anxiously as Lacroix began to call the airlines.

'I have never wanted to be more wrong in all my life,' said Kari.

Solonge and Kari listened to Lacroix talk to the airline operator, who was able to confirm that Joey had boarded a flight to the UK that afternoon. They all breathed a huge sigh of relief. However, Kari's relief dissipated as he realised that this confirmed that Joey had left him.

'Think about the flight time, she would have had to get to the airport between two and three - what time was Tak Tun on the phone?' Lacroix asked Kari.

Kari thought for a moment, 'I guess around two, perhaps three?' Slowly, things began to make sense. 'You're right… they were phoning my parents to ask if it was okay to round up the meeting, ensuring the coast was clear.' Suddenly, Kari got up, 'Joey didn't write this note; I know she didn't. Like you, I can't hear her when I read it. It's so formal, and that's not the Joey I know.'

'I'm afraid to ask, but, what now?' Solonge asked.

'I need to find Joey; I have to hear from her that she doesn't want to be with me. I know I shouldn't act like this, but I can't leave any stone unturned.' Kari looked at Lacroix and Solonge; he knew it was time to be honest with them both - he needed their help. He placed his glass on the table and sat down, opposite them both. 'I have never felt this way about anyone before. I gave her my feather. I'm prepared to leave the life that I know, just for the possibility of being with her. I just wish I'd told her that myself.'

'But, the tribe will disown you.' Lacroix worried.

'Maybe, but I need her. She'll be off volunteering soon and then I'll never be able to find her.' Kari said, the desperation ringing in his voice. 'I want to write a new legislation for the tribe that I will put out for proposal.'

Solonge looked at Lacroix who was engrossed by what Kari had said. 'What are you proposing, Kari?' Solonge asked, nervously.

Kari looked focused and determined as he explained. 'I'm proposing to update the relationship treaty.'

'Did you know about this, Lacroix?' Solonge asked her fiancé.

'No.' Lacroix answered, quietly.

'Luca is the only person I have discussed this with and I have his full support. Can I also count on you?'

'You know we will support you, Kari, in whatever you choose. It's time the tribe moved into the twenty first century and you're the man to lead us. The tribe would be stupid to remove you. Whatever it takes, whatever you need, we will be behind you for the entire journey,' Lacroix said to Kari.

'Thank you.'

'I can help by going to England and finding Joey.' Solonge said. 'I'm more flexible than you both. Kari, you have to stay here and write the legislation and Lacroix, you need to look after Kari.'

'I can't ask you to go to England, Solonge.' Kari said.

'I'm not asking for your permission Kari, I'm telling you, I'm going. I'll head off in a couple of days, once I've got a few things in order here. I'll still have plenty of time before the wedding to tie loose ends.'

'Solonge, if you need anything, anything, you must ask.' Kari said, as he walked over and enveloped her in a warm embrace. 'It means a great deal to know that you will do this for me, and thank you, Lacroix, for letting her go. I am also very grateful that you have not judged the relationship I had with Joey. I don't know if we ever had a future, but I'm not content to leave it like this, you know I hate unfinished business. I'll call Luca tomorrow and ask him to come home. I need his support, now more than ever and he'll need to take over some of my duties, whilst I work on the new treaty.' He sighed quietly as he continued, 'Also, he needs to be prepared to take over the tribe, if necessary.' He pulled Joey's letter out of his back pocket. 'Solonge, can I ask one more thing of you?'

'Of course.'

'When you find Joey, please can you show her this letter. I need to know if she wrote it.' Kari handed the letter to Solonge.

'You'll be able to ask her yourself. She will come back to you. She will.' Her voice rang with sincerity.

They talked into the early hours and re-scheduled Kari's meetings for the next week, allowing him time to concentrate on the new legislation. He wanted to call a meeting with The Elders, by the end of the week, to discuss the new proposal.

Chapter 27

Gahenge was working in his study when he heard the front door open. He recognised the sound of Kari's footsteps, quickly followed by Lacroix. He was relieved to hear them; he wouldn't have blamed his son if he had flown to England to find Joey.

'Kari?' He called out.

Kari entered his father's study, closely followed by Lacroix.

'I'm glad to see you have returned home. We were worried about you.'

'You needn't worry about me father; I'm a grown man.' He turned to leave but stopped. 'Oh, but I forgot,' he added as he returned his attention back to his father, 'you and the tribe are there to make all the decisions for me, are they not,' his voice dripping with sarcasm.

'Do not speak to me like that!' said Gahenge, outraged.

'Then I have nothing more to say, for now.' Kari said and stalked off to his study, further down the hall.

Once inside the sanctuary of his own study, Kari phoned Luca. He was aware of the time in France, but he had to talk to him because he needed him to come home immediately. Kari spoke frankly and Luca agreed to be on the next flight, which meant he would arrive later that evening.

Lacroix got them both coffee and some breakfast; Kari wasn't hungry, but he appreciated the coffee. They shut themselves away all day, working endlessly. Even when Lacroix left to collect Luca from the airport, Kari continued to work. He tirelessly researched his campaign. He was passionate for it to succeed, if not for him, then maybe for future generations.

In the past two years, he discovered that the tribe had ousted fifteen members because they had fallen in love with *an outsider*. Kari thought that this sacrifice of tribal members was an incredible loss. Instead of gaining fifteen new members, and subsequently any children they were fortunate to have, the tribe would rather lose their own for fear of changing tradition.

Kari struggled with visions of Joey. He wondered how she was, what she was doing, did she think he was weak as her letter suggested. He also fought against the urge to fly to England, he knew he had to stay and work on the changes he felt the tribe needed. Solonge and Joey had become good friends, he hoped she would bring Joey back to him.

Luca arrived with Lacroix late that night and it felt like a breath of fresh air. Kari greeted his younger brother warmly. He missed Luca and wished he lived nearer, but he respected that Luca had been fortunate enough to be able to choose his own path in life – until now.

After many more cups of coffee, Kari relayed the whole story to his brother, keeping it brief but careful not to omit any details.

'I know she means so much to you Kari, I never thought a woman would live up to your expectations, but I do believe this *Joey* does. Did Father and Mother not see that?'

'They did, and that's why I'm in this situation now. You know I came to you before in Paris saying I wanted to set up the project?' Kari asked Luca.

'Uh huh,' Luca replied, drinking coffee whilst mentally noting that Kari looked extremely tired.

'I was hoping to take things a little more slowly, but circumstances have forced them to proceed quickly.' Kari rubbed his weary eyes. 'In an ideal world, I would have got a long way into the legislation and our family would welcome Joey.'

Luca noticed the tremble in his brother's voice as he said Joey's name. He could see Kari loved her very much. Why weren't his parents helping Kari, rather than driving his love away.

'So, let me get this right, they would risk losing you, rather than welcome Joey?' Luca asked.

'Exactly.'

'The next step would be for me to step into your shoes. What if I don't want to? What if I don't marry a native girl? Have they considered this dangerous ground that could be exposed.' Luca said, in a matter-of-fact tone.

'I don't think they have, until now. If neither of us become Chief of the Kutan Tribe, the next in line is Henrique, being father's younger cousin, and from there Arabella!' Kari shook his head in despair.

Luca ran his hand over his chin. 'I'll do whatever it takes Kari, there is no way Henrique is taking over the tribe. It's going to be hard, harder than I think we realise. But I'm also going to be honest with you...' Luca stopped, unsure if he should speak the truth.

'What is it?' Kari asked, curious to know what was on Luca's mind.

Luca drew a sharp breath between his teeth, 'I have absolutely no desire to become Chief of the Kutan. We have to get this legislation passed, you have to remain in power.'

The following week passed quickly. Solonge flew to England whilst Kari, Lacroix and Luca worked tirelessly on the new legislation. Occasionally, Luca accompanied his father to meetings because Kari had refused to attend any. Kari wanted his father to appreciate what he did for the tribe and to experience what life would be like if he were excommunicated for pursuing Joey.

Gahenge was very concerned by how events were unfolding in his family's life. He didn't expect Kari to be so obstinate. He thought, with time, he would get over Joey and eventually find a *suitable* soul mate.

He'd also never witnessed his son act so violently towards Henrique. He knew there wasn't a lot of love lost between the two men, but he was taken aback by how earnestly Kari had fought for Joey's honour. He knew his son was proud, and passionate, but he wasn't aware quite how much. Maybe they should have left Kari and Joey alone – but the tribe could not accept an outsider; it would ruin the tribe and everything they believed in. They were a pure blood First Nations Tribe and he intended for it to stay that way.

Then, Gahenge thought of Luca. He had come to his brother's side when asked - they had a wonderful bond. He just wished Luca were more in tune with the needs of the tribe. Gahenge had taken him to a few meetings and clearly Luca was out of his depth. If Kari did step down from his responsibilities, Luca would have to take Kari's place. Gahenge shook his head as he thought of where the tribe could be in years to come if that was the case. He loved Luca dearly, but Luca was dreamy, artistic and didn't have a real concept of life.

And, what if Luca didn't want to become Chief, what then? He knew his cousin was waiting in the wings for this opportunity. Henrique believed he would make a great leader, and in many ways he would, but he is not a people person.

Gahenge decided to take the afternoon off and ride his horse to the Sacred Mountains where he intended to ask the Spirit Gods for guidance. He needed their wisdom like never before. Many times he'd asked for advice, and as yet they have never dismissed or forsaken any prayer he'd sent, but today would be different. He was unsure if they'd even acknowledge his need for answers, and if they did was he really prepared for the potential outcome? He was torn. He was a great leader, but that was mostly because of the support from his wonderful son, Kari.

Chapter 28

'Excuse me, is it possible to see Joey Lewis, please?' Solonge asked the receptionist at Stones Architects.

'I'm sorry, she no longer works here. She left nearly two weeks ago.'

'Of course, I remember now. You don't happen to know where she works now, do you?' Solonge asked, hopefully.

'I'm afraid not. Sorry.' The receptionist stared blankly at the beautifully exotic lady, who was looking expectantly at her.

Solonge smiled and left the building.

What now? She thought, sitting on a bench outside the Abbey and watching the world go by.

She was in a strange country and she felt incredibly lonely. Solonge hated being alone, she thrived on the company of others. She looked across the square and, on the opposite side, was an elderly lady looking equally lonely. Solonge walked over to her, hoping to pass time with some company.

'Do you mind if I sit down?' Solonge asked the elderly lady.

'No, not at all, help yourself, my dear. I'm just sitting here watching all these busy people rush by. I bet half of them never stop and watch what's going on around them.' The old lady smiled at Solonge, 'You're not from round here, are you, dear?'

'You're right. My name is Solonge,' she said as she shook the lady's hand, 'I'm from Canada.'

'Nice to meet you Solonge, I'm Nancy. Canada, now that sounds like a grand place. I've never been. Alfie always said we should have travelled more, but somehow, we never left the country. England is a wonderful country, mind you. It's a shame not enough people appreciate it.' Nancy said. 'Are you on holiday, honeymoon maybe?'

'No, I'm trying to find a friend but I've just been to where she works and they told me she'd left. I feel a bit stuck now!' Solonge said, looking into the distance.

'That's a shame. Maybe she doesn't want to be found.' Nancy said, with a matter-of-fact tone.

'I think you may be right, Nancy. It's a long story…' Solonge started.

'Oh, don't worry about me, I've all the time in the world and I love a good story.' Nancy grinned at Solonge.

Solonge found herself telling this complete stranger a simplified version of the love story between Kari and Joey, without mentioning any names.

'Why can't people mind their own business! If this man loves this girl then he should hold onto her and never let go. You only have one life and mine is nearing its end. I hope I'll meet with Alfie again, but you can't be sure.' Nancy said, with a wistful look in her eye before saying, 'Why isn't *he* here, looking for her?'

'It's difficult to explain, but he has a family commitment that he has to attend to. Trust me, he wants to be here, but instead, it's me, with a plane ticket to fly her back to him. The problem is, I don't know how to find her.'

'I can see your problem, dear.'

Solonge liked the way this old lady called her *dear*. She wished her family and tribe were more affectionate – instead, everyone was so uptight and tense. *Kari needs to make lots of changes!* Solonge thought.

'I've just had an idea!' Nancy beamed at Solonge. 'Does this girl have a local she goes to?'

'A local?' Solonge looked confused.

'Like a pub, restaurant, gym, park, club, that sort of thing?'

'Nancy, you are a star,' and Solonge kissed the older lady.

'Steady on my dear, you haven't found her yet.'

'But, I will. She used to go to a pub, it was named after an animal, The Fox, The Sheep.'

'I've heard of The Pig's Head, but not the others.' Nancy said.

'The Pig's Head! That's it! Could you tell me where it is, please?'

Nancy told Solonge where to find the pub and, after many thanks, Solonge hurried off to find it.

Solonge found the pub and went inside. It was small, dark and smelt of stale ale. She went to the bar.

'Yes, love?' The barman enquired.

'Oh, hi, I wonder if you can help me, please? I'm looking for a friend who I believe comes in here. Her name is Joey Lewis?'

The barman looked at her, blankly. 'No, I've never heard of her, we are a very popular pub. Have you got a photo?'

'No, sorry, I don't. Is there anyone else working here who may know her?'

'Here, Jack, have you heard of a *Joey Lewis*?' The barman shouted to the other bar man who was at the other end of the bar.

'Why, who's asking?' Jack said as he walked towards them.

'This lady, here,' the barman pointed to Solonge.

'Yeah, I know Joey Lewis. She and her friend used to come in here, quite regularly actually, but I haven't seen much of her lately. Come to think of it, I haven't seen her for a good couple of weeks or so.'

'Oh, okay. I'm just visiting from Canada and I would have liked to have met up with her.' said Solonge, sounding jaded.

'Her friend Lucy comes in. I can give her a message, if you like?' Jack offered.

'What time does Lucy normally come here?'

'Straight after work, not long after five thirty.'

'Of course.' Solonge murmured. 'In that case, I'll wait and speak to Lucy myself, if you don't mind pointing her out to me, that is. I'll have an orange juice whilst I wait.' Jack poured Solonge an orange juice and she took herself off and sat in the corner.

Solonge watched as gradually, the pub became busier. There were lots of businessmen, talking loudly and laughing. Several kept looking at her, making her feel slightly uncomfortable. But, she remained where she was; she had a mission to complete.

Lucy walked into the pub and ordered her usual glass of white wine. She missed Joey and wished she still worked at Stones and had never met those controlling Canadians who'd changed her life so much.

'Hey, Lucy, there's someone here waiting to talk to you.'

Lucy raised her eyebrows, quizzically.

'She's in the corner, under the dancing sheep painting.'

Lucy turned and walked towards the corner. As she pushed her way through the crowds, she saw a beautiful, native woman, nursing her empty glass. Lucy began to walk back to the bar, however, Solonge had spotted her.

'Lucy.' Solonge shouted, 'It is Lucy, isn't it?'

'Yes, I am Lucy. Who are you?'

'I'm Solonge, a friend of Kari's. Please, can I talk to you for a moment?' Lucy didn't move. 'Please?' Solonge asked, again.

Reluctantly, Lucy joined Solonge. 'How is Joey?' Solonge asked.

'A mess, thanks to your friend.' Lucy's response was sharp.

'I'm really sorry to hear that. If it's any consolation, Kari is too.'

'Shame I can't see *that* for myself.' Lucy said, coldly. Who was this woman, why was she here and what did she want from Joey?

As Solonge began to tell Lucy why she needed to see Joey, Lucy found herself warming to Solonge. She was surprised but secretly pleased to hear that the big, strong Kari was hurting.

Lucy wasn't sure what to do. If she told Joey Solonge was here and wanted to talk, she knew Joey's pride would get the better of her. But, as Joey's best friend, she knew that Joey needed to hear what Solonge had to say.

'If I take you to where Joey lives, I am taking a huge risk in losing a very close friend.' She sighed, 'But I think she should hear what you've just told me.'

'I understand, and I really appreciate your help. All I need is some time with her, if she decides she doesn't want to come back to Canada, then we will respect her decision. Kari needs to know if she chose to leave or was forced.'

'From what I understand, Joey said she felt she had no choice,' Lucy said, sadness emanating from her voice. 'Come on, I'll take you now, before I change my mind.'

Chapter 29

Fifteen minutes later, Lucy pressed the button for Joey's flat.

'Hello?' Joey answered.

'Joey, it's me, Lucy. Can I come up for a chat?'

The buzzer sounded and Lucy pushed open the door. Solonge followed her up numerous flights of stairs to the top, through an open door, into a flat.

'Joey, hear me out before you say anything. I have someone here to see you.' Lucy said, as Solonge stepped from Lucy's shadow, into the flat.

'Hi, Joey.'

Joey's eyes welled with tears. She rushed forward and fell into Solonge's open arms, crying. Silently and tactfully, Lucy pushed a note into Solonge's hand. The note contained her phone number, in case she could help any further. Solonge mouthed *thank you* and Lucy shut the door quietly behind her, leaving Joey alone with Solonge.

Joey sobbed for a while and Solonge gently rocked her in her arms. She waited until Joey's sobbing subsided, before pulling back and assessing her. Lucy was right – Joey did look a wreck. If this it's what it's like to have your heart broken, she never wanted to experience it.

'How did you find Lucy?' asked Joey.

'That's a long story, but it doesn't matter right now. I have so much to tell you, I don't know where to start.'

Joey took Solonge into the lounge and, together, they sat on her small sofa. Joey knew she looked awful, so, thankful it was Solonge and not Kari she was sitting in front of. If Kari saw her like this, he'd run for the hills, for sure.

Solonge proceeded to tell her what she knew, as Kari and Lacroix had explained it to her. When she got to the part where Kari collapsed in the meeting, Joey started to cry again. Solonge assured her that he was fine now, well, at least he hadn't collapsed again.

'I'm here because Kari wanted to know if you decided to leave, or, if you were persuaded. And,' Solonge said, handing Joey the note, 'is this the letter you wrote?'

Joey took the familiar envelope Solonge handed, but when she took the letter out and saw it she said with confusion, 'Solonge, this is not the letter I wrote. Mine had smudges across the page where my tears had fallen as I cried with each heart rendering word. I hated writing it. I wanted to wait until Kari returned so we could talk properly. I had so many questions. But, I was told the sooner I realised there was no point in continuing our relationship, the better it would be for everyone.'

'Kari thought as much. We're not sure, but we think the Paterson meeting was deliberately extended to allow the necessary time for you to be taken out of the picture. Lacroix and I tried to call you over those two days, but for some reason, your phone didn't register. I even called at the house, but they wouldn't let me enter, fobbing me off with a story that you had gone walking in the meadows.'

'They were right, though. There was no future for Kari and me. I know we weren't engaged, I mean, he hadn't even told me he loved me. Mind you, I never told him either, but... I'm in love with him and I fell further, harder each day. The longer I left it, the more painful I knew it would be when he eventually ended it.' Joey said, gazing into the distance.

Solonge moved to kneel at Joey's feet. She held Joey's hands in hers and said, 'Joey, he gave you his feather necklace.'

'I know, I gave it back to his mother.'

'And, she has given it back to him, but that's beside the point. Do you understand the significance of the feather necklace?' Solonge asked.

'Kari said it means a great deal to him, that's all.'

'Within our tribe, it means unequivocal love; he is in love with you, and the necklace symbolises that you are taken, that nobody else can have you. Look,' Solonge pulled out the feather that hung around her neck, 'Lacroix gave me his feather after the Nice ball, when he realised that he was in love with me.'

'Oh my God.' Joey put her hand to her mouth, 'I had no idea.'

'I'm surprised Kari never explained. But then, most men aren't great at showing emotion and, unfortunately, Kari has bucket loads of restraint and pride. He needs to loosen up a bit; I thought he had, since meeting you. Joey, do you understand what I've just said, Kari is in love with you.'

'But, he never said...'

'Not in as many words, but I know he has *physically* shown his love!' Solonge replied and Joey blushed.

'Kari wants you to come home. He wants to see you, talk to you.'

'I can't, Solonge. This still doesn't solve the problem that Kari and I cannot be together. If he's hurting half as much as I am, surely the best thing is to continue and, with time, the pain will ease. Kari has to find a wife from within the tribe who will be an equal to the Chief of the Kutan Tribe. I can't take him away from his life. It's everything he's ever worked for. I couldn't live in a bubble, knowing that one day he could turn around and say that he hated me, when he realises he gave everything up, just to be with me. I'm sorry, but I can't and I won't do it.'

'Joey, don't you think Kari has the right to make that decision? You're denying him the opportunity. Besides, Kari would never hate you. He knows what he's doing.'

Solonge told Joey about the new legislation Kari was currently writing, and although Joey was impressed, she said it wouldn't help them, but it may at least help others.

Solonge had one, final card left to play. 'Lacroix and I want you to come to our wedding, without you, our circle will not be complete. You were there the night Lacroix and I became one, you need to be there at our wedding to complete our circle. If you're not there, it would create a weak link in our marriage.' Solonge explained.

'Solonge, I can't come. What if I promise to think of you all day and send you love and best wishes? Please don't ask me to come. If I see Kari, I may not be able to hold back.'

'Please, Joey, you don't have to be an active part of the ceremony, just be there, hide behind a tree if necessary, but Lacroix and I need you.' She paused. 'I'll leave my direct line, if you change your mind, please call. I can arrange everything and you won't have to speak to Kari.'

'I may be in Africa by then, Solonge,' replied Joey.

'We'll cross that bridge, if it comes to that. But, all I want you to do for me is to think about what I've just said. Ideally, you'd come home with me now, but please, think about it. I'm leaving the day after tomorrow. Call me if you change your mind, but failing that, at least come to my wedding. We need you.' Solonge she said, looking sincerely at Joey.

Joey nodded and hugged her friend goodbye. It would be so easy to say yes, but she had to be strong. It hurt like hell, but surely time would lessen the pain. She wandered into the kitchen and pinned Solonge's number on her notice board…

Chapter 30

Kari threw himself into his work in an attempt to erase Joey from his mind. He didn't succeed. Joey continued to haunt him during the day and vividly whilst he slept. He hadn't slept properly for days, instead choosing to nap in an armchair or rest his head on his desk.

One night, he had dreamt that Joey was in the room, teasing him and then running away to hide from him. He had searched everywhere for her, he could hear her laughter but, despite frantically looking, he could never find her. He also dreamt they were making love - in France - he could smell her, taste her, touch her and, oh, how he had wanted her. He'd woken up, sweat pouring from his face, his body physically aching for her touch.

He continued to avoid his parents and worked hard. He was learning lots of interesting facts that, until now, he'd been unaware of; one of the most interesting, was that his great Grandfather's brother, Ahote, had been destined to become a great Tribal Chief but, he was dismissed from the tribe because he fell in love with a Canadian woman. His brother Hok'ee took over as Chief and the bloodline changed from that moment. If Ahote had remained Chief, Kari would probably have never been in line for the title. Ahote was a proud and brave man and had decided love was a greater cause than the tribe.

Lacroix continued to update Kari with the information Solonge was able to find out. So far, things weren't looking promising.

Lacroix was concerned for Kari's well being. He knew that Kari hadn't slept properly for days, was hardly eating and, in fact, wasn't sure if he'd been showering at all, his stubble was even beginning to thicken. Kari was bad tempered and, if someone so much as looked at him the wrong way, he jumped down his or her throat. Lacroix suggested once to Kari that he should take a breather for an hour and use the time to eat and shower, Kari had glowered at him and Lacroix hadn't mentioned it again.

It was very early one morning when Lacroix entered Kari's study, bringing news from Solonge. Kari left his desk and sat on the sofa to intently listen to Lacroix's information.

'Lucy took Solonge to Joey's flat.'
'How did she find Lucy?'
'Using The Pig's Head.'

Kari nodded with polite restraint; he desperately wanted to skip to Joey's answer.

Lacroix continued. 'Joey told Solonge that she wasn't forced to leave, but she was encouraged. She understood there was no future for your relationship, she said she could not ask you to leave the tribe, just for her.'

'Is that not my decision to make, *if* needs be?'

'She didn't make the decision to leave lightly. As far as Joey understood, she felt it was better to break off the relationship sooner, rather than later.'

Kari sighed, passing no comment.

'Solonge showed her the letter and, like we thought, she said she hadn't written it, there is another, one that was written through tears.'

Kari closed his eyes as he saw an image of Joey crying, his heart began to ache again.

Lacroix continued, although he hated to see Kari hurting. 'She is in a lot of pain and misses you like crazy, but hopes that time will heal the wounds. She accepts that you need to find a suitable wife to support your lifestyle.' Lacroix stopped, he hadn't wanted to break the last piece of news, but he knew he had to. 'Kari?'

Kari opened his eyes and looked at his friend.

Lacroix was momentarily shocked to see the amount of sadness, emanating from Kari's eyes. He took a deep breath and said, 'Joey will not be returning to Canada.'

Kari winced, putting his head in his hands and sat in stunned silence.

Lacroix waited, patiently.

'So, that's that,' Kari said, finally. He rubbed his hand over his scratchy stubble. 'She wrote a different letter to the one I received. She was encouraged to leave, and even though I want her, she doesn't want to come back. What else can I do?' Kari looked imploringly at his friend.

Lacroix had never seen Kari so flat. He looked like someone had taken the wind out of his sails. 'I'm not sure.'

The minutes ticked by. 'I'm not giving up on this legislation. It may be too late for me but it will help future members. No one should have to choose between love and family, it's not right.' Kari got up and went back to his work. 'Thank you, Lacroix, but, if you don't mind, I need some time alone.'

Lacroix nodded and quietly left the room, leaving Kari in peace.

Kari didn't know what to think. Perhaps if he'd told Joey he loved her, they would still be together. The simple fact was, he needed her love and support.

Friday evening came and Solonge was due home, waited for by a desperate Lacroix. Kari could see he had missed her so much this past week, and felt guilty for having separated them. He was so grateful for everything that both Lacroix and Solonge had done for him, one day he hoped to be able to repay them. He suggested that Lacroix take the weekend off and spend quality time with Solonge. He knew more than anybody else, just how precious love is.

Kari was in the kitchen making a sandwich to eat at his desk, when his mother walked in.

'Kari, how are you? I haven't seen you for days.' Aiyana said.

'You know, Mother, trying to adjust to being alone again, without anyone to care for. Discovering what I believe in to be a farce… but, apart from that, life is great.' Kari turned on his heel, intending to leave Aiyana in the kitchen. He couldn't bear to be in the same room as his mother, her betrayal had cut him like a knife.

'Kari, I only did it because I love you.'

'No, Mother, you did it because you thought Joey was wrong for me, you thought she didn't love me for who I was, but because you believed she wanted my title and money. You did it because the future, as you knew it, could collapse.' He looked pointedly at her, ensuring she understood what he had said.

'I know she loved you. I was scared. One day when you have children of your own, you'll understand, you'll do anything to protect them. You'll hate to see them suffer; you want everything to be perfect. But, I now see, that's not always possible.' Aiyana trailed off.

Kari turned back to look at his mother, 'If you knew she loved me, why did you treat her so appallingly? Why couldn't you respect her, make her feel welcome, learn to like her? Was it really because she is not of the same ethnicity?'

His mother didn't speak, but nodded. Kari sighed and walked out of the room. Aiyana watched him leave. Her baby, her first-born was ashamed by her behaviour. He loved a woman other than her. She'd hardly seen him this past week, and she knew that he wasn't looking after himself. It was so unlike Kari, who was normally so tidy and methodical. She knew she had to ease his pain somehow, but *how*? She had an idea.

Kari was in his office when he heard a gentle knock on his door.

'Come in.' Kari said, wearily. The door opened and his mother stood in the doorframe.

'May I come in, Kari?' She asked with trepidation.

Kari gestured to the sofa, inviting her to sit. He saw his mother was nervous. 'What can I do for you?' Kari asked.

'It's more, what can *I* do for *you*?' She said, quietly. 'Kari, there are things I need to tell you. Things you need to know about Joey's last day here. If your father knew that I were here, he would be furious, but you're my son. I love you and all I want is for you to be happy.' She looked at him with pleading eyes. Kari got up and walked over to the sofa to sit beside her.

'I hate to see you so upset. I had no idea you felt this strongly about her. If I'd have known, maybe I could have prevented things happening, but please understand, all I saw was my son being taken away from me and from our tribe, by an outsider, no less. I had to do something.' Aiyana tried to explain.

'You didn't even give us a chance. You treated Joey with no respect, I was surprised she agreed to come back to Canada for a second time, a lesser woman wouldn't have.' Kari said, wearily. He was so tired that he was unsure of what he was saying.

'If only you could meet a young, tribal woman, like Arabella. You loved her once, why not again?'

'I didn't love her, Mother. I never felt an ounce of what I feel for Joey.

'But, you did have a relationship with her. If you united with Arabella, we would have the best and strongest tribe in Canada.'

'We had a relationship that was more off than on. We tried to make it work, but there was no love, at least, not from me. She was a companion at times, but nothing more.' Kari said, firmly, before moving to go back to his work. Aiyana put her hand on his arm, halting him.

'I have a lot to say, please, allow me to finish. I may not have the courage to do so again.' She waited for Kari to nod. 'Did Joey ever tell you she loved you?'

Kari shook his head.

'Did you ever tell her you loved her?' Kari shook his head again.

'But, you gave her your feather and you made love, our way.'

Kari should have been embarrassed but, instead, he brazenly nodded in agreement, proud of his love.

'I know Joey was in love with you, not only because she let you go as she thought she was doing the right thing for you, but I saw it in her eyes that final afternoon she was here. I could see her heart breaking in front of me. Everything within me wanted to tell them to stop, but it was already too late.'

Kari was beginning to feel apprehensive, but he said he wouldn't interrupt.

'When she came down with her suitcase she looked at me and asked if I could help remove your feather, she had tried, but couldn't. I tried but you had tied a knot so tight, even I found it difficult to untie. Henrique suggested we cut it off and both Joey and I sharply said *No!* I persisted and managed to release the necklace from her. The look in her eyes was innocent and pure love, I knew then, she wouldn't have done anything to hurt you.'

'She was brave, very brave. If I were her, I would have probably thrown myself at our feet, begging to see you. But, she stood tall, held her head high and looked defiantly at your portrait and said *He will make a wonderful Chief,* and then left, accompanied by Henrique.'

Kari swallowed deeply, attempting to hold back the tears that were forming in his eyes. His mother was describing *his* Joey, the one he knew so well.

Aiyana continued. 'Shortly after she left, we received a call from Tak Tun, he said you'd taken ill, collapsing in the meeting with a great pain. He said he was going to round up the meeting and get you home as soon as possible.'

Aiyana took a deep breath. 'We had asked Tak Tun to deliberately prolong the meeting, giving us time to remove Joey from your life. We knew you would never leave her, but we also knew that there was a chance she'd leave, if she loved you enough to set you free. When your father and I heard of your collapse, we knew it was because your hearts had bonded, spiritually. You may not known this, but your souls would have become one when you made love, our way.'

Kari looked at his mother, confused.

'It means our ancestors, in our spirit world, have joined your souls and spirits together. You have been fused together, becoming one. It is called *One Love*. If one were to leave, the other left behind would suffer immense pain – as if their heart had been ripped in half – *One Love*, broken. With time it will heal, but you will probably never love another, not like you loved Joey. It is an extremely rare and intense love. I have heard of these tales before, but I have never witnessed it happening, and now it has happened to my own son.'

'Joey desperately wanted to see you and talk, but we said it wouldn't help. You hadn't called her, hadn't returned home and you wanted her to leave you. We tampered with her phone, so Lacroix couldn't contact her and she couldn't contact you either. We knew if you spoke to her, you'd convince her to stay and we couldn't risk that. We were acting in the best interest of the tribe. But, I feel you have lost Joey, and that we might lose you. I don't know how to make it right?' Aiyana looked at her son, tears were falling down her face.

Kari wanted to soothe his mother's pain, but he couldn't. He felt sick. He wanted more than ever to see Joey, to touch her, kiss her, hold her. He loved her so much and he'd never even told her.

'I wouldn't blame you, if you left the tribe and went in search of Joey. You know we want you to stay, but I will understand if you decide to leave, remember, we also only did what we did because we love you too. We know you will make the best Chief the Kutan Tribe has had in generations.'

His mother took his hands. 'Thank you for listening, I know this is no consolation, but I kept the letter Joey had written for you. I didn't want to forge one, but Henrique said we had to.' Aiyana placed Joey's real letter in his hands. She kissed her son's forehead before leaving him to read his private letter.

Kari sat in disbelief. He hadn't interrupted his mother; to be honest, he couldn't, he'd been lost for words. What was he going to do now that he'd lost Joey; his mother had said he would never love anyone else.

He looked at the letter folded in his hand, as he opened it, he could see watermarks where Joey's tears had fallen onto the paper. The words swam before his eyes as tears began to fall down his cheeks. He wiped them away as he hungrily read the words she had written, it may be the last thing he'd ever hear from her.

Dearest Kari,

If you are reading this, you will have realised that I have left. I have loved our time together, words cannot explain the pleasure and joy you have brought to me. You are the most honourable, sincere and kindest man I have ever had the pleasure of loving.

I'll admit when I first saw you, I was scared. You appeared cold and aloof but that perception changed so quickly, as we began to spend time together. You mean everything to me – you are the centre of my world. You make me happy, you make me cry, you make me laugh. You have taught me to love, unconditionally and unequivocally. It's for these reasons, I have to let you go. I realise that we cannot be together. Our worlds are too different and it's a matter of time before we both realise this. After spending time here in Canada, your true home, I see we can never be together. I know we are only 'dating' each other and that we haven't talked of marriage, but I now see that you must marry someone from your tribe, soon. So, I'm letting you go before I fall deeper. It's hard enough to leave, already.

Please don't contact me, I will shortly be beginning my new life in Africa. I hope with time, the pain I am feeling, will lessen.

Remember I said I'd had my heart broken before? That was nothing compared to this. I never had the chance to tell you Kari, but I love you. I love you more than words can say, that is why I have to let you go, and I love you too much to watch you throw your life away. I have so much respect and admiration for you, and I just know that you will make the most incredible Chief given the opportunity. Please don't throw it away on me. If I can ask one last thing of you, make me proud and become the greatest Chief the Kutan Tribe has ever and will ever have.

All my love,
Joey x

Kari re-read the letter and wept. He wanted someone to hold him, comfort him, but there was no one. He was entirely alone. Whilst reading the letter, he'd heard Joey say she loved him and that was why she was letting him go. Eventually, Kari fell into a fitful sleep on the sofa.

Chapter 31

That night, Kari had a dream, so vivid he believed his Great Grandfather's brother, Ahote, visited him. He dreamt he was sitting on the veranda of the cottage in the Sacred Mountains, when a man rode up to him on horseback. At first, Kari was surprised to see a man he didn't recognise on a private part of their land. As Kari moved towards the man to ask him to leave, the stranger held up his hand.

'Kari, I am Ahote, the restless one. You must take my advice.' His accent was heavy, difficult to understand and he wore old-fashioned clothing. In native tongue, Ahote explained that Kari must continue to fight for his legislation. It was the only way forward, because without it, future members of the tribe would be limited. Ahote explained that Kari would become Chief, but that the road ahead would be difficult, often causing sadness and danger. Kari would have to be strong.

Ahote then turned his horse, riding away into the distance. Kari noticed that he had been wearing a black, sacred feather around his neck, similar to his own.

The dream evolved until Kari was kissing Joey. They were in the mountain cottage, lying in front of a raging fire. The heat radiating from the fire was hot, very hot. Kari watched, mesmerised, as Joey opened the door and left the cottage. He shouted her name, but she didn't answer. In his dream, he ran like a man possessed, trying to look for her, but he just could not find her. He awoke with a jolt. Heart racing and breathing heavily, he was glad to wake from his hell.

For the first time in almost a week, he went upstairs to shower and shave, feeling incredibly fresh afterwards. The dreams had refocused his mind; he had to pass his legislation and then find Joey.

He wanted to present his legislation to The Elders by next week so that he could then focus on his normal work, which had apparently not gone according to plan in his absence this week. After Lacroix and Solonge's marriage, he would find Joey. He would leave no stone unturned until he found her.

The following week passed in a haze for Kari, he felt as if he were operating on autopilot. Everyone seemed to be relieved that he was looking after himself again. He listened and passed comments on conversations about the tribe at the dinner table. Of everyone, Kari thought Luca was the most pleased to have Kari back.

Luca had clearly hated making the decisions that Kari found so easy. Luca loathed the meetings where he had to sow seeds in people's minds and slowly nurture them into fruition until a decision was finally made. Luca liked quick results. He didn't like having to wait for a group to make a verdict.

Having stepped into Kari's shoes these last few weeks, Luca had a newfound respect for his older brother. How Kari did this on, a daily basis,

Luca couldn't understand. Luca wanted Kari to return completely to his job, so he could go back to Paris, to his life and his lover. He desperately missed France and ached to return.

One afternoon, after a particularly long meeting, Luca rang Kari and asked how much longer he would need to stay, but Kari wasn't sure. The sooner he could get The Elders on board, the better. Luca understood and promised to help Kari where possible. Kari smiled, Luca's lack of interest in the tribe confirmed that Kari was the only viable option as future Chief.

At last, the day arrived for the presentation of Kari's new legislation. All of The Elders congregated at Cha Tik Warro. There was a flurry of excitement in the air – not only because a new proposition was going to be discussed, but also because Kari would be present. They missed his passion and energy, his commitment and honesty. The Elders were excited to hear his new project.

Lacroix was the most animated. He had worked hard with Kari to deliver this legislation, which would offer bright and exciting futures for the tribe. It was equally fantastic to see Kari charged up again – the Kari that he knew and respected.

Kari, Luca and Lacroix were already in the Great Hall as the Tribal Elders entered. The Elders were a small group of incredibly wise and well-respected leaders. They supported the Chief and helped maintain order of the day to day business and welfare amongst the tribe. The group consisted of Isi, Hok'ee, Kangee and Matwall. Although Henrique was not an Elder, he was a direct descendent of the Kutan bloodline and was considered a figure of great dominance, therefore, he was permitted to attend these private gatherings. Women however were not permitted, except one, Macawi. Macawi represented her husband, who had been an Elder, but died three years previously. It was believed his spirit still ran through her soul, guiding her. Even though she was nearly eighty years old, she's still sharp witted and Kari had a lot of respect for her.

The air chilled as Gahenge entered the room, and everyone stood to welcome him.

Gahenge remained standing, motioning for the others to sit. 'We are all gathered here today because my son, Kari Kutan, has a new legislation he would like to propose. We will listen to what he has to say and then, and only then, will we let him know our thoughts. Like you, I have not read the legislation so, I ask you to be patient and listen.'

Gahenge then sat, indicating that Kari should begin.

Luca and Lacroix looked at Kari as all eyes turned to him. He stood tall and proud, not showing any signs of nerves. Taking his time, he looked intently at each principle Elder that sat before him, including his father.

'Thank you for coming today to listen to what I have to propose,' Kari began. 'Each and every one of you knows me extremely well, you have watched me grow from a boy to a man, and I hope you believe that I have always put the interests of our tribe first. I have dedicated my life to our tribe and I hope to continue to do so for years to come. I am passionate about what we do, and I strive to reach the goals we aim to achieve. Occasionally, I may disagree with what people say, but this is only because I try to look at the larger picture; I want what is best for all of us, not just one person.' Kari stopped to make sure everyone understood what he had said so far. Everybody around the table seemed to be giving him his or hers undivided attention.

'Very recently I was forced to look into our relationship law, and was shocked to see how out dated and rigid it truly is. I would like to take a moment to read it to you now -

"A member of the Kutan Tribe is not permitted to seek a relationship outside of the Kutan Tribe for pleasure or marriage. If an individual does, then he or she will be instantly excommunicated, without the possibility of ever returning. For all intents and purposes, this person will cease to exist in the eyes of the tribe." This law was agreed centuries ago and put into written law in 1878. Today I want the tribe to consider re-evaluating this law. Bring the Kutan Tribe into the present day.

In the last two years alone, we have lost fifteen members of our tribe. Let me say that again – *fifteen* members of our tribe. This is because they had a relationship and furthermore married a person from a different ethnicity. So, we chose to dismiss our own people, rather than welcome the people they fell in love with. We could have gained fifteen *new* members and any children that are born to them.' Kari stood in silence.

If we carry on like this, within the next two generations, we'll no longer have a tribe to protect. We are driving our people away and I don't intend to push anymore of my family away, I want to *welcome* newcomers.'

Suddenly, The Elders were muttering under their breath, Kari knew they wouldn't like change and they definitely wouldn't like the enormous change that he was proposing.

'Please, hear me out,' Kari said loud enough so he could be heard above the noise. 'I'm proposing that we welcome *outsiders* as our tribe calls them. If the relationship turns into marriage, the outsider has a welcoming ceremony into our tribe. During this ceremony, they will take an oath that binds them to our beliefs and ways. The marriage will be a traditional Kutan ceremony and any children, born from that union, will be raised within our culture.

My Great Grandfather's brother, Ahote, was a victim of excommunication. He simply found his love and soul mate in a Canadian woman. Histories say that he would have been a fantastic Chief, but the love he felt for Miss Walker was too strong for him to give up. He was forced to choose between love and the tribe. He chose love. He was instantly dismissed from the tribe and never seen again. Nobody should be forced to choose between love and family. I talk of *family* because I believe our tribe is a family.'

Kari inhaled deeply and closed his eyes. He knew what he was going to say next would be extremely difficult. He released his breath, opened his eyes and began. 'Very recently, I became involved with a woman who was not from our tribe. I knew it was wrong, and whilst I tried to stay away from her, I don't believe you choose who you fall in love with, it just happens. The harder I fought to keep my distance, the more impossible it was to stay away. I knew a relationship with her was not permitted, but I couldn't deny that I was falling in love with this woman. I had to know if there was any chance I could be open and honest with my feelings for her. As I mentioned, I found the original legislation, which confirmed everything I was brought up believing, but it doesn't mean it is right. The world has changed since the relationship law was last written – society has evolved and I want our tribe to evolve with it. It's too late for the fifteen members that I mentioned before, and it's too late for me because I've already lost the woman I love, but I don't intend for another member of my *family* to go through the same pain. We have to change the law, or we will not have a tribe in the future.'

He looked at the stunned faces, staring up at him. 'Frankly speaking, I have been looking for a companion and wife. I'm thirty-four and still single. There is not one woman within the tribe here in Canada or Pontrains that I feel I can love the way you should love your soul mate. I had stopped looking when I found Joey, and now she has gone. But, if my chance came again and if I had to choose between love and family, I'm not sure what I would choose.' He stopped momentarily, sadness swelling in his throat, preventing him from continuing. He took a sip of water and continued. 'Ahote was strong to leave his family for his love, but I want to be stronger. I want my family and my tribe to accept the woman I love, regardless of her ethnicity. I want my tribe to accept other individuals who will fall in love with our tribe members.' Kari looked around the room at the bewildered faces.

'I have said my piece. Thank you for listening.' He sat down ready for the onslaught of questions.

No one uttered a word. Nobody knew where to start. Finally, Macawi took a breath and spoke, the only woman in the room. 'Thank you for such an informative and passionate speech, Kari. Whilst I recognise that some of what you say makes sense, I am concerned that we would weaken our blood line if we let *outsiders* in.'

'I understand, Macawi, but if we keep pushing our own away, pretty soon there will be no tribe to continue, we only have a little over three thousand people as it is.' replied Kari.

Isi then spoke. 'Kari, you should lead by example. If the Tribe's heir marries outside of our culture, what sign does that give other people of the Kutan Tribe?'

'But, what if I don't find a wife within our tribe. The bloodline would still not be continued.'

'In that instance, Luca would produce heirs.' Isi said, firmly.

Luca raised his eyebrows, 'But, what if I don't produce heirs?'

'Then, the bloodline would have to change, falling to the next in line, which would be my daughter, Arabella, and the children she would bear.' Henrique said with a smirk.

Kari's blood ran cold.

'But, what if she doesn't produce an heir?' suggested Kari. 'We could continue like this indefinitely and that is beside the point. The point I'm trying to make is that we desperately need to amend the relationship and marriage law.

We cannot continue to push our people away; we must welcome new blood. It's simple.'

The discussions went round and round in a circle, ending each time with Kari enforcing his point; the tribe must change to survive in the modern world.

Gahenge observed the meeting and he was immensely proud that his son had put his point across so well. He understood where Kari was coming from. Whilst he hated to admit it, in his heart, he knew Kari was right. He'd seen his son go through hell during these past few weeks, simply because he couldn't be with the woman he'd fallen in love with.

At the end of the day, it shouldn't be that difficult. Gahenge loved his tribe, but he loved his son more. He knew the tribe needed Kari to take them forward; it had to be Kari, because otherwise, the tribe would fail.

Kari began to draw the meeting to a close as he felt he had given everybody enough to ponder.

'I have printed copies of my proposal which I ask you to read before we recommence. After Lacroix and Solonge's wedding on Saturday, I would like a meeting next Tuesday to discuss further questions you may have?'

Again, silence fell in the massive hall. Everyone nodded in unison, lost for words. Lacroix handed everybody a copy of the proposal and The Elders filtered out, with the exception of Kari, Lacroix, Luca and Gahenge.

Kari turned to his father, 'Father, do you think I'm asking something unreasonable?'

Gahenge looked at his son proudly, 'I believe you can do anything, if you really put your heart into it, Kari.'

'Thank you, father.'

'You're welcome.' he replied, before leaving the room with his copy of the proposal.

Luca looked at Kari and Lacroix and said, 'Well, at least he didn't say no.'

Chapter 32

Solonge was so excited for Saturday, she was unaware of anything else happening around her. She had her Hen party earlier in the week and the dress had its final alterations and fitted perfectly. Everything was going so well, except for the fact she missed Lacroix. How she missed the intimacy they had shared for such a brief time. She didn't know how she had survived before without his touch, kiss or gentle words of encouragement. The phone rang and breezily she answered it.

'Hi Solonge, it's Joey.'

Solonge stopped her cleaning and sank into the nearest chair. Joey was the last person she had expected. 'Joey, how are you?'

'I've been better. I was wondering… if it's still okay, I'd like to be there for you and Lacroix on your wedding day… to complete your circle.' Joey added.

'Oh, Joey, that is the best news I've heard all day.'

'There is one condition - Kari can't know I'm there. You can tell Lacroix, but that's it. The situation still hurts like hell, but I want to be there, for both of you. I can't start this healing process all over again, it's too difficult.'

'Of course, I understand. Oh Joey, this is wonderful news; Lacroix will be over the moon, thank you. When can you get here?' Solonge asked urgently.

'Whenever you need me?'

'Can you catch a flight which would get here for tomorrow morning?'

'Yes.'

'Excellent, text me the times and I'll collect you from the airport. You can stay with me on Friday and I'll take you to the ceremony on Saturday. That way, you won't have to see anyone you don't want to, but you'll be there for Lacroix and me. We can talk about your return journey when you're here. Oh Joey, you don't know how happy you have made me.' Solonge grinned, giddily.

Meanwhile, Kari was driven by the knowledge that his own father believed his new legislation could succeed; even if it didn't help him, he knew he could potentially help others. Also, after the wedding, he was going to fly to England to find Joey and see if he could persuade her to be with him again.

Kari was looking forward to his friends' wedding, he was extremely happy for them both. He loved them very much and wished them nothing but happiness. His only regret was that Joey would not be there with him. He still missed her enormously and dreamt of her every night. Sometimes, she was hiding and he couldn't find her, other times they were making love and, just as they were about to climax, he would wake up; he needed her now more than ever.

Joey had been in a dream like state since ending the phone call with Solonge. She couldn't believe she had agreed to go to Canada for the wedding. How would she feel when she saw Kari? She knew it was going to be unbearable to see him yet not be able to touch him. However, she had to do this for her friends – Solonge and Lacroix. Lucy had convinced her to call; after all, what did she have to lose… apart from her heart again! She packed a simple dress and her essentials into the dogged suitcase.

Solonge hugged, a very anxious and nervous, Joey when she met her at Vancouver airport, early Friday morning. Solonge reassured Joey that she hadn't told Kari, before telling her the plan for that evening.

They would be staying in an apartment in the city, with a few of Solonge's other girl friends. The plan was to have a relaxing girls night – do each other's nails whilst sharing a bottle of wine.

Joey felt so happy to be back in Solonge's company again, realising how much she had missed her. She wanted to ask how Kari was, but promised herself she wouldn't, because it hurt too much to think about him, let alone to talk about him.

Solonge took Joey to a very modern, minimalist and large apartment in the city. Three very close, childhood friends of Solonge - Kachina, Eyota and Misae - were already there, waiting for them. They were also going to spend the night at the apartment and help Solonge get ready for the wedding in the morning. They made Joey feel very welcome and eased any remaining tension she felt.

Throughout the day they ate pizza, slouched in casual clothes and generally talked girl things. Eyota was the only one married and Solonge asked her about her wedding night.

'It was amazing.' Eyota enthused. 'You're both so charged from the events that have happened throughout the day, as well as abstaining for the month previous, that when you finally get a moment to yourselves, you practically explode.'

'Not to mention all the other couples, doing it to!' added Misae.

'True, there is a certain degree of expectation!' Eyota agreed, 'Don't worry, Solonge, I won't let you down.' She said, winking.

'I knew I could count on you.' Solonge said, picking up another slice of pizza.

Kachina nodded in agreement, 'If I can help, you know I will.'

'Things not so good between you and Teck'na?' Eyota asked, concerned for her friend.

'So, so. One minute he's hot, the next he's cold. But, I'll suffer another night, if it means Solonge conceives the baby she so desperately wants.'

Joey sat and listened intently as the women talked so openly about Solonge's wedding night. She still found it bizarre that every couple was actively encouraged to have sex that night. She couldn't imagine her sister and mum being so open about such a taboo subject in her house.

'You alright, Joey?' Solonge asked concerned, as Joey had been very quiet.

'I think it's great how you're all so open about what's expected tomorrow night.'

Eyota shrugged, 'It's what we do. Besides, if we didn't have sex and procreate there would be no future generation.'

'I appreciate that, but, it's just... everyone is expected to *play* their part. Even older people.' Joey said, trying not to imagine Gahenge and Aiyana...

'It's not just lust, it's values and tradition,' said Misae. Her thoughts then wandered before adding, 'I heard Luca was back. I wonder if he'll be partaking in tomorrow night's activities!'

'Forget Luca, it's Kar, ow!' Kachina said, before Solonge poked her hard in the ribs, stopping her from saying anymore.

'Solonge, are you looking forward to tomorrow night?' Eyota said quickly, noting Joey's decidedly uncomfortable face.

'You bet. This abstinence thing is not easy.'

'So, come on, Solonge, what is Lacroix like?' asked Misae.

'I'm not telling you!'

'Come on, we're your closest friends. It's only right we know if you're going to marry a stud or a duff!' teased Misae.

A haze fell over Solonge's eyes as she thought of Lacroix. 'He is amazing - like no other man I have been with before. It just feels so right with him. He's caring, careful, obliging and tentative to my needs.' Solonge said, with a girlie laugh. 'What about you, Eyota? You're an old married woman with children, does it stay the same?'

'Oh yes, it gets better with age. Of course, you lose the initial lust where you just want to do it all the time and everywhere, but it becomes something deeper, more satisfying, in a way. Look at me, baby number four on the way and we're still going strong.'

Joey suddenly realised, this was *Eyota* - Kari's first love! *Oh great, this could be tricky!* Joey thought as she made a mental note to avoid all conversation about Kari. She thought she was doing well, until Eyota turned directly to her and said, 'I'm sorry to hear things didn't work out for you and Kari.' Eyota smiled, warmly, 'I know he's Kari Kutan, future Chief and all the rest of it, but underneath all that bravado, he's just a really decent guy.'

Joey tried to smile but tears instantly sprang to her eyes.

'Rumour has it, Kari's been totally torn up since you and he broke up.'

'I guess it wasn't meant to be.' Joey muttered.

'Hey, that's right, you've both had Kari Kutan!' Kachina piped up. 'Now, I bet he is amazing in bed, but... then again, maybe not, seeing as you both let him go.'

Eyota looked at Joey before replying. 'Kari and I dated a long time ago; we were young and didn't know what we wanted.' Eyota took Joey's hand in hers, 'I love Kari as a friend, nothing more. I loved him, but I realised I wasn't *in* love with him.'

'Wasn't he your first?' asked Kachina.

Eyota looked at Joey, not sure how to answer such a direct question in front of her. 'Yes, he was my first love so I couldn't compare him to anyone until I met Hoi Tog. All I can say is, I'm in love with Hoi Tog and I want his children, you can't compare the two.'

'But, Kari is totally fit. His body is gorgeous!' Kachina looked away, dreamily. 'I can't wait to see him tomorrow, and if I ever had the chance to be with him, I wouldn't let him go. He looks the sort of guy who's interesting in bed, too.' Kachina looked at Eyota.

'No comment.' Eyota said, getting up and stretching her legs and all eyes turned to Joey.

Joey blushed; she wasn't sure what to say, 'Why are you all looking at me?'

'Because… we want the gossip on Kari! Why hasn't he secured himself a wife yet? Is he as good in bed as he looks? Come on. We have two of his previous lovers in this room and neither are exactly raving about how good he is!' Kachina said, with a wicked glint in her eye.

'Please, Kachina, I have to work for the guy.' Solonge said as she poured more wine for everyone. 'And, I can't imagine he'd want us talking about his private life.'

'Also, leave Joey alone, if she doesn't want to talk about Kari, then we should respect her wishes and not pry.' Eyota said, sitting back down.

'I can only assume your silence means he doesn't live up to expectations.' Kachina added, before she took a large mouthful of wine.

'Maybe I can't answer your question.' Joey said, coyly.

Solonge smirked and looked away knowing full well that Joey and Kari had slept together.

'I saw a picture of you both, holding hands!' Kachina said, indignantly.

Joey smiled, realising suddenly that she liked to talk about Kari. 'In which case, I can tell you about how he holds my hand, but there is no *proof* that we were physically anything more than that.' She answered, smirking.

Eyota laughed, she liked Joey. She was the sort of character she imagined Kari would want to be with.

'Yes, but Kari doesn't hold hands with anyone, period.' Kachina grabbed her mobile and began to quickly search Google. 'Kari doesn't even smile at women, in case he gives them the wrong impression. Look,' she said triumphantly as she held up her phone for everyone to see. The screen revealed a picture, taken a few weeks ago, of Kari and Joey holding hands. 'Here, we have photographic evidence that he held your hand in public whilst looking adoringly at you. You can't tell me that handholding was as far as your relationship went!'

Joey sighed, it seemed Kachina wasn't going to drop the subject until she got an answer. 'That picture was taken in France. As you may or may not know, Kari invited me there for a no-strings holiday. Everything was great until one morning, I looked out of my window and saw him getting out of the pool in his Speedos – I thought I was going to melt on the spot!' Joey reminisced.

Misae and Kachina giggled as they imagined what Joey explained.

'But, Kari is much more than just a great body. He is the most special man I have ever met. He's warm and giving. Kind and generous.'

'And?' Kachina probed.

'And what?' Joey asked, feigning innocence as she knew exactly what Kachina was asking.

'Is he as good in bed as I think he'd be?' Kachina asked, frankly.

Joey took a deep breath and she could feel herself blushing. 'What do you think?'

'Well, I *hope* he's as good as he looks.' Kachina said, honestly.

'Not only is he beautiful to look at, but he's also bloody fantastic in and out of bed.' Joey said with a wicked giggle.

The others laughed with her. They liked Joey; she was easy to talk to, not at all what they'd imagined. They thought she only wanted Kari because of who he was, but, as they got to know her, they began to see that she really cared for him.

'Joey, there's something we have to discuss.' Solonge said, pulling the subject away from Kari again.

Joey's mind raced. Had Kari met someone else already? 'Sure.' Joey said, tentatively, unsure what Solonge wanted to talk about.

'If you want to remain relatively inconspicuous tomorrow, we strongly suggest a good layer of fake tan.'

Joey almost spluttered on her wine in relief. 'What!'

'And dying your hair,' Misae added.

'Really?'

The four women all nodded at Joey, who stared back at them, open-mouthed.

'You can borrow my traditional dress tomorrow but you'll still stand out with your fair skin and brown hair.' Solonge said, kindly.

'You're kidding, right?' Joey asked, still not sure if the women were teasing or not.

'We're not kidding, Joey.' Eyota said as she produced a carrier bag that had been hidden from view until now. 'I went to the drug store earlier and bought some fake tan and hair dye.'

Joey sat in stunned silence as Eyota passed her the bag.

'It's temporary and washes off in an instant,' Eyota added, concerned by Joey's silence.

'Good job there's no rain forecast for tomorrow!' Kachina muttered, quietly.

'And, you think this is a good idea?' Joey said, reading the two boxes of potions.

'If you want to remain inconspicuous, then, yes,' Solonge said, encouragingly.

'What if it turns my skin orange and streaky?'

'We'll make sure it doesn't.' Eyota said, taking one of the boxes from Joey.

'Come on, between the four of us we'll have you looking less…' Kachina said, trailing off, not sure how to explain what she meant without insulting Joey.

'Pale?' Joey offered.

'English Rose!' Eyota said as she put on the see-through gloves.

'I can't believe I'm doing this!' Joey said as she allowed Solonge and Misae pull her to her feet and drag her through into the bathroom.

Solonge chuckled, 'Come on, we had better make a start as I'm not sure how many coats we'll need to apply.'

'Oh, crap!' Joey groaned as she striped down to her underwear and let the four, excited women transform her.

As evening approached, Joey was sat alone and her mind wandered to Kari, as it so often did. What would he think if he saw her now? She must admit the transformation had been relatively successful and felt more optimistic about blending in tomorrow.

She was deep in her own world and wasn't even aware Eyota had sat next to her until she heard her say, 'Is everything okay, Joey?'

Joey sighed, 'I'm fine. I was thinking of Kari, that's all.'

'I hope you don't feel awkward because I have also dated Kari.'

'No, not at all. I know that he had a life before he met me. He has talked about you, and always with the greatest of respect. He said you married a very dear friend of his.'

'That is kind. I can safely say Hoi Tog is the love of my life. Kari was an experiment.' Eyota laughed, warmly. 'I do wish Kari would find his soul mate, though. He is such a decent person. Hoi Tog told me that he had never seen Kari so happy as when he was dating you. Kari was a changed man. It's such a shame you can't be together.'

'Leaving him was the hardest decision I've ever had to make.'

'Me too.' Eyota said, quietly.

'Listen to us.'

'Poor guy, having both of us walk out on him!'

Joey nodded. 'You don't have to tell me if you don't want to, but why did you leave him?'

'Like I said, we weren't *in* love with one another. Even though he could have given me everything I'd ever wanted, it still wasn't enough. For a relationship to stand a chance of surviving, you need to not only love one another, but also be in love with each other. When I broke it off with Kari, I already had feelings for Hoi Tog, not that Kari knows that, mind you. Did you love him?'

'I loved Kari more than I have ever loved anyone. That's why I left. It hurt like hell, and still does, but I couldn't take him away from his tribe, he would end up hating me and I couldn't bare that.' Joey replied.

'Kari would never leave his tribe but I don't think he could hate you either. Oh, come here!' Eyota said, wrapping Joey in a warm embrace as she saw Joey's eyes fill with tears. 'You'll be okay; he's a tough one to get over. But you will, you'll be okay.'

'I'm sorry.' Joey mumbled as she wiped her tears away, 'I told you it was hard but I'm getting there.' Gaining control of her emotions, she took a deep breath, 'Come on, this is Solonge's night, where's the music?'

It was a day of mixed emotions. They talked non-stop, painted each other's nails and danced. They talked about what the men would be doing and they all agreed eating, drinking and smoking the peace pipe.

Much later in the evening, Joey asked Solonge where she would be sleeping. Solonge told her they would be sharing a room, and led Joey to it. 'I know you miss Kari, but just remember, tonight when we share this bed, I'm not him!' Solonge smirked to Joey and left her alone to sort out her things.

Joey wondered over to the window to look at the bustling city, twenty stories below. It was true that some cities never slept; it was as busy now as when she arrived hours earlier. She sat on the massive bed and looked around the room. Suddenly, the aroma struck her – she could smell Kari! She turned around, half expecting to see him, but there was nobody else in the room with her, but she could smell him, why? She thought she was going mad.

She went to the toilet and, as she washed her hands, she recognised the aroma of the soap – it was definitely the same as Kari's. Her eyes threatened to shed further tears, but she forced herself to get a grip and went back into the bedroom. As she passed a chest of drawers, something caught her eye. On top of a small pile of magazines, she saw the picture that was taken of her and Kari at the Nice ball. They looked so happy, even though at the time, Joey was oblivious to whose arm she held. Gasping, she put her hand to her mouth and sank onto the bed. She looked around the room; it had to be Kari's room, this was Kari's apartment. The urge not to snoop through the drawers and closet was difficult to ignore, but she did. She sat on the bed, hypnotised by the picture she held delicately between her hands.

She had no idea how long she had sat on the bed unable to move, but it must have been a while as Solonge came back, looking for her, worried that something had happened.

Solonge found Joey holding the picture. 'I should have told you this is Kari's apartment. He keeps it as a bolthole. He kindly offered me the use of it tonight, before I knew you were coming; I promise you, he still has no idea that you're here.' Solonge knelt on the floor, in front of Joey, holding her hands and said gently, 'You probably don't want to hear this Joey, but I have never known him to love another like he loved you. He was so happy when you were seeing each other. These past few weeks he has been so desperately unhappy, depressed even. For the first week, I don't think he ate properly, he lived on coffee, and he didn't sleep in his room, preferring to nap in his office. He didn't shower or shave - he was a wreck. He is finally returning to normal, but he's a shadow of the man he was when he was dating you.' Solonge paused and searched Joey's eyes before saying, 'I have to ask, if I don't I'll never know, but is there any chance you'll speak to him tomorrow?'

'I can't.' Joey replied. 'I can't go through this again because it hurts too much. I can't ask him to choose between me or his tribe, I just can't.'

'I know, but maybe if you could just talk?'

Joey shook her head. 'I'm here for you and Lacroix, not me or Kari. After tomorrow, I wont bother you again. I only want you and Lacroix to have a wonderful marriage.'

Solonge and Joey hugged for a long time. Eventually, all the women retired to bed because they had a long day ahead of them.

As Joey lay quietly in Kari's bed, she wondered what he would say if he knew she was there.

Chapter 33

The next morning, the apartment erupted into a hive of activity. The girls persuaded Joey to wear the tradition costume, convincing her it would give her a better chance of blending in. Joey still felt uncomfortable wearing it - it felt morally wrong. Eyota wolf whistled as Joey came out of the bedroom, feeling incredibly self-conscious. 'You look great, Joey.' Joey didn't care what she looked like, so long as she was there for Solonge and Lacroix.

Solonge looked incredible. The traditional, native wedding dress was beautiful and made from soft, cream animal hide. Various precious stones were sewn down the body of the dress, enhancing delicate embroidery. Soft tassels dusted her arms and around her neck, she wore layers of heavy beading and feathers. Solonge explained that the Kutan Tribe truly believed that eyes are the windows to the soul. Nothing was allowed to obscure or detract attention from the eyes of the couple that were marrying. Their souls were to be laid bare, ready to be united by the Spirit Gods.

Joey watched with interest as Eyota braided the very front sections of Solonge's hair whilst the other two women chanted softly. The simple braids were then secured with a large turquoise stone and feather at the back of Solonge's head, leaving her face and eyes free from any wisps of hair.

The other women, Solonge's bridal companions, wore similar native dress to Joey's, the only difference being, Joey's was beige and theirs cream, to compliment Solonge. They were all so beautiful and Joey felt decidedly drab in comparison.

A chauffeur driven car collected them and drove them to Cha Tik Warro. It was decided they would find a discreet area where they could drop Joey off. She would then make her way to the gardens at the rear of the house where she could watch the ceremony, out of sight.

Joey carried a small bag that contained her mobile, purse and the number of a taxi she would call to collect her when she was ready to leave. The taxi would take her back to the apartment where she could change and collect her things. A key had been left for Joey with the security guard at the concierge of the apartment block.

Meanwhile at Cha Tik Warro, Lacroix was itching for the ceremony to begin and Kari had already had to ask him to calm down many times. He'd made sure Lacroix knew what he was doing today – what dances he would be performing and what to say at the appropriate time. Lacroix was like a small child on his birthday. He just wanted everything to start, immediately.

Kari smiled at his dear friend and wished one day, he could also experience happiness like Lacroix's. As ever, Kari's mind wandered back to Joey. Today would be hard; she should be here, joining in with the excitement. He wondered what she was doing, whether she was thinking of him? Possibly not, but he was sure she would at least be thinking of Solonge and Lacroix.

Joey made her way, as discreetly as possible, to the main gardens behind the house. Thousands of fellow natives made their way to pay their respects and join in with the ceremony. Joey walked with her head bowed, attempting to keep her face hidden as she walked among the massive crowd.

Everyone seemed to be in high spirits as they were ushered along a path that wound around the right side of the house. As a large group surged through the side gate, Joey made her way towards the stables. Her plan was to wait there until more people arrived and then stealthily make her way to a thicket of trees overlooking the marriage. From there, she would be able to watch the ceremony in peace, completing the circle for Lacroix and Solonge. Solonge said she would tell Lacroix that Joey was there, but only when the time was right, and he would swear that he wouldn't tell Kari.

Kari looked out of the first floor windows, waiting patiently for Lacroix who had gone to the bathroom again. So many people, so many of his father's tribe – would they ever be his people? If that were the case, there would have to be changes. He loved the idea of one large family, supporting each other in times of need and celebration. There were thousands of people present, but not one woman amongst them interested him, romantically speaking.

The chanting began and everyone's spirits were high as they waited for Solonge and her bridal companions to arrive.

He knew everyone was eager to celebrate Solonge and Lacroix's union, but it was also a time when a number of single young women would try to catch his or Luca's eye in attempt to win their hearts.

'Okay, I'm ready,' Lacroix said, entering the room.

'Excellent, let's go!' Kari said, turning Lacroix towards the door, 'No, that way. I'm not letting you look out the window or you'll be off to the bathroom again.'

Lacroix laughed nervously as they made their way downstairs to meet Luca and Gahenge. They would be the last to join the ceremony.

Joey watched behind the camouflage of the trees, she knew she was safely out of sight. Nobody had seen her and no one could see her. To one side a huge totem pole dominated the far end of the dry, sandy earth clearing. Below the totem pole was a large chair with two cushions laying on the ground either side of it. The imposing Kutan family house, Cha Tik Warro, framed one side of the clearing and thousands of natives congregated around the edges, vying for the best vantage spot to watch the sacred ceremony. There were many hog roasts turning on their spits, mouth-wateringly tantalising in their smell. The sound of chanting alongside the dull thud the natives feet made, as they persistently beat the dry earth, was like nothing Joey had ever witnessed before. A massive fire was burning profusely and eerie sound of a wooden flute filled the silence in the air. Joey didn't really know what to expect. Would a priest be present?

Suddenly, a howling sound shattered the peace as Solonge and her bridal companions walked into the clearing. They stood in the open space facing the fire. As Kachina, Eyota and Misae danced and circled Solonge, they scattered petals. The beautifully vibrant petals added to the beauty of the scene as they swirled slowly to the earth. Solonge looked radiant.

The natives chanted, stomping their feet in time with the drumbeat, it was a truly magnificent sight and Joey began to wonder what else would happen during a tribal wedding. Her heart started to quicken with excitement as she watched the ceremony unfold. The crowds reaching a frenzy of expectance, the atmosphere highly charged.

The sound of a breathy, single wooden flute soared above the chaotic chanting and ceased all activity. Tension mounted. Joey didn't even want to breath. Another sound reminiscent to beads being shaken broke the otherwise silent arena. In the distance, she heard a war cry. Everyone, including Solonge, bowed their heads. The sound of a haunting flute and the beat of a single drum broke the silent air. *This is it!* Joey thought as she took a deep breath and tried to mentally prepare herself to see Kari again.

The beat on another drum began to harmoniously wind with the first rhythm, creating a steady build in tension as the wedding party drew closer. Other instruments began to join the melody and one native, who was stood below the totem pole, sang a chant over and over again. Movement caught Joey's eye as Gahenge entered the clearing. He looked intimidating but magnificent. He wore a full headdress of feathers and tribal paint was smeared down his cheekbones. He walked towards Solonge with his arms folded, kissed her on both cheeks, before sitting on the large chair.

Everything went a bit fuzzy for Joey as Lacroix entered the clearing, followed by Kari and she assumed Luca. Everyone looked at Lacroix, as the impressive threesome walked towards the waiting women, but Joey couldn't tear her eyes away from Kari. She had never seen Kari look more sensational. He looked exactly like his portrait; spectacular, magnificent, but with a coldness emanating from his eyes. Joey had never seen him look so native and she felt slightly scared of him.

She watched in stunned silence – she couldn't have moved, even if she wanted to. The three women moved out of the way as the three men surrounded Solonge, dancing around her, each hitting their spear on the ground to the beat of the drum. Lacroix smiled at his beautiful Solonge, Luca had a look of complete concentration and Kari looked entirely in control, as if he did it everyday.

All three men were dressed in the same clothes, but Joey couldn't tear her eyes from Kari. His torso was naked and she could see he had lost weight. However, his body rippled as it moved with grace and control from position to position. He was wearing a short breechcloth of animal hide to keep his modesty. Layer after layer of precious stones, beads and feathers were worn around his hips, weighing down the cloth. Leather straps were wrapped around his wrists and ankles as he danced, barefoot. Like Gahenge, war paint was smeared down Kari's cheekbones, enhancing his already chiselled features.

Each man wore different headwear. Lacroix had a modest feather, fastened to the bandana he wore around his head. Luca wore his hair tied back with feathers erupting from the base of his ponytail whereas Kari wore his hair completely loose with one large feather on the side. In their right hand, they each held a spear.

As the chant ended, Solonge and Lacroix couldn't help but beam at each other. The warmth that flowed between them was evident for everyone to see. Joey could see their breathing was rapid and shallow compared to Kari's deep and even breath. Luca looked at Kari and grinned. When Kari smiled back at his younger brother, Joey's heart melted, she had missed his familiar smile.

The drumming and flute surged into a new song. Eyota took the three spears from the men and stood next to Gahenge. Lacroix took Solonge's hands, Luca took Kachina's and Kari took Misae's. Joey felt a stab of jealousy as she watched Kari hold another woman's hands.

Slowly, in time to the music, the three couples began to move in a formation dance. They interlinked, turned and changed hands, before swapping partners. An older native chanted and sprinkled them with blessed water. Joey wished she knew what it meant.

Lacroix and Solonge never took their eyes off each other, even when they we partnered with others. Luca appeared to be having fun, whereas Kari was deadly serious. As the song ended Luca, Kachina, Misae and Kari left Solonge and Lacroix alone. Joey saw Solonge whisper something to Lacroix. He looked surprised, but soon, a smile slowly spread across his face. Joey wondered if Solonge had told him Joey was there.

Joey glanced across to Kari and noticed that he and Luca were now either side of their father, seated on massive cushions.

The arena space was suddenly full of young people, dancing and chanting around Lacroix and Solonge. The music swelled and the beautiful young people danced in formation, in time to the beat. The elder native chanted as he placed his hands on Solonge's and Lacroix bowed heads. Kari watched with intent.

The music evolved into a soft lullaby that was sang by a woman. Solonge and Lacroix danced, other couples surrounded them and danced also. Joey could tell from the delicacy of the music and the way the young woman softly sang, it was a love song. Luca turned to talk to his father often, but Kari remained silent and stone-faced. Joey remembered seeing that look, when she first saw him, all that time ago back in The Pig's Head. She would have loved to know what he was thinking. Gahenge said something to Kari, but he shook his head and continued to watch the dancing young people.

Kari wished that, more than anything, he could be dancing with Joey, to this beautiful love song. His father had just asked him to go and find a dance partner but Kari couldn't, it wouldn't feel right. He was happy to watch Solonge and Lacroix, who looked so happy and in love.

As the song ended, crowds formed an orderly queue as they waited for food. Thankfully, Lacroix and Solonge would join his family and they would be brought some of the great feast.

The food smelt so enticing it made Joey's mouth water. People helped themselves to the roasted pork as it was sheared off and passed to waiting people. More and more food was brought out to everyone. There were plates and bowls of freshly cooked fish, rice and vegetables. Joey tried to ignore the hunger pangs in her stomach and instead, concentrate on Kari. She noticed that he wasn't eating the quantity he normally ate. Perhaps he wasn't hungry; maybe he didn't like the food that had been chosen for him.

Something bothered him. He had felt it when he walked into the ceremony earlier and now he could feel it again. He knew he would sound mad if he mentioned it to his father, so, he thought better of it and remained quiet. But, as he sat quietly trying to eat his food, there was no denying he felt like he was being watched. Maybe it was the Spirits of their past loved ones, but it seemed more than that. He could feel heat emanating from behind the thicket of trees in the lower garden. An invisible force seemed to draw his eyes to that specific area of the garden.

It was almost too much for his curiosity to bear, but he knew he'd have to dance again in a short while. In the meantime, he assessed the trees from where he sat - as long as no, unfortunate, woman thought he was looking at her.

Joey's heart raced; Kari was staring intently in her direction. She tried to physically blend into the trees. What if he'd seen her? Impossible. His concentration was only broken when Lacroix said something to him, to which Kari nodded.

Lacroix kissed Solonge's hand before walking out into the middle of the arena, followed closely by Kari and Luca. One by one, all of the men filtered into the vast space and stood behind Lacroix, who now was facing Solonge.

Joey watched transfixed, as heavy drumming demanded the men to dance in unison. Lacroix led the dance. It was incredible to watch as gradually, Lacroix began to raise its intensity. It was not a beautiful dance - it was aggressive, the drum beat unforgiving. The men began to sweat from the passion and enthusiasm that Lacroix demanded. As the dance ended, only half the men remained, many had dropped out through exhaustion.

Joey watched as Solonge walked to Lacroix and kiss him gently. Luca slapped Lacroix on the back and grinned at Kari. Kari returned Luca's smile and raised his eyebrows to Lacroix who laughed quietly under his breath. There was obviously a private joke going on between the three men.

It wasn't long before the drums began to beat a new fast rhythm and Joey watched as most of the tribe moved into the large open space to prepare to dance. This time, the men faced the women. There must have been around three hundred dancers, filling the now crowded space. At the forefront, Solonge faced Lacroix.

As the music churned through the native bodies, Joey was mesmerised by how graceful Kari was. He placed each foot on the ground with delicacy and precision.

Aiyana and Gahenge looked so proud as they watched the dance unfolding in front of them. Joey noted Henrique stood, removed from the celebration, towards one of the edges. Like Joey, he appeared to be watching Kari. Henrique had an air of arrogance, he didn't look majestic - he looked sinister.

Whilst everyone was dancing, Joey seized the opportunity to move to a new place of hiding. Kari must not find her. It was going to be hard enough to leave as it was, but she couldn't cope if they came face to face. Cautiously, she made her way to the small outbuilding to her left.

As Kari danced, his eyes kept being drawn to the thicket of trees. Everyone was everywhere, music turning their bodies into a frenzy. A number of women discreetly touched his arm, but he ignored them. How he yearned more than ever for Joey, especially as this particular dance was aphrodisiacal.

When he looked towards the trees, he was certain he saw movement. It could be paparazzi intruding in their private and special celebration, even though they had been given strict instructions.

As discreetly as possible, he made his way through the throng of people, towards the thicket. One of his roles was to protect his family and friends; he could not put them at risk, all of his senses were telling him to investigate. As he approached the trees, he sensed the heat had moved. His body and soul were on autopilot, something had taken over his body and he allowed himself to be drawn towards wherever he needed to go. He wasn't scared, although his heart quickened. Spurred on by an invisible force, he walked towards the old, derelict outbuilding.

Joey looked around the edge of the building and saw, to her absolute horror, that Kari was walking towards her. She tried the door but it was locked, she was trapped. She squashed her body into the wall, hoping the darkness of the evening would camouflage her. She couldn't do anything else but hope he would turn back. The chanting and music drowned out any sound Kari made. She couldn't hear any footsteps or broken twigs, but then again, Kari was a trained hunter, and right now she was being hunted. Her heart was beating so fast she thought she might pass out. She closed her eyes and held her breath.

Kari approached the old out-building, feeling slightly stupid. The last thing he wanted was to stumble across a passionate couple. But, his legs kept moving, uncontrollably spurring him on. The only concern he had, was his ever-increasing heart rate. As he looked around the edge of the building, he noticed a shape in the dark. It was a woman. He stared at her, and finally she opened her eyes and the beauty radiating from within them, took his breath away.

'Joey?' He heard a voice say, not recognising it as his own. Time stood still. In the dark shadows, the woman looked like Joey but she had black hair, dark skin and was wearing native clothes. But, her eyes… It couldn't be Joey; she wasn't here. Was his mind playing tricks? Was this some kind of a sick joke?

'Yes?' The question hung in the hallow space between them.

Kari legs buckled beneath him, as he lost all strength. Thankfully, the wall of the building supported his frame as he fell against it. He couldn't speak. He couldn't breath.

'I'm sorry; I had to come for Lacroix and Solonge. I didn't mean… I didn't intend… I… I'll go now,' Joey said, trying to pass him.

Kari reached out and gently held her upper arm, preventing her from leaving. He turned his head to look at her and whispered, 'Am I dreaming?'

She looked into his big, dark eyes that seemed to penetrate her soul. 'No…' Joey managed to say before he brought his mouth crushing down on hers. He kissed her as if his life depended on it, and she kissed him back with as much urgency. They needed to touch each other, to kiss without coming up for air. Kari thought his heart was going to pound out of his chest, it raced so fast. He felt a slight stabbing sensation and then all the pain he'd been feeling for the past three weeks suddenly stopped.

He held Joey's body tightly to his as his hands ran from her head to her bottom. He wanted to make love to her; his body was reacting violently to feeling her again, smelling her again, kissing her again. With amazing strength, he pulled back and looked at her. Her lips were bruised from his harsh kisses, but she had never looked more beautiful. Her eyes were dark and oozed love.

'It really is you?' Kari said, his hands gently touching her face. 'But, your skin and hair.'

'I wanted to blend in.'

He kissed her again and between kisses he said, 'I have missed you. I need you more than I ever thought possible, Joey. I need to show you how much I've missed you.'

Joey pulled away, 'We can't Kari, we can't.'

'Why not?' Kari looked into her beautiful eyes, and tried to resist the temptation to kiss her again.

'Because, it hurts too much, I can't…' A sob caught in her throat before she could continue and tears began to fall down her cheeks.

'Oh, Joey,' Kari said, resting his forehead on hers. 'I know it hurts; I've never experienced pain like it. This is why I have to show you how much I need you, how much I want you. Please?' Kari searched her eyes, he could feel his own, filling with tears. He looked imploringly into hers and eventually she nodded. He cupped her face gently and kissed her, tenderly.

'I must say goodbye to Solonge and Lacroix, but… I'm afraid you'll be gone before I get back and I will not take that risk.' He took her hand and led her towards the edge of the building.

Joey pulled him back, 'No wait. You must say goodbye to Lacroix and Solonge. I will wait.'

Kari looked at her unsure whether to trust her. 'Do you promise not to leave me again?'

Joey nodded, offering a compromise she said, 'I promise I'll wait.'

He kissed her gently on the lips before leading her discreetly to the main house. They passed behind trees, ensuring they weren't seen by anyone. 'Once I've said my goodbyes to Lacroix and Solonge, I'll come for you.'

Joey couldn't help but smile at what Kari said, but he seemed oblivious.

'I can't tell you how wonderful it is to see you smile,' said Kari before he kissed her again. 'Wait here, by this window. Give me five minutes.' He turned to go but before he left he said, 'Promise you'll be here, waiting for me?'

'I promise I will be here. Wish Solonge and Lacroix well from me.' Joey said.

'I will.' Kari said with a smile and, after one final kiss, he left to quickly find Solonge and Lacroix hoping with all his might, Joey would still be there when he got back.

Chapter 34

What just happened? Joey thought. One minute she had been hiding from Kari, and the next she was melting into his arms. Like thieves in the night, they had scurried down the side of the house. Now she was waiting for him to let her into the house where they were clearly going to spend the night together. It felt like her head might explode with happiness. She couldn't go now. She didn't want to go, she wanted to feel safe in his arms again. For him to kiss her and tell her he missed her. When reality came crashing down again, she would deal with it. For now, she didn't want to think of tomorrow, she focused on the slice of truth that Kari was going to return in a few minutes and they would spend the night together, even if it were just for one more night.

It didn't take long for Kari to find Lacroix and Solonge. They were talking to another newly-wed couple. He excused himself for having interrupted their conversation and explained that he needed to talk to Solonge and Lacroix immediately. The young couple hastily retreated to give the heir of the Kutan Tribe and his protectors some privacy.

'What's wrong, Kari?' Lacroix asked, concerned to see his friend slightly shaking.

'I'm sorry but I'm going to have to say goodbye now and I wish you a very happy and wonderful honeymoon.' Kari said, embracing each of his dear friends in turn.

They were slightly surprised – it was still relatively early in the evening. 'Are you feeling okay, Kari?' Solonge asked, beginning to worry.

'I'm absolutely fine, never better.' Kari started to grin he couldn't help himself. Solonge and Lacroix looked at each other confused. Kari leant in closer to them so only they could hear him say, 'Joey wishes you great happiness too.'

'You've seen her?' Solonge asked, quietly.

Kari nodded and with a huge smile on his face he turned and walked into the house.

Solonge jumped into Lacroix's arms and he spun her around, celebrating. People standing watched their exultation with mild surprise before dismissing it as part of the wedding celebrations.

Kari felt as if he were still in a dream. He didn't want to allow himself to believe it was true. He hurried down the west wing corridor, entered the far end room and quietly pulled the door shut behind him. Without turning on the lights, he ran to the window and yanked it open. He looked out and at first his heart sank as he couldn't see Joey… then, from behind a large bush, she emerged.

'Tell me, how am I supposed to get up there?' Joey asked with a grin on her face.

'Just pull yourself in.'

'Just pull yourself in?' Joey mocked Kari's matter of fact voice. She tried to pull herself through the open window, but ended up laughing and losing all the strength in her arms.

'Suddenly, I'm reminded of our horse riding experience!' Kari said, sighing. 'Okay, lean over and I'll pull you in.' She stretched her arms up and Kari pulled so hard that he went flying backwards as he overestimated her weight. Holding her securely in his arms, he lost his balance and crashed into a nearby chair before falling onto the floor which resulted in Joey lying on top of him. They both collapsed into laughter fits, made worse as they tried to laugh quietly.

'This is not quite how I imagined our reunion!' Kari said, chuckling, 'Not that I'm complaining.'

'Are you okay?' Joey said, trying to stop her laughter at the same time, realising that if were caught, they were in a compromising position.

Kari ran his hands up her thighs, 'Almost perfect, thank you.' They looked wantonly at each other and both realised they needed to find somewhere more private, and quickly. Joey clambered off Kari and helped him to his feet. He took her hand and led her back down the long corridor and up the stairs to his room.

Once they were inside Kari's room, he drew the curtains but left the windows open. It was a very warm evening and he wanted to enjoy the joyous atmosphere and chanting that filled the still air of the night.

Joey stood in the middle of the room, suddenly conscious that she was unsure of what to do next.

Kari wrenched the feather from his hair and dropped it to the floor as he walked towards her. His hands shook as he reached for her and as soon as their bodies touched, they were unstoppable. They had managed to be restrained outside, but now in the privacy of his room, there was no need. With haste, they made their way to his bed, hands touching one another's bodies and mouths constantly searching each other's.

Kari backed onto the bed first and Joey followed his lead. They knelt opposite each other, indicating they were going to make love the Kutan way. Excitement and adrenalin pulsated through their bodies. They buzzed like wires and electricity flowed between them as they tried to restrain themselves.

They mirrored each other's touch until every fibre of Joey's being was desperate for Kari to savage her in pure lust, but he clearly wanted to take his time, even though it was slowly killing her.

As he untied the leather straps from around his wrists and ankles, he looked looking imploringly at her.

Joey was unnerved and mesmerised by the burning passion from within his dark, brooding eyes.

His eyes remained focused on hers as he ran his hands over her body, down to the hem of her dress and pulled it up and off her body. She heard him take a deep breath in an attempt to regain control; she could tell restraint was hard for him too.

Joey ran her hands over his torso and down to the animal skin around his waist. She felt for the fastener to remove the heavy jewellery from around his waist but couldn't find an end or a beginning. Kari's hands moved to hers and together they undid the heavy jewels. He dropped them to the floor with a thud. Again, with her hands in his, he found the ties that held the breechcloth together; she undid it and pulled the cloth away. To her amazement, he was completely naked underneath it, displaying how much his body desperately wanted hers. Her eyes shot to his and they absorbed his.

Kari expertly removed her knickers so she was left wearing only her bra. He closed his eyes, fighting to gain control as he found it increasingly hard to resist her. He unfastened her bra and slipped it from her shoulders. Kari released a groan of anguish, and after a moment, his hands began to explore her body, whilst Joey mirrored his touch. They trembled, each yearning to complete their bond. He lifted Joey onto his lap. The intensity of his gaze was so deeply filled with lust, she could only imagine hers reflected the same.

He used every ounce of self-control; he never knew he was capable of such restraint. He wanted her so badly, but he also wanted this moment to be perfect, he needed to know she wanted him as much as he wanted her.

Joey was beginning to move into a different world when she heard Kari ask if she was still on the pill.

'Yes, why?'

For a long time Kari gazed at her beautiful face cupped between his large hands. He replied, 'I don't want to use any other form of contraception. I want to make love to you. I want us to feel the full pleasure of being as one, skin to skin, my seed released in you. I have never allowed myself this freedom with anyone before, but I want this with you.' Kari's eyes were sincere and full of honesty.

He kissed her gently before lifting her gently and pulling her onto him. As he sank deeply into her, they both released moans of bliss, feeling each other skin-to-skin, creating a first time experience. Tenderly, Kari moved in and out of her as he whispered in his native tongue. Joey didn't understand what he said, but the feelings flowing through her body were unimaginable. He controlled their movements and held Joey's hips firmly between his hands.

As Kari kissed her neck, she dropped her head back, allowing full access as he began to softly bite and suck the tender, soft skin of her neck. When he moved his mouth back up to hers, she pulled his hair back leaving his neck vulnerable, for the first time in her life Joey gave someone a love bite. She enjoyed hearing him moan with pleasure and his sound fuelled her desire. She also noticed he'd pulled himself free from her and was trying to control his breathing. She held his face in her hands and kissed him seductively, teasing him incessantly with her tongue.

He laid her down before lying beside her. They looked wantonly at one another; the passion and need for each other evident. Both their bodies shook, each wanting to bring heightened pleasure to the other, pushing to the brink, neither wanting it to end. Kari wanted Joey to reach complete fulfilment and gently he roused her further with his fingers. Slowly, he beckoned her to satisfaction and she gasped, her muscles tightened deeply within her, causing her body to explode. She begged him to come with her.

Quickly, he pulled her legs around his hips as he sank deeply into her. She cried his name as he thrust harder and faster. She clung to his body as she orgasmed and Kari relentlessly drove through her clenching muscles. The moment intensified as she felt him release deeply within her. Neither of them had experienced anything like it before. After they were spent, they lay gently trembling in each other's arms; Kari kissed her head and stroked her body tenderly.

A long while later, Joey said finally, 'I think I've died, I can't move.'

'Me too.' Kari said, huskily, aware though they were both still firmly linked. He couldn't move even if he wanted to. They lay for a while, waiting for their breathing to steady. Eventually, Joey turned to look at him; Kari kept their legs entwined so their lower bodies remained as one.

'What was it you kept saying?' Joey asked Kari.

Kari smiled and pulled her closer. His gaze was intense as he looked deeply into her eyes, 'It translates as – my Gods, my Spirits, I love her, I love her.'

Joey stared back, not quite sure she heard correctly.

'I love you.' Kari said, simply.

Joey's eyes widened with his honesty and replied, 'I love you, too.'

They kissed with ferocious agitation and he began to thrust gently into her. They held each other tightly, not wanting to ever let go. This time they made love slowly and gently. Their lovemaking was breath taking, eyes locked on each other and slowly their moans turned into cries of pleasure. As their bodies crashed over the edge and the pleasure rolled over them in waves, Kari cried out, 'Oh Joey, I love you, I love you.'

Chapter 35

Joey woke up to a muffled noise. As she came around from her deep sleep, she realised she could hear faint moaning sounds. 'Goodness!' she exclaimed as she remembered it was a night fuelled by sex for the native tribe. She looked over at Kari who slept quietly next to her and couldn't help grinning to herself. He loved her. He actually said he loved her. As she propped herself up on her elbows, she realised she really needed to go to the toilet. Unfortunately, the sound coming from the couple next door was even louder in the bathroom.

Joey heard Kari call her name. Quickly she washed and dried her hands when she heard him call her name again, this time with more urgency. She came out of the bathroom to see Kari sitting on the edge of the bed about to leave it. 'Sorry, needed the loo and you were fast asleep.'

The look of relief on his face was palpable. 'I dreamt you had been here and then you were gone.' He held his hands out to her.

'I was woken by our neighbours…' Joey said as she tilted her head to the wall on the right.

'Oh. They seem to be having a good time!' Kari replied and pulled the duvet back for Joey to re-join him in his bed. He put his arms around her and they snuggled closely to each other.

'They've moved it up a gear.' Joked Kari.

They couldn't help but listen to their neighbours. 'Oh no, she's not… she is.' Joey said.

'What?'

'Listen, she's pretending to orgasm, wait, she'll be shouting yes, yes, yes in a moment.' And sure enough, the woman began screaming *yes* in ever increasing volumes, just as Joey predicted. 'It's like that scene from '*When Harry met Sally*'.' Joey sniggered.

They then heard great high-pitched squealing and a deeper groaning from a man also shouting yes. Kari's eyes widened with mock horror as he said, 'I think they've… finished.' They both chuckled. 'She sounded pretty convincing to me…' Kari added.

'No way, trust me, I speak from experience, that was fake.'

'Oh, really?' Kari muttered as he kissed her. 'You are a great actress, Miss Lewis, I must try harder.' He began to kiss her neck and proceed further down her body.

'No, not with you, I've never once pretended with you.' Joey said, trying not to giggle as he gently nibbled her collarbone.

'Would you tell me if I didn't satisfy you?' Kari's muffled voice came from under the duvet.

'Yes, I would. And you, would you tell me?' Joey was slightly nervous to ask.

Kari re-emerged from under the bedding. He looked her fully in the eyes and simply said, 'I'm no actor. What you see is what you get. You satisfy me more than I thought humanly possible. Now, can we show next door how it's really done?' With that Kari, went back under the covers to continue where he'd left off.

A while later, they lay in each others arms, gasping for air as their bodies recovered from another round of passionate love making. They became aware during their union that their neighbours were banging on the wall - not through their own pleasure but because they were letting Joey and Kari know they could hear them. Kari had gone beyond caring at this point, besides it was his house.

'I think they may be a little jealous.' Kari said as he held Joey tightly. 'I hope I don't know them well.'

'Please don't tell me it's your mother and father?'

'No, they live at the far end of the house. It could be anyone.' Kari said, before planting a kiss firmly on her head. 'Is this permanent?' Kari asked as he twisted a lock of Joey's hair.

'No. I was assured that a shower would remove the hair dye and fake tan.'

'Good. I'm not apposed to the new look but I prefer your natural look, if I'm honest.'

'I give you permission to scrub me clean.'

'Oh, I will, trust me, every last inch of your body.' Kari said as he kissed her tenderly on the lips. 'We may need to change the sheets, too.'

'What... oh!' Joey said as Kari pulled the covers back to reveal the streaked linen. 'Oops, sorry.' Joey said guiltily as she saw the mess that her fake tan had made. 'But... if you didn't get me so hot and sweaty, this wouldn't be an issue.

They lay contentedly with each other for a while, neither needing to fill the silence, until a low grumble came from Joey's stomach and she realised she hadn't eaten anything for nearly twenty-four hours.

'Is now a good time to get some food?' Kari asked.

'Sorry, all this exercise and no food isn't a great mix.' Joey looked sheepish.

'Stay here don't go anywhere, okay? I don't want to return with a mound of food to discover that you've gone.' Kari said, looking intently at her beautiful body.

'Why would I go anywhere when I know you're coming back... *with* food!'

Kari went to the bathroom and a moment later came out with a towel, wrapped around his waist. 'You did a good job by the way!' he said pointing to the bite mark she had given him. 'We're a matching pair.' Kari grinned as he left the room.

Kari reappeared quickly, carrying a tray laden with a variety of foods; he placed the food on the bed and walked back to close the door.

Just as Kari was about to shut the door, a woman emerged from the room next-door and said, 'Excuse me. Do you mind keeping the noise down in here, we're trying to sleep.'

Joey froze under the covers and then slowly pulled the duvet down from her face so she could see who was talking to Kari.

'We could ask the same thing.' Kari said, leaning on the doorframe.

'Oh. Kari, I didn't realise it was you.'

'It's my room, who else would be here?' Kari replied, coldly.

'Well, clearly you're not alone.' The beautiful native woman said as she tried to look further into the room. 'If you don't mind being just a little quieter, we'd really appreciate it.'

'The thing is, Arabella, when you're in the throws of deep love, you're unaware of what sound comes from each other's body, you're enticed into pleasing your partner. All we're doing is responding naturally to the pleasure we both feel. If I could be quieter, I would, but when you're don't fake pleasure, it's very hard to control it. Now, if you don't mind, I feel the need to make more *noise,* as you put it.'

Without another word Kari closed the door on the open mouthed, red-faced woman, concisely shutting her out of his life in more ways than one.
The look on the woman's face was priceless as Joey stuffed the corner of the duvet in her mouth to stop herself from crying out loud with laughter.

Kari climbed onto the bed and tugged the duvet free from her mouth.

'I can't believe you just did that, Kari!' Joey said as tears of laughter rolled down her face. 'Do you know her?'

'Yes, that was Arabella, my ex.' Kari replied as he passed her a cup of coffee.

'No... Oh God, and she... Oh God, no.'

Kari nodded.

'And, we heard... Oh crap, no.'

Kari nodded again and passed Joey some food, 'At least she knows I've moved on.'

'Yes, but... she's going to wonder who was in here last night.'

'Correction, who is still in here this morning,' Kari said, taking a bite of his toast.

'Fair enough, but isn't she just the littlest bit curious, won't she talk to your parents?'

'Oh, trust me, she's curious. Why do you think she almost barged her way into my room?'

'Did she know this is your room?'

Kari looked pointedly at Joey.

'Okay, stupid question, of course she knows it's your room.'

Kari swallowed, quickly. 'She was a long time ago; she is not my present or future, in any way, shape or form. If I had my way, I'd have wanted you to sit proudly in my bed for her to see.'

'I can't, I'm not meant to be here!' Joey worried as she helped herself to some toast.

'But, thankfully, you are.' Kari said simply. They ate in silence.

'Will she tell your parents you had someone in your room last night?' Joey asked.

'Yes, without a shadow of doubt. Arabella was never one to shy away from awkward situations. If she can spread some gossip, then, she will. She may throw a spanner in the works though as she may have seen the bite mark and therefore think it was native woman I was with last night. I can almost hear her running down stairs to spread the word.' Kari said, tucking into some fruit.

'Well, I guess it takes the scent off me for a while, but what will you tell your parents when they ask?'

'Nothing.'

'Okay, I guess they don't need to know. It's none of their business.' Joey tried not to look dejected.

Kari removed the remainder of the food from the bed and placed it on the table before sitting on the edge of the bed next to Joey. He put a finger under her chin and lifted her face up so he could look into her, now sad, eyes. 'We need to talk.' Kari said, gently.

Joey nodded, suddenly a lump formed in her throat, she knew her bubble was about to burst. She fought bravely to stop the tears that were beginning to prick her eyes.

Kari could see tears begin to well in her eyes, and he knew he needed to reassure her, and quickly.

Before he could begin, Joey said, 'It's okay, you don't need to explain anything. I have a number of a taxi firm; if I can just have five minutes, I'll be out of your hair for good. We can leave everyone guessing as to who you were with last night, I won't say anything I promise, no-one need never know…'

The whole time Kari was shaking his head, willing her to stop, but she didn't, in the end he gently placed a finger to her lips, 'Ssh, please.' Amazingly, she did.

'Three weeks ago, my world fell apart when my mother handed me your feather and letter. I believed you had left me because you didn't want to be with me anymore.' Joey went to speak but Kari put his finger back on her lips, silencing anything she was about to say and smiled.

'I was unable to function. I couldn't eat, or sleep. I was foul to everyone. I was low, pretty low. I wanted to fly to England, find you and ask you come back to me. Lacroix and Solonge intervened and that was when Solonge took my place and went to England. We agreed I'd be better working on the new legislation I was writing. I started writing the new legislation after our time in France. Remember I went to see Luca?'

Joey nodded.

'I needed to tell him what I was proposing and I needed his support. I knew I had to do something, I was falling head over heels in love with you and I was not prepared to choose between you or my tribe.' Joey sat in stunned silence as he told her how the tribe has to change, not necessarily for his benefit, but for the future of the tribe. He told her about his Great Grandfather's brother who had been dismissed from the tribe generations before.

'I understand that you left me as you felt there was no choice – I had to choose either you or the tribe. You believe I would end up regretting my decision and hate you. Joey, I could never hate you, besides, don't I deserve to make that decision for myself?' Kari looked intently at her.

Joey knew what he was saying made sense, but she still didn't want him to risk losing everything for her.

Kari continued, 'The tribe must move with the times in order to survive. Of course, now that I have first hand experience, I feel more passionate than ever to get this new legislation passed. My mother and father reacted badly because they are scared. They don't want to lose me and they realise I have never been this serious about anyone before.'

Kari got up and walked to a chest of drawers and pulled out the folded pouch of leather.

Joey recognised it instantly. She put a hand to her mouth in an attempt to hide her gasp.

'I want you to wear my feather again, Joey.' He placed the leather pouch in her lap. Looking into her eyes, he said, 'I love you, Joey, more than I have ever loved anyone. I *need* you by my side. I never want to experience the loss I felt when you left me again.' He held her face in his hands and wiped her tears. His eyes were gentle and pleading. 'Please, say you'll wear my feather?'

Joey choked, 'Yes', and he pulled her face towards his and kissed her lips, extremely softly. He then took the feather necklace and tied it securely around her neck. Once it was safely tied, he kissed her again and held her tight. He didn't want her to see the relief on his face. His relief was immense and he blinked away the tears that threatened to escape.

They held each other for a good while, no sound from either of them.

Joey was the first to pull away. 'So, what happens now?'

'I want to spend the day in bed with you, loving you.'

It was around lunchtime when Kari asked where Joey's clothes were.

'In your apartment, in the city,' Joey replied.

'Ah, my bachelor pad. I hardly ever use it. It's more an investment but it comes in handy when I need to escape from here.' Kari suddenly stopped mid-flow. 'So, you were with Solonge the day before she got married with her bridal companions?'

Joey nodded. She could see Kari trying to work working something out in his head.

'I'm not sure what your thinking, but yes, I met Eyota and she's lovely, I slept in your bed with Solonge, and I saw the picture taken of us, at the Nice ball.'

'You know me so well. Did you like the apartment?'

'Very modern! I thought it belonged to a man but didn't know it was yours. When Solonge showed me where I would be sleeping, I could smell you, but it could have just been the soap in the bathroom. But, when I saw the picture of us, I knew it had to be yours, I can't imagine why anyone else would want it.

Solonge told me it was in fact your apartment, but was concerned I wouldn't want to stay if I'd have known. The weirdest thing was that I felt nearer to you than I had in weeks and I was more than happy to stay.'

'And Eyota?'

'Like you said she is lovely. She is sincere and very caring, and before you ask, no, we did not compare notes!' Joey said as she poked him in the ribs.

'I wasn't even thinking it!' Kari yelped in protest.

'So, I need to get your clothes sent here. I can't have you eating supper tonight, naked in front of my family.' Kari got out of bed and pulled on a pair of jeans and a t-shirt.

'Wait, what do you mean have dinner with your family? Wouldn't it be easier if I just leave and let you carry on with your legislation before coming back into your life?'

'No.' Kari answer, firmly and left the room, leaving a gaping Joey in his bed.

Kari finally located Luca at the stables, brushing down the horse he'd just ridden.

Luca looked up as he saw Kari approach. 'Ahh, the Cracken awakes!' Luca teased.

'I've been busy.'

'So I hear, and now see.' Luca pointed to his neck to signify the bite mark on Kari's neck.

'Let me guess, Arabella has spoken to you?' Kari enquired,

'You've got it in one. She left before I went riding saying she couldn't sleep, there was too much noise coming from your room.' Luca raised his eyebrows. 'Who is the unfortunate female to fall victim to your charm, anyone I know?' He didn't see Kari with anyone yesterday, but maybe he needed a woman to help ease the pain from losing Joey.

Kari smiled at his younger brother wondering whether to tell him straight away or to wait until dinner tonight. He had always been honest with Luca and decided not to change the habit of a lifetime. Luca was staring at him, expectantly.

'Joey.'

'No! *The* Joey?' Luca questioned with an excited tone.

'Well, how many Joey's do you think I've been sleeping with?' Kari picked up a brush and helped brush down the horse that was starting to get impatient.

'I had no idea she came to the wedding.' Luca responded, taken aback.

'Neither did I. She was there to complete the circle for Solonge and Lacroix and hid throughout the ceremony. It wasn't her intention to be found.'

'I don't understand?' Luca questioned.

'She arrived with Solonge and intended to leave without me being any the wiser.' Kari sighed.

'How did you find her?' Luca was intrigued.

'It's hard to explain. It's going to sound very odd but I was drawn to her. It was almost as if I sensed her.'

Luca looked at Kari, sceptically.

'I know it's hard to understand, but something, I'm guessing spiritually, drew me to her. I found her hiding behind the old log store. She tried to leave but I stopped her. Then, the rest, well, how shall I put it...'

Luca raised his hands, 'It's okay; I don't need to know anymore. Suffice to say, I heard enough from Arabella.' Luca smiled fondly at his older brother. 'What happens now?'

Kari stopped brushing and rested his hand on the horse shoulder, 'I'm not entirely sure, but I know Joey needs her suitcase from my apartment. Would you mind getting it for me, please?'

'Sure, no problem.'

Kari handed Luca his keys.

'But, then what?' Luca asked.

Kari smiled, 'An interesting time. I want Joey to stay until Wednesday morning so that I can then take her to France for a short holiday.' Kari went back to brushing the horse. 'I had been planning to flying to England to find her anyway, but now she's here, I think the best thing for us is a short holiday, together. I have the meeting with The Elders on Tuesday and I hope for a positive result, now more than ever.'

'Me too!' Luca replied, quickly. 'Otherwise, you and Joey could get very serious and before we know it, you'll be dismissed from the tribe and I'll be expected to fill your shoes.' Luca shuddered. 'I know you love your job, Kari, but I've had a taster these last few weeks and I can't tell you how much I'm wanting to go home to my life. We have to get this legislation passed.'

Kari nodded. He knew his brother had his own life that he was aching to return to, however, he was eternally grateful for Luca being here.

'I'll tell you what though, I'm very much looking forward to meeting the woman who's stole my big brothers heart.' Luca smirked at Kari.

'Don't you go getting any ideas!' Kari pointed his finger at Luca in mock threat.

'Have I ever trodden on your toes? If your flying out on Wednesday, maybe we could fly together?'

'I'd like that.' Kari smiled at his younger brother.

'Right, I'd better go and run your errand. I'll leave Joey's suitcase outside your bedroom door.' Luca said as he began to walk away, tossing the keys in the air as he walked. 'Oh, Arabella bumped into mother as she was leaving, so she knows you had a visitor last night.' Luca smiled and turned to walk to the cars.

Kari smiled to himself. He knew he had an interesting time ahead, a rough time perhaps, but he knew with Joey by his side, he would succeed. He led Luca's horse back into the stables and gave it a long drink before leaving it in peace.

Chapter 36

True to his word, Luca left Joey's suitcase outside Kari's bedroom door. When Joey opened it, she realised she didn't have much to wear. She chose what she thought was the most acceptable pair of trousers and she and Kari walked downstairs to have dinner with Gahenge, Aiyana and Luca.

Kari had spoken at great length to Joey before leaving the safe haven of his room. He tried to reassure her that all would be okay and he wouldn't leave her side for one moment. She didn't look very convinced, if anything, she looked petrified!

Together they walked towards the dining room, a room that was filled with horrible memories for Joey. Kari looked at Joey and noticed her faced had paled. They stopped. 'Are you okay?' he asked.

'No.' Joey said, nervously, as her voice strangled in her throat.

Kari took her hands. 'Wait here a moment,' he said as he stooped down to look into her eyes.

Joey nodded and watched Kari walk away and into the dining room. The little courage she had evaporating with each distancing step.

As Kari entered the room, three pairs of eyes looked at him. He asked the server to arrange another setting because he had a guest. The server nodded and without a word, hurried to arrange another setting at the table.

'Kari, we were beginning to wonder where you were!' Aiyana looked fondly at her elder son. He had made her so proud yesterday at the wedding. He looked magnificent; she only wished it had been his wedding. She also knew he'd had a woman stay the night in his room, Arabella had told her earlier. Aiyana would not normally be happy with the fact he'd moved so quickly to the bedroom, but it meant he was hopefully getting over the English woman.

'Sorry, I've been busy.' Kari explained. 'I have invited someone to dinner. Please, I ask you to make her feel welcome.' He looked at his mother and father and waited for them to nod. Luca began to grin.

Kari left the room to get Joey and found her standing exactly where he'd left her, too scared to move. He gently grasped her clammy hand and led her into the dining room. Kari smiled back encouragingly.

Together they walked into the room. 'May I introduce, Joey.' He stood with his arm protectively around her waist - Aiyana and Gahenge were stunned and sat open mouthed.

Luca got up from the table and walked towards his brother and Joey. 'I am very pleased to meet you, Joey,' shaking her hand and smiled reassuringly at her.

Joey felt a little more confidence after Luca's warm welcome but she didn't even want to look towards Kari's parents. She could feel the cold, unwelcoming atmosphere emanating from them.

Luca went back to his seat and Kari walked Joey to her place at the table. He held her chair out for her and once she was seated he sat next to her. He was going to be with her every step. He was proud of how she was trying to hold her head high, even though she was clearly and understandably very apprehensive.

Joey knew she had to remain dignified. 'Good evening Mr and Mrs Kutan.' Joey said, acknowledging them both. They still sat open mouthed and stared at her.

Nobody said a word. The silent air fell heavy in the room. Aiyana moved her hand across to Gahenge and placed it on top of his. He looked at her and she looked at him, communicating through their pointed glances.

Finally, Gahenge turned to Joey. 'Welcome Joey.' Aiyana smiled at her.

Joey didn't realise until that moment, she'd been holding her breath. She returned their smile and felt Kari squeeze her knee.

Whilst the food was served, Kari took a moment to reflect upon the people sitting at the table. The four most valued and loved people in his life. The anguish he'd witnessed in his mother's eyes just a couple of week's prior had faded and was now replaced with hope, love and sincerity. His father sat proud, his mouth set with the ever present rigid determination, yet there was warmth in his eyes betraying the softness of his character which he kept so well hidden. His brother Luca had an enviable ease of character that never failed but lighten any situation. Amusement danced around his warm eyes, a smile always present to his mouth. And then there was Joey. She looked a little short of petrified, and understandably so. He could watch her all day and never tire. He observed her fast and shallow breathing. Suddenly she turned her head and smiled at him, as if knowing he was watching her. Instantly he was drawn to her radiant smile and beautiful eyes, showing him the depth of her soul. He knew it wasn't possible to love another as he did her.

Once the delicious food was served, conversation started to flow. Nobody raised a question as to why Joey was at the table. She was relieved, because she didn't want to answer any difficult questions.

Aiyana and Gahenge noticed Joey wore Kari's sacred feather, and that both her and Kari had the love bite associated with their special lovemaking. They knew that their spirits would again be bonded, and neither of them wanted to put their son through pain again.

'What are your plans next week, Kari?' Gahenge asked.

'I have meetings all day tomorrow and then on Tuesday we meet with The Elders to discuss the new legislation.' Kari put down his knife and fork. 'I would love Joey to stay here during this time, if not, we will go to my apartment.'

Aiyana answered, 'Joey is most welcome to stay here.'

'Thank you, I appreciate you making us feel welcome. I was going to take a week's holiday as of Wednesday, originally to fly to England to find Joey, but now I don't have to, as she's here.' He squeezed Joey's hand and smiled warmly at her. 'However, I would still like to take the weeks holiday and fly to Nice to spend some quality time with Joey.'

Gahenge chewed his food slowly, allowing him time to answer appropriately. 'I know you need a holiday, Kari, and of course you may use the

Villa. Enjoy your time together; I will look after things here in your absence. Who knows, by then you may have the answers you need for your legislation.'

Kari appreciated what his father had said, it meant a great deal to see his parents were trying to accept Joey.

'So, dare I ask what you're going to do, Joey, whilst Kari is tied up in meetings?' Luca asked.

'I'm not sure. I wouldn't mind visiting the city to buy some clothes. I didn't bring much with me.'

Kari answered, 'I could live to regret this but, can I suggest spending the day with Luca tomorrow? I'm sure he can find ways to entertain you. However, on Tuesday, Luca will be with me, but I can arrange for you to get to and from the city?'

'Oh Kari, you're going to let me spend the day with Joey and you don't think I'll be tempted to tell her all your dark secrets?' Luca teased.

'That's what concerns me.'

'It all sounds great to me!' said Joey. 'Besides, I'm sure there's nothing that bad!'

'Oh, you just wait, Joey,' said Luca grinning. Kari shook his head in despair.

'Only believe half of what he says!' Kari grimaced at Joey.

'Then, I'd suggest you had better make that half juicy, Luca!' Joey laughed.

Gahenge and Aiyana couldn't help but notice the relaxed nature they saw in Kari. They couldn't remember him being so at ease with anyone before. Luca clearly liked Joey too. Aiyana also thought it would be helpful for Luca to spend time with the woman that had stolen Kari's heart. She knew he'd honestly answer any questions she intended to ask him tomorrow.

As the meal ended Joey couldn't fail but notice the warmth and acceptance she was beginning to feel from Aiyana and Gahenge towards her. There was no denying there wasn't still a degree of apprehension, but now she saw warmth and hope where before there was none.

After a very pleasant meal, Gahenge and Aiyana retired to their living room. They said they were tired, but the other three knew it was so they could talk about Joey. Luca, Kari and Joey sat in the main living room, comfortably chatting and talking about places Luca could take Joey tomorrow.

Joey was excited to be spending time with Kari's younger and very easy-going brother. Kari was pleased to know that Joey would be looked after and he wouldn't return tomorrow and discover she'd been pushed back to England.

That night Joey and Kari made love tenderly. There was no hurry, just an expression of their love. They slept soundly – Joey because she was exhausted and Kari because he saw hope in his parents that he hadn't seen before. Maybe, just maybe, and with time, they would see what he saw in Joey.

Chapter 37

Kari rose early and quietly woke Joey. 'What time is it?' Joey asked, sleepily. 'Early. I just wanted to let you know I have to go to work but I will be back for dinner.'

'Okay.' Joey mumbled, her voice sleepily thick.

Kari kissed her gently on the forehead, 'Sleep well, my beautiful Joey, and don't believe everything Luca tells you.'

'Uh huh.' Joey replied, huskily.

'All I ask is that you're here when I get home tonight.'

'Uh huh.'

'Joey, promise me you'll still be here?'

'Promise…' She replied, although she was almost asleep.

He tucked her hair behind her ear, 'I love you, Joey.' Kari whispered and kissed her one more time, before leaving her in peace.

A couple of hours later, as Joey ate breakfast; she wondered where she would find Luca when suddenly, he emerged through the main doorway from the garden.

'Kari said I'd find you in here, eating!' Luca teased Joey.

'He knows I like food.' Joey replied with a smile. 'So, what are we doing today?'

'Is there anything you'd like to do?'

'Actually, there is. Could you give me some tips on how to ride a horse?'

'I'm not sure if Kari would like that. I'm a good rider but not to the standard of Kari, he should probably teach you. If you had an accident, he'd never forgive me.'

'Please, just a basic lesson would be fantastic. I have been out with Kari but I can't even get on the horse without help!'

Luca was unsure. He didn't want to risk her hurting herself but she looked desperate. 'Okay, but only the basics… I'm not going to take you galloping or anything like that.'

'Thank you, I'll listen to everything you say and I promise if it gets too much, we'll stop.'

'Let's just hope I don't live to regret this…' Luca muttered under his breath. 'Ready to go?' She nodded and together they walked to the stables. Luca felt decidedly more nervous than Joey.

As they approach the stables, Luca said, 'So, apart from the one time with my brother, have you ever ridden a horse before?'

'Once. My friend had a pony and I tried to ride it, but unfortunately I ended up slipping between the horse's legs as the girth wasn't done up tightly enough!'

This didn't reassure Luca. 'Okay, stay here.' He went off to talk to a groomsman and a little while later Luca emerged from the stables leading a horse. Thankfully, the horse didn't look that big. Luca called her over and as she walked nearer to them the horse seemed to grow before her eyes – it looked massive; suddenly, she didn't feel so brave after all.

'Joey, allow me to introduce Pallo. He's really gentle and I think should be good for you to learn the basics on.'

'Hi, Pallo,' Joey said, gingerly stroking his neck. The horse moved its head up and down very quickly in response. Joey hoped he liked her and wasn't telling her to bog off.

'Let's go to the training ring.' Luca said as he led Pallo. 'We normally take new horses in there, to break them in.' Luca explained.

'Except today you're going to break me in.' Joey couldn't help herself.

Luca laughed, 'Kind of.'

They turned a corner and came face to face with a large fenced off area of sandy earth. Luca opened the gate and led Pallo and Joey in. 'We're going to take it very slowly.' Luca explained. 'Firstly, put your foot in the stirrup and throw your other leg over behind the horse. I won't let go of the reins, I promise.'

Joey did as Luca instructed and, after a couple of attempts, she managed it. She sat on the back of the horse and suddenly felt like she was about ten feet off the ground. Luca attached a leading rein and handed Joey the main reins.

'Hold the reins tight like this.' He showed her. 'Excellent. Now, I will lead you around the arena.' As they began to walk, Luca reminded her to keep the reins taut and heels pushed down in the stirrups. 'Excellent, you're doing really well. How do you feel if we take it up a notch?'

'Fine.' Joey replied through gritted teeth.

'I will jog next to you. I'll keep hold of the leading rein but I'll need you to take the weight in your feet and rise and fall to the rhythm of Pallo.' After initial, unsuccessful attempts, Joey felt she was beginning to get the hang of it. Her thighs were beginning to ache. No wonder Kari's were rock hard!

'How are you feeling?' Luca asked, slightly out of breath.

'Great. It all feels good.'

'You're looking great. Maybe lessen the hold on the reins a bit, not too much, the more you give the more he'll drop his head and before you know it you'll be cantering around the ring. That's it, excellent. We'll make a horse rider of you yet.' Luca was pleased with how Joey was responding already.

'Pull gently on the reins and say *whoa*!' Luca instructed Joey. She did and the horse responded by slowing to a walk. 'Fantastic!' Luca said, out of breath. 'If Kari could see you now, he'd be really impressed.'

Joey smiled, she felt pleased with herself.

'How do you feel taking it up another gear?' Luca asked.

'Sure.'

'I'm going to attach the long leading rein and I'll stand in the middle of the arena whilst you circle me. I can't keep up this running, I'm not as fit as Kari.' Luca said before walking to the middle of the ring. 'Walk on!' he called out to Pallo, gently pulling the rein. Pallo moved as instructed, a gentle walk. 'Joey, gently tap his sides with your heels and remember the rhythm you had just now,

I expect him to start to trot. Excellent, you're doing perfectly.' Luca allowed them to complete a fair few circles around him. Joey was doing brilliantly, he felt confident she could try more. 'Okay, say whoa and again pull gently on the reins, that's it perfect,' Luca encouraged as Joey and Pallo stopped.

'If you can jump off Joey, I'm going to show you what to do next.'

'Luca, how do I jump off?' Joey asked.

'The reverse of how you got on. Take your right foot out of the stirrup and then swing your leg back behind you, and whilst holding onto the saddle, ease yourself to the ground, slowly, that's it, perfect. Can you stand over there and watch what I do?'

Joey sat on the fence and watched as Luca gracefully mounted Pallo and geed him up into a trot. 'See how I take my body weight into the stirrups, and see how I move so that when Pallo rises, I do as well, otherwise I'd end up crashing down on him, and trust me, he wouldn't like that. You were doing brilliantly and I'd like you to take him into a canter. This time see how I level my body out, leaving him full movement. My weight is distributed through both my legs and I have a tight hold on the reins. He hardly has any room to pull his head. If I let go a little more, watch what happens!' Luca lessened his hold on the reins just a bit and Pallo had full use of his head and took advantage, suddenly, they were galloping around the arena. Luca had full control but it showed how quickly things could change.

He pulled the horse to a stop. 'You see it's very important not to let the horse get the better of you. You need to stay in control. Don't worry, I'm not expecting you to get to that stage today. But, I wanted you to be aware that if you're not in control, things can change very quickly, and trust me, Kari would not like that to happen to you!'

Joey nodded, she understood. She got back on the horse, this time with relative ease. She held the reins confidently in her hands and Luca re-attached the leading rein.

'When you're ready, take him to a trot again, that's it, perfect, excellent!' He hadn't expected her to be this comfortable so early on in the lesson. 'Right, gently dig your heels into his sides and we'll go up to a canter. Perfect, I know it feels fast but keep the rhythm, you're doing really well. That's it take the weight in your feet.'

'My thighs!' Joey exclaimed as they began to burn from the exercise. She was desperately trying her best to concentrate and not fall off, but her legs felt like they were on fire.

'Three more circles, excellent!' Luca shouted. He was really impressed but didn't want to push her any further. 'Okay, say *whoa* and pull on the reins gently. Excellent, see how he's responding, come back to trot and then take him down to a walk.' Pallo was breathing heavily, he wasn't used to such exertions these days.

Joey pulled Pallo to a complete stop and grinned at Luca.

Luca could see why his brother had found Joey so endearing, she also had an amazing smile. 'You were brilliant!' Luca said to Joey. 'I think that's enough for today, I don't want you to get over confident. But, you should be really pleased with yourself.'

'Shall I get off?'

'Yep, the same as before.'

Joey dismounted from Pallo with ease this time. She went around to the horse's neck and slapped him kindly. 'Thank you Pallo, you were very patient and I hope I wasn't too restricting!' Joey said as she gently rubbed his neck. He seemed to like it as he whinnied moving his head up and down with excitement.

'You have another fan of the Kutan household.' Luca murmured, taking the reins and leading them back to the stables.

'Thank you, Luca. I wouldn't blame you if you hadn't have wanted to take me riding, but thank you, I really appreciate you taking the risk. At least now I can get on and off a horse with out looking like a complete muppet.' Joey smiled warmly at Luca.

They walked in companionable silence, Joey trying to remember everything Luca had taught her and Luca beginning to see what his brother saw in Joey.

Luca passed Pallo to a groomsman and turned to Joey and said, 'So, what now? Rock climbing? White water rafting? Any other surprises you'd like me to teach you?'

'No, I think I've used all my bravery for the day, but I'll hold you to it for another day.'

'How about something more leisurely? A walk to the lower woods, perhaps? The view is amazing from up there - it's the base of the Sacred Mountains. We can take a picnic and I'll tell you all of Kari's secrets?' Luca grinned.

'I'd like that. Don't keep anything from me.'

They went back into the house to freshen up. Luca asked her to meet him outside in half an hour.

Chapter 38

'I have enough food to feed an army!' Luca exclaimed as he emerged from the back door, half an hour later. Joey noticed that he had a large rucksack. She knew she liked food, but this was something else.

'How many days are we going for?' Joey teased.

'I told you, Kari said you liked food and he also said Madame Dupre mentioned you needed fattening up.' Luca teased her. 'Ready?'

'Can I help at all?'

'You can take that if you like?' Luca said as he pointed to the rucksack.

Joey bent to pick it up, *woah it's heavy*!

'No, I'm joking!' Luca laughed, 'I think you probably would have taken it if I insisted.'

They walked in companionable silence through the lush green meadow. Joey had walked here before but never as far as the woods in the distance. It looked a fair distance, but she was happy to be with her guide.

Joey liked Luca. He was similar to Kari, but at the same time, very different. They both had an exotic look, but Luca was much slighter in frame. He was not as tall or as muscular as Kari, he was leaner. Luca's face was softer too, he didn't have the sculptured cheekbones and jaw line that Kari had, she guessed he looked more like his mother. Joey also noticed that Luca's eyes were a lighter brown colour, rounder and not as deep set. One thing they both shared was the shape of their mouths, with the prominent cupids bow. Luca's hair was shorter and slightly wavy unlike Kari's, which was poker straight. Luca had a lovely nature. He seemed more relaxed than Kari, more like Kari when he was alone. She did imagine though that Luca could flare up at a moment notice and possibly not remain as controlled as Kari. He seemed less tame. Maybe it was the artistic streak in him, she wasn't sure. But, she liked his company and was glad to be spending the day with him. She hoped he liked her.

Like Kari, Luca divulged many interesting facts. He told her about the different birds and wildlife they came across and what importance they held to their environment. Not only did Luca teach Joey how to ride a horse, but he also taught her how to say something in the Kutan native language that would please Kari.

A good hour later, with the sun streaming down, they stopped by a stream to have a drink.

'It is truly beautiful here.' Joey acknowledged, looking around at the view.

'This is nothing. You should see the view from the mountain!' Luca said, pointing upwards.

'When did you last visit the Sacred Mountain?' Joey asked.

Luca was quiet as he thought. 'Well, I haven't been home for a good while, so I'm guessing possibly this time last year. No that's a lie; it would have been two years ago. Yes, definitely the latter.'

She felt there was more that Luca wanted to say.

In time, Luca continued, 'I had some questions that I needed answering so I visited to see if the Spirit Gods could help.' Luca stopped and looked thoughtful.

'Did it help?' Joey felt she had to ask.

'I guess you can say it did,' Luca reflected with an air of sadness. Joey didn't want to probe; she decided to let Luca tell her if he wanted, it was not her business to ask.

After a short break, they continued on their hike.

'Kari and I used to spend days and weeks up in the mountains when we were younger.' Luca smiled to himself, reliving memories.

Joey smiled back at him.

'We used to pack food and provisions, ride our horses and stay in our own little world for days at a time.'

'Were you very close when you were younger?' Joey asked.

'Yes, we still are. We may not see each other much, but we'll always be there for each other, no matter what.'

'Like you are now?' Joey asked.

'Exactly. Although, I'll be honest I have no desire to do what Kari does. He's amazing at his work and I totally respect him. But, if I'm expected to fill his shoes, well… let's just say I'm not willing.' Luca explained.

Joey didn't know how to answer that so decided to remain quiet.

Luca noted the lack of response; he knew she didn't want Kari to choose between her and the tribe. She'd already walked once and he didn't want to be the reason for her going again. He decided to change the subject.

'Let me tell you some things about Kari you may not already know.'

'Oh yes, and don't hold back! I'm stronger than I look.'

Luca told her about how they used to spend hours fishing in the stream that runs near the mountain cottage. How Kari taught Luca to spear fish. Kari was always much more successful, primarily because Luca didn't like to kill the fish, so, he often let them swim away.

He also told her how they used to make dams in the river and make deep pools to swim in. Their father used to tell them off because they were messing with nature, but they did it year after year anyway.

Kari also taught Luca how to dive off the great rocks through the waterfall. Incredibly dangerous, but great fun! Joey was beginning to see that Kari was in fact, a risk taker.

There was also the time, when Kari was about fifteen and Luca twelve and they had been careless in not disposing of the fish's heads and bones. Whilst they ate their catch, a large brown bear came investigating, a low deep growl reverberating from its chest heightened Luca's anxiety. Luca said he wanted to run back to the cottage and hide, but Kari told him to remain still and wait. He told Joey he wept, as he believed the bear was going to kill them as it gradually stalked closer and closer. Kari remained calm and in control the whole time and tried to reassure Luca that they'd be okay. Luca remembered that Kari reached for the gun they constantly carried. Joey asked would Kari have shot the bear? Luca said he would have, if he had to. Thankfully, the two boys stood their ground and after the bear ate all of the fish and bones before turning and disappearing into the woods. He explained that if he'd have ran to the cottage, the bear almost definitely would have chased him and probably killed him. Kari had saved his life and he would never forget it.

They finally reached the beginning of the woods and Luca opened the rucksack and unpacked a blanket for them to sit on. Joey also noticed he removed a rifle from a side pocket and lay it on the ground.

'Um, Luca, have you brought me here to finish me off?' Joey asked with a nervous laugh.

'Oh, God no. I'm sorry. We always carry a rifle if we come this far up to the woods. You never know when Mr Bear may return.' He laughed, 'I'm so sorry, it must look bad but I promise, I have not brought you here to shoot you.'

'Phew, you had me worried for a moment!' Joey replied.

Luca laid out the feast and he really had thought of everything. There were rolls, pieces of meat, cheese, salad, fruit, cakes, biscuits, crisps and finally, wine!

'You seriously think we're going to eat all of this?' Joey asked, an unmasked element of surprise in her voice.

'I hope so, I don't want to carry this load back!' Luca exclaimed.

'In that case, we had better get started.'

Luca poured them both a glass of wine and together they tried to make some form of headway through the food.

'Has Kari told you about his first crush, Shelby?' Luca cheekily asked Joey.

'No.'

'Let me think, he was about ten years old when he had his first crush on his school friend, Shelby. She was pretty, blonde and very, very Canadian. The kind of girl boys wanted to be with and girls wanted to be. She was top girl in every capacity. A member of the cheerleading team, class rep, you name it, she was 'the girl'. All the boys in the class fancied her and Kari knew he wasn't alone in fighting for her affections. I was very young but I remember the day when he came home from school and asked our nanny how they managed to keep the sheets so white, she informed him they added a little bleach to keep them crystal clean.' Luca stopped and began to chuckle. 'About an hour or so later, Kari came running back into our playroom, tears streaming down his very red blotchy face.' Luca was now laughing hard and wiping away tears of laughter from his eyes and continued, 'He'd only gone and found the bleach and had been applying it to his skin! Nanny was furious and after a considerable amount of diluting and a trip to the hospital, we discovered he'd been trying to turn his skin white.'

'Apparently he'd asked Shelby to the park and she'd refused him because he was dirty and brown, and she only liked white boys.' Luca shook his head. 'I think that is the only time a female has rejected Kari. It hit him hard and he didn't look at another girl for years. I wonder what's happened to Shelby?'

'Poor Kari, he's lucky he didn't permanently scar his skin!' said Joey, shocked and saddened by the story.

'Thankfully, he'd diluted the bleach like they did for the washing; otherwise he would have damaged himself. It was a hard lesson. Women are difficult to please but deep down we can't change the colour of our skin, no matter how hard we try.'

'But, he's a beautiful colour, you all are. Compared to me, pale and uninteresting.'

'Not to Kari you're not!' Luca looked intently at her.

It was the same look Kari often gave her.

'Whoever my brother decides to spend the rest of his life with they will be a very lucky woman. I'm not just saying it because he's my brother. He truly is amazing. I wish there were more men like him in the world.' Luca reflected.

'I remember a time when were about twelve and nine and we were playing chase round and round our parents private sitting room. We shouldn't have been in there and certainly not playing chase. Anyway, as boys do, it got a little out of control and I ended up falling into a table which sent one of mother's prize ornaments crashing to the floor!'

Joey grimaced as she pictured the event.

'Suffice to say, it was in a fair few pieces. I looked at Kari and promptly burst into tears, again! I knew we'd both be punished, but I more so because I'd knocked it over. Mother came rushing into the room and saw her beautiful ornament, smashed into a million pieces. I opened my mouth to explain when I heard Kari say it was his entire fault. He said he'd dared me to go in there and he knocked the ornament over by accident. I stood in silence as my brother took all the blame. I still feel guilty now. Why didn't I say something? It wasn't his fault. However, he was thrashed twelve times, one for every year of his age and grounded for two weeks, including not being allowed to ride. That was the worst part of punishment. Mind you, he couldn't have ridden even if he wanted to. It took him three days before he could sit, and even then it was with a cushion.' Luca looked at Joey and he saw the horror in her eyes. She held her hand to her mouth to hide her look of shock.

'Kari and myself swore there and then that we would never inflict pain on a child ever, no matter what crime had been committed. In sympathy, I didn't ride either. I still can't shake the feeling of great remorse I still hold today.' Luca said sadly.

Joey poured another glass of wine for them both and, as the wine took effect, they began to open up more.

'Have you mentioned how you feel to Kari?' Joey asked.

Luca shook his head, 'Do you see what I mean, though? He was and still is the best brother ever. I love him and I want him to be happy.' Luca stopped and looked at Joey. 'I can see you make him happy, Joey. I haven't seen him this… alive in years. I know he has never questioned his position before.' He saw the discomfort in Joey's eyes as she listened. 'I know it makes you uncomfortable, but believe me when I say Kari doesn't make decisions lightly. If he says he wants to be with you, then he does – 110%. I've seen the way he looks at you, it's as if you're his masterpiece. I think he was beginning to think he'd always be alone. I've never seen him so in love before.' Luca smiled warmly at Joey.

Luca wanted to reassure her that Kari was deeply in love with her and he understood why. He'd really enjoyed Joey's company and she was easy to talk to. They didn't feel the need to fill the silences. She didn't probe Luca for information and seemed genuinely interested in what Luca had to say. Luca could also see vulnerability in Joey's personality too. Maybe she had a deep wound that still needed to heal, he didn't know what it was, but he was sure Kari did. She was also very nervous around their mother and father, understandably after the way they treated her last time she visited. She was interesting and there was certainly more to her than meets the eye. He witnessed how determined she was at learning to ride the horse, he could only imagine she was like it in other areas of her life too.

Joey wasn't sure if she should pry but she was only going to ask one simple question, leaving it up to Luca to say more if he wanted. 'What about you Luca, is there someone special in your life?'

Luca turned his wine glass round and around in his hand, clearly deciding how to answer her direct question. Finally, he answered, 'Yes, there is.'

'Does she live in France?' Joey asked.

Luca was quiet for a long time and Joey was about to change the subject when Luca looked at her intently and answered, 'Yes, he does.'

He saw her register what he had just said, 'So, what's his name?'

'Pierre La Rouse.' Luca smiled. Joey noted the spark in his eyes when he said Pierre's name. 'I have been seeing Pierre for over two years and I've never told a soul until now.' Luca looked again at Joey.

Joey smiled, but not to question further. If Luca wanted to tell her more then she would listen, but she didn't feel that it was her place to ask.

'We met at the Louvre in Paris. I felt his presence before I even saw him. But, when we finally met each other, we both knew instantly that we were meant to be together. It all happened so fast, I don't really know if I was on earth for a few months. That was when I came back here, to ask my Spirit Gods for advice. I wasn't dating a member of the tribe, but to top it all, I was in love with a man.' Luca stopped and took in a deep breath.

'I stayed for five whole days but I didn't feel a thing. I believed they had deserted me. I guess they hadn't come across a gay native before.' Luca smiled, but Joey could see the pain in his eyes. 'I returned to Paris. I was lost. I couldn't talk to anyone; I would surely be rejected from my own family if they ever found out. You've seen how mother and father have treated you. Imagine how I would be treated, their own son, dating a white person and a man at that?'

'I can't imagine. Surely you can talk to Kari?' Joey suggested.

'No. I couldn't bear to see him look at me with disgust. He is a very proud man.'

'Yes, but he's seeing me and I'm not exactly ideal.'

'But at least you're a woman!' Luca replied.

'But, he's your brother. Granted, he'll be shocked, but in time, he'll understand.' Joey tried to explain.

'He would hate me. I'd revolt him and I couldn't bare that.'

'Luca, he could never hate you. I haven't known Kari long but I know he would never hate you.' Joey put her hand on his arm reassuringly.

Luca placed his hand on hers, 'Thank you for your kind words but I think I'll just live in ignorance for now. Maybe when things have calmed down, I'll talk to Kari, but not now. There's too much happening as it is.' Luca stopped and then chuckled; 'The tribe think I'm the back up plan if Kari leaves.' He stopped and smiled, 'Oh, what a big mistake they could be making.'

Joey smiled fondly at Luca.

'In many tribes I would be called *two-spirit* and I'd be honoured, respected even. But, oh no, not the Kutan Tribe – being attracted to the same sex is as taboo as dating another race.'

They talked about Luca's other passion, which was art, and Joey said she'd love to see his work one day. Luca hoped she would still be around to show her. He really liked Joey and he was going to fight with Kari for her acceptation within the tribe.

Chapter 39

Much later that afternoon a slightly merry Luca and Joey made their way back to the house with a relatively full rucksack of food. Luca took her to the games room where he tried to teach her how to play a games console. They were so engrossed in their game they didn't hear Kari enter the room.

'It's alright for some to spend the day having fun, some of us have to work,' teased Kari.

Joey threw down her controller and ran into Kari's arms. They hugged each other tightly and Kari drew back to kiss her gently on the lips.

'Have you missed me or have you had too much fun?' Kari asked, smoothing her hair behind her ears not losing contact with her eyes.

'Yes, I did miss you but Luca has kept me entertained all day. I didn't realise the time.'

Kari kissed her nose as she tilted her head up to maintain eye contact.

'Do you believe all the sordid tales Luca told you?'

'Of course.' Joey's smile spread into a grin as she said, 'Have you seen Shelby recently?'

'Oh no, I'd forgotten about Shelby.' Kari groaned, looking at his brother, 'Luca, what stories have you been telling?'

'Only the truth, Kari, only the truth.' Luca smiled and looked affectionately at the relationship between both Joey and Kari. He wished one day he could share his relationship with Pierre with his family. 'Are you going to desert me, now my good-looking, older brother has returned? Am I left to defeat the aliens alone?' Luca asked Joey whilst trying to concentrate on his game.

Joey was about to reply when Kari said, 'No, make the most of Joey. I'm off to shower and change. I look forward to hearing all about your day,' he said quietly to Joey before he kissed her slowly. He pulled away but desperately wanted Luca to disappear so he could show her exactly how much he had missed her.

Kari came back a little while later and with Joey's insistence, took over her controls. She enjoyed watching the two brothers trying to defend earth. She imagined how inseparable they must have been as children and the fun they must have had. Thanks to Luca's tales that afternoon, she was beginning to understand Kari's history. She also hoped one day Luca would be able to confide in Kari about his sexuality.

The two men were laughing and working together when the supper-bell rang. Luca turned off the console and the three of them went to leave the room. As Joey followed Luca, Kari pulled her back and closed the door. He pulled her into a firm embrace and kissed her passionately. How he had missed her today, his hands began to wander to intimately dangerous places on her body.

'Kari, we're going to be late…' Joey gasped between kisses.

'Right now, I really don't care.'

'No, you know what they say – the best things come to those who wait.' Joey gently pushed him away, re-opened the door and walked towards the dining room.

Kari couldn't believe what he'd just witnessed. He stood there, turned on but alone as Joey walked off, mid-kiss. He stood stunned for a minute then ran his hand over his chin, shook his head and followed Joey down the hallway.

He entered the dining room to see a smirking Joey and Luca, and his baffled mother and father.

Kari sat next to Joey and looked at her questioningly. Joey smiled in response as the dinner ritual of Aiyana tasting the food before dinner began.

Luca dominated conversation throughout dinner as he enthused about the day he and Joey had spent together. He didn't mention the riding lesson he'd given Joey. He felt it would be best for her to tell Kari, if she wanted to.

During the meal, Joey felt Kari's eyes burning into her, his energy burning into her soul demanding her attention that she look at him, but she didn't. She knew he was taken aback that she had left him mid-kiss and he was clearly questioning why.

Joey wasn't the only one to notice Kari's bewildered glances. Aiyana saw that Kari had hardly eaten and he looked longingly at Joey, but it appeared Joey was trying her best to ignore him.

The subject of tomorrow's meeting came up and Joey discovered it would be held in the Great Hall at Cha Tik Warro. The meeting would start at 10 o'clock continuing indefinitely.

Kari had arranged for Joey to have a driver and protector all day who would take her to the city and escort her. She was unsure of how she felt about this and would have been very happy to leisurely wander around the shops alone.

As Gahenge suggested they retire Joey stopped them and repeated what Luca had taught her earlier. Her bravery diminished as she looked at the stunned faces of Gahenge and Aiyana. She heard Kari cough, trying to hide his laughter and Luca began to snigger. Joey felt herself blush.

'Did I not pronounce it correctly?' Joey asked, concerned she'd mispronounced something and offended Kari's parents.

'No,' Luca said between laughing, 'you said everything perfectly.'

'Thank you. I am pleased,' Kari said trying to retain a bubble of laughter that threatened to explode at any moment.

'Aiyana, shall we smoke the pipe before we retire?' Gahenge said, breaking his wife's startled stare.

'Yes, yes I think it's a wise idea. Please, excuse us.'

Joey watched as Kari's parents hurried out of the room. They couldn't get away fast enough.

Once they were alone, Luca and Kari burst into fits of laughter leaving Joey none the wiser.

'What?' Joey said concerned she'd really upset Aiyana and Gahenge.

'Oh, Joey,' Kari sighed as he pulled Joey into his arms and kissed her forehead. 'There is never a dull moment with you.'

'All I said was *"Thank you, Kari, you make me really happy".*'

Luca's laughter erupted again.

'Joey. Sweet, innocent, trusting Joey, I told you not to believe everything my brother tells you,' Kari said, trying to maintain his laughter again.

Joey was suddenly weary. 'Luca, what did you teach me to say?'

'Thank you.'

'And?' probed Joey, knowing there was more.

'In my defence, I thought you wanted to surprise Kari.'

'Luca…'

Kari coughed, regained his composure and said, 'You pronounced every word beautifully.'

'Okay, but what did I say?' Joey asked Kari.

Kari translated for her. 'Thank you, Kari. You're the best lay I've ever had.'

'Give or take a word or two,' Luca added quietly.

'Oh no.' Joey mumbled as she put her head in her hands. 'I can't believe I just said that to your mum and dad of all people.

'As I said, it was spoken beautifully and, I hope, truthfully,' said Kari.

'Luca, you git!' Joey said as she began to laugh. 'How am I ever going to face them again?'

'Don't worry. It could be worse, at least they think Kari satisfies you.' Luca said as he got up from the table and walked towards the sitting room followed by Kari and a red-faced Joey.

Once they were in the sitting room, Luca and Kari sat opposite one another on the large comfortable sofas – but Joey chose to curl up in a small armchair by the fireplace.

Kari looked at Luca, and then to Joey, and then back to his brother. Joey seemed oblivious to Kari, waiting patiently on the sofa for her to join him. He even sat with his arm resting on the back of the couch. It took an immense amount of control not to stride over and physically place her next to him. He needed to feel her, he'd missed her so much and now they were finally together, there were metres of space between them.

Luca could feel the sexual tension, which was hanging in the air between his brother and Joey. He could see Kari was trying to maintain a level of control, unlike Joey who looked cool and collected. After an agonising half an hour Luca couldn't take the sexual tension any longer and excused himself, leaving Joey and Kari alone.

As soon as Luca had closed the door behind him, Kari leapt up to turn the key in the lock.

Joey could see the desire in his eyes and she started to tremble with anticipation.

He slowly walked towards her. With every step he took, he could see the yearning in her eyes. He stood in front of her and said, 'I have been patient long enough.' He dropped to his knees and pulled her body to his and kissed her deeply, his lips and tongue demanding her mouth. She let out a moan of desire, which was muffled by his mouth.

Kari groaned and kissed her again passionately. 'I was already turned on but hearing you say that, in my language, makes me want to…' he finished his sentence with a phrase from his own language. Before she could ask for a translation, he held her face and kissed her. He needed her and he couldn't wait any longer. He positioned her towards the edge of the chair and pulled her jeans and knickers down. In one swift movement he undid his jeans and thrust into her, causing them both to cry out with pleasure. It wasn't long before they both reached the point of climax. The waiting time had heightened their desire.

'Dear God, Joey, I love you,' Kari said as he looked into her eyes adoringly.

'I know.' Joey whispered.

'I've wanted to do that all day but you left me waiting earlier and it drove me to distraction. I hardly ate a thing!' Kari laughed. 'I've discovered one thing, if I want you, I have to have you, otherwise, I can't concentrate.' Kari kissed her passionately.

'Why do you think I sat over here?'

Kari looked at her confused, 'Why did you sit away from me?'

'Because, I don't think I could have stopped myself either. Luca had been so good all day the last thing I wanted to do was disgrace myself in front of him.'

Kari laughed quietly.

'However, if you don't take me to bed very soon, I'm afraid I can't be held accountable for my actions!' Joey replied, kissing him seductively.

Kari didn't need to be told twice. They rearranged their clothes and hurried up the stairs, Kari practically dragging Joey behind him.

That night Gahenge slept restlessly. During the night he woke with a start from a vivid dream. Aiyana was disturbed from her slumber as she felt Gahenge sit bolt upright.

'Gahenge, Gahenge, it's okay, my love, it was just a dream,' she soothed.

'Oh, Aiyana, it was more than a dream. The Spirit of Ahote visited me. He said the new legislation, which Kari has proposed, has to be passed. If not, the tribe will not be able to continue. Kari is the Chief to succeed all Chiefs; we have to believe in Kari and to support him. So, you see Aiyana, I have to sign the legislation and I have to help Kari convince the others.'

Chapter 40

When Kari entered the Great Hall with Luca, all The Elders were already present. They formally greeted Kari and Luca and waited in silence for Gahenge.

A few moments later Gahenge arrived and took his place at the head of the table and the meeting began. 'I'm glad we are all able to make it today as there are many important matter to discuss.' He turned to his elder son, 'Kari, I will hand over to you, for now.'

'Thank you, Father.' Kari replied. 'I would also like to thank everyone for coming today. I hope we can end the day with a decision, one way or the other.' He then looked each Elder directly in the eye; Henrique was the only one to look away.

'We are here today to discuss the Relationship Legislation I presented last time we met. Have you all read the documents outlining the proposal?'
Various murmurings of yes were followed by a few nods of the head.
'Excellent. I believe it was very straight forward, but I welcome any feedback or questions.'

Kari waited patiently for the first person to talk. He thought that as soon as someone started, he would be flooded with questions. He looked around the room with encouragement, waiting for the first person to speak.

Kangee cleared his throat. 'Kari. Isi and I took the liberty to meet and discuss the new proposal you put together. I believe I can speak for both of us when I say that at first we were very defensive about what you suggested – we didn't understand the need for change. It's worked for our tribe for centuries, why alter things now? But, as is often the case, you're right. We no longer live in the fifteenth century. Times have changed and it's time our tribe evolved with inevitable change. If we don't rethink our rules now, we run an enormous risk of not having a tribe in a couple of generations.' Kangee stopped to make sure everyone had correctly heard what he had said.

Kari sat quietly, without betraying any emotion, nodding occasionally.

Isi continued, 'Kangee and I have signed and agreed to your new legislation. It's the only way forward, you have our total backing.' Both men passed their signed documents to Luca.

'Thank you, Kangee and Isi. That is very understanding of you both and I thank you for your trust in me. If the legislation is passed, I will endeavour to do all I can and will not let you down.' Kari replied, he hoped his tone was neutral.

Matwall was the next to speak. 'I have also read the document and it makes a very believable solution to what could be a problem for you, Kari. I can't help but believe you want this legislation passed for your own benefit. So what. We have lost fifteen members of the tribe these past two years, but they knew the rules. If they truly believed in our traditions they would not be interested in finding love elsewhere.'

Again, Kari sat there and noted what had been said. But, before he could reply, Hok'ee continued, 'I agree with Matwall. You want this legislation in place because you are finding it difficult to find a woman to marry. I have two possible solutions.'

'I'm interested to hear what they are, Hok'ee,' Kari said sincerely.

'One, we find you a suitable wife.' Hok'ee noticed Kari's eyes widen at his suggestion.

'And the other option?' Kari asked.

'You don't have to marry but we find you a suitable woman in the tribe who can bear your heirs.' Hok'ee said with a degree of pride in his voice.

Kari blew the air from his lungs and sat and smiled. He didn't quite know how to address those interesting solutions.

Luca looked at Kari. He didn't know if he could prevent his manic laughing that threatened to escape.

Gahenge sat in silence and waited for his elder son to react. He was impressed that he hadn't raised his voice at the absurd suggestions.

Finally, Kari spoke. 'Tell me, what message does it give the rest of the tribe for me to marry a woman I don't love, or have bastard children with a surrogate?'

Hok'ee was quick to defend himself, 'It shows that you want the tribe to remain true blood and strong. That you want to keep the bloodline clean.'

'I can think of two other solutions,' Kari said calmly, 'my legislation gets passed or I remove myself from the tribe.'

A hushed whisper broke out around the table.

Luca couldn't believe what he was hearing. He couldn't just sit there and listen to it anymore. 'Can I just say, I can't believe you would even consider the possibility of allowing Kari to step down from his deserved role, I have seen what my brother does and it amazes me that he has the strength to continue most days. I have had to go to meetings in his place and I am totally baffled. With the greatest of respect, I really don't think you appreciate exactly what he does and who he is.'

Gahenge interrupted, 'Luca, please.'

'No, Father, I haven't finished.' He retorted sharply rising from his seat, 'If you think for one minute that I'm a suitable substitute, you are very wrong. What if I don't want to marry? What if I can't have children? Are you telling me you'll be satisfied with Henrique or, worse still, Arabella?'

'Luca, that is enough!' Gahenge said and thumped his hand on the table to stop his youngest son from saying anything further. Silence hung heavy in the air as Luca sunk into his chair with simmering agitation.

Kari smiled at Luca and said, 'Thank you,' very quietly.

Macawi was the next to speak. 'Kari, you know I have watched you grow into the fantastic man you are today, and I for one appreciate all that you do for the tribe. I love you like I love my own son and I take on board any suggestion you make, I always have done and I will continue to do so.' Macawi looked fondly at Kari.

'I have read your legislation and it is true, it is a large change. For years, I have hoped you would find a suitable soul mate, like I did when I met Ka Tich Ne. However, the years have passed, and not one tribal woman has caught your interest in the way I believe Joey did yours.'

'At our last meeting, I could see the despair in your eyes as, clearly, you had your heart broken with Joey leaving. It saddened me greatly. At Lacroix's wedding I could see you had regained most of your strength and it pleased me. I think we all can agree on what a fine job you did at the wedding. It showed what a great leader you are, you remained dignified and respectful the entire day, even though you must have thought like many others – when will it be my day?' Macawi looked at Kari.

Kari didn't move a muscle. True, he had wondered if he'd ever have a wedding day of his own, but he didn't want to disclose this with The Elders.

'I don't feel that Kari wants this legislation for his own good. He is no longer with Joey.' Macawi said to everyone in the room.

Kari felt Luca look at him, but they both remained silent.

Macawi continued, 'I am sorry, Hok'ee, I could never agree with your ideas. It would be absurd to expect Kari to marry without love. What would be the point in that marriage? And as for Kari being a sperm donor, well, I can't say what I'd really like to, but let me just say, it's probably the most ridiculous suggestion I have ever heard!' Macawi looked pointedly at Hok'ee and shuddered.

The meeting went back and forth for hours. They discussed leaving the situation unchanged, and with time, Kari may meet a tribe woman, fall in love and marry. Every time this was suggested, Kari reminded them it was not solely for his benefit, it was for the tribe. A change had to happen. They could not continue like they have been.

They discussed Kari stepping aside and allowing Luca the chance to meet a tribe's woman and fall in love and marry. Luca pointed out again that he had no desire to step into Kari's shoes. Hok'ee thought with time Luca may grow to like the role and could potentially become a better Chief than Kari.

They also discussed Henrique taking over as Chief when Gahenge retired. However, Henrique was only a few years younger than Gahenge. Henrique assured everyone he was more than willing to fulfil the requirements of the role. He explained that Arabella intended to marry and have children of her own, and would never consider a match outside the tribe.

Kari also brought new information to the table. He told The Elders about other tribes that had already done as he was suggesting. Gahenge read the information carefully, pleased to see his son had completed extensive research. He was aware there were many other tribes who had broadened their horizons but he didn't know what the lasting effects were.

Gahenge listened to everyone, wondering when he should say his piece. He watched as Luca became more agitated, apart from the one outburst he had, up until this point, managed to control his temper. Kari on the other hand was relaxed. It was a sign that Kari was extremely content in his private life – he hadn't been this relaxed at the last meeting.

Food came and went, refreshments were served throughout the day and it was nearing 3 o'clock when Henrique finally spoke. 'I notice Kari hasn't mentioned something. I have waited all day hoping he would confess but it appears he is holding back.' Everyone turned and looked expectantly at Henrique. 'We may have nothing to worry about after all.' Everyone looked at Henrique, including Kari.

Kari was wondering what Henrique was implying. He didn't trust Henrique and he was likely to cause a problem where none existed.

Henrique looked squarely at Kari. 'I have it on good authority you were not alone after Lacroix's wedding.' He noted the muscle in Kari's cheek twitch, but still he remained silent.

Henrique continued, 'My daughter, Arabella, said you and your... *companion* shall we say, kept her awake with all the noise coming from your room. Now, I know Joey wasn't at the wedding; there were only tribe's people. So tell me, do we know this woman you spent the night with?' Henrique sneered at him.

Without even looking up, Kari knew everyone, including his father and brother, were looking at him expectantly. He looked at his hands then with his head high he replied, 'Some of you do, yes.'

Macawi responded with much excitement, 'I knew you had a sparkle back in your eyes, and fire in your belly. The sort you only get when you're in love. Who is she?'

Kari took a sip of water, swallowed and replied, 'It's Joey.'

Gasps were heard around the room. Gahenge lowered his head; he knew he now had an uphill battle on his hands.

Kari was quick to speak, 'Before anyone jumps to the wrong conclusion, I had no idea Joey would be at the wedding. Solonge had quietly, unknowingly to everyone else, including Lacroix, ensconced Joey into the grounds. Joey was there simply to complete the commitment circle. We were both there when Solonge and Lacroix fell in love. Joey told me she only came to complete their circle.'

'You're a bigger fool than I thought, if you believe that.' Henrique said, venom dripping from every word.

'I can assure you, I am no fool, Henrique.' Kari glared at him. 'What I'm about to say will probably be hard to understand. During the ceremony I could feel a presence behind a thicket of trees. After a few hours, my curiosity got the better of me and I had to investigate. I thought it might be paparazzi, I wasn't sure. But, I knew it was my duty to the tribe to investigate anything that wasn't right.'

Kari stopped and reflected on that night. 'As I approached the thicket, the presence moved and radiated from the old wood store. I moved as quietly as I could, not making a sound. As I turned the corner, I could not believe my eyes. I thought I was delusional. I knew I missed Joey more than I can explain, but I had no idea I would start to imagine her being there. I called her name. The woman had nowhere to go, I'd trapped her. The figure walked towards me and tried to get past, she wanted to leave. But, it was Joey, it really was. I could smell her. Feel her soul. If she thought for one minute I was going to let her leave me again, she had another thing coming.' The room was silent and everyone witnessed the catch in Kari's throat as he said the last sentence.

Kari looked around the room. 'Believe me, Joey wanted to go. She knew we shouldn't be together. She knew I would have to choose between her or my tribe and we had both suffered immense pain already.' Kari appeared to have drifted away reliving the moment and quietly he said, 'But, I kissed her, and once I kissed her, I knew she couldn't go.' Kari trailed off.

The room remained silent. Then, as if awakening from a dream, Kari continued, 'Yes, Arabella is right. Joey did stay in my room that night and I made love to her again and again, I wanted to show her that I needed her and I love her more than anything else.'

Luca sat with his mouth slightly open. Tribal members were not meant to speak about their intimate feelings, yet here was his brother, who was normally so reserved, openly confessing to The Elders his love for Joey. He had never heard his brother speak so frankly and passionately about anything before.

Nobody spoke for a while. Gahenge used this silence to begin his speech. 'I'd like to say something. As Chief of the tribe, when I discovered Kari was dating an English woman, I knew I had to put a stop to it. I persuaded the young girl to leave Kari; I said if she loved him she would go. To my amazement, she did. She left because she put my son first. I can't tell you how I wanted in that moment for her to be a First Nations woman, she was the kind of woman my son needs to support him throughout his life. She was strong to leave, so very strong. I can see why Kari fell in love with her. But, our Spirit ancestors had already bonded their hearts and souls. I have witnessed first hand that you don't need to be from our native tribe in order for this to happen. When Kari's feather was removed from Joey, Kari suffered immense pain. Kari's heart and soul was torn apart. Our Spirit ancestors had bonded them and we ripped them apart. If one were to leave, the other would suffer immense pain.'

Gahenge turned to Kari, 'Kari, I imagine the pain lessened with time but it would never truly have gone unless you re-bonded with Joey. How is the pain now and tell me honestly?'

'I felt immeasurable pain during the Patterson meeting, and in truth, I continued to feel discomfort until recently.' Kari said. 'I thought my heart was going to leap from my chest when I investigated the presence I felt at Lacroix's wedding, it beat so hard and fast. Since then I have been with Joey the dull ache has stopped, and I've felt fine.'

'That is because you're hearts and souls have bonded again. You are fortunate to be given the incredible and rare One Love. You will never love another like you love Joey.'

Gahenge turned back to the shocked group. 'Today, I have listened to different suggestions, varying from the possible to the absurd. I love both of my sons very much, and believe either could make wonderful Chiefs when I retire. However, Luca does not want the role and Kari does. The answer to me is simple. When I retire I will hand over to Kari. If he chooses to marry and have children then so be it. We can only talk hypothetically about the future. We need to deal with here and now. Right now we have a law that is old and out of date. It needs to be modernised, and I proudly return my signed and approved legislation document back to Kari. Simply, we cannot lose anymore tribe members and I'm certainly not going to lose my son.'

As Kari took the document he noticed his hand shook slightly.

Gahenge said to Kari, 'Son, I knew from the moment I saw your mother that she was the one for me. I could never love another. It's not our business to know if you feel that way about Joey, we will find out in due course if that is the case. But, I assure you I will support you.'

Gahenge looked at his tribal leaders. 'We have to make changes and Kari has to become the next Chief. If there is a woman who loves him by his side then he will be even stronger. But, I can say this, I will not dismiss my son for loving a woman from a different race.'

Macawi sat and clapped. She then got up from her seat and went over to give Kari a huge hug and he looked up at her surprised. Macawi explained, 'I've been waiting for your father to approve your relationship with Joey. I have been aware the whole time; Ka Tich Ne's spirit has been my constant confident throughout this whole process. Of course I support you Kari, I'd be a fool not to. You only get one chance at life and, if you are lucky enough to experience One Love, then I say, go for it.'

'Thank you, Macawi, Father. I cannot express my gratitude to you both. I am stunned. Thank you. I will not to fail you.'

Gahenge nodded in agreement with Kari. 'Henrique, Hok'ee and Matwall, I strongly suggest that you reconsider your views. We are one tribe, and we work best when we work united.' He paused, 'We cannot afford to lose any more members; it is time we welcome newcomers. We will encourage them to see the benefits of becoming part of our tribe, to raise their children in our culture. When we succeed, we will make a bigger and stronger tribe than we have ever known.'

Gahenge turned to Kari and continued, 'Kari, you also need to inform the other world leaders of our potential change. We need to provide them with the legislation documents outlining the new measures we are proposing and ask them to respect our new tribe values.'

Kari nodded. He knew with Isi, Kangee, Macawi, Luca and now his father, he now had the majority vote. He only had Henrique, Hok'ee and Matwall to convince from his own tribe. If it came to it, they could over rule them anyway. The road was far from over, but he hadn't felt this positive since he decided to get this new legislation under way.

Kari finished the meeting. 'Thank you for coming, Elders. I feel we have made great progress today and I only hope we can continue. I will be taking a short break for a week but I can assure you I will return and conclude this situation. I am sorry for those who feel I have let them down by continuing my relationship with Joey, but the feelings I have for her go beyond love.'

Isi, Kangee, Luca and Macawi all stood and clapped Kari. Henrique, Hok'ee and Matwall remained seated with their arms crossed. Kari thanked them all as they left.

When it was just Luca, his father and himself, Kari turned to his father and said, 'Thank you for what you said and did today.'

'You're welcome.' Gahenge looked proudly at his son and smiled.

Chapter 41

Joey had been oblivious to the day's events unfolding at Cha Tik Warro. She'd had an incredible day. She woke earlier than Kari and watched him sleeping. He looked so peaceful. There were no signs of uncertainty or restlessness, he seemed completely at peace. He eventually stirred and it wasn't long before they gave into their body's desires.

Whilst they took a leisurely shower together, Kari explained where to find the best shopping areas and places to have lunch. He'd insisted on giving her a small fortune in cash – she'd never held so much money. He didn't want her to spend a cent of her own money. She could have his money, but on the condition that she bought some seductive underwear. Joey wasn't sure how she would master this ultimatum with a protector following her every move! Kari's smile was broad when he told her to have fun.

During breakfast a friendly looking middle-aged man named Maska, introduced himself as her protector for the day. He explained that if there was anything she needed or anywhere she wanted to go she merely had to say. His smile was warm as he left her alone to finish her breakfast, saying he'd wait patiently in the drawing room assuring her there was no need to hurry.

Neither Maska or Joey spoke as he drove the sleek black Mercedes away from Cha Tik Warro. The calm tranquillity of the lush green countryside soon disappeared as the bright, busy, bustling city of Vancouver loomed before them. They approached downtown Vancouver via the Granville Street Bridge. Joey spent the morning soaking up her surroundings. She noted the varied ethnic and linguistic mix of people, creating such wonderful and contrasting images before her. The buildings were as diverse as the people that inhibited them. The revolving doors of the office towers beckoned the focused and busy business workforce, in and out like a steady flowing stream. The wonderful designer boutiques, art galleries and restaurants heralded the tourist and Vancouverites. Joey was pleasantly surprised. Even though the city was busy, it didn't seem crowded and the air was fresh as the streets were spotlessly clean.

As she meandered along the Burrad Inlet waterfront, she became mesmerised by the prominent white sails of Canada Place. Suddenly she tripped and would have landed on her face if it hadn't have been for Maska's lightning reactions. He caught her arm and steadied her just in time, thankfully preventing her from being pavement splat! She thanked him profusely. He smiled and suggested that maybe she should have something to eat.

She had a leisurely lunch at one of the wonderful Japanese restaurants Kari had suggested. It felt strange sitting on her own whilst her protector sat a short distance away. As she ate the wonderful selection of small Izakaya tasty dishes, Joey wished she wasn't alone. She decided it was the kind of meal you'd generally share with another, passing comments on the delicious sushi treats. She looked to the front of the restaurant and saw Maska sitting quietly, drinking what she assumed was a coffee. He seemed deep in thought and she wouldn't want to make him feel uncomfortable if she asked him to join her. She imagined this was what it must be like for Kari every day, but at least Lacroix was a friend. It made her laugh to think about it, Lacroix was there to protect Kari, but if it came to it, Kari was clearly much bigger and stronger and she wasn't exactly sure how Lacroix would be able to protect Kari. Joey shuddered at the thought of Kari in danger; she didn't want to imagine it. She sighed quietly to herself as she resigned herself to eating alone. However, she enjoyed the tiny morsels of food that ignited her taste buds causing an explosion of intense flavours in her mouth.

In the afternoon she wandered around many different designer boutiques and department stores. She bought many beautiful clothes and accessories aware she still had to fulfil her promise in purchasing a very sexy lingerie set. Thankfully, Maska maintained a very respectful distance as she wandered around the lingerie store on her own. A sales adviser suggested items, but she found the perfect piece to allure Kari and looked forward to showing him when the time was right.

She also wanted to purchase something for Kari. He'd been so very generous, but wasn't sure what to purchase. She found a lovely photo frame but she felt it would be a bit pretentious to give him that with a picture of her in it. She was walking past a jewellery counter when she saw a selection of lucky charms. A delicate little horseshoe made from platinum caught her eye. She knew he loved riding and thought he could do with some luck at the moment.

It was mid-afternoon when Maska drove back to the peace and tranquillity of the house. She'd had a busy day and decided to rest whilst she waited for Kari. She had no idea how long the meeting would last.

Kari took Luca to his office for a quick de-brief after the meeting. As Kari shut the door, he turned to Luca and said, 'I am amazed by father's reaction today. I'm overjoyed.'

'Me too, Kari. Father is not stupid, he knows what the tribe needs to do to survive and I'm just pleased he appreciates everything that you do. I'm also pretty sure Hok'ee and Matwall will agree and sign. It just depends if they're allowed to make their own decisions or will continue to be influenced by Henrique.' Luca began to laugh, 'I didn't know how you were able to remain so cool when Hok'ee suggested you become a sperm donor!'

Kari laughed and shook his head, 'It would never happen so I found his suggestion merely comical.'

'What are your plans from here?'

'Whilst I'm in Cap Ferret, I intend to meet with Hokyana and tell him about the proposed changes. I also need to inform the other world leaders. If I can't see them in person, I'll at least conference call them. I want to get this legislation sealed as soon as possible.' Kari looked at Luca intently. 'The End of Summer Dinner is due shortly and ideally I'd like to have everything completed by then. If not, the dinner will at least give me a chance to speak to those I have been unable to meet.' Kari took a deep breath; he knew he was beginning to climb a mammoth mountain.

'If that's all I can help with for now, I'm going to make the most of my last few hours here and go for a ride.' Luca stood to leave. 'I'm guessing you'll find something to do between now and dinner!'

Kari smiled as he watched his brother leave. He needed to make some phone calls to a few tribal leaders; he wanted to invite them to the End of Summer Dinner. These leaders were heads of reformed tribes, the sort of tribes Kari had in mind for Kutan. He hoped it would inspire confidence in his father and The Elders to meet tribal leaders from other tribes who were open to mixed relationships and marriage.

It was around 5 o'clock when Kari let himself into his bedroom. He was pleasantly surprised to see Joey lying on his bed, fast asleep. He closed the door quietly behind him and made his way silently to the bed. He sat on the edge of the bed and gazed at Joey.

He loved her so very much. He was beginning to wonder how he'd got to thirty-four without her by his side. He felt incomplete when she wasn't around. She was lying on her side, facing the middle of the bed, hugging his pillow. She looked so peaceful. Her thick lashes brought together in sleep, closing her stunning eyes to the world. Strands of her beautiful hair were swept across her face.

He allowed his eyes to absorb her body. He was glad her sexual appetite matched his. He felt stirrings in his groin, reminding his brain they were alone and had a couple of hours of privacy.

Gently, he tucked the loose strands of hair that fell over her face behind her delicate ears. Joey murmured something illegible and swatted at the air by her face.

Kari smiled. He lowered himself gently onto the bed but the large plump pillow blocked his view of her. He raised himself up onto one elbow and this time trailed his little finger down her cheek. Again, Joey swatted at his hand, but slowly she began to wake up as her hand hit his.

'Hello, sleeping beauty,' Kari smiled at her.

'Kari. What time is it?'

'Just past five.' Kari said and he kissed the tip of her nose.

Joey pushed the pillow behind her and onto the floor and snuggled into his warm embrace. They had at least two hours before supper, and she wanted to enjoy this quiet time with him. 'So, if you're here now, how did the meeting go?'

'Really well, thank you,' replied Kari, pulling Joey tighter. 'Most of The Elders approved, including my father.'

'Really?' Joey questioned and pulled back to look at Kari.

'Uh huh,' said Kari, beginning to shower her face with delicate kisses.

'Are you saying your father is okay with us seeing each other?' Joey enquired.

'Uh huh,' Kari said as he began to remove Joey's clothing.

'So, what exactly does this mean?' Joey asked, baffled.

'They know,' said Kari, between kisses, 'that... we are together... and... we don't care what anyone thinks.'

Joey didn't know what to think. On one hand she didn't want to believe she'd pressured Kari into this new legislation but on the other she wanted to whoop for joy.

'What do we do now?' asked Joey.

Kari stopped his exploration and looked Joey straight in the eyes; 'Right now I want to love you with absolutely no guilt.' Joey could see the depth of his love radiating from his soul as he looked directly at her. He looked at her for a few moments before succumbing to the feelings that were raging around his body.

They made love gently and sincerely. Each giving as much as the other gave. Kari had an immense feeling of relief and wanted Joey to know he loved her very much.

Afterwards they lay holding each other - legs entwined and Joey resting her head on Kari's chest. He didn't remember ever feeling this content.

'How did the shopping trip go?' Kari asked.

'Brilliantly, thank you. It's a great city.'

'And did you spend the money wisely?'

'I didn't spend it all don't worry, I'll go and get the...' Joey said and made a move to give the remainder of the money back to Kari.

Kari pulled her back, 'No, you misunderstand me. I don't care how much or how little you spent.' He looked at her seductively; 'I wanted to know if you bought anything special?' and he kissed her shoulder.

'Ah, I understand,' Joey said as she snuggled back into his embrace. 'In answer to your question, yes I did and I look forward to showing you.'

'Not as much as I'm looking forward to seeing you in it.' Kari smiled.

'I wouldn't have thought sexy underwear was your thing.'

'No, it's not to be honest. But, I want to experience everything with you. I love you whatever you wear – dressed or undressed. I liked what you did the other night by teasing me and I'd like you to know that maybe you could tease me further.'

Joey was quiet for a while.

'What are you thinking?' Kari asked Joey.

'I'm just thinking of other ways I can tease you.'

'Hmm, what have I let myself in for...' Kari sighed.

'Oh, trust me, I think you'll like it,' and Joey looked up at him giving him her most wanton look.

'Don't look at me that way, otherwise I can't be held accountable for my actions!' Kari said hoarsely and kissed her deeply.

Joey pulled away. 'Wait, I bought something for you today.'

Kari sighed heavily and rolled onto his back. 'What have I started?'

Joey scrambled across the bed, grabbed her bag and removed a small box from inside it and handed it to Kari.

'You didn't need to buy me anything.' Kari said but took the box she eagerly presented to him.

'I know. But, you've been so generous and I appreciate all that you're doing, I really do. And besides, it's a gift of love. It's small, but I hope you like it.' Joey suddenly felt nervous.

Kari smiled warmly at her. He had no idea what she would have bought him and he appreciated she had bought him anything at all. He opened the box to discover the delicate horseshoe. He took it gently out of the box and held it in his palm.

Joey knew the horseshoe was small but suddenly it looked positively tiny lying in the palm of his hand.

'Thank you, it's beautiful.' Kari lifted his hand to look closer at the tiny horseshoe. 'It's perfect.'

'It's not much, I know, but I wanted you to have something to remind you of me. I know you love horse riding and where I come from a horseshoe…'

'Means good luck,' Kari finished for her. 'I need all the luck available at the moment.' He picked it up between his forefinger and thumb, 'Thank you, I love it.' Kari leant over and kissed her.

'I wanted to say thank you for all you've done for me, but what do you buy a man who has everything?' Joey added.

Kari held her chin in his hand and tilted her head up so he could look her squarely in the eyes and said, 'You don't need to buy me anything. You have already given me all I could possibly want. You've told me you love me. I have everything I need right here.' As Kari lifted her onto his lap he noticed Joey wince. Kari looked at her concerned, 'What's wrong, you're hurt?'

'Oh, it's nothing,' Joey said dismissively, happy to be held by Kari and not wanting to break the moment.

'If you're hurt I need to know, perhaps I can help?' He insisted.

'Yesterday I asked Luca to teach me to ride.' She noticed Kari frown. 'I'm okay. Luca didn't really want to teach me as he thought you'd like to but I insisted. I guess I'm just a bit saddle sore and my thighs are on fire.'

'Yes, I would rather teach you. Horse riding can be very dangerous but I know how persuasive you can be.' he gently scolded her. 'You should have said earlier that you were sore, I'd have been more gentle.'

'Really, I'm fine it's just when I move quickly or sit like this,' Joey moved to show Kari, but he stopped her before she hurt herself again.

'It's okay, you don't need to show me,' he held her firmly. 'I have a good idea though, wait here.' Kari moved from underneath her and walked to his bathroom. Joey listened as he ran a bath. He came back into the room a little while later, 'Mademoiselle, if you would like to follow me?'

Joey got up and tried to walk as normally as possible. Kari watched her and he couldn't help chuckling. 'Please tell me you didn't walk around the city like that?'

'No, once I get going, I'm fine.'

Joey walked past Kari and into the semi-dark bathroom. Kari had drawn the blinds and lowered the lighting to create a relaxing atmosphere. The bath was filled with inviting bubbles and beautifully scented warm water.

Joey turned to Kari, 'Oh, you are good.'

'I try to be,' Kari replied.

Joey eased herself into the divinely scented water and shuddered, it was blissful. She looked at Kari who knelt by the side of the bath as he reached for a natural sponge. 'Are you not joining me?' Joey said innocently.

'I didn't want to intrude. I'm happy to stay here,' Kari said, not very convincingly.

'Well, I'd be happier with you in here. If you insist on sponging me you can do it just as well from in here.' Joey looked at him willingly. She watched as he stood up and removed the towel from his waist. God, he was beautiful she thought as her eyes devoured his lean, muscular body as he climbed into the bath and lowered himself opposite her. He manoeuvred her legs so they rested on top of his. Joey thought the bath was massive but suddenly with Kari, it seemed to shrink.

'What else did you get up to yesterday with Luca?' Kari asked as he began to massage her soapy feet.

'Well, I rode Pallo. Luca was very patient and he only allowed me to canter.'

Kari stopped what he was doing, 'Canter! You cantered?'

'Yes. I managed to get on and off the horse, walk, trot and eventually, canter. Luca kept Pallo on the leading rein the whole time so don't worry. He wouldn't go any further as he didn't want to push me. I was happy to do more but I don't think his nerves would have stood it.' Joey smiled proudly.

'I'm impressed,' said Kari warmly.

'Thank you, I wanted to surprise you next time we go riding. But, I still need a lot of training, so if you're up for the challenge, I'm willing to learn.'

'I'm willing to teach you anything,' Kari said seductively, 'especially riding.' He raised his eyebrows and looked at her suggestively. 'But we'll have to wait until next time you're here as I need your sore muscles to recover.'

'I agree, horse riding can wait, but I'm happy for you to teach me other riding techniques…' Joey said huskily.

Kari pulled on Joey's calves sliding her along his legs towards him with ease. 'As much as I love my brother, I'm not going to allow him to teach you this sort of riding.'

Making love in the warm bath was a new experience for both of them share. Kari allowed Joey to set the pace; he didn't want to hurt her bruises further. The warm water, sloshing over their wet limbs, heightened the intensity of the moment.

Once they were both spent, Joey turned over and nestled herself between his firm thighs and lay back in his arms. He kissed her head and told her he loved her.

Joey sighed contentedly. 'Any idea what the time is?'

'I have no idea; I'm guessing six thirtyish. We'll have to go to supper soon. It's our last night here for a while and I'd like to leave on a good note, especially as my father seems to have accepted our relationship.' He said before kissing her head again.

'Absolutely.'

'How are the bruises?'

'At this moment in time, I can't feel them. But I may need help getting out of the bath.' Joey chuckled.

'Your wish is my command.' Kari said quietly in her ear.

Joey laughed. 'Oh, you are so going to wish you hadn't said that,' she said mischievously, 'I am notching up a fair few things to tease you with already.'

She noted Kari take in a deep breath and exhale slowly. 'I am so looking forward to our holiday,' he said seductively.

Joey had been thinking the same thing.

Chapter 42

Supper was the most relaxed meal Joey had experienced at Cha Tik Warro. Aiyana welcomed Joey whilst Gahenge warmly smiled at her as she and Kari entered the dining room.

Everyone was relaxed. Luca was excited to be returning to France and Kari assumed he was relieved he wasn't going to have to step into his shoes. Joey also knew Luca was ecstatic about returning home to Pierre.

After supper they retired to the sitting room, this time Gahenge and Aiyana joined them. It made Kari happy to see all of his favourite people in the same room getting along. He knew his parents still had a few reservations but they were making a tremendous effort. That was all Kari could ask.

Kari noticed Joey sat delicately on the sofa and before easing herself slowly into the seat.

Luca noted the discomfort on Joey's face. 'Has all the riding caught up with you at last, Joey?' Luca asked.

Joey blushed, she knew he was talking about horse riding but her mind was on such a different track. She noticed Kari stifle a laugh.

'Yes, it appears it has, Luca. Not that it's put me off. I'm willing to keep trying, but think it's best if I allow myself time to recover before doing it again. Thank you for your concern, though.'

'That's a shame. I was going to see if you fancied a ride tomorrow morning?' Luca said to both Kari and Joey.

Joey laughed, 'Thank you but there's no way I'd keep up with you. Besides, you don't want to be standing in the training ring with me going round and round in circles.'

'Thanks Luca, but I'll give it a miss too,' said Kari.

Joey detected the slight disappointment in his voice. 'Just because I'm a wuss doesn't mean you can't both go out and ride.' Kari looked at her. 'Go on, why don't you both go out in the morning, our flight isn't until midday.'

'But, I don't want to leave you?' Kari said.

'Kari, you'll only be gone a few hours; we're going to be together for five full days. You don't know when you'll next see Luca.' She then looked suggestively at him and said, 'And, I know you love to ride.'

Kari noted the tone in her voice and he smiled at her. 'If you're sure then yes, I'd love to.' Turning to Luca he said, 'I'll meet you at seven, at the stables. We can ride for a few hours and be back in time to shower and change before leaving for the flight.'

Aiyana noted the exchange between Kari and Joey and she understood that all they wanted to do was be with each other, but she respected Joey for encouraging Kari to spend time with his brother. She wished Luca would come home to live. She missed him and his passionate ways. Maybe once this new legislation had been finalised she could ask Luca to return home. Now wasn't the right time.

Gahenge cleared his throat and said, 'Kari, I just wanted to say how proud I was of you today in the meeting. You held yourself with dignity and I was very impressed. I don't think it will take long before the others agree to your proposal, apart from perhaps Henrique. However, if it comes to it, it will be him against us and I know who will succeed.' Gahenge said proudly.

He then turned his gaze to Joey. 'Joey, I'd like to apologise for the way we treated you when you first came to our home. We were incredibly rude.'

Kari placed his hand on Joey's knee protectively whilst his father spoke to her.

Gahenge continued, 'I'd like you to know that you are very welcome here. I know Luca is fond of you. He's only said nice things about you to Aiyana and myself since he spent the day with you yesterday. It appears you have captured Kari's heart. I have never known him talk so candidly as he did today. I also believe you only want what is best for my son and the fact you were prepared to leave if you felt it was in his interests, staggered me. I can see you love him equally. All I ask is that you look after Kari, he is my son and I love both my sons dearly. One day I hope Luca finds someone who loves him just as much as you love Kari.' Gahenge held his head high.

Kari and Luca had never heard their father speak with so much affection. They both sat in relative shock.

Luca got up and walked over to his father and hugged him warmly. 'We love you too, Father.' Gahenge stood woodenly, he wasn't used to being open with his feelings. He'd always been taught to restrain his emotions.

Kari hadn't taken his eyes from his father and slowly he raised himself from the sofa and walked over to him. Kari was a good deal taller than his father and he looked down at him. Placing his hands on his father's shoulders he said, 'Thank you, Father, you have no idea how I appreciate all that you just said. I love you all very much and I didn't want to have to choose between my family and Joey.' Kari then pulled his father into a warm embrace.

Joey felt tears threatening to escape and she had to wipe her eyes quickly before anyone noticed. Thank goodness all eyes were on Kari and his father, giving her the opportunity to compose herself.

'I think we will leave you young ones to it,' Gahenge said and he looked at Aiyana for assistance. He didn't expect to find himself so emotional but suddenly he found he was close to tears and he wanted to leave the room before he broke down. Aiyana walked towards him, kissed both her sons on the cheek before taking Gahenge's hand.

As the older couple left the room Kari and Luca both sighed deeply in relief. Luca, who was used to being emotional, wiped the tears from his cheeks. Kari smiled affectionately at him. He walked over to his younger brother and enveloped him too in a big hug, 'Whilst I'm in the mood, I should tell you also that I am so grateful for all you have done for me. I love you so much, Luca, and if I can ever do anything for you, please ask.' Kari said warmly.

Joey couldn't take anymore and she let the tears fall freely down her cheeks.

'Kari, I can't even begin to pay you back for all you have done for me over the years. The fact you're in line for Chief is so selfless of you. You know I love you and I'll continue to support you.'

Kari pulled back but kept his hands on Luca's shoulders, 'One day you'll find someone to love who will love you as you deserve.'

Luca looked at Joey, and then back to Kari, 'I know.'

Kari then saw Joey with tears streaming down her cheeks, 'Oh, Joey, I didn't mean to make you cry.' He went over and sat her on his lap; she winced as the bruises screamed. Kari apologised as she repositioned herself. Kari wanted to hold her and be this relaxed with Joey in front of his brother.

They all talked for a couple of hours about the flight tomorrow, France and the places Joey should visit. Joey told them both about her passion for art and explained that would love to see Luca's work.

In the morning Kari woke before Joey and crept from the bedroom to join Luca for the horse ride. They enjoyed every moment of riding through the meadows they both knew so well, allowing the horses run as hard as they wanted before quenching their thirst in the stream.

Joey watched from a window as she saw the two men return. Neither horse wore a saddle. Apart from at the wedding, she had never seen Kari look so native and alluring. The horses galloped down the lower meadows with the men whooping in excitement, clearly loving the exhilarating thrill of riding.

A short while later she saw Luca and Kari enter via the kitchen, she ambled over to meet them.

Kari's eyes were electric as she looked at him. They were clearly buzzing with adrenalin.

Kari kissed her. 'Good morning, beautiful, how are you this fine morning?'

'Good, thanks,' Joey said as she hugged him back. 'Urgh, you're all sweaty.'

'It's a good workout,' replied Luca. He took some food and wandered out of the kitchen. 'See you at ten.'

'Come on, I need to shower and pack,' said Kari as he picked up a selection of food.

Kari was a master at showering and packing quickly; Joey noticed how he carefully packed the little horseshoe safely in a section of his wallet. Within half an hour he was finished. He took their bags downstairs to the waiting car and, shortly afterwards, Luca joined them. Gahenge and Aiyana wished them well on their travels and tried to persuade Luca to visit soon.

The three of them arrived at the airport with their security guards. Unlike any other time Joey had been to an airport, their car drove directly onto the runway and to a private jet.

Kari noticed Joey looking at him puzzled as they pulled up to the plane, but he didn't say anything until they boarded and were preparing for take-off. 'Sometimes we hire a private jet, especially if there is more than one family member travelling.' Joey looked at him with her eyes wide. Kari smiled, 'I know it's extravagant but it lowers the media attention. Imagine the headlines if we were to fly on a public plane today! Besides, I had this plane on standby as I was expecting to fly to England today to find you.' Kari said as he pulled her hand to his lips and kissed it.

'I'm surprised you don't fly privately all the time?'

'Now that would be extravagant,' Kari smiled. 'We do use private jets, but not all the time. I'm also not allowed to travel by any means with my father. The Chief and his heir can never travel together, in case of… well you know.'

Joey nodded. She understood.

As the plane took off for Paris, Kari realised he'd never flown with Joey before and he had no idea she was such a nervous flier. She held his hand tightly throughout the entire journey and closed her eyes for both take-off and landing.

Joey knew Luca couldn't wait to get home but she noticed he was sad to say goodbye to his brother. Luca hugged both Joey and Kari as he disembarked and asked them to come and visit him soon, to which Kari replied that they definitely would.

'I'll miss Luca.' Joey said as the plane taxied down the runway.

'Are you not looking forward to spending some time alone?'

Joey looked at him mischievously, 'Of course.' She then shut her eyes tight as the engines roared to life and the plane began to speed down the runway. At least this time it would be a very short journey to Nice, Joey thought, squeezing Kari's hand tightly.

Chapter 43

It was very late when the taxi stopped outside the beautiful villa. Kari carried the bags, turned off the alarm and closed the door on the outside world. At last, he was alone with Joey, and he intended to make the most of their time together.

'Hungry?' Kari asked Joey.

'Not really,' she said as she looked at him coyly.

'Me neither. Follow me.' Kari picked up the bags and walked upstairs. Joey followed obediently. He walked to his bedroom door, opened it and strode into the room. He placed the bags on the floor, and without turning on the lights he walked over to Joey and said, 'How exactly are your bruises?'

'We haven't tried them out today, I think they're easing a little.' Joey walked into his embrace and looked up at him, expectantly.

'Perhaps we could test them out?' Kari murmured as he bent to kiss her lips.

'I'm willing if you are.' Joey returned his kiss and before long the bruises were all but forgotten as they re-consummated their souls.

For the next two days neither of them left the villa. They rejoiced in the liberty of making love as, when, or where the mood took them - which was pretty frequent. They didn't dress properly. Joey often wore Kari's t-shirts and he wandered the house in just shorts.

It was on the second day of their holiday, whilst Joey and Kari were lying in each other's arms after making love on the large, wicker lounger, when Joey turned to Kari and said, 'You do realise that I bought clothes especially for our holiday and, so far, I haven't worn a thing I brought.'

'I was wondering when you were going to surprise me with my other gift…' Kari asked eagerly.

'Oh, yes, that gift… well, what are our plans for tomorrow?'

Kari looked at her intently, 'Well, I'd prefer not to be blunt… so to put it nicely, I'd like to carry on with what we've been doing these past two days.'

'Go on, what would you say if you were being blunt?'

Kari repeated most of the phrase Luca had taught her.

'Really! You want to *lay* with me.' Joey looked at him suspiciously, 'Why do I get the feeling that you're sugar coating it? What does it really mean?'

'Pretty much that I want to sleep with you.'

Joey narrowed her eyes, 'I get the feeling you're still not telling me the whole truth.'

'Your ears are too delicate…' Kari hugged her, hoping she would drop it.

'Go on, I can assure you, I'm not that delicate,' Joey retaliated.

'Nope.'

'Please? Not even if I tease it out of you?' Joey said suggestively.

'You've never heard me talk that way and I'm not sure you'd like it.' Kari said, indicating he no longer wanted to continue that conversation.

'Okay. You've slammed the door shut to that subject!' Joey muttered under her breath before saying, 'So, back to my original question, do you fancy going out tomorrow? Maybe for lunch?'

'Why?'

'Just an idea I've had...' Joey said innocently.

'I'm intrigued. If you'd rather go out than allow me to ravish your body then who am I to argue?'

Joey raised her eyebrows but said nothing.

'In that case, I'll take you out for lunch if *my* cooking does not meet *your* high standards.'

'No, your cooking is amazing and I am very impressed. You wait until I tell Lacroix how fortunate I have been to have eaten food prepared and cooked by your own hands.' Joey smiled as she kissed his hand. 'I wonder how they are?'

'My hands?'

'No! Lacroix and Solonge'

'Hopefully, in about nine months' time, we'll meet baby Lacroix or baby Solonge.'

Joey smiled at the thought. She knew Kari would make a fantastic father. 'I know you want children, well, more that you're expected to have children one day, how many would you like?'

'Is that a proposal?' Kari teased whilst interlocking his fingers with hers.

'No!' Joey quickly said but noticed Kari looked taken aback by her sudden rejection. 'I didn't mean it to sound so negative. Yes, I'd love children... one day, but no, not yet and I would like to be married first. Not that marriage means anything.' Joey finished sadly.

Kari noted it wasn't the first time he heard her be so negative about commitment from a man. 'Joey, not every man leaves their wife.'

'Maybe, but take you for example; you're supposed to produce an heir, a male heir at that. Sometimes, it's just not possible.'

'I understand. I can't speak for every man but when I decide to marry, I will mean it. I would never walk out on my wife and children, even if they had three legs and two heads! Whatever the outcome, we'd be together, forever.' Kari looked at Joey, 'This is a distinct difference with our beliefs. Not only are we joined by a wedding ceremony, but our souls are intertwined, never to be broken.'

'Like ours?'

'Yes, I believe our spirits and souls are joined.'

'But... what if you meet your true love? The one you're meant to be with. What happens to our souls then?' Joey was nervous of his answer.

'Joey. Dear Joey how else can I tell you, I love you so very, very much. With all my heart, body and soul.' He looked imploringly into her eyes, 'I'm not sure what I would do without you.'

Joey could see the sincerity in his eyes and she wanted to believe him but there was still something that prevented her from doing so. 'My father probably said the same to my mother, and look what happened.'

'I'm not your father.' Kari reminded her gently, trying with all his might to reassure her. 'Don't push me away, Joey, trust me.'

As Kari held her in his arms, she couldn't shake the feeling of insecurity. Kari was being incredibly patient but, if she wasn't careful, she knew she would end up pushing him away like she had done to so many men before him. But, she also knew Kari meant so much more to her than any other man. 'I do trust you, Kari, it's just… I'm scared.'

'How about me, don't you think I'm also scared? My comfort is knowing you wear my feather.'

Joey touched the sacred feather. 'Solonge told me it meant you loved me.'

Kari moved so he could look directly in her eyes. He saw the uncertainty in Joey's eyes. 'Do you understand the significance of the necklace?'

Joey nodded but he still saw the questions in her eyes.

'Forgive me, I assumed Solonge had told you. Yes, it's a symbol of love, from one man to a woman. The Kutan Tribe believes a boy turns into a man on his sixteenth birthday. On that day, there is much celebrating. Our spiritual leader, Negan, blesses and presents the young man with two identical feathers – one for him to wear from that moment and another to give to the woman he loves. For my ancestors it was their equivalent of an engagement ring. They married much younger in those days, often to their first love. It was a sign to any other suitor that any woman who wore a feather was taken. In days gone by many tribes didn't believe in monogamy, but the Kutan Tribe *always* has. As time passed, each generation evolved. Today, a woman can wear many feathers – one at a time of course – but it doesn't mean marriage. It means the couple are very much in love and are committed to each other.'

'Visually letting everyone know you love each other but are not engaged.'

'Exactly. Of course, no man, or woman for that matter, wants someone who has worn many feathers during their young life, but it's not uncommon for a woman to have worn a handful.'

'So, sometimes a necklace could be worn and then passed on four or five times?'

'Yes.'

'Oh, they must get damaged then? The feather is so delicate.'

'They do get repaired and cleansed. For example, if a relationship ends, the spiritual leader cleanses and blesses the necklaces. Also, every year of the man's birth day, both necklaces are removed and given to our spiritual leader to bless. If he needs to replace the feather or cord then he will, but the central jewel remains intact.'

'And each pair is different to any other?'

'Yes. You will notice that Luca and I have similar necklaces to our parents. Often a design or colour is passed down from generation to generation.'

'Do the necklaces get handed down?'

'No. We wear them eternally.'

Joey digested what Kari told her.

'So, now the feather you are wearing, is a huge comfort to me and I hope of comfort to you. I love you, Joey.' He kissed her softly wanting to eradicate the questions and concerns he could still see flickering through her mind. 'Talk to me, Joey.'

'Oh, it's nothing, really…' she replied flippantly.

Kari looked at her suspiciously, 'Nothing, *really*?'

She took a deep breath, 'I'm just curious that's all…'

'Go on,' Kari encouraged, as Joey seemed reluctant to continue.

'Are the men also circumcised on their sixteenth birthday?'

Kari laughed, 'Ouch, no. It's performed when the baby is a few days old.'

'Every baby boy?'

'Yes.'

'What about the girls? Does anything happen to them?'

He lay on his side, resting his head in the palm of his hand as he looked at her. 'No. What else is going round and around your head?'

Joey blushed and looked away.

'Joey,' he said gently as he encouraged her to look at him.

'How… I mean when… who teaches you how to make love… your way.'

Kari couldn't help but grin, 'Our mothers.'

'Really?'

'No!'

'Then who?' Joey was intrigued. 'I've personally never come across anything like it.'

'Until roughly hundred and fifty years ago the Kutan Tribe had no outside educators what so ever - everything was taught by our Elders and spiritual leader. As I explained before, we were and still are a unique tribe.

'Today Kutan children go to mainstream school but we also have additional spiritual lessons where The Elders and spiritual leader teach the young people about traditions, values and histories. Part of the Kutan education is how to love another wholly and satisfy their needs, as well as procreate. Legend proclaims that previous generations of my tribe only ever made love the Kutan way. When books and a wider education became more available, recent generations became interested in the more … familiar ways. But, it is believed that when a tribal couple becomes much older, they only ever make love the Kutan way, it is deemed more precious.'

'I'd agree. I feel connected to you in that moment as if we were one being.'

Kari spoke in his native tongue, 'It translates as to become one, one love.'

'To become one.' Joey said quietly and snuggled into Kari's body. For her, it seemed he was her one and only love. She couldn't imagine ever feeling at one with another human soul.

Kari was aware Joey had fallen asleep as the tension left her body. He had to convince her he loved her more than any other woman, he wanted to erase all her insecurities.

During the evening, they worked together to cook a delicious meal. It reminded Joey of the first time they'd cooked together. How nervous she had felt around him, how she wanted to touch and kiss him. Yet now, she was sure if she asked him to make love to her at that precise moment, he probably would.

After dinner Joey told Kari about the story Luca had told her when Kari took the blame for the broken ornament.

'I'd do anything to protect my brother.' Kari said simply.

'Yes, but the punishment was so harsh.'

'It was how we were brought up,' Kari said as a matter fact. 'My parents were lenient compared to most. It doesn't change the fact that Luca and I vowed that we would never inflict that sort of punishment on another human being, especially a child.' Kari said seriously.

'Did you often suffer that kind of punishment?' Joey asked.

'Not really. We were smacked if we did something *very* wrong, but generally, we were banned from riding. How about you?'

'My mum couldn't bear to tell us off, let alone give us a punishment. I guess I learnt a lot from Emily. I was possibly wiser and got away with more. But, Mum was our friend; she didn't want to turn us against her. We were all she had.'

'Would I like your mum?' Kari noted Joey called her *Mum*, not Mother.

'Oh yes, she's a bit wacky, kind of trendy. I know she'd love you. Well, I told you about her reaction when she saw our picture in that magazine?'

Kari smiled at the memory.

'Mum desperately wants Emily and me to be happy and to find a man that can worship her daughters like she does. Emily has found someone who ticked all the boxes. Emily is strong. She loves her husband and has two beautiful boys. All of this by the time she was twenty-seven. Here I am, on the other hand, thirty, finally met a man I love but we're from opposite sides of the world.' Joey tried to shrug it off but Kari noticed. 'I want to make my mum as proud of me as she is Emily. I know I can never be as successful as Emily, but I can try.'

Kari leaned towards Joey, 'I can't imagine anyone being better than you in any circumstance.'

'You haven't met Emily.'

'I'd like to. I'd like to meet your mum too. Do they know how we feel about each other?'

'Not really. Mum knows I'm here with you now and that I went to Canada, but she doesn't know how serious I am about you.'

'Why not?'

'Because I don't want to have to explain if it all goes pear shaped.' Joey looked at Kari. He didn't say anything, he just looked at her. 'Everything is going so well at the moment, I'm just wondering when it's all going to change.'

'Joey, I've finally convinced my family how I feel about you and they've accepted it. It now appears I have to convince you!' He got up and crouched at her feet, 'I can't stand the thought that you're waiting for this to end.' He looked at her intently. 'Tomorrow you can use me in any fashion you like. Think of me as your servant, I will be at your beck and call. I'm excited and I want you to be too. But right now, I'm taking you to bed and I'm going to love you.'

Kari picked her up in his arms and carried her to the bedroom. They made love his way, both feeling much more secure. Kari was attentive to every need of Joey and made sure she was totally satisfied before submitting to his.

Chapter 44

In the morning Kari made love to her again. He wanted to make sure Joey knew exactly how much he wanted, needed and loved her.

He looked at her, lovingly, 'Remember, I'm yours.' He kissed her delicately on the lips, 'So, what is your first request?'

Joey smiled, feeling better now she was in control. 'I would like you to take me out for lunch. Wear something comfortable, but there is one rule…' She looked at him cheekily, 'You are not allowed to wear underpants.'

'But, I was going to wear my white linen trousers so I have to wear underwear otherwise they don't hide a great deal.'

Joey chuckled, 'Exactly. Wear them but with your white shirt left to hang loose outside? That way you can keep your dignity but I will know differently.'

Kari liked the fact she'd obviously thought about it. 'What about you, what are you wearing? Are you wearing my gift?'

'You'll see.' Joey replied as she threw back the bed covers and got up to shower. Kari joined her.

A short while later Joey left Kari shaving as she went into the bedroom to get dressed. She decided to wear her new black, halter-neck dress. The dress was flattering to her shape with a pinched waist and a floaty, knee-length skirt. On her feet she wore a pair of high wedged sandals. She normally didn't wear high heels, but today she wanted to look fantastic. She wore her hair loose because Kari preferred it like that. The only jewellery she wore was Kari's feather. She looked at her reflection and felt pleased.

She was looking out of the window when Kari walked back into the room. He wolf whistled at her; he'd never done that before. Startled, she turned. His smile was broad across his face. 'You look stunning.' he said as he walked towards her wearing only a towel around his waist.

'Why, thank you, all for you!' and she twirled for him. 'And to match you, I have absolutely no underwear on.'

'Oh God, and you expect me to go out today?' He pulled her into his arms and ran his hands up her back.

'Yep,' she smiled back.

He ran his fingers through her still damp hair and sighed, 'It's going to be a fun lunch.'

Whilst they had breakfast on the terrace, Joey brushed past him and he felt his body react knowing there wasn't a lot of cloth between them, and nothing to hold him in place. *How was he going to survive the day?*

Kari drove them to a remote town in the hills. It was a beautiful, hot day without a cloud in the sky. They strolled hand-in-hand around the beautifully quiet and ancient, cobbled streets chatting about various places of interest and historic buildings. It was much cooler in the shade, a welcome relief from the heat of the rising sun.

At one point Joey took Kari's hand and pulled him up a flight of steep steps between two old buildings. Once they were safely out of sight from any passers-by, she pulled him into a hidden alcove and pushed him hard against the wall. She kissed him passionately and pressed her body into his. It was at this point she reminded him she had no underwear on and how easy it would be to take him. Kari almost gave in to temptation when Joey pulled away and began to walk down the steep steps to the cobbled street. Kari took a moment to right himself before jogging to catch up with her. When he did, he looked at her pleadingly, suggesting he couldn't take this teasing. Joey simply smiled back at him.

They found a quiet restaurant off the beaten track of the tourists; it sat opposite a small, quaint church.

A middle-aged lady ushered them to a quiet table, tucked away in the corner. The table was dressed with soft, white linen and four empty glasses were patiently waiting to be filled.

Joey opted to sit next to Kari instead of her usual position, opposite him. He knew her intention was to tease him today and he had a feeling she wouldn't pass up any opportunity but he was happy not to question her.

A young waiter explained the menu, there were three options and Kari looked expectantly at Joey.

'What?' Joey asked.

'You're in control today, so, I'm leaving lunch up to you.' Kari smiled warmly at her.

Joey cleared her throat; she can do this she thought. 'Pardon Monsieur, um, *again* s'il vous plait?'

She heard Kari cough in an attempt to hide his laughter.

The young waiter explained the choices again and waited patiently for Joey to respond.

Joey's mind raced. She understood *terrine* and *confit du canard,* so asked for two of each dish. The waiter offered a carafe of wine but Joey declined and instead asked for a bottle of still water.

As the waiter walked away, she glared at Kari who was clearly finding it difficult not to laugh.

'I'm sorry,' he said, 'it's the way you said *again* in English, but with a French accent, as if it would help.'

Joey tried to remain straight faced but found it impossible.

The waiter returned with a bottle of still water and a basket of bread.

'Are you expecting me to feed you too?'

'I like the sound of that.' Kari beamed at her.

Joey poured the water and handed Kari a piece of bread, 'I give you permission to feed yourself.'

Kari looked at her dejectedly but accepted the bread she offered.

The first course arrived and it was beautifully presented with a sprig of oregano resting against the terrine, pesto delicately drizzled around the plate with cinnamon dusted around the outer edge. Kari complimented Joey on her choice of food.

He was oblivious to Joey's next teasing test as she rested her right hand on his thigh. They talked quietly to each other as they waited for the main course. When the succulent duck arrived he became aware that Joey's hand had wandered and slowly began to tease him intimately. With only the lightweight fabric of his trousers to form any kind of barrier, it wasn't long before he was aroused. He put down his knife and fork and gazed at her. He couldn't believe she continued to eat heartily; seemingly unaware of his needs.

He felt very turned on and was close to moaning out loud. Kari placed a hand on hers halting her movement. When she looked at him her eyes were full of mischief. He didn't need to say anything; the look in his eyes begged *no more…*

Joey stopped. Whilst she waited for Kari to eat more of his main course she reflected it was the first meal they had shared together where she had finished first. She watched Kari push the food around his plate and eventually give up eating altogether. She smiled to herself; he'd obviously lost his appetite as he often did when he wanted her.

After a brief pause the waiter returned and was concerned to see Kari had hardly touched his food. Kari assured him the food was delicious and was looking forward to the dessert. The waiter smiled politely as he removed the plates leaving both Kari and Joey alone again.

Joey looked at Kari but said nothing.

'Yes, Miss Lewis…' Kari leant back in his chair and returned Joey's gaze.

'I didn't say anything!'

'You didn't need to, your eyes say it all.'

'So, why ask if you already know what I'm thinking.' Joey teased as she sat further back in her chair to be level with Kari.

He gently ran his finger down her cheek and said quietly, 'The answer is yes, I do.'

Again, she was hypnotised by his deep, dark eyes, unable to see anything else but him. They were so entranced by each other's gazes that they failed to notice the waiter return with desserts. He politely coughed breaking the spell cast between them.

'Merci, monsieur, cela semble merveilleux,' Kari said enthusiastically to the waiter who, once again, smiled before leaving them both in peace.

'You know, my mum always said I wasn't allowed to eat dessert if I didn't finish my main.' Joey pointed out as Kari began to eat the delicious raspberry tart and sorbet.

Kari finished his mouthful before replying. 'I owe it to this establishment to at least try and eat more of the delicious food they have prepared.' Joey placed his hand on her thigh. Kari was fine until she encouraged his hand to move up her thigh to the top of her legs. At which point, he was reminded she was not wearing any underwear. He closed his eyes and shook his head. 'But, then again…' he sighed as he put down his spoon.

Joey giggled as she tucked into her food.

'You are a bad woman, Joey.' Kari said devilishly quietly.

'I'm just glad we chose a restaurant with adequate table clothes to hide your…' Joey words caught in her throat as she felt Kari's fingers stroke her. Slowly, Joey expelled her breath and continued to eat.

'How do you do it?' Kari asked amazed she was still able to eat, especially as he began to arouse her further.

'As a woman, I can multi-task,' Joey replied breezily as Kari took her desires to another level. 'Besides, how bad would it look if we both left our food. The chef would fear for their reputation.'

Kari was impressed, to a passer-by no one would have a clue how turned on Joey was becoming. She had a mild flush to her cheeks but that could also appear as a healthy glow from the sun. She wiped her mouth with her napkin when she had finished her last mouthful. 'Delicious,' she said as she licked her lips and placed her hand on his groin pleased to find he was hard and erect.

He groaned, almost silently, to himself as he felt her squeeze him a little.

'Although,' Joey said as her breath caught in her throat. 'Now would be a good time to stop, unless you really want me to repeat that scene from *When Harry met Sally.*'

A muscle twitched in his cheek and his dark eyes sparkled in the dimly lit restaurant as he placed his cutlery on his plate, indicating he had finished.

After a short while the waiter returned but was still concerned to see that Kari hadn't eaten a great deal. Again Kari apologised and said it was no bad reflection of the food the restaurant had produced, merely he didn't have much of an appetite today. The waiter offered café but Kari declined.

She noticed Kari's hand shook as he poured himself some fresh water and drank it quickly. She liked teasing him.

'If it's alright with you, can we move on?' Kari asked clearing finding it hard to control his desire.

'Sure,' Joey replied. 'I'll buy you an ice-cream later,' she said as she excused herself and went to the toilet.

When she returned she discovered Kari had paid the bill and was very insistent they move on.

As they walked out of the quiet restaurant the owner bide them a happy holiday.

Joey took Kari's hand as they crossed the street towards the small church.

'Would you like to go in? Kari asked.

Joey wasn't sure how comfortable Kari would feel going into a place of Christian worship, 'Do you mind?'

'Not at all.' Kari reassured her and led her into the cool church.

Kari watched as Joey lit a candle. She came back to his side and explained, in a hushed voice, various pieces of architecture and religious artefacts as they walked around the quiet church.

'Are you a Christian?' Kari asked Joey.

'Yes.' Joey noticed a flicker of dismay cross Kari's face. Then as they stood in front of a beautiful stained glass window she said, 'But a lapsed one.'

Kari didn't comment to Joey admission but she could see unanswered questions in his eyes. As they left the cool, dark confines of the church and stepped out into the heat of the sun, Joey asked, 'Is there a problem with me being a Christian?'

'No.' Kari replied but he didn't convince Joey.

'Is it another reason why you can't be dating me?'

'I'll be honest, it's not ideal but it's who you are.'

'I'm not ideal?'

'No. Yes. Oh, you know what I mean. You are perfect in every way but you know I'm only meant to date a tribal woman.' He pulled her to a stop. When she eventually looked at him he said, 'Would you ever consider another belief?'

She didn't answer immediately but eventually said, 'Yes, if I believed in their values. There are some religions I really don't understand, but I'm pretty open minded.'

Kari kissed her forehead and took her hand as they began to walk towards the park. He didn't want to push the subject any further at the moment. He was aware though that if their relationship developed then he'd have to ask her to take on the values of the Kutan Tribe - to become one of them in principle, if not through birth.

As promised, Joey bought Kari an ice cream to make up for his lack of food at lunchtime. She knew she couldn't tease Kari too far in public, as he didn't normally even hold hands, let alone kiss. However, today he was very relaxed and as they sat on the bench he put his arm around her and pulled her towards him. Joey could feel his eyes watching her as she licked her ice-cream and eventually he said, 'Can we go home?'

'Already, but it's still early!'

'I don't care.' Kari shook his head.

'But, I thought you were in my hands today,' teased Joey.

Kari gave up with his ice cream and offered it to Joey, 'Do you want the rest of this?'

'No thanks. Have you had enough?'

'Yes. Of every level of your torture!' he pleaded.

She could see he was suffering. 'Okay,' she said as she took the remainder of his ice cream and threw it in the bin nearby.

Kari watched her intently as she walked back to him and held out her hand so they could walk back to the car. 'You're driving me insane...' he said as he looked at her through hooded eyes.

'That's what I wanted to achieve, but we haven't finished yet.' She smiled when she heard Kari sigh. 'We can walk side-by-side if you prefer?' Joey suggested.

'No, I want to hold your hand.'

They walked through the cobbled back streets heading towards the parked car. Joey couldn't resist a final temptation. Noticing they were totally alone, she pulled him into an embrace and ran her hands over his firm bottom. Kari reacted instantly and she felt his hardness against her stomach. He moaned into her mouth as his hands stroked her bare back. His body ached for hers, knowing she was naked underneath the dress. It took tremendous strength but he managed to pull apart from her, gasping as he did. The look in his dark, dark eyes was one of sexual desire. He wanted her. He needed her. She took his hand and led him back to the parked car. Once in the car he drove off in haste.

On the way Joey noticed a lay-by sign. She asked him to pull over. Kari stopped the car. He closed his eyes fighting the sexual urge to ravish Joey's body. He felt his seatbelt slacken as Joey unfastened it.

With her hand she turned his face to look at her, she could see he was fighting a losing battle of will. She knew she had turned him on, but she wanted more. He looked back at her with total lust. He was trying desperately to keep some level of control. She knelt on her seat and leaned across to kiss him. At first, gentle, suggestive kisses, but then slowly she deepened the intensity. Her hands moved over his chest and under his shirt. He couldn't help it but groan with joy from the relief of her touch. When his hands swept up her thighs he heard her mew expectantly. To say they were both turned on was an understatement.

'Oh, Joey, I want you so badly. I can't take much more.' Kari said quietly.

'I know, I didn't plan on doing this but I want to.' Joey stopped kissing him and got out of the car. Kari did the same. He thought he knew what she meant. She walked up to him and without uttering a word he took her hand and led them away from the car, through the dense trees lower down the hill.

When he was sure they were out of sight from any passing car or person he stopped. He pulled Joey into an embrace and kissed her deeply. He lifted Joey, wrapping her legs around his hips as he pushed her firmly against a tall, thick tree. His mouth never left hers as he thrust quickly into her again and again, their cries silenced by their kisses. It wasn't long before they both reached climax, heightened by the excitement of the gentle teasing all day but also by the knowledge that they were in public, in broad daylight.

As they leant against the tree Kari smiled at Joey and said, 'So, that wasn't in the plan?'

'No, I didn't think this bit through.'

'I love your surprises!' Kari laughed, still trying to catch his breath.

They kissed one another lovingly before Kari took her hand and led her back up the hill towards the car.

Chapter 45

He rested his hand upon Joey's thigh as he drove back to the villa. 'What now?' Kari asked as he parked the car on the driveway to the villa.

'I'd like you to go and relax in the garden as I am cooking dinner tonight.' Joey said as she got out of the car and walked towards the villa.

Kari locked the car and whilst walking to the front door he joked, 'Am I worthy of eating one of your specialities.'

'Cheeky! Go and relax… you're going to need your strength for later.'

Mischief glinted in his eyes as he began to ascend the stairs.

'Ahem, where do you think you're going?'

'To change into some shorts.'

'Did I say you could change?'

'No.'

'Well,' Joey looked at him with pursed lips then laughed, 'go on, but make the most of it because upstairs is out of bounds until I say so from the moment you come back down.'

'Yes, ma'am,' he said as he jogged up the stairs.

'There's a bottle of Champagne you could open for me.' Joey shouted to his retreating back before heading to the kitchen to prepare the dinner.

After Kari had changed he poured them both a glass of Champagne and strolled around the garden reliving the day's events. He smiled to himself, he had never been so reckless but he liked it. Joey really did bring out a more wild and adventurous side of his character.

Meanwhile, in the kitchen Joey was busy making a prawn and chorizo risotto. She didn't think she was a great cook, not compared to Kari. Whilst it simmered she ran up to the bedroom and prepared for what she had planned. As she closed the shutters she saw Kari sitting by the pool, drinking his champagne. Whoever would have thought all those weeks ago, when she saw him in those very tight Speedos, she would be preparing to give him a night to remember. She loved him so very much, and wanted to make love to him tonight, in a different way.

She removed the duvet from the bed but left the pillows in place with the scarves she needed to hand. The glow from a small light added to the seductive scene.

Putting on the sexy underwear she felt a rush of excitement and was eager for the night to begin. Wanting to conceal the underwear for the time being, she wore a loose maxi dress. Quickly she dragged a brush through her hair… so far, so good!

'I was beginning to think you'd gone for a lie down.' Kari was re-filling their glasses as she rushed into the kitchen. 'Is there anything I can do?'

'Dinner will be ready in five, if you want to take a seat.' Joey said as she ushered him from the kitchen.

A few moments later Joey emerged from the villa carrying two enormous plates of risotto. Kari looked eagerly at the food she placed in front of him. He said it looked delicious and began to eat heartily. Although he may have liked what she'd cooked, she also guessed he was hungry.

Neither mentioned the day's events as they chatted whilst they ate. Kari was aware Joey had more plans and although he was dying to know what they were, he was more than happy for Joey to take the lead.

Throughout the meal Joey topped up their drinks, she needed Dutch courage for what she was aiming to achieve later. 'And now, for dessert…' Joey said suggestively to Kari.

Kari was about to say he was full, when, to his amazement, Joey stood up and began to lower the straps of her dress. Joey felt incredibly self-conscious and glad she'd drunk a few glasses of Champagne as the dress dropped to a soft pool of fabric at her feet. She said nothing.

He sat in stunned silence. He gulped and found his heartbeat hammered in his chest. He said nothing as his eyes swept up and down the contours of her body, drinking in the vision before him.

She wore a black basque that was perfectly sculptured to hug her hips, caress her small waist and push her bosom up into two soft, fleshy mounds. Underneath he could see she wore knickers that were made from the same lace as the basque, which was seductively accentuating her figure.

He wanted to touch her. But he found he couldn't move, he couldn't even breathe.

Taking a deep breath to calm her nerves, Joey took the initiative and walked towards him. She bent over to give him a full view of her cleavage and said, 'Do you like your gift?'

Kari could only nod.

Joey smiled as her confidence grew. Sitting astride him she looked deeply into his eyes. She was pleased to see the effect she was having and she hadn't even started what she had planned. She held his face in her hands and ran the tip of her tongue across his lips. She heard him moan with desire. 'I love you,' she whispered and began to kiss him, starting with his closed eyes, nose, cheeks before finishing at his full lips.

At last he regained control of his body as his hands grasped her waist. He touched her softly, his hands gently running over the silky material and delicate lace. He kissed her neck before blowing gently in the hollow causing her to shiver with delight.

Joey's fingers and hands explored the incredible body beneath her. She ran her hands over Kari's taught shoulders and onto his chest. She managed to undo the buttons of his shirt with relative ease and remove it from his body. She marvelled at the firmness of his chest. His skin was soft and very, very warm. 'Dear God, I love you,' she said before she kissed him. 'Take me upstairs, Kari.' Her voice husky with desire as she stood and held her hand out to him.

Kari gladly accepted the hand she offered as she led him into the villa and upstairs. He entered his room and observed the changes she had created regarding the bedding and lighting. She pulled him over to the bed and encouraged him to lie down. He did as instructed, intrigued by what she had planned. She then gave him a knowing smile. He looked back, expectantly. She gently took one of his hands and tied one end of a scarf around his wrist before tying the other end around the bedpost. She pulled it tightly, but not so as to hurt him. Joey looked across at Kari and he smiled back at her, encouragingly. Joey then got off the bed and tied the other arm.

Kari felt incredibly vulnerable, but very turned on. He had never experienced anything like this before.

Joey walked to the end of the bed and, in a cat like manner, crawled onto the bed between his knees. She looked seductively into his eyes and could see the vulnerability in them. 'If you want me to untie you at any moment, just say and I... wont.'

As she kissed him, Kari found he instinctively went to hold her but his arms were held back by the restraints. She kissed and licked his neck, his chest and shoulders. It reminded him of earlier in the day when he had watched her lick the ice cream. She was now doing to him what he wanted her to do earlier. Her hands seemed to be everywhere at once, and yet he was unable to move his arms. He found his body instinctively arched to meet hers. He desperately wanted her. She rubbed her body against his as she moved further down his torso, clamping his legs beneath hers as she licked and kissed his abdomen. Kari was beginning to wonder what she might do next - his mind raced.

Joey moved further down his body, undid his shorts and removed them, throwing them to the floor. She stood at the foot of the bed and removed her beautiful lace knickers. Kari watched and released a deep sigh.

She crawled back between his legs to kiss him; their tongues explored each other's mouths. Joey's hands quickly went back to where they had been just moments before. She felt him freeze as she reached his abdomen. 'Are you alright?' Joey asked, looking back up to him.

Kari tried to say yes but his voice had been muted by his desire, so instead he nodded. Little by little she continued to kiss him, moving lower and lower down his body. He thought he would explode when he felt her take him in her mouth and gently suck. Slowly Joey intensified the pleasure, her lips moved up and down, gradually applying more and more pressure as her tongue teased his very tip and her hand pumped him firmly. He couldn't help but release gasps of pleasure throughout the intense moment, which was then magnified as her other hand gently squeezed his testicles. He cried, 'Oh, sweet... oh!' Still she continued to tease him further until he said, 'Joey, I need you, please...' His body began to tremble, his breathing was rapid and shallow, he was so very close to release.

Joey also knew he was close to orgasm, she was beginning to read his signs well. She released him from her mouth but continued to kiss him down each leg before crawling back up his body to sit astride his stomach. She saw his knuckles were white where he grasped the restricting scarves. His eyes, the darkest of blacks, were flooded with adoration as he watched her.

Kari looked at Joey in wonder. No one had ever taken him to the edge like that and stopped so suddenly leaving a gnawing pain in his loins. He watched as she undid her basque with a painfully slow pace and threw it to the floor. She looked beautiful and the look in her eyes as she gazed at him was one of love.

She bent to kiss him fully on the lips as she lowered herself onto him, they both gasped as she gradually accepted all of him. Gently Joey moved to a steady rhythm, not sure it would take much before Kari reached the edge again. She was incredibly turned on and knew it wouldn't take long before she climaxed also.

Kari said her name over and over, as well as a word in his native tongue. He thrust up as she pushed down, increasing the penetration. *Oh God!* Joey thought as wonderful sensations surged throughout her body.

'Kari, what are you saying?' she asked quietly.

He was beginning to lose control. He heard but shook his head in answer.

'Tell me!' Joey urged as she bent to kiss him.

'No...' Kari groaned as his body ached to release, his arms fighting the natural urge to hold and touch Joey.

'Please,' she said into his open mouth.

'Argh.' Through gritted teeth he replied, 'Release... me.'

With one quick pull on the scarves Joey freed Kari in an instant. He grabbed her and rolled her onto her back with himself still firmly embedded inside her. She wrapped her legs around his waist and cried his name as he took control.

He lifted her bottom as he pounded into her. 'I want to fuck you, Joey... Oh God... Joey... I love you... fuck... I love you...' Kari groaned loudly, his body trembled like Joey had never witnessed before. He physically shook and repeated her name and I love you over and over.

Joey clung to Kari with all her strength as she climaxed.

He rested his forehead on hers and they looked wondrously into each other's eyes, both gasping for breath.

Kari had no energy to move - he was totally spent. Eventually he rolled onto his side and took Joey with him. He smiled at her and sighed, 'Wow.'

She searched his face, hunting for clues that he was all right with what they had just done - what she had just done to him. His face was relaxed, not a single frown upon his brow. His eyes were bright and full of life, his smile genuine.

'I know you said you were thinking of ways to tease me, well, I can honestly say, you did. That was amazing. Never have I ever experienced anything like that. Thank you.' He kissed her hard on the lips. 'But... I'm sorry if what I said offended you, it was said in the heat of the moment.'

'Don't be sorry,' Joey was quick to reassure him. 'To be honest, it turned me on even more, if that is even possible.'

Kari raised his eyebrows in question.

'Honestly, swear as much as you like.'

'I don't generally swear, but what you did to me tonight drove me insane. I loved it - totally.'

Joey grinned at him. 'From what I know of you, you're bloody passionate! It sounds familiar, was that the word Luca taught me to say?'

Kari nodded, 'The closest translation to what Luca taught you is *thank you Kari, you are the best fuck I have ever had.*' He looked directly into her eyes and said, 'One thing I can truthfully say is I'm passionate about you, Joey.'

'As I love you, Kari… in fact, I'd go as far as to say, I fucking love you.'

Kari grinned.

'Or aren't ladies supposed to be as obscene with their choice of words?'

'I don't think ladies tie their lovers up and do what you just did to me!'

'I'm no lady, Kari, trust me.'

'But you are and you're my beautiful lady.' He looked directly into her eyes and said, 'I love you so fucking much.' His eyes searched hers before pulling her towards him and kissing her passionately.

Joey was relieved her teasing had paid off; she'd have to think of more things to experiment with Kari.

Chapter 46

As he awoke, he looked at Joey sleeping peacefully and reminisced about the day and night they had shared. He lovingly trailed his fingers down her face, along her back until resting temptingly upon her naked bottom. So delicate the touch her body instinctively shivered with delight. He watched as a smile began to spread across her face and slowly her eyes flickered open.

'Good morning,' Joey smiled at him.

'A very good morning to you,' replied Kari smiling back. 'I need your help?'

'Hmm, of course, what can I do?'

Kari took her hand and placed it on his throbbing erection and watched as a grin spread across her face.

'Oh,' was her reply.

Kari nodded and raised his eyebrows. Looking back at her, he said, 'Never have I ever woken to find myself so…' he tried to think of a suitable word, 'aroused.'

'Oops, sorry.'

He looked at her and said, 'I need to make love to you, Joey.'

'Who am I to turn away someone in need of my help,' she replied as Kari pushed her back and kissed her. Joey welcomed his deep, loving kisses.

They made love slowly, their eyes locked on each other as they moved in time with one other.

Afterwards Kari rolled onto his back taking Joey with him, holding her tightly. She lay on his chest and listened as his heartbeat returned to normal.

'Better?' Joey asked.

'Much. Thank you,' he said and kissed the top of her head.

'So, as it's our last full day here, what would you like to do?' Joey asked.

'I really need to meet Hokyana from the local tribe. Do you remember Pontrains, I took you to a restaurant there for lunch?'

'How could I forget! I was amazed to see an entirely different community down here in the South of France. Are you going to tell him about the legislation?'

'Yes. The tribe is a division of the Kutan Tribe, and therefore my father is responsible for them. Hokyana is like a Sub-Chief if you will, I need to introduce him to the new legislation. I know it will have a profound effect on things here. You are more than welcome to join me. By that I mean have something to eat whilst I meet with him.'

'Thanks but I do need to phone my mum and I can tidy up here whilst you're gone.'

'Are you sure? I'm happy to help tidy up later and I don't like the thought of you being left here on your own.'

'How long do you think you'll be?'

'I reckon I'll need a few hours; I really should catch up with Hokyana whilst I'm here.'

'That's fine. You go ahead and I'll make us a late lunch.'

Kari looked at her to make sure she meant what she was suggesting.

'Honestly!' Joey said quickly.

'If you're sure.' He watched Joey nod. 'I'll just call him to see if he's free today.' Kari jumped out of bed, pulled on a pair of shorts and left the room. Joey lay quietly in bed, bemused by Kari's sudden decision.

He returned a short while later and said, 'Yes, he is free and can meet me within the hour. If I go now I can be back by noon. Are you sure you're okay with this?'

'Absolutely. I'll be fine, honestly,' Joey said as Kari disappeared into the bathroom she listened to the powerful jets of water gush from the shower.

A little while later he came out of the bathroom. 'Don't worry about making lunch, I'll bring something back for us from that amazing fish restaurant. By the way, are you planning on staying there until I come home?' Kari asked huskily.

'No, I'm going to get up once you've finished.' She watched him dress in smart, caramel-coloured trousers and a white, linen shirt. As he tucked the shirt into his trousers and did up his belt, Joey summarised that the trousers showed off his long strong legs whilst the white shirt made him look particularly healthy. She didn't think she could ever get tired of watching him as he brushed his hair and tied it in a loose ponytail at the nap of his neck. 'I take it you've recovered from your earlier problem?' teased Joey.

Kari stopped what he was doing and walked towards the bed. 'For now, yes, but, ask me again when I return...' He said before kissing her sensually. He came very close to cancelling the meeting and instead opting for another round.

Joey watched him leave and wandered onto the balcony. She suddenly felt very alone as his car started and drove away from the villa. *Keep busy*, she told herself as she walked into the bathroom to shower.

Later, Joey tidied and cleaned the villa whilst she played music on her iPod. She found the music comforting and it didn't make her feel quite so alone. She gave the kitchen and adjoining terrace a spring clean, hoping Madame Dupre would be pleased. Joey didn't want to think that tomorrow was their last day here, she never knew when or if she would see Kari again.

Joey then made herself a coffee and carried it out to the bistro table and sat languidly on the sun soaked terrace as she dialled her mum's telephone number. Margaret was excited to hear from her. 'How is the Dark Prince?'

'He has a name, Mum. He's fine, just fine. Dare I say it... he's pretty much perfect!'

'Is he there with you now?'

'No, he's popped out, but he'll be back soon.'

'Good, I wouldn't want him to hear that you think he's perfect or, before you know it, he'll be gone.'

Joey didn't pass comment on what her mum said, she ignored it, although the snide remark bit her, re-opening a wound that had failed to heal.

Margaret filled the silence by asking, 'Has he whisked you off to any fancy events this time?'

'No.'

'No? Why ever not?'

'We've spent the whole time alone, enjoying each other's company,' Joey clarified.

Margaret could hear the affection in Joey's voice as she spoke of Kari and, although it was a joy to hear, she was also aware that Joey could soon be going to Africa. 'Don't get too comfy, Joey, you know how things can change.'

Joey closed her eyes as she listened to her mum. 'I know, but for now I'm really enjoying my little slice of happiness that fate has handed me.'

'Fate can quickly change!' Margaret was quick to say. It seemed her daughter was falling in love with this mysterious Prince and she'd never met him. She didn't want Joey to get hurt, her daughter's infatuation with this man was concerning because any future together was difficult to perceive. 'A letter arrived for you from the African Embassy.'

'I did wonder. Do you mind opening it for me?'

'Hang on.'

Joey listened to the strange muffled sound coming down the line; she imagined her mum was balancing the phone between her chin and shoulder as she tore the envelope open.

'Dear Miss Lewis, blah blah blah, oh… oh, that's wonderful!'

'What, what's wonderful?'

'You've been offered a placement in Sudan. They've listed the vaccinations you are advised to take, and… can you contact them to arrange a necessary start date, the sooner the better.'

'That's great,' Joey said, desperately trying to sound enthusiastic. The reality was that although she was going off on the adventure she'd always wanted, her and Kari would be indefinitely apart.

Margaret knew Joey was having second thoughts and possibly because of Kari. 'Darling, it's exactly what you wanted.'

'I know, it's just…'

'You carefully researched volunteering, Joey. Just because a man has stepped into your life doesn't mean you should stop all plans you had prior to him. If I remember correctly, this trip was seeking a break from men.'

Joey reflected; it seemed a lifetime a go that she felt that way. 'I did, but now I don't know. The timing sucks.'

'Perhaps, depends on how you look at it. The timing could be perfect. It will give you both time apart to realise if you do want to be together.' After a short while Joey still hadn't responded. 'Joey, you only have one life and, from what I have learned, you have to put yourself first. You cannot rely on others, especially men.'

'I know.'

'Stay with me whilst you get organised for your trip, it will be lovely to have you home. I know the Craig family are looking for help behind the bar, perhaps you could give them a hand before you go to Sudan and save some money. I won't charge you any rent.'

'Possibly.'

'Also, Emily and family are coming at the weekend and it will be so lovely to all be together.'

'Great,' Joey replied trying to sound enthusiastic. She loved her sister and family but it also meant that the already small cottage would become incredibly tiny and she'd have to share her mum's bed.

'We'll talk more when you get home. I'm so proud of you, Joey, going to help those less fortunate than yourself.'

'Thanks, Mum. Anyway, I'd better go.'

'Of course. See you soon, my dear.'

'Bye, Mum, love you.'

'Love you too.'

Joey hung up feeling confused. She was excited to be offered the placement but what about her relationship with Kari? She needed to think carefully. She wasn't sure how much longer Kari would be, but for now she felt she'd worked hard and deserved a rest as she settled herself on the large wicker recliner.

Kari had a very successful meeting with Hokyana who welcomed the change as he had lost many tribal members in the last few years through forbidden love. He asked Kari whether it would be possible to welcome them back into the tribe, if they were willing to abide by the new tribal laws. Kari couldn't see why not. He liked Hokyana. Maybe it was because he lived in this beautiful part of the world, but he found him incredibly relaxed and not uptight like his father and Elders.

On his way back to the villa Kari went via his favourite fish restaurant and ordered two fish of the day, to go. The owner of the restaurant greeted him warmly and asked for whom the extra meal was for? Kari didn't answer, but the owner saw the twinkle in his eye.

Just after midday Kari arrived back at the villa and noticed how clean and tidy the place looked. He was impressed by how hard Joey must have worked. Leaving the food in the kitchen he walked outside to find Joey and spied her sitting by the pool, legs dangling in the water.

'You're back.'

'Not much later than I thought,' he said rolling back his sleeves as he walked towards her.

Joey stood up just as he reached her and he pulled her to him and kissed her. 'I have missed you,' he embraced her and breathed in her scent deeply.

'Me too,' she replied.

'I come bearing gifts – fish of the day,' Kari grinned at her. He lazily draped his arm around her shoulders as they walked back into the villa.

Whilst eating Kari told Joey about the successful meeting and he was pleased with the encouragement Hokyana gave him.

He asked if Joey was okay, as she seemed to have something on her mind. She said she was fine and he didn't like to probe further. He knew she would tell him in her own time.

'Right, I'm off to change,' Kari said as he got up from the table. 'Shall I meet you by the pool?' Kari noticed again Joey seemed to have wandered off into a world of her own. Joey didn't answer. 'Or, I could just strip off and swim naked?'

'Sorry, what did you say?' Joey asked looking confused.

'Nothing. I'll meet you by the pool in a moment,' Kari smiled and left to change.

Joey was aware she had been a little distant, she just wasn't sure what to do about her trip to Sudan. If the opportunity arose she would talk to Kari, but she didn't want to spoil their last day here.

She stacked the plates into the dishwasher and returned to the pool to wait for Kari. He appeared after a few moments wearing Speedos with a towel casually thrown over one shoulder. He still took her breath away as she watched him. He sighed contentedly as he lay next to her on the large wicker chair.

'You've done a great job cleaning the villa, thank you.' Joey was sitting upright so he kissed her upper arm, which happened to be the same level as his face. 'Madame Dupre will be very impressed, I never normally leave it this clean…'

'I spoke to Mum this morning,' Joey suddenly interrupted.

'That's great. Is she okay?' Kari wondered if this was what was on her mind.

'Yes, she's fine, pleased to hear from me.' Joey stopped for a moment then said, 'A letter arrived from the African Embassy. They've offered me a place in Sudan and they want me to start as soon as possible. I need to have certain vaccinations, anti-malaria medication and so on before I go.'

Kari didn't say anything; he just nodded appropriately. He was now certain that this had been playing on her mind.

Joey paused. 'Mum said I can stay with her until I leave for Sudan, maybe get a local job in a bar or something to make some money and fill my time before leaving…' Joey trailed off. There, she'd said it. The problem was Kari hadn't responded.

Joey moved down the lounger and lay on her side to look at him. He returned her gaze, his face devoid of emotion, not giving any indication of how he was feeling.

'Well, what do you think?' She asked.

To be honest, Kari didn't know what to think. He was hoping in a selfish way they would have refused Joey, but he was a fool to think that. He didn't want her to go to a third world country, risking her health and life. Kari wanted her to be with him, but he wouldn't steal her dreams. Aware she was waiting for a reply from him, he swallowed and inhaled a deep breath. 'That's great. It's what you wanted.'

Joey nodded. It was what she wanted, once, but not now. Now she wanted Kari to say *don't go, stay with me*. But, her mum was right she had to look after herself. Besides it wasn't very long ago she decided she needed a life change, experience new cultures, help those in need. The problem was she felt fine with everything except the last fact, she didn't want a break from Kari.

'I'm guessing I'll be ready to go by the end of the month.' Joey thought she saw Kari's eyes widen slightly in amazement as she told him. But still he didn't say anything. 'When I get home I'll find out more details.' They were both very quiet. For the first time since she first met Kari she didn't know what to say and the silence between them became heavy.

Kari also felt the silence and knew he had to say what was weighing on his conscience. 'I'm really pleased for you. I know you want to travel, live and help others in need, you should be proud of yourself. You'll be great.' He paused, he didn't want to say the next bit, it seemed to get stuck in his throat. He cleared his throat as it tightened with a flood of emotion. 'I also remember you said you wanted a clean break, to get away from everything, including men.' He returned his eyes to hers. He was aware his heart was beating fast.

Joey looked into his open eyes and noticed a certain vulnerability that she'd never seen before. 'I know,' she replied falling into his dark eyes. 'It's going to be really tough to keep in contact.' She sighed, 'With everything you're trying to achieve. Do you think we should put our relationship on hold?' Her voice wavered as she said it. She knew she was doing it again, pushing the man she cared for away.

Kari was staring at her intently, not quite believing what he was hearing. He was about to tell her how he truly felt when, suddenly, he felt a sense of darkness, a foreboding overshadowing their conversation. Not liking what he sensed, he sat up quickly, his heart pounding in his chest.

'Kari, are you alright?' Joey asked, her voice full of concern.

'Something's not right.' Kari said so very quietly that Joey had nearly missed what he had murmured. He got up and started to walk towards the villa. She watched him not sure if it was what she'd said or something else. Suddenly she heard the villa phone ring and watched Kari sprint towards the house. He was very quick and she assumed he'd managed to answer the call as it stopped ringing a few seconds after he entered the villa.

She got up and followed him. As she entered the cool villa she could hear him talking in his native tongue to someone on the other end of the line. She couldn't understand what he was saying, but she could hear the concern in his voice. She heard him mention Luca's name a few times but that was all she understood. She stood waiting patiently for him to finish the call.

A short while later Kari switched off the phone. Although he stood with his back to her, but she could see from his stance he looked like he had the weight of the world on his shoulders.

'Kari, what is it? Who was that on the phone?' Joey asked urgently.

He turned to look at her and she noticed the blood had drained from his face he looked ashen. 'That was Olowan, my father's private secretary. My father's had a suspected heart attack.'

Joey's hand went to her mouth. She walked over to Kari and put her arms around him and held him as firmly as she could. In return, he held her tightly. He wasn't sure what he should do. Joey had just suggested they put their relationship on hold and his father had possibly had a heart attack. Despite their earlier conversation he desperately needed comfort from Joey.

'What can I do?' Joey asked.

Kari ran his hand into her hair and breathed in her delicious smell. He wanted to say *don't leave me*, but pride got the better of him. 'I need to get back to Canada as soon as possible. He let go of Joey and walked to the phone running his hand through his own hair. 'I also need to call Luca and Madame Dupre.'

'Where's the computer, I can at least re-arrange your flight.'

Kari pointed to a room Joey had never been in. She found the computer and turned it on. 'What time is your flight time tomorrow and who are you supposed to be flying with?'

'I had a private plane booked but that's probably not available today so it will need to be cancelled. I don't mind who I fly with or what class, I just need to go tonight.'

Joey nodded and began to trawl through flights.

Kari was talking to Luca on the phone and he spoke mainly in English accompanied with the occasional French phrase. She didn't want to impose and listen in on their private conversation so grabbed her mobile and phoned the airline. Thankfully they were very accommodating and were able to get Kari on a plane later that evening. Joey wondered how else she could help and decided she was happy to stay in the villa as planned, and wait until Madame Dupre returned tomorrow. She would then get a taxi to the airport and return to England.

Things in Kari's life were about to take a dramatic change. A life he wasn't quite prepared to embrace just yet. Kari came off the phone from Luca and said, 'Luca will fly to Canada as soon as he can, probably a flight in the morning. How did you get on with our flights?'

'I managed to get you on the flight that leaves at quarter to eleven. Don't worry about me I've kept mine the same. I'm happy to stay here and villa-sit until Madame Dupre returns tomorrow. But, if you don't mind calling her to explain why I'll be on my own that would be great. Our sign language is good but not great.' Joey smiled weakly.

He had thought to ask her to go to Canada with him. He wanted her by his side, now more than ever. Yet he was flying back to Canada alone, with the possibility of becoming Chief of the Kutan Tribe imminently and Joey was returning to England and then moving to Africa. His head was spinning.

'If you're sure?' was all Kari said. Joey nodded. Kari dialled Madame Dupre's phone number and fluidly explained the situation. Joey had always loved the French accent; to her, it was an incredibly sexy language. To hear Kari speaking it so fluently made her feel slightly lightheaded, but she reminded herself that now was not the right time to feel this way.

When the conversation was finished he explained to Joey that Madame knew everything and he'd asked Madame to order a taxi for her tomorrow to take her to the airport when Joey requested.

'Thank you,' Joey replied simply.

'I guess I should go and pack.' Kari said flatly and walked out of the room.

'Kari,' Joey called after him. He turned to her voice, but his eyes held no expression. He waited for her to say something, but she didn't. He walked away, his legs feeling like lead.

Chapter 47

Kari was on autopilot as he changed into jeans and a t-shirt and packed his suitcase. As he worked he placed clothes that needed to be washed in the linen basket – he always left clothes at the villa for when he visited. He was going through the motions but couldn't get a grip on reality.

He glanced over to the bed. The bed where they had so passionately made love, just a few hours ago. The bed was made and the room tidied, but if he closed his eyes he could imagine being back in that moment. He sat wearily and put his head in his hands. *How could things change so quickly?* He thought.

Joey walked into the bedroom with two coffees and found Kari sitting on the edge of the bed. She wondered if she should leave him. She placed his coffee on the bedside table and turned to leave him in peace, but something stopped her. Joey looked again at him, walked over and knelt at his feet, sitting on her heels facing him. Unsure of what to say, she asked, 'What did Olowan say?'

Still with his head in his hands Kari answered, 'Father had a meeting with Henrique this morning. They were going to discuss a family who wanted to move to a different location and decide as to whether the move was acceptable. Olowan said he heard raised voices and father getting very angry. The next moment, all was quiet. He saw my mother rush into the study and then she began screaming. When Olowan went in, he found Henrique administering CPR to my father and my mother crying for an ambulance.'

Kari stopped and took a deep breath. 'I don't know how long father was unconscious but Henrique and Olowan continued with CPR until the paramedics arrived. Apparently it took a while but eventually they started his heart again. He is now in City Hospital undergoing assessments. I'm not even sure if he's gained consciousness. If Henrique hadn't have been there, my father may not have survived this long.'

Joey allowed Kari to talk, she placed her hand on his and waited for him to finish. She felt there was more to come.

Kari looked at her, he wasn't crying but tears glistened in his eyes, threatening to spill over. 'I find it amazing the rollercoaster of emotions I have been through recently. Yesterday I was the happiest man alive and yet... right now I feel... lost.' Joey searched Kari's eyes for what he was trying to say. She didn't have to wait long when Kari said, 'Not only could I lose my father, but I could be losing my freedom and the only woman I have ever truly loved.' Joey could see a muscle twitching in his cheek. She could see he was desperately trying to hold himself together. All she wanted to do was hold him tightly and say everything was going to be all right, but she couldn't, because she wasn't sure if it would be.

'I may have to become Chief of the Kutan Tribe sooner than I thought,' Kari said, 'I'm not ready.'

Joey moved to sit next to him on the bed, she felt hideously underdressed in just her bikini. 'Kari, you are, you so are. You know you will make the best Chief the tribe has ever had. But let's hope you don't have to just yet. Your father is strong, he's fit and let's hope he'll be okay.'

'But what if he's not?'

'Don't think like that.'

Kari continued to look at the floor. If he looked at Joey he might break down, desperately he tried to be strong and not give in to the emotions he was feeling. He wanted Joey to hold him and for her to softly tell him that everything was going to be all right. He needed her strength, because right now he didn't have a lot.

'Maybe my move to Africa has come at the right time for us,' Joey said. 'Now more than ever you need to focus on the tribe and make sure everyone stays united. At least if I'm away for a while, you won't need to worry about me.'

Kari couldn't take it anymore. He got up from the bed and walked to the other end of the room. He felt like screaming. She really didn't get it. He faced the wall and took deep breaths to calm the emotion that threatened to erupt.

Joey watched as Kari walked away. She wanted to make it easier for him to focus on his family and tribe. 'With me out of the way you can finalise your new legislation, you'll be able to give the tribe your full commitment until your father recovers.' Still Kari didn't answer her, she didn't know what else to say. She was giving him every opportunity for him to thank her for being so reasonable, but maybe he didn't understand. 'We could put us on hold and I will wait for you Kari, but I'd also understand if you want a complete break, giving you the opportunity to meet some...'

'No!' Kari shouted hitting the wall with his fist before he turned and faced Joey. He shook as the adrenalin pumped through his veins. 'You don't get it do you?' he shouted.

Joey was taken aback. His face was stern and his eyes were jet black. Joey began to feel a little scared, and hugged her knees to her chest trying to comfort herself.

Kari looked at Joey with his piercing stare and he could see he'd frightened her. He was making the situation worse, the last thing he had wanted to do was scare her. He put his hand to his face and attempted to rub away his expression and pull himself together before he spoke again. His hand remained by his mouth, trying to prevent him talking.

'You don't understand,' Kari said much more calmly and quietly. He could feel the tears welling again in his eyes and he tried his best to stop them from falling.

'I need you now more than ever, Joey. I need your support and strength. I need your love. Without you, I'm nothing.' Kari could hear his voice waver and crack. He clenched his teeth in a last ditched attempt to stop the tears. 'Please don't leave me, one way or another we can sort it out. But don't leave me, please?' He couldn't hold back anymore. He'd fought hard but the tears began to fall. This was probably the first time he'd cried in front of a woman, except of course his mother and nanny. Kari reached out for Joey.

Joey was stunned by the courage that Kari had shown, he'd tried to remain in control but eventually it was too much and she saw the raw emotion he had fought so hard to hide. She had tears in her eyes as she watched him silently fight the tears from falling down his beautiful cheeks. She got up and walked over to where he stood. As soon as she reached him he enveloped her in a warm embrace, and he sobbed into her hair. Joey held him equally as firmly and cried into his warm body. She knew Kari needed her, and she was going to be there for him.

Kari felt like he'd been run over by a train. The varying degree of emotions he'd been through these last twenty-four hours was unbelievable. His pride normally didn't allow him to be so open with his emotions, but he could not hold his pride in place today. As he held Joey in his arms he was able to regain a level of control again. He pulled back so he could look in her eyes. He wiped away his tears before wiping away Joey's with his fingers.

'I mean it, Joey, when I say I love you. I need you more than ever. I need your love.' He looked adoringly into her eyes, 'I need to feel your love. I need you to make love to me?' He searched her eyes for an answer, 'Please?'

Joey nodded and very slowly he bent to kiss her. She responded and hungrily he kissed her back. His hands were in her hair and gently he nudged her legs backwards towards the bed. As her legs touched the bed they fell together, Kari catching their combined weight with his outstretched hand. They kissed passionately as Kari removed his t-shirt, he wanted to feel her naked skin on his and he didn't want anything to get in the way. He undid his jeans and removed them along with his underpants.

Joey also felt the urgency and removed her bikini. He looked hungrily at her and scooped her up into his arms. Slowly they began to move, equally making love to one another as the pleasure of being one overtook their bodies.

As their passion moved to a higher level their urgency increased. 'I love you, Joey, never leave me, please never leave me. I need you, I need you.' Kari repeated over and over as Joey made love to him.

When it was over Joey sat astride Kari and lovingly they kissed. Their emotions were raw and they needed to reassure each other.

Eventually, Kari held Joey as he laid her back onto the vast bed, her legs wrapped firmly around his waist.

'I love you,' Kari said again and pulled her tightly to him.

'I love you too.'

'I'm proud that you're going to follow your dreams and I'll support you, like you've supported me all this time,' said Kari. 'But I'm not going to finish our relationship or put it on hold. I'm not saying it's going to be easy but if we want to make it work then we can. If it helps, I'll insist I need a mobile phone so you can contact me anytime.'

Joey laughed, 'Not sure the mobile networks are that great where I'm heading, but I'm sure we'll find a way to stay in touch.' She looked at him, 'Why don't you own your own mobile?'

'I've never needed one before. There has never been a moment where I needed to talk to someone privately or urgently. I have people to make calls for me. There is also the fact phones are hacked very easily.'

'Not sure I could live without my phone. Sudan is going to be challenging in more ways than one.'

'You must get breaks, we'll just have to fit around them.' Kari tried to sound positive but inside he still didn't want her to go, but he wouldn't ask that of her, she'd been so understanding of him.

'I'm more than willing to try. If it doesn't work then we'll talk about what we can do to make it work,' she looked at him for reassurance.

He nodded then kissed her.

'Can I ask one thing?' Kari asked

'Of course.'

'You believe you may be going at the end of the month.' Joey nodded to Kari's question. 'The tribe has its annual Summer Dinner coming up, I'd would truly love it if you could be my official, strings date?'

'Really. But what about your dad?'

Kari said sadly, 'Whatever happens with Father, it's an annual event and it has to proceed. I would love you to come back to Canada with me tonight but I appreciate you have things to arrange.' Kari had a faraway look as he continued, 'You're probably right, my family and tribe need me more than ever right now.' He then looked at Joey and said honestly, 'But that doesn't mean I don't need you, because I do, and don't you forget that.'

Joey smiled at him, 'In that case, I would love to be your official date and feel free to do whatever you wish to me. We'll have a lot of catching up to do and a lot of time to prepare for.' She kissed him fully on the lips, 'I love you so much, Kari.'

Kari kissed her back and within moments he had rolled her onto her back and this time he made love to her, slowly and sensually, making sure she was fully satisfied first.

Chapter 48

It was early evening when they finally got out of bed, showered and dressed before the subject of how Kari would get to the airport arose.

'It's okay,' said Kari, 'you stay here and I'll call for a car.'

'Or I can drive you there.'

'But you'll never make it back. You'll get lost,' Kari reasoned.

'No, I won't.'

'Yes you will!'

'No I won't!' Joey said defiantly.

Kari smiled at her knowingly.

'Okay, I would get lost. But I want to be with you for as long as possible. I can't wave you off from here!' Joey said despairingly.

'How about we both go to the airport, the car can wait for you and bring you back here when I have to go through to the departure lounge.' Kari suggested.

'It will cost a fortune!'

'If it means I can be with you for an extra hour, it's worth it for me.'

'If you think that's the best option.'

Kari called a private car hire and explained what he wanted it to do. He arranged a set fee and paid for it in advance.

Whilst waiting for the taxi to arrive Kari and Joey sat in the sitting room. Joey sat on Kari's lap and he twisted a section of her hair round and around his fingers. She insisted that he call her as soon as possible to let her know how Gahenge was feeling. He said he would and he promised to keep her up to date regarding the legislation.

Joey also promised to tell Kari how her plans were developing regarding Sudan. She was also pleased to hear that Kari was fully inoculated to travel to Africa because he needed to be able to fly anywhere in the world at the drop of a hat.

As the car approached Kari pulled her into a deep embrace. Joey knew he wouldn't be able to do this at the airport so she made the most of this final hug and kiss from him.

Kari held Joey's hand in the car as it sped towards the airport, and as they drew closer he tightened his grip further. How he'd wished he'd asked her to travel with him to Canada. He didn't want to face what waited for him alone. Kari looked out of the window and he saw Joey looking at him in the refection. He turned back to look at her and smiled. He hoped he looked braver than he felt.

The taxi stopped outside the departures hall. Kari spoke to the driver in French; the driver nodded and replied. Kari turned to Joey and reassured her that the car would be waiting over by the collection point.

They left the safety of the car and the driver retrieved Kari's suitcase, smiled at Joey and said in a thick French accent, *ovvvvverrrrrr zeeeerrr*, and pointed to the collection point.

Joey smiled and replied, 'Merci beaucoup.' Kari took his case from the driver and to Joey's surprise held her hand as they walked into the departure hall. Not that Joey minded, but they were in a very public place where paparazzi were commonly found. She looked up at Kari but he didn't notice, his eyes were focused on where he had to go. His face was stern as he walked. Joey noticed people actually moved out of the way for him as he approached their space. She thought it must be amazing to have that effect on people.

They got to the check-in desks and Kari spoke in hushed French tones to the attractive airline stewardess. Joey noticed how the steward blushed slightly as she replied. Kari responded when needed otherwise kept his face devoid of any expression. Joey stood a little way away from Kari. She could feel countless pairs of eyes watching them. Some possibly wondering who he was, just like she had all those months ago and some recognising him, silently pondering if they could ask for an autograph or a selfie.

Kari thanked the check in stewardess and turned to find Joey a few paces behind him. He smiled at her and walking towards her said, 'I have twenty minutes before I have to go into the departure lounge.'

'What do you want to do?'

She heard Kari sigh and leaning into her he said in her ear, 'I know what I'd like to do but it's a little too public here.'

Joey laughed, 'My thoughts exactly.' She noticed people were now looking at her, wondering to whom this extremely handsome man was talking.

'You can go through if you like.'

'Oh no, I'm not leaving you a second sooner than I have to.' To Joey's total astonishment Kari then put his arms around her and kissed the top of her head. She found she was beginning to blush from all the people staring.

He pulled back, took her hand and walked towards the departure lounge.

They walked comfortably hand in hand, some people looking, some oblivious. As the departure lounge loomed closer, Joey could feel her heart start to sink and to her horror she felt she might cry. Internally she told herself off, desperately trying to hold herself together.

Kari looked around for two spare seats, but there were none free so they had no option but to stand. They stopped and Kari turned to face her. At that moment he didn't care who he was, he wanted to be a normal guy saying a fond farewell to his girlfriend as it would be weeks before they see each other again. He took her in his arms and held her tightly. Out of the corner of his eye he saw the first flash bulb, but he didn't care.

'Are you okay?' Kari asked Joey.

'No.'

'Me neither,' Kari said quietly into her hair, and he kissed her head. He wasn't going to let go of her until he had to. He felt her arms snake around his waist and he smiled as she held him tightly. At that moment he felt they were the only two people in the world.

'I am so going to miss you.'

'I know, me too.' Joey replied. 'When do Solonge and Lacroix come back from their honeymoon?'

'They were supposed to have another week, but unfortunately circumstances will have forced them to leave a week early.'

Joey understood. She felt Kari squeeze her that little bit tighter for reassurance.

'Give them my love, won't you?' Joey asked Kari.

'I will.'

They were then quiet for a long while, oblivious to the onlookers.

'Kari, how do you feel? I mean, are you worried?'

'Yes,' Kari said quietly, 'I didn't think I'd be starting down this road for many years, so yes, I'm scared.'

'You'll be okay, though, won't you?' Joey asked.

'I'll be okay if I know I have you loving me.' He pulled back to look at her and smiled. He could see the tears in her eyes, he hated goodbyes and this was one of the worst he'd ever experienced. But then, he guessed, it could be worse. At least they'd agreed to stay together, not put the relationship on hold as Joey suggested.

He looked into her eyes and saw a tear escape. He wiped it away without saying anything. He knew Joey was finding it as hard as he was. He smiled at her trying to reassure her as best he could, and she half smiled back, but it was broken by a sob that escaped from her mouth. She put her hand up to her mouth to hide the emotion that was about to spill out, but Kari moved it away and bent down to kiss her fully on the lips. It was not a deep kiss, but a kiss of great emotion and feeling. She responded back to him and held him as tightly as she could.

He heard his flight being called and he rested his forehead on hers. 'I have to go,' he said reluctantly.

'I know.'

Kari sighed and gave her another warm hug, he wanted to remember how it felt to hold her. He didn't want to let go.

Joey was doing exactly the same thing. *How was she going to survive until she next saw him?* She felt guilty because he had a mammoth mountain to climb and he needed to know she was going to be all right. She needed to reassure him that he didn't need to worry about her.

Kari released Joey from his hold, held her hand and walked towards the departure gate. As he found his pass, he turned to Joey and said, 'I'll be in touch as soon as possible.'

Joey nodded as she was too choked to talk. She was battling the tears that threatened to flow and not stop.

Kari looked at her and hugged her tightly and said, 'Thank you for last night. It was the best night of my life. I love you so very much, Joey Lewis.' He kissed her fully on the lips before walking through the gates leaving her alone with paparazzi taking photos.

The staff checked his boarding pass, acknowledged him through and Kari began to put distance between them. Before he left from view, he turned and mouthed *I love you*, to Joey. By now, Joey had tears streaming down her face, but she saw what he said and she mouthed *you too*. He smiled and disappeared.

As she wiped the tears from her eyes she could hear a mix of accents shouting, *Joey, it is Joey, isn't it? Oi, Joey, where's Kari going? Joey, over here, love! Are you and Kari officially dating now?* Joey turned to see a blaze of flashbulbs and somehow she managed to find the exit and the peace of the waiting taxi. That's not to say she wasn't followed, because she was by the paparazzi.

She sat back in the safety of the car and thought of the journey ahead for Kari. She wanted to be with him, but understood he needed to concentrate on his family and tribe. However, she was going to miss him like hell.

The driver was as good as his word. He drove Joey directly back to the villa, wished her a good night and drove away. She let herself back into the villa, went into the kitchen and poured herself a glass of wine. She wandered out to the terrace, but the villa, the view and her life seemed incomplete. Returning to the kitchen, she poured the wine down the sink and instead took a glass of water to bed. Joey washed, brushed her teeth and climbed into the massive, lonely bed. She could smell Kari, oh God, how she missed him already. She pulled his pillow close to her and sobbed, crying until she fell into a fitful sleep…

The Feather Necklace Series

By Gabriella Marshall

The Feather Necklace – One Love is the first novel in the series. The story continues introducing more memorable characters. Facets of Kari's and Joey's personalities are revealed as they live in varying degrees of the highs and lows of a most incredible love story.

Are Joey and Kari destined to be together or has Kari merely been a pawn in a game his Spirit Gods are playing?

Printed in Great Britain
by Amazon